Spring

Published by Hesperus Nova
Hesperus Press Limited
28 Mortimer Street, London w1w 7RD
www.hesperuspress.com

This edition first published by Hesperus Press Limited, 2014

Cilla and Rolf Börjlind assert their moral right to be identified as the authors
of this work under the Copyright, Designs and Patents Act 1988.

First published by Norstedts, Sweden

Copyright © Cilla and Rolf Börjlind 2012 by Agreement with Grand Agency.

English language translation © Rod Bradbury, 2014

Designed and typeset by Fraser Muggeridge studio

Printed in Great Britain by CPI Group (UK) Ltd, Croydon, CR0 4YY

ISBN: 978-1-84391-515-7

Cilla and Rolf Börjlind

Translated by Rod Bradbury

Late summer, 1987

In Hasslevikarna, the coves on the island of Nordkoster on the west coast of Sweden, up near the border with Norway, the difference between high tide and low tide is usually between five and ten centimetres, except when there is a spring tide. That phenomenon that occurs when the Sun and the Moon are in line with the Earth. Then the difference is almost fifty centimetres. A human head is twenty-five centimetres in height, give or take.

Tonight there would be a spring tide.

For the time being the tide was out.

The full moon had sucked the reluctant sea back many hours before, and exposed an expanse of damp sand. Small, shiny crabs scuttled back and forth across the sand glowing in the steely-blue light. The limpets clung on particularly hard to the rocks, biding their time. All the life exposed on the shore knew that the tide would wash over them once again.

Three figures on the beach knew too. They even knew exactly when it would happen – in a quarter of an hour. Then the first gentle waves would roll in and wet those parts that had dried out, and soon the pressure from the dark rumble out there would push up wave upon wave until the flood of the tide had reached its maximum.

A spring tide; meaning that the beach would be covered with fifty centimetres of water.

But they still had a little time. The hole they were digging was almost finished. It went straight down, almost one hundred and fifty centimetres, with a diameter of about sixty centimetres. A body would fit perfectly. Only the head would reach over the top.

The head of a fourth figure.

The head belonging to the woman who was standing some way away, quite still, with her hands tied.

Her long dark hair fluttered gently in the intermittent breeze, her naked body shone, her face muted without any make-up. Her eyes revealed a strange lack of presence. She looked at the digging further down the shore. The man with the spade pulled the curved blade out of the hole, tipped the last of the sand onto the pile next to him and turned around.

He was finished.

Seen from a distance, from the rocks where the boy had hidden, there was a weird stillness about the moonlit beach. Dark figures on the sand far away on the other side of the beach, what were they doing? He didn't know, but he heard the approaching roar of the sea and saw the naked woman led out across the wet sand, seemingly without offering any resistance, and saw her lowered into a hole.

He bit his lower lip.

One of the men shovelled sand into the hole. The dripping sludge settled around the woman's body like wet cement. The hole was soon filled. When the first scattered waves rolled in towards land, only the woman's head stuck out. Her long hair became wet, slowly; and a little crab became caught in a dark strand. She herself was staring at the moon, without uttering a sound.

The figures moved back a little, up amidst the dunes. Two of them were nervous, uncertain, the third was calm. They all watched the solitary moonlit head out on the sand.

And waited.

When the spring tide came at last, it came in rather fast. The height of the waves increased with every surge and washed over the woman's head, into her mouth and up her nose. Her throat was filled with water. Whenever she turned her head away, a new wave hit her face.

One of the figures went back out to her and crouched down. Their eyes met.

From his vantage point, the boy could see how the level of the water was rising. The head sticking out vanished and then reappeared and vanished again. Two of the figures had now disappeared, the third was on its way up the beach again. Suddenly he heard a horrific scream. It was the woman in the hole who had screamed, hysterically. The scream echoed around the shallow cove and bounced against the boy's rock, before the next wave washed over the head and the scream was silenced.

Then the boy started running.

The sea rose and became still, dark and shiny. Under the surface the woman shut her eyes. The last thing she felt was another kick, little and gentle, against the inside of her belly. Then her waters broke.

Summer 2011, Stockholm

One-eyed Vera actually had two healthy eyes and a gaze that might halt a hunting falcon in mid-air. Her vision was excellent. But she argued her point with the subtlety of a sledgehammer. Started with her own opinion and then battered away so that any counterarguments were flung out in every direction.

One-eyed.

But loved.

Now she was standing with her back to the setting sun, with the last rays sliding across Värta bay, bouncing off Lidingö Bridge and reaching the park at Hjorthagen with enough strength still to create an elegant backlit halo around Vera.

'It's my *world*, that's what this is about!'

The passionate way she said this would have impressed any parliamentary gathering, although her husky voice would have seemed out of place in a chamber. And maybe her clothes too – a couple of soiled, different-coloured T-shirts on top, and on the bottom a tulle skirt that had seen better days. And barefoot. But now she wasn't standing in a parliamentary chamber, she was instead in a little out-of-the-way park near the Värta docks and her audience consisted of four homeless people in varying states, spread out on some benches among the oaks and ash trees and bushes. One of them was Jelle, silent and tall, he sat by himself as if in his own world. Benseman sat on another bench and next to him, Muriel, a young druggie from Bagarmossen. She had a plastic bag from the co-op next to her.

Arvo Pärt was snoozing on the bench opposite them.

At the edge of the park, hidden behind some thick bushes, two young men were crouched down. Wearing dark clothes, their gaze fixed on the benches.

'It's my world, not theirs! Right?'

One-eyed Vera gestured towards a distant spot.

4

'They just come and bang their fists on the caravan and I've hardly got my teeth in and there they are standing outside the door! Three of them! And how they stared! "What the hell is this about?" I said.

'"We're from the council. Your caravan needs to be moved."

'"Why?"

'"We're going to develop the land."

'"For what?"

'"An illuminated track."

'"A what?"

'"A running track, it's going to go right through here."

'"What the hell d'you mean? I can't move this! I haven't got a car!"

'"Regrettably, that isn't our problem. The caravan must be gone before next Monday."'

One-eyed Vera stopped to catch her breath and Jelle took the opportunity to yawn, discreetly. Vera didn't like you yawning when she was ranting.

'Don't you get it? There's three blokes standing there looking like they were grown in a filing cabinet in the Fifties, and telling me that I should go to hell! So that some overfed idiots can run off their flab right over my home? Of course that really pissed me off, right?'

'Yeah.'

Muriel was the one who hissed an answer. Her voice was rather lacerated, thin and grating, and she would never draw attention to herself unless she'd had a hit.

Vera brushed aside her thinning reddish hair and started up again.

'But this ain't about some fucking running track, it's about all them folks out walking their furry little rats who don't like someone like me being there, in their posh surroundings, I don't fit in with their neat and tidy world. That's what it's about! They don't give a fuck about us!'

Benseman leaned forward a little.

'But you know, Vera, it could be that they…'

'Right, let's be off, Jelle! Come on!'

Vera took two big steps and prodded Jelle on the arm. She couldn't care less what Benseman thought. Jelle got up, shrugged his shoulders slightly and followed her. He didn't really know where to though.

Benseman gave a bit of a grimace. He knew his Vera. With slightly shaking hands he lit a crumpled cigarette butt and opened a can of beer. A sound that caused Arvo Pärt to come to life.

'Now is fun.'

Pärt was a second-generation Estonian, his parents having come to Sweden as refugees during the war. He had his own special way of speaking. Muriel watched as Vera left, and then turned to Benseman.

'Well, it's right, a lot of what she said, as soon as you don't fit in, then they want you out of the way… ain't it like that?'

'Yes, I suppose so…'

Benseman was from the north of Sweden, best known for his unnecessarily firm handshake and for the way the yellows of his eyes seemed to have been marinated in vodka. He was a big man, with a distinct northern dialect and rancid breath which oozed out through the gaps in his teeth. In a previous life, he had been a librarian up in Boden, with a large appetite for books and an equally large appetite for alcoholic beverages. The whole nine yards, from cloudberry liqueur to some of the extremely potent products from an illicit distillery. Ten years of alcohol abuse had completely wrecked his social life and ended with him driving down to Stockholm in a stolen van. Down in the capital he just scraped by as a beggar and shoplifter, like flotsam that had been washed ashore.

But he had read a lot.

'…we are dependent on charity,' said Benseman.

Pärt nodded in agreement and reached out for the beer. Muriel pulled out a little pouch and a spoon. Benseman reacted immediately.

'You were going to lay off that crap, weren't you?'

'I know, I will.'

'When?'

'I will!'

And she did, immediately. Not because she didn't want her fix, but because she suddenly caught sight of two youths who were sauntering towards them through the trees. One had on a black hooded jacket, and his mate a green one. Both of them were wearing grey tracksuit bottoms, heavy boots and gloves.

They were out hunting.

The homeless trio reacted fairly quickly. Muriel grabbed her plastic bag and ran off. Benseman and Pärt stumbled after her. Benseman suddenly remembered the second can of beer he had hidden behind the bin. That could mean the difference between getting some sleep or being awake the coming night. He turned back and accidentally tripped up in front of one of the benches.

His balance wasn't at its best.

Nor was his reaction time. When he tried get back on his feet he got a hard kick right in his face and fell onto his back. The youth in the black jacket stood right next to him. His mate had pulled out a mobile and switched the camera on.

That was the start of an exceptionally brutal assault, filmed in a park from which nothing could be heard on the outside and where there were only two terrified witnesses hidden in some bushes quite a way away.

Muriel and Pärt.

But even from that distance they could see the blood running from Benseman's mouth and an ear, and hear his muffled groans after each kick to his midriff and face.

Time after time.

After time.

What they didn't get to see was how some of Benseman's few remaining teeth were kicked into the flesh of his cheeks, poking out the other side. What they did see was how the big northerner tried to shield his eyes.

The eyes he used for reading.

Muriel cried, silently, and pressed the crook of her arm – full of scars – across her mouth. Every part of her emaciated body shook. In the end, Pärt took the young girl by the hand and pulled her away from the disgusting scene. There was nothing they could do. Or rather, they could call the police, they could do that, Pärt thought, and dragged Muriel with him as quickly as he could down towards Lidingövägen.

It was a while before the first car approached. Pärt and Muriel started to shout and wave their arms when it was about fifty metres away which resulted in the car swerving away into the middle of the road and then accelerating past them.

'Fucking bastards!' Muriel shouted after them.

The next driver had his wife in the passenger seat, a well-groomed lady in a pretty cerise dress. She pointed through the windscreen.

'Now don't run over those drug addicts, remember you've been drinking.'

So the grey Jaguar, too, whooshed past.

By the time one of Benseman's hands had been stamped on till it was a bloody mess, the last of the sunlight had sunk into Värta bay. The youth with the mobile turned the camera off and his mate picked up Benseman's hidden can of beer.

Then they ran off.

They left behind them the dusk and the big northerner on the ground. His smashed hand was clawing feebly at the gravel, his eyelids were closed. *A Clockwork Orange*, the book title was the last thought winding through Benseman's brain. But who the hell wrote it? Then the hand stopped moving.

The covers had slipped off and exposed her naked thighs. The rough warm tongue licked its way a bit along the skin. She moved in her sleep and felt it tickle. When the tongue turned into a little nip on her thigh, she sat up and pushed the cat away.

'No!'

It wasn't really aimed at the cat, more at the alarm clock. She had overslept. Well and truly. And to make it worse, her chewing gum had fallen off the bedstead and firmly attached itself to her long black hair. Semi-crisis.

She leapt out of bed.

She was an hour late and that put pressure on all of her morning timetable. Her multitasking capacity was going to be tested. Especially in the kitchen: the milk for her coffee was about to boil over at the same time as the toast started to burn and her bare right foot trod on a patch of transparent cat vomit just at the same time as she got a call from an insufferably intimate telephone salesman who started with her first name and guaranteed that it wasn't about selling something, only an invitation to a course about financial consulting.

Almost a total crisis now.

Olivia Rönning was still stressed when she rushed out of the door on Skånegatan. No make-up, with her long hair quickly put up in something reminiscent of a bun. Her light suede jacket was unbuttoned, a yellow T-shirt showed under it, somewhat frayed at the bottom, her washed-out jeans ended in a pair of well-worn sandals.

It was sunny today too.

She stopped for a moment to decide which way she'd go. Which was quickest? Off to the right. She started to half run while glancing at the billboards outside the supermarket:

ANOTHER ROUGH SLEEPER BADLY BEATEN.

Olivia carried on running.

She was on her way to her parked car. She had to go to Sörentorp out in Ulriksdal. To the Police College. She was twenty-three and this was her third term. In six months she would be able to apply to be taken on as a police trainee at a station in the Stockholm district.

After a further six months she would be a police officer.

A little out of breath, she reached her white Mustang and pulled out her car keys. She had inherited the car from her Dad, Arne, who had died of cancer four years earlier. It was a convertible, a 1988 model, red leather upholstery, automatic, and a straight-four which roared like a V8. The apple of her dad's eye for many years. Now it was hers. Not in mint condition, the rear window had to be secured with gaffer tape now and then, and the paintwork had the odd blemish. But it nearly always sailed through its MOT.

She loved the car.

With a few simple moves she lowered the roof and sat down behind the wheel. She nearly always noticed the same thing, a smell, for a second or two. It wasn't from the upholstery, but from her dad: the inside of the car smelt of Arne. Only for a couple of seconds, then it was gone.

She attached her headphones to her mobile, selected Bon Iver, turned the key in the ignition, put the car in drive and drove off.

The summer holidays were on their way.

* * *

A new issue of *Situation Sthlm*, the magazine for the homeless, was now ready for sale, Issue 166. With Princess Victoria on the cover, and interviews with Sahara Hotnights and Jens Lapidus. The editorial office on Krukmakargatan 34 was filled with homeless sellers who were buying their copies of the new issue. They could buy them for twenty kronor each, half the retail price on the street, and keep the difference when they sold them.

A simple deal.

And it made all the difference for many of them. The money they got from selling magazines kept them afloat. Some of them spent it on their addictions, others to pay back money they owed. Most of them quite simply used the money to buy food for that day.

And to have some self-esteem.

It was, after all, a job they were doing, and they got paid for it. They weren't nicking things, or shoplifting, or mugging pensioners. They only did that if everything got fucked up. Some of them. But the majority were actually proud of the way they performed their sales job.

And it was quite hard work.

Some days, you could stand at your pitch for ten or twelve hours and hardly manage to flog a single copy. In rotten weather and icy cold winds. Then it wasn't much fun creeping into an outhouse somewhere with no food in your stomach and trying to get to sleep before the nightmares seized you.

But today there was a new issue coming out. That was usually a cause for celebration for all those in the room. With a bit of luck they'd manage to flog a whole bundle on the first day. But there was no sign of merriment in the office.

On the contrary.

A crisis meeting was taking place.

Yet another of their mates had been badly beaten up the previous evening. Benseman, the northerner, the guy who had read a hell of a lot of books. He had broken bones all over his body. His spleen had ruptured and the doctors had struggled all night to stop the internal bleeding. The guy in charge of reception had been to the hospital earlier in the morning.

'He's going to survive... but we won't be seeing him here for quite a while.'

People nodded a little. In sympathy. Tense. This wasn't the first attack of recent times, in fact it was the fourth, and the victims had all been homeless people. Rough sleepers, as they had been called in the papers. And it had been the same each time. Some youths had sought out one of them at a well-known meeting place, and beaten them up. A really nasty beating. And they also filmed the whole bloody thing and then posted it on the Net.

That was almost the worst part of it.

So fucking humiliating. As if they were nothing more than punchbags in a 'reality' documentary about violence as entertainment.

And almost as hard to deal with was the fact that all four had been sellers of *Situation Sthlm*. Was that just a coincidence? There were about 5,000 homeless people in Stockholm, and only a tiny proportion of them were sellers.

'Are they just picking on us?'

'Why the fuck would they do that!'

Of course there was no answer to that. Yet. But it was unpleasant enough anyway to frighten the group in the room – and they were already shaken.

'I've got hold of some teargas spray.'

That came from Bo Fast. They all looked at him. Everybody knew Bo, his name sounds pretty stupid and when pronounced as one word it meant something completely different, *bofast* means 'permanent resident'. They had given up teasing him about that years ago. Now Bo held up his powerful spray for all to see.

'You know it's illegal,' said Jelle.

'How d'you mean?'

'A spray like that.'

'So what? How legal is it to beat people up?'

Jelle didn't have a good answer to that. He was standing by a wall with Arvo Pärt next to him. Vera stood a bit to one side. For once, she had kept her mouth shut. She had taken it really badly when Pärt phoned and told her what had happened to Benseman just a few minutes after she and Jelle had left the park. She had been convinced that she could have prevented the assault if only she had stayed behind. But Jelle didn't think so.

'What the hell would you've done?'

'Fought them! You know how I floored those guys who tried to grab our mobiles out in Midsommarkransen!'

'But they were pissed out of their minds, and one of them was almost a midget.'

'Well, in that case you'd have had to give me a hand, wouldn't you?'

Now Vera didn't say a word. She bought a bundle of magazines; Pärt bought his bundle, while Jelle could only afford five copies.

They went out onto the street together and suddenly Pärt started to cry. He leaned against the rough façade and put a dirty hand up to his face. Jelle and Vera looked at him. They understood. He had been there and had seen it all and not been able to lift a finger.

Now it was all coming flooding back.

Vera gently put her arm around Pärt's shoulders and bent his head down towards her shoulder. She knew how frail he was.

His real name was Silon Karp and he was from Eskilstuna, the son of two Estonian refugees. But during a nocturnal heroin trip in an attic office on Brunnsgatan, he had caught sight of an old newspaper with a picture of the shy composer and been struck by the amazing likeness. Between Karp and Pärt. He saw his double, quite simply. And during the next fix he had slipped into his double, and two became one. He was Arvo Pärt. Since then, he had called himself Pärt too. And seeing as the company he kept couldn't care less what people were really called, he became Pärt.

Arvo Pärt.

He had worked as a postman for many years and had delivered letters in Stockholm's southern suburbs, but weak nerves and a craving for opiates had dragged him down into what was now his rootless existence. As a homeless magazine seller for *Situation Sthlm*.

Now he stood here crying against One-eyed Vera's shoulder, inconsolable, he cried because of what had happened to Benseman, because of how bloody awful everything was, all the violence. But most of all he cried because life was the way it was.

Vera stroked his matted hair and looked up at Jelle, and Jelle looked down at his bundle of newspapers.

Then he left.

* * *

Olivia turned in through the college gates at Sörentorp and parked her car immediately to the right. It stuck out a bit, among the dark grey saloon cars of various types. She had nothing against that. She glanced up at the sky and wondered whether she ought to put the roof up, but decided against it.

'What if it starts raining?'

Olivia turned around. Ulf Molin. A guy the same age as her, and in her class too. A guy who had a remarkable talent for always turning up in Olivia's vicinity without her actually noticing. Now he had appeared behind her car. I wonder if he'll follow me, she thought.

'Well then I'd have to put the roof up.'

'In the middle of a lesson?'

This sort of totally meaningless conversation got on her nerves. She took her bag and started to walk off. Ulf followed her.

'Have you seen this?'

Ulf was by her side holding a swish tablet.

'It's that assault last night, the rough sleeper.'

Olivia took a look and saw a bleeding Benseman being hit by several kicks to various parts of his body.

'It's posted on that same site again,' said Ulf.

'Trashkick?'

'Yes.'

They had discussed the site the previous day, at college; everyone had been very upset. One of the teachers had explained how the first film and a web link had been posted on 4chan.org, a site that was visited by millions of young people. The film and the site had been flagged pretty soon and removed, but a lot of people had already seen the link and so it spread. The link went to the trashkick.com site.

'But can't they close it down?'

'It's probably hosted by an obscure web hotel, not entirely easy for the police to track down and close.'

The teacher had told them that.

Ulf put away the tablet.

'That's the fourth film they've posted now... it's so fucking sick.'

'What, that they get beaten up, or that it's out on the Net?'

'Well... both of them.'

'And which do you think is worse?'

She knew that she shouldn't start up a conversation, but they had about two hundred metres to the college building and Ulf was going the same way. Besides she liked to make people say what they thought. She didn't really know why. It might just have been a way to keep her distance.

Attack.

'I think it's all connected,' said Ulf. 'They beat people up so they can post it on the Net, and if there wasn't a site to post it on then perhaps they wouldn't beat them up.'

Well done, Olivia thought. A long sentence, coherent thinking, sensible reflection. If did a bit less sneaking around and a bit more thinking then he would definitely rise a couple of notches in her estimation, and she had her standards. Besides, he was pretty trim and half-a-head taller than her, with dark brown curly hair.

'So what are you doing this evening? Fancy a beer or something?'

Ah, now he was back at his old rating.

The classroom was nearly full. There were twenty-four students in Olivia's class, divided into four basic groups. Ulf wasn't in her group. Åke Gustafsson, their tutor, was standing beside the blackboard. A man in his early fifties with a long police career behind him. He was very popular in college. Some people thought he went on a bit. Olivia thought he was charming. She liked his eyebrows, the bushy type which seem to have a life of their own. Now he was holding up a file in one hand. There was a whole pile of them on the table next to him.

'Since we are going to go our separate ways in a few days, I've thought up something – and this is a bit outside the course – something that you could do during the summer holiday, and it's completely voluntary. This is a file with a number of old unsolved Swedish murders, I put it together myself, my idea is that you can choose one of them and make your own analysis of the investigation, look at what could have been done differently with modern police methods, DNA, geographic analysis, electronic surveillance, and whatnot. This is a little exercise in how cold cases can be tackled. Any questions?'

'So it isn't compulsory?'

Olivia glanced at Ulf. He always had to ask something just for the sake of asking. Åke had already said that it was voluntary.

'It's completely voluntary.'

'But it might boost our marks a bit, right?'

When the lesson was over, Olivia went to the table and picked up a file. Åke approached and nodded at the folder in her hand.

'Your dad worked on one of those cases.'

'Did he?'

'Yes, I thought it'd be a bit of fun to include it.'

Olivia settled down on a bench some distance from the college building, next to three men. All three were silent – they were made of bronze. One of them was Handsome Harry, a notorious conman from the old days.

Olivia had never heard of him.

The other two were Tumba-Tarzan and Constable Björk. The latter had a police cap in his lap. Somebody had balanced an empty beer can on top of it.

Olivia opened her file. She hadn't been intending to spend any time on college work during the hols, and this was voluntary too. But it got her out of the classroom so she wouldn't have to listen to Ulf harping on about nothing.

Now she was curious though.

Her dad had been involved in one of the cases.

She quickly thumbed through the file. The summaries were very brief. A few facts about methods, places and dates, a bit about the investigations. She was quite used to police terminology. She had heard her parents discussing legal cases at the kitchen table throughout her childhood. Her mother, Maria, was a criminal lawyer.

She found the case almost at the end of the list. Arne Rönning had been one of the people in charge of the investigation.

Detective chief inspector in the national crime squad.

Dad.

Olivia looked up and let her gaze take in the view. The college was situated in the midst of almost unspoilt countryside, with large well-kept lawns and beautiful woodland areas that stretched right down to the bay, Edsviken. An extremely serene setting.

Her mind was on Arne.

She had loved her dad, deeply, and now he was dead. And he'd only made it to fifty-nine. That wasn't fair. And now the thoughts were back. The ones she had suffered from, often, and which she could almost experience as a physical pain. The thoughts about her betrayal.

Her betrayal of him.

They had been extremely close all through her teens, and then she had let him down when he suddenly fell ill. She'd gone off to Barcelona to study Spanish, work, chill out... have some fun.

I just ran away, she thought. Although I didn't realise it at the time. I did a bunk because I just couldn't get to grips with the fact that he was ill, and that he could get worse – that he could actually die.

But he did. When Olivia wasn't there. When she was still in Barcelona.

She could still remember the phone call from her mum.

'Dad died during the night.'

Olivia rubbed her eyes gently and thought about her mum. About the time after her dad's death when she had returned from Barcelona. A dreadful time. Maria had been devastated and was locked up inside her own grief. And that grief had no room for Olivia's guilt and anguish. Instead they had tiptoed around each other, not saying anything, as if they were afraid the whole world would shatter if they gave voice to their emotions.

Eventually, things settled down, of course, but it was still something they steered well clear of talking about.

That was putting it mildly.

She really did still miss her dad.

'Have you found a case?'

It was Ulf, who had materialised in front of her in his own unique way.

'Yes.'

'Which one?'

Olivia looked down at her file.

'A case from the west coast.'

'When was it?'

'Eighty-seven.'

'Why did you choose that one?'

'Have you found anything? Or perhaps you're not going to bother? I mean, it wasn't compulsory.'

Ulf gave a slight smile and sat down on the bench.

'Does it bother you if I sit here?'

'Yes.'

Olivia was quite good at speaking her mind. Besides, she wanted to concentrate on the case she had just picked out.

The case that her dad had worked on.

It was a rather spectacular case, as it turned out. Åke had written such an interesting summary that Olivia wanted to know more straight away.

She drove to the National Library and went down into the basement to the reading room with all the old newspapers on microfilm. The woman behind the counter showed her how to find things on the shelves and which microfilm readers she could use. Everything was arranged meticulously. Every single newspaper from the Fifties onwards was now on microfilm. All she had to do was to choose which newspaper and which year, sit down at the reader and get going.

Olivia started with a local newspaper that covered the island of Nordkoster. *Strömstads Tidning.* She had the date and the location of the murder from the file. When she launched the search function it didn't take long for the headlines to fill the screen: MACABRE MURDER ON ISLAND SHORE. The article had been written by a fairly excited journalist but did actually provide some hard facts about the time and place.

She was hooked.

She spent the next few hours working her way through the regional papers, *Bohuslänningen* and *Hallandsposten*, and then widening her scope bit by bit. The Göteborg newspapers. The Stockholm-based evening papers. The big national dailies.

And she made notes.

Feverishly.

Major features as well as details.

The case had really attracted nationwide attention. For several reasons. It was a deliberately brutal murder, the victim was a young pregnant woman, and the perpetrators were unknown. They hadn't got any suspects. No motives had come to light. They didn't even have a name for the victim.

The case had remained an unsolved mystery ever since.

Olivia became all the more fascinated. Both by the case as a phenomenon, but above all by the murder itself. It had taken place on a moonlit night in the Hasslevikarna coves on the island of Nordkoster. A diabolical method of murdering a naked pregnant woman.

With the tide.

The rising tide?

That was quite simply torture, Olivia thought. An extreme form of drowning. Slow, hellish.

Why?

Why that spectacular method?

Olivia's imagination was in overdrive. Were there links to the occult? Tidal worshippers? Moon worshippers? The murder had taken place late in the evening. Was it some sort of sacrifice? A rite? A sect? Were they going to cut out the fetus and sacrifice it to some lunar god?

No, mustn't get carried away, she thought.

Olivia turned off the reader, leant back and looked down at her full notebook: a mishmash of facts and speculation, truths and guesses, and more or less credible hypotheses by various crime reporters and criminologists.

According to one 'reliable source', traces of a drug had been found in the victim's body. Rohypnol. Rohypnol is a classic rape drug, Olivia thought. But wasn't she in the final stages of pregnancy? Had she been sedated? Why?

According to the police, a dark cloth coat had been found up in the sand dunes. Hairs matching the woman's had been found on the coat. Where were the rest of the clothes if that was her coat? Had the murderers taken them but forgotten the coat?

They had tried to ascertain the woman's identity via Interpol but this had led to nothing. Strange that nobody missed a pregnant woman, she thought.

The police described the woman as between twenty-five and thirty years old, possibly of Latin American extraction. What was meant by 'Latin American extraction'? How large an area did that cover?

The entire sequence of events had been witnessed by a nine-year-old boy named by a local reporter as Ove Gardman. The boy had run home and told his parents. Where was he today? Could she get in touch with him?

According to the police, the woman was unconscious but still alive when Gardman's parents came to the beach. They tried to resuscitate her but when the air ambulance arrived the woman was dead. How far away did the Gardmans live? she wondered. How long did it take for the helicopter to get there?

Olivia got up. Her brain was battered with impressions and reflections. Halfway up, she almost lost her balance.

Her blood pressure had fallen through the floor.

She sank down into the car on Humlegårdsgatan outside the library and felt her stomach protesting. She dealt with that by taking a PowerBar from the glove compartment. She had been sitting for several hours in the library reading room and was rather surprised when she realised how late it was. Time had simply vanished down there. Olivia glanced at her notebook. She realised just how fascinated she had become by the old beach case. Not just because Arne had worked on it, that was an extra fillip, but for all its remarkable ingredients. Above all, one specific detail had fastened in her mind: they had never established the identity of the murdered woman. She was, and remained, unknown. For all those years.

That spurred Olivia on.

She wanted to know more.

If only her dad had been alive, what could he have told her?

She pulled out her mobile.

Åke Gustafsson and a middle-aged woman stood out on the neatly tended lawn outside the Police College. The woman was from Romania and was in charge of the college's catering. She offered Åke a cigarette.

'Not many people smoke nowadays,' she said.

'No.'

'It must be because of cancer.'

'Quite likely.'

And then they smoked.

Halfway through his cigarette, Åke's mobile started ringing.

'This is Olivia Rönning, hi. Well, I've chosen that case at Nordkoster, and I'd like…'

'I thought you might,' Åke interposed, 'your dad was involved in that…'

'Yes, but that's not why.'

Olivia wanted to keep them separate. This was about her and now. It had nothing to do with her dad. At any rate not as far as her tutor was concerned. She had chosen a project and she was going to do it in her own way. That's what she was like.

'I've chosen it because I think it's interesting,' she said.

'But pretty difficult.'

'Yes, that's why I called you. I'd like to look at the real murder investigation paperwork, where is it?'

'Probably in the central archives in Göteborg.'

'Oh really? That's a pity.'

'But you wouldn't have been able to look anyway.'

'Why not?'

'Because it's an unsolved murder and it's still within the limitation period. Nobody is given access to an open investigation if you're not a member of the investigation team.'

'Yeah, right… so what do I do now? How can I get some more information?'

There was silence at the other end.

Olivia sat at the wheel with her mobile against her ear. What's he thinking? She saw a female traffic warden approaching who looked as if she meant business. The car was parked in a space reserved for disabled drivers. Not a good idea. She started the engine just as she heard Åke's voice again.

'You could try speaking to the person who was in charge of the investigation team,' he said.

'He's called Tom Stilton.'

'I know.'

'Where is he?'

' Haven't a clue.'

'At police headquarters?'

'I don't think so. But you could ask Olsäter, Mette Olsäter, she's a detective superintendent. They worked together quite a lot, she might know.'

'And where can I find her, then?'

'At the national crime squad, in C-building.'

'Thanks!'

Olivia pulled away right under the nose of the traffic warden.

* * *

'*Situation Stockholm*! Latest issue! Read about Princess Victoria and support the homeless!'

One-eyed Vera's voice had no difficulty in reaching out over the hordes of affluent residents of the chic Sofo district in southern Stockholm who were going into the market hall complex to stuff their bags full with a mixture of junk food and luxury. She had the appearance of someone perfectly suited to perform at the National Theatre. Like the actress Margaretha Krook when she was in her prime, although Vera looked rather shabbier. But she had that same sharp gaze, a commanding presence and a charisma that you couldn't help but notice.

Her copies were selling.

Half of her bundle was already gone.

Arvo Pärt hadn't been as successful. He wasn't selling any-thing. He stood leaning against a wall a little distance away. This wasn't his day, and he didn't want to be alone. He looked at Vera out of the corner of his eye. He admired her strength. He knew a lot about her dark nights, most of the people in her circle did. Yet now she was standing there as if she owned the world. Homeless. Unless you counted a decrepit old grey caravan from the 1960s as home.

But Vera did.

'I'm not homeless.'

Which is what she told a customer who bought a magazine and wanted to peep into the world of the dregs of society. Social porn?

'I'm in between homes.'

Which was partly true. She was on the council's special 'Housing First' list, a political project to give the impression they were improving the situation for the city's homeless. If she was lucky, she'd be allocated a flat in the autumn, they'd told her. A trial flat. If she behaved well, she might be able to keep it.

Vera intended to behave well.

She always did behave well. Almost always. She had her caravan and a disability pension of just over 5,000 kronor a month. She scraped by with that but it only covered the most basic essentials. To get the rest, she had to go rummaging in skips.

And she was doing OK.

'*Situation Stockholm*!'

Now she'd sold three more copies.

'Are you really going to stand here?'

The question came from Jelle. He seemed to turn up from nowhere with his five copies and had now parked himself quite close to Vera.

'Yeah? What about it?'

'That's Benseman's pitch.'

Every seller had their own spot in the city. It was written on the plastic card that hung around their necks, and had their name too. On Benseman's card it had said 'Benseman/Söder Market Hall'.

'Benseman's not going to be here for a while,' said Vera.

'It's his pitch. Have you been allocated it temporarily?'

'No, have you?'

'No.'

'Well then, what are you doing here?'

Jelle didn't answer. Vera took a step in his direction.

'Anything against me standing here?'

'It's a good pitch.'

'Yeah.'

'Can we share it?' said Jelle.

Vera gave a slight smile and looked at Jelle. The sort of look that he backed away from as quick as he could. Like now. He looked down at the ground. Vera came right up to him, leant over and tried to catch his eye from below. About as easy as catching a trout with your hand. Hopeless. Jelle just twisted away. Vera let out that hoarse laugh which immediately caused four families with little kids to swerve away with their designer pushchairs.

'Jelle!' she laughed.

Pärt moved away from the wall. Was there trouble brewing? He knew Vera was a temperamental woman. Jelle was more of an unknown factor. It was said that he came from the archipelago, far out somewhere. Rödlöga, somebody had said? His father had hunted seals! But there was so much talk, and there was so little substance to it. And now the supposed seal hunter was standing outside the market hall having an argument with Vera.

Or whatever it was they were doing.

'What's the row about?'

'We're not having a row,' said Vera. 'Jelle and me, we never have a row. I just say how it is, and he stares at the ground. Don't you?'

Vera turned towards Jelle but he had already moved off. Now he was fifteen metres away. He wasn't going to argue with Vera about Benseman's pitch. Really he didn't give a damn about where Vera sold her magazines. She could decide that herself.

He was fifty-six years old, and really he didn't give a damn about anything.

* * *

Olivia steered her car through the late summer's evening, on her way to Söder. It had been an intense day. A poor start, Ulf Molin had pestered her as usual, but then she'd found that murder case. And things were suddenly going very nicely. For several reasons. Private and otherwise.

The hours she had spent at the National Library had left their mark.

Weird how things turn out, she thought. It wasn't at all how she had planned things. She would soon be on summer holiday after a tough and intense spell. At college on weekdays, and working weekends at the Kronoberg remand centre. After that she was going to take things easy. She'd managed to save a bit of money so that she could stay afloat awhile. A cheap last-minute charter flight was the rough idea. Besides, she hadn't had any sex for almost a year. She was going to do something about that too.

And then this comes along?

Perhaps she should skip the murder-case project after all? It was voluntary, right? Then Lenni phoned.

'Yeah?'

Lenni was her best mate from her final years at school. A girl who drifted around and desperately tried to find something to cling on to so she wouldn't sink. As always, she wanted to go out in town, see what was happening, afraid to miss out. Now she'd got together with four other mates so that she wouldn't miss Jakob, the guy she was interested in just now. She had read on Facebook that he was going to the Strand at Hornstull this evening.

'You've got to come along! It'll be great! We're going to meet at Lollo's at eight o'clock and…'

'Lenni…'

'Yeah?'

'Can't make it, I've got to… it's some college work, I need to sort it this evening.'

'But Jakob's mate Erik is going and he's been asking about you several times! And he's dead handsome! Absolutely perfect for you!'

'Yeah but I can't make it.'

'Livia, how can you be such a pain in the arse? You really need to get laid if you're going to get back into form!'

'Another time.'

'That's what you always say nowadays! OK then, but don't blame me if you miss out!'

'Promise. Hope it works out with Jakob!'

'Yeah, keep your fingers crossed! Hugs and kisses!'

Olivia didn't have time to say hugs before Lenni had hung up. Lenni was already on her way somewhere else, somewhere with a bit of action.

But why had she really said no? She had been thinking herself about guys just before Lenni phoned. Had she really become as deadly boring as Lenni claimed? College project work?

Why had she gone and said that?

Olivia put some fresh cat food in the bowl and emptied the litter tray. Then she sank down beside her laptop. What she really would have liked was a bath, but there was something wrong with the drains which meant that the water ran out over the floor when she let the plug out of the bath and she simply couldn't deal with that just now. She'd do something about it tomorrow. Put it on her things-to-do-tomorrow list. A list that she had neatly pushed ahead of her most of the spring.

Instead she opened Google Earth.

Nordkoster.

She was still fascinated by the possibility of sitting at home in front of a screen and just hovering down almost to the window level of buildings and dwellings all over the world. She always felt spy-vibes when she was doing it. Almost like a peeping Tom.

But now they were a different sort of vibes, she noticed. The more she zoomed in on the island, the landscape, the small roads, the houses, the closer she got to her goal, the stronger the vibes became. And then she got there.

Hasslevikarna.

The coves on the northern part of the island.

Almost like a little bay, she thought. She tried to get as close as possible. And that was pretty detailed. She could see the sand dunes above, and the beach. The beach where the pregnant woman had been buried. There it was in front of her, on the screen.

Grey, grainy.

She immediately started imagining where. Where had the woman been buried?

Was it there?

Or there?

Where did they find the coat?

And where had that little boy been sitting when he saw it all? Was it over there by the rocks on the west side of the beach? Or on the east side? Up by the trees?

She suddenly noticed how irritated she had become because she couldn't get any closer. All the way down. Almost with her feet on the beach.

To be there.

But she couldn't. This was the best she could do. She turned off her computer. Now she was going to treat herself to a beer. A beer like Ulf had gone on about a couple of times. But she was going to have a beer on her own, at home, without having to rub shoulders with her classmates in the pub.

On her own.

Olivia liked being single. It was entirely her own choice. She had never had any problem with boys, on the contrary. Throughout her childhood and teens she received confirmation that she was attractive. First, all those cute photos of her as a little girl, and Arne's mass of holiday videos starring little Olivia. Then there were all those admiring glances as she stepped out into the big world. For a while she amused herself by wearing sunglasses and observing all the boys she met beneath them. How their gaze would seek her out wherever she went and wouldn't let go until she had passed. She soon tired of that. She knew who she was and what she had. In that respect. It gave her a sense of security.

She didn't have to go out hunting.

Like Lenni.

Olivia had her mum and her little flat. Two rooms painted white, with wooden floors. It wasn't hers for real, she rented it from a cousin who was working for the Swedish Export Council in South Africa. He'd be there two years. Meanwhile, she was living here. Amidst his furniture.

She just had to put up with that.

And she had Elvis, of course. The cat that had been left after an intense relationship with a sexy Jamaican. A guy she had bumped into at Nova Bar on Skånegatan, first she'd felt surprisingly horny and then she'd fallen in love with him.

The version she told him was the opposite way round.

For almost a whole year they had travelled and laughed and shagged and then he had met a girl he knew from 'back home', as he put it. And she was allergic to cats. So the cat stayed on at Skånegatan. She had named it Elvis after the Jamaican moved out. He had called it Ras Tafari, after Haile Selassie's name in the 1930s.

Elvis was more to her taste.

Now she loved the cat almost as much as her Mustang.

She finished her beer.

It was good.

When she was about to open a second beer she happened to notice the alcohol content and realised it was much stronger than the first, and that she hadn't had any lunch. Nor dinner for that matter. When she got going, food became low priority. Now she felt she ought to give her stomach something to work on, to counter the slight spinning sensation in her brain. Should she nip down and get a pizza?

No.

The slight spinning sensation was actually quite nice.

She took the second can with her into the tiny bedroom and sank down on top of the bedspread. A thin long greyish-white wooden mask hung on the wall opposite her. One of her cousin's African art objects. She still hadn't made up her mind if she liked it or not. There were nights when she woke up from some cold dream and saw the moonlight reflected from the mask's white mouth. That wasn't exactly pleasant. Olivia let her gaze wander up towards the ceiling and suddenly realised: she hadn't checked her phone for several hours! That was not like her. Her mobile was a part of Olivia's outfit. She never felt fully dressed if she didn't have her phone in a pocket. Now she grabbed it and unlocked it. Checked her emails, messages and calendar and ended up on the Swedish TV site. A bit of news before she slid away, that would do nicely!

'But what are you going to do then?'
'I can't stand here and reveal our plans.'

The person who couldn't stand there and reveal anything on the evening news was called Rune Forss, a chief inspector with the Stockholm police, fifty-something she guessed. He had been tasked with dealing with the repeated assaults on rough sleepers. A task that hardly made Forss jump for joy, she thought. He seemed to belong to the old school. That part of the old school where they thought that lots of people only had themselves to blame. For one thing or another. Particularly when it came to the mischief-makers, and even more particularly when it came to folk who couldn't pull their socks up and get a job and behave like everybody else.

They only had themselves to blame, to a very large extent.

That definitely wasn't an attitude that they taught at the police college, but everyone knew it existed. Amongst some people. Some of Olivia's fellow students had already been infected by the same jargon.

'Are you going to go undercover among the rough sleepers?'

'Undercover?'

'Yes, be like a rough sleeper, blend in among them. So you can catch the perpetrators.'

When Rune Forss finally understood what he was being asked, he seemed to have difficulty in suppressing a smile.

'No.'

Olivia turned her mobile off.

* * *

If it had been a heart-warming story, then one of those homeless people would have been sitting on a simple chair at the bedside of the badly wounded man. Her hands would have smoothed the man's blankets and tried to give him a sliver of fragile hope. But in the true story, the one that is true to what actually happened, the staff at the hospital reception had phoned security the very moment One-eyed Vera had cut across the hall on her way to the lifts. The security staff had caught up with her in a corridor not far from Benseman's room.

'You are not allowed in here!'

'Why not? I'm just going to visit a mate who...'

'Come along with us!'

And Vera was then removed from the premises.

Which is a euphemistic way of saying that the security people marched off with a protesting Vera, past staring people, right through the entrance hall and more or less threw her out on to the street. They did this in an unnecessarily brutal and deeply embarrassing manner, despite the fact that she reeled off all her human rights. Or her own version of them.

Out she went.

Into the summer night.

And that marked the start of her long walk to her caravan in the woods in Solna.

Alone.

On a night when violent young men were at large and Chief Inspector Rune Forss had fallen asleep comfortably on his stomach.

2

The woman who had just popped a large forkful of marzipan cream layer cake into her mouth had red-painted lips, a lot of fuzzy grey hair and 'volume'. That's how her husband had put it on one occasion: 'My wife has volume.' Which meant that she was quite wide. A fact that sometimes pained her, sometimes didn't. During periods of the first instance, she would try to shrink the volume, with hardly noticeable results. During the latter she just liked being who she was. Now she was sitting in her spacious office in C-building at the National Crime Squad and surreptitiously eating a cream layer cake, half-listening to a news bulletin on the radio. A company called MWM, Magnuson World Mining, had just been named Swedish Company of the Year Abroad.

'The news has been greeted with strong protests in many quarters today. The company has been severely criticized for its methods in connection with coltan mining in the Congo. This is what the managing director, Bertil Magnuson, had to say to his critics...'

The cake-eating woman turned off the radio. She was familiar with the name Bertil Magnuson in connection with a disappearance in the 1980s.

She directed her gaze at a portrait on the edge of her desk. Her youngest daughter, Jolene. The girl smiled at her, with a peculiar smile and enigmatic eyes. She had Down syndrome and was nineteen years old. My darling Jolene, the woman thought, what does life have in store for you? She was reaching out for the last piece of cake when there was a knock on the door. She quickly pushed the cake behind a couple of box files on the desk, and then turned towards the door.

'Come in!'

The door was opened and a young woman peered in. When she looked at you her left eye was not completely parallel with her right eye – she had a bit of a squint. Her hair was set up in an untidy black bun.

'Mette Olsäter?' the untidy bun asked.

'What is it about?'

'Can I come in?'

'What is it about?'

The untidy bun seemed uncertain as to whether that meant that she should come in, or not. She stopped in the door frame, the door half-open.

'My name is Olivia Rönning and I'm a student at the Police College. I'm looking for Tom Stilton.'

'Why?'

'I'm doing a project on a case that he was in charge of and need to ask him about a few things.'

'What case is that?'

'A murder on Nordkoster in 1987.'

'Come in.'

Olivia stepped in and closed the door. There was a chair in front of Olsäter's desk but Olivia didn't dare sit on it. Not without an invitation. The woman behind the desk was not only obviously large, she had a very commanding presence.

Detective superintendent.

'What does the project entail?'

'We're looking at old murder investigations and examining what could have been done differently today, with modern methods.'

'A cold-case exercise?'

'Sort of.'

The room fell silent. Mette looked at her piece of cake out of the corner of her eye. She knew it could be seen if she asked the young lady to sit on the chair, so she kept her on her feet.

'Stilton's left,' she said bluntly.

'Oh, right. When did he leave?'

'Is that relevant?'

'No, I... but perhaps he could answer my questions. Even if he's left. Why did he leave?'

'Personal reasons.'

'What's he doing now?'

'No idea.'

Like an echo from Åke Gustafsson, Olivia thought.

'Do you know where I can get hold of him?'

'No.'

Mette Olsäter looked at Olivia without moving her eyes. The message was clear. The conversation was over as far as she was concerned.

'Well, thanks anyway.'

She found herself making an almost unnoticeable bowing gesture before going to the door. Halfway out, she turned round and faced Mette.

'You've got a bit of something, some cream or something, on your chin.'

And then she pulled the door shut behind her, fast.

Mette – just as fast – wiped her chin with her hand and removed the little blob of cream.

So annoying.

But a bit amusing too, Mårten would have a good laugh at that this evening, her husband. He loved embarrassing situations.

But she was less pleased about Rönning's hunt for Tom. She probably wouldn't find him, but even just mentioning his name had stirred things up inside Mette's head.

She didn't like people stirring things up there.

Mette was of an analytical bent. A brilliant investigator with an overactive intellect and an impressive capacity for doing lots of things at the same time. That wasn't boasting, it was what had got her where she was today. One of the most experienced murder investigators in the country. A woman who kept a cool head when softer colleagues got caught up in irrelevant emotions.

Mette never did that.

But there was a place in her head where you could stir things up. On rare occasions. Those occasions almost always had some link to Tom Stilton.

Olivia left Mette's office with a feeling of... yes, what? She didn't really know. As if that woman hadn't liked her asking about Tom Stilton. But why? He had been in charge of the investigation of the Nordkoster murder for several years, and then they had closed the investigation. And now he had left the police. Big deal. Surely she could get hold of that Stilton on her own. Or let go of the case, if it was going to be so complicated. But she wouldn't do that. Not yet. Not that easily. There were still several ways to get hold of information now that she was in the police headquarters anyway.

One was Verner Brost.

And now she half ran down a dreary office corridor, several metres behind him.

'Excuse me!'

The man slowed down a little. He was just under sixty and on his way to a slightly delayed lunch. He didn't seem to be in the best of moods.

'Yes?'

'Olivia Rönning.'

Olivia had caught up with him and held out her hand. She had always had a firm handshake. She herself hated shaking something the consistency of a Danish pastry straight out of the oven. Verner Brost was a Danish pastry. He was also the newly appointed head of the cold-case group in Stockholm. An experienced investigator, with a suitable patina of cynicism and a genuine calling, all round a good civil servant.

'I just wanted to find out if you're doing anything on the beach case.'

'The beach case?'

'The murder on Nordkoster in 1987.'

'No.'

'You're familiar with it?'

Brost had a good look at the pushy young woman.

'I'm familiar with it.'

Olivia ignored the decidedly guarded tone.

'Why isn't it on your agenda?'

'It isn't accessible.'

'... accessible? What do you mean by...'

'Have you eaten lunch, Miss?'

'No.'

'Nor have I.'

Verner Brost turned on his heel and continued on his way to the Plum Tree, the staff canteen in the police building.

Don't pull rank, Miss Olivia thought, and felt herself just as patronised as she had cause to feel.

Not accessible?

'What did you mean by "not accessible"?'

Olivia had followed Brost, two steps behind him. He had homed in on the canteen like a robot, put some food and a beer on a tray, and then found a seat without losing momentum. Now he was sitting at a small table totally concentrated on eating his food. Olivia had sat down opposite him.

She soon realised that this man had to get some food into him, quickly. Proteins, calories, sugar. This was obviously a large scale problem.

She waited a while before saying her piece.

She didn't have to wait very long. Brost dealt with the intake at impressive speed and sank back on his chair with a barely concealed burp between his lips.

'What did you mean by "not accessible"?' she asked again.

'I meant that we have no justification for opening the investigation again,' said Brost.

'Why is that?'

'How much do you know about this sort of thing?'

'I'm in my third term at police college.'

'You don't know very much, in other words.'

But he smiled when he said that. He had seen to his bodily needs. Now he could allow himself a short conversation. Perhaps he could persuade her to treat him to a mint biscuit with his coffee.

'If we are going to take on a case, a basic requirement is that we can apply something to it that they haven't been able to use before.'

'DNA? Geographic analysis? New witness statements?'

She does know something then, Brost thought.

'Yes, that sort of thing, or some new technical evidence, or if we find something that they missed in the old investigation.'

'But you haven't in the beach case?'

'No.'

Brost smiled indulgently. Olivia smiled back.

'Would you like me to get you some coffee?' she asked.

'Yes, that would be nice.'

'Anything to go with it?'

'A mint biscuit would be tasty.'

Olivia was soon back. She had the next question on her tongue before the coffee was on the table.

'Tom Stilton was in charge of the case, wasn't he?'

'Yes.'

'Do you know where I can get hold of him?'

'He is no longer with the police, he left many years ago.'

'I know, but is he still in Stockholm?'

'I don't know. For a while it was rumoured that he was moving abroad.'

'Oh right… gosh… then it'll be hard to get hold of him.'

'Indeed.'

'Why did he leave? He wasn't that old, was he?'

'No.'

Olivia saw how Brost stirred his coffee with the obvious intention of avoiding her gaze.

'So why did he leave?'

'Personal reasons.'

I ought to stop here, Olivia thought. Personal reasons were not really any business of hers. It had no connection at all with the college project.

But Olivia was Olivia.

'What was the mint biscuit like?' she said.

'Delicious.'

'What were the personal reasons?'

'Don't you know what "personal" means?'

The mint biscuit hadn't been that delicious, she thought.

Olivia left the police building on Polhemsgatan. She was irritated. She didn't like it when she came up against a brick wall. She got into her car, pulled out her laptop, opened a search site and typed 'Tom Stilton'.

Several articles were listed. They all had some connection with the police, all except one. A report from a fire on an oil platform off the coast of Norway in 1975. A young Swede was feted as a hero after saving the lives of three Norwegian oil workers. The Swede was called Tom Stilton and was twenty-one years old. Olivia downloaded a copy of the article. Then she started looking up Tom Stilton on all the directory sites. He wasn't on Eniro, the online national address registry. Nor had she found any trace of him on the other sites. No results. Not even on Birthday.se. As a joke she checked the national vehicle registry too. Same there.

The man did not exist.

Perhaps he had moved abroad? Like Brost mentioned. These days he could be sitting in Thailand with a cocktail and boasting of his murder investigations to some drunken hotties. Or maybe not. Perhaps he had other inclinations?

Homosexual?

No, he wasn't that.

At any rate not in the old days. Then he had been married to the same woman for ten years. Marianne Boglund, a forensic generalist, a sort of coordinator. Olivia had finally found Stilton in the tax authorities' register of marriages.

He was listed there.

With an address but no telephone number.

She made a note of the address.

* * *

Almost on the other side of the world, in a little coastal village in Costa Rica, an elderly man was sitting and painting his nails with transparent nail polish. He was on the veranda of a most remarkable house and his name was Bosques Rodriguez. From his vantage point he could get a glimpse of the sea on one side. On the other, the rainforest climbed up the side of a mountain. He had lived here all his life, in the same place, in the same remarkable house. He used to be known as 'the old bar-owner from Cabuya'. Nowadays he didn't know what people called him. He rarely went into Santa Teresa, where his old bar was. He thought the place had lost its soul. It was probably because of the surfers, and all the tourists who flocked in and forced up the prices of everything that could be forced up.

Including the water.

Bosques smiled a little.

The foreigners always drank water from plastic bottles that they paid scandalous amounts for and then threw away.

Then they put up posters urging everybody to take care of the environment.

But the big Swede in Mal Pais isn't like that, Bosques thought.

Not at all.

3

The two boys sat quietly in the sand under a wind-ripped palm, with their backs facing the Pacific Ocean. Some way from them sat a man with a closed laptop on his lap. He sat on a simple bamboo chair in front of a low building with a peeling façade of blues and greens, a sort of restaurant which sold home-caught fish and booze at irregular hours.

For the moment it was closed.

The boys knew the man. One of their neighbours in the village. He had always been kind to them, played and dived for shells. Now they understood that they must sit quietly. The man was only wearing a pair of thin shorts, nothing on top. Barefoot. His blond hair was thinning and tears ran down his heavily tanned cheeks.

'The big Swede is crying,' one of the boys whispered, in a voice that disappeared in the warm wind. The other boy nodded. The man with the laptop was crying. He had now been crying for many hours. At first up in his house in the village, in the last hours of the night, then he had needed some air and gone down to the beach. Now he was sitting here facing the Pacific.

And still crying.

Some years earlier, he had ended up here in Mal Pais, on the Nicoya peninsula in Costa Rica. A few houses along a dusty coast road. The sea on one side and the rainforest on the other. Nothing to the south; to the north lay Playa Carmen and Santa Teresa and some other villages. Backpackers flocked to them. Long fantastic surfing beaches, cheap lodgings and even cheaper food.

And nobody who asked who you were.

Ideal, he had thought at the time. For hiding. For starting afresh.

Unknown.

Going by the name of Dan Nilsson.

His reserve capital had hardly kept him afloat until he was offered a job as a guide in a nearby nature reserve, Cabo Blanco. That suited him perfectly. With his quad he could be up there in half an hour, and with his fairly decent knowledge of languages he could deal with most of the tourists who found their way to the reserve. There weren't that many at first, more in the last year, and now enough to keep him busy four days a week. The other three days he mixed with the locals. Never with tourists or surfers. He wasn't a water person, and wasn't interested in getting high. He lived a very modest life, in most respects, people hardly noticed him, a man with a past that was going to remain in the past.

He could have turned up in any one of Graham Greene's books.

Now he was sitting on a bamboo chair with his laptop on his knees and crying. With two small boys sitting worried some way away and not having a clue as to why the big Swede was so sad.

'Shall we ask him what's wrong?'

'No.'

'Perhaps he's lost something that we can find?'

But he hadn't.

He had, however, reached a decision. At last. Through the tears, a decision he had never thought he would need to make. Now he had done it.

He got up.

The first thing he got out was his gun, a Sig Sauer. He felt the weight of it in his hand while keeping an eye on the window. He didn't want the little boys to see it. He knew they had followed him, keeping their distance. They always did. Now they were sitting in the bushes waiting. He lowered the gun and went into his bedroom and closed the shutter. With some effort he pushed the wooden bed to one side and exposed the stone floor. One of the slabs was loose and he lifted it up. There was a leather bag under the slab. He lifted the bag up and put the gun in the empty space and lowered the slab again. He noticed that he was acting with precision, efficiently. He knew that he mustn't end up off course, start thinking, and risk changing his mind. He took the leather bag into the living room, went up to his printer and lifted up an A4 sheet of paper. It was filled with closely spaced text. He put the sheet of paper into the bag.

There were already a couple of other items in there.

When he stepped out of his house, the sun had climbed over the trees and now bathed his simple veranda. The hammock swayed lazily in the dry breeze and he realised that he would raise a lot of dust on the road. An awful lot. He looked about him to see if the boys were around. They had gone. Or had hidden. Once he had come across them under a blanket at the back. He thought that a large monitor lizard had sneaked in and he pulled the blanket away with some caution.

'What are you doing there?'

'We're playing at lizards!'

He got onto his quad with the bag in one hand and rolled off down the road. He was going to Cabuya, a village some distance away.

He was going to visit a friend.

There are houses, and houses, and then there is Bosques' house. And there is only one of those. It had originally been a fishing shack, knocked together by Bosques' dad, an eternity ago. Two small rooms. Then the Rodriguez family had grown, indeed grown considerably, and with the arrival of each new baby Daddy Rodriguez had insisted on building a little extension. Eventually the supply of legally acquired timber dried up, and then he had to improvise, as he called it. Built with whatever he could lay his hands on. Sheets of metal and laminates and various sorts of netting, driftwood sometimes, and bits from a wrecked fishing boat. Daddy Rodriguez had reserved the bow for himself. A projection on the south side where he (with some difficulty) could just squeeze in and lose himself in bad liquor of one sort or another and read Castaneda.

But that was Old Man Rodriguez.

Rodriguez Junior, Bosques, had been left on his own in the house in the end. His sexual orientation had not given him any children and his latest lover had died a couple of years earlier.

Bosques was now seventy-two and he hadn't been able to hear the cicadas for many a year.

But he was a good friend.

'What is it you want me to do? With the bag?' he said.

'You should give it to Gilberto Lluvisio.'

'But isn't he a policeman?'

'Yes, that's why,' said Dan Nilsson. 'I trust him. He trusts me. Sometimes. If I'm not back here by the first of July, then you should give it to Lluvisio.'

'And what should he do with it?'

'He should make sure it gets to the Swedish police.'

'How?'

'There's a piece of paper in there which says how.'

'OK.'

Bosques poured some rum into Nilsson's glass. They sat at the front of the remarkable house on what you could only call a veranda – for want of a better term. Nilsson had washed down the worst of the road dust with tepid water. Now he brushed away a swarm of insects and lifted the rum to his mouth. As already mentioned, he was moderate in his habits, and Bosques had been rather surprised when Nilsson had asked if there was any rum in the house. Now he looked at the big Swede with a degree of curiosity. This was an unusual situation. Not only on account of the rum; there was something about the Swede's entire attitude. He had known him since the very first day he came to the area. Nilsson had rented his sister's house in Mal Pais and eventually bought it off her. That had been the beginning of a long and close relationship. Bosques' sexual orientation had never rubbed off onto Nilsson, it wasn't that. But something about the Swede's way of going about things had appealed to Bosques.

A lot.

Nilsson didn't take anything for granted.

And nor did Bosques. Various circumstances had taught him to take care of what you had. Suddenly it might be gone. It's fine as long as you've got it, but then there is nothing.

Like Nilsson.

He was there. Things were fine. Soon he might not be around any more, Bosques suddenly thought.

'Has something happened?'

'Yes.'

'Something you want to talk about?'

'No.'

Dan Nilsson got up and looked at Bosques.

'Thanks for the rum.'

'*De nada.*'

Nilsson remained standing in front of Bosques. Long enough for Bosques to feel that he too must get up, and once he was on his feet Nilsson put his arms around him. It was a very brief hug, the sort that many men quickly exchange when they part. What was special about it was that they had never hugged each other before.

And would never do so again.

4

One-eyed Vera had a radio. A little transistor radio she had found among the rubbish in a house on Döbelnsgatan, with an aerial and everything. The casing was broken, but it worked. Now a gang of them were sitting in Glasblåsar Park listening to Radio Shadow, a radio programme made by and for the homeless and broadcast one hour a week. The programme was about the recent attacks. The sound was a bit rasping, but everyone knew what it was about. Benseman. Trashkick. And about the fact that some sadists were going around looking for new victims.

Among them.

To beat them up and post the film on the Net.

They were being targeted.

'We must stick together!'

Muriel shouted that out. She had taken something that took away her inhibitions and she thought she could say her bit. Pärt and the four others sitting on the benches looked at Muriel. Stick together? What did she mean?

'You what? Stick together?'

'Be together! So that they can't, so that you're not alone and giving them the chance to beat you up... when you're by yourself... alone...'

Muriel quickly turned down her voice when they all looked at her. She directed her gaze at the gravel. Vera came up and stroked her striped hair.

'That's good thinking, Muriel, we shouldn't be alone. If we're alone, we're afraid, and they'll scent that straight off. They're like dogs. They sniff out them that's afraid, and beat them up.'

'Exactly.'

Muriel raised her head slightly. In another time she would have liked to have had Vera as her mum. A mum who stroked her hair and who came to her defence when people looked at her. She had never had a mother like that.

Now it was too late.

Now it was too late for most things, Muriel thought.

'Did you hear that the cops have created a new group to hunt down those bastards?'

Vera looked around her and saw that a couple of the others nodded. But with little enthusiasm. All of them on the benches had their own private experiences of the cops, from old times and recent times, and none of those experiences gave them cause to feel any great degree of enthusiasm. Would the cops devote any more time to protecting the homeless than the minimum necessary to satisfy the media? No, none of them thought that for a nanosecond. They knew their place on the scale of priorities, and it wasn't at the top.

It wasn't even at the bottom.

It was on the back of a kebab serviette that Rune Forss had wiped his mouth with.

They knew that much.

* * *

The lecture hall at the Police College was almost full. It was the last day of the spring term and they had some visitors from SKL, the National Laboratory of Forensic Science in Linköping. A lecture about specialist techniques and methodology.

A long lecture. With pauses for questions.

'There have been demands that we should take more DNA swabs, what do you think about that?'

'We think it is positive. In England they swab perpetrators even of break-ins, which means they have an enormous national DNA database at their disposal.'

'And why don't we do that here?'

The question came from Ulf, as usual.

'The problem, if we want to see it as a problem, is our privacy laws. We are not allowed to create that type of database.'

'Because?'

'Personal integrity.'

They went on like that for a couple of hours. When the subject turned to the latest developments with regard to DNA analysis, Olivia became especially attentive. She even asked a question, which Ulf noted with a little smile.

'Can you establish paternity from the DNA of an unborn fetus?'

'Yes.'

It was a simple answer and it came from one of the lecturers, a redhead in a simply cut bluish-grey dress. A woman who had attracted Olivia's attention as soon as she was introduced.

Her name was Marianne Boglund, forensic generalist at SKL.

It hadn't taken many seconds for the penny to drop, but when it did Olivia found herself thinking 'wow'. This was the woman who had been married to Tom Stilton.

Now she was standing up there beside the podium.

Olivia wondered whether she should take a gamble. Only the day before, she had checked out the address that had been given for the Stiltons. There was no Stilton there now.

She decided to take a gamble.

* * *

At a quarter past two the session was over. Olivia had seen Marianne Boglund following her tutor, Åke Gustafsson, into his office after the lecture. Now Olivia stood outside in the corridor and waited.

And waited.

Ought she to knock on the door? Was that being a bit too pushy? What if they were having sex in there?

She knocked on the door.

'Yes.'

Olivia opened the door, apologised for disturbing, and asked if she could possibly have a minute or two with Marianne Boglund.

'Just a moment,' said Åke.

Olivia nodded and closed the door again. They hadn't had sex. Where had she got that idea from? Too many films? Or because Boglund was a decidedly attractive woman and Åke Gustafsson had his eyebrows?

Marianne Boglund came out and stretched out her hand.

'What can I help you with?'

Her handshake was firm and dry, her eyes very formal, she was hardly a woman in close contact with her emotions. Olivia was already regretting this.

'I'm trying to get hold of Tom Stilton,' she said.

Not a sound. Definitely not close contact.

'I can't find any address for him, nobody knows where he is, I just wanted to ask if you might happen to know where I can get hold of him.'

'No.'

'Could he have moved abroad?'

'No idea.'

Olivia gave a little nod, thanked her briefly, turned round and went off along the corridor. Marianne remained standing where she was. Her gaze followed the young woman. Suddenly she took a couple of strides after her, then stopped.

Marianne Boglund's answer tumbled around inside Olivia's head. She had heard that answer several times now from different people. Obviously practical. At least when it was about Stilton. She was feeling rather disheartened.

And that she had behaved rather badly.

She had trespassed into people's private sphere, she was aware of that. Boglund had definitely got that proverbial speck in her eye at the mention of Stilton's name. And that was a speck that was absolutely none of Olivia's business.

What on Earth was she playing at?

'What are you playing at?'

It wasn't her inner voice that acquired life. It was, of course, Ulf. He caught up with her on her way to the car and smiled.

'Err, what?'

'DNA of an unborn baby? Why did you want to know that?'

'Curious.'

'Is it about the Nordkoster case?'

'Yes.'

'What's it about?'

'A murder.'

'Olivia, I've twigged that.'

And now she won't say any more, Ulf thought, as usual.

'Why are you always so damned secretive?' he said.

'Am I?'

'Yes.'

Olivia was taken by surprise. Both by the personal nature of the question and the whole awkward situation. What did he mean, secretive?

'What do you mean?'

'That you always slip away, in some way, have an excuse or a…'

'You mean with the beers?'

'Yeah, that too, but you never follow up. You ask questions and get answers and then you're on your way.'

'Oh, am I?'

What was he after? Ask and answer, and on her way?

'Well, I suppose that's what I'm like,' she said.

'Apparently.'

Now Olivia could have gone on auto-pilot and driven off, but suddenly she came to think of Molin senior. Ulf was the son of one of the top people in the national crime squad, Oskar Molin. Which was hardly his fault. At first, it had irked Olivia a little. She didn't really know why. Perhaps a suspicion that Ulf had a bit of an advantage over the rest of the class. Which was silly of course. He would have to do the same, and get the same grades as all the others. Besides, he probably had more pressure on him from home. But of course he would probably have greater possibilities to move up. With a dad who could help him over the highest thresholds.

But what the hell.

'Do you have any contact with your dad?' she asked.

'Yeah, of course. Why do you ask that?'

'I'm looking for an old detective who's no longer in the force and nobody seems to have any idea where he might be. Tom Stilton. Thought your dad might know something.'

'Stilton, you said?'

'Yes, Tom.'

'I'll ask.'

'Thanks.'

Olivia climbed into her car and drove off.

Ulf remained where he was and shook his head a little. A difficult lady. Not stuck-up, but difficult. Always kept her distance. He had tried to get her to join him in a pub crawl with some others from the class, but no, she always had an excuse. She'd be studying, she'd be going to the gym, she'd be doing stuff that everybody else did but still had time to have a beer. A bit secretive, Ulf thought. But pretty, a bit of a squint, lovely full lips, always straight shoulders, no make-up.

He wasn't going to give up.

* * *

53

Nor was Olivia. Not on the beach case, nor on the vanished detective. Perhaps there was a connection there? He might have found something out and was stopped and pushed off abroad? And why would he do that? He left for personal reasons, didn't he? Was that the speck in Boglund's eye?

Olivia noticed she was getting carried away. That was the downside of having been born with imagination and growing up with parents who solved intrigues at the kitchen table. She was always looking for a conspiracy. A connection.

An enigma she could ponder while she fell asleep.

The white car drove out onto the Klarastrand road. The music in her earphones was muffled and suggestive, this time it was the Deportees. Olivia liked lyrics that said something.

When she passed the slope with all the rabbit warrens she smiled to herself. Here was where dad always used to slow down and glance at his daughter in the rear mirror.

'How many are there today?'

And little Olivia would count them as fast as she could.

'Seventeen! I can see seventeen!'

Olivia suppressed the memory and pressed the accelerator. There was surprisingly little traffic. The holidays had begun of course, she thought. People will have started going off to the countryside. This led her to think about their old holiday house out on Tynningö Island. The family place, where she had spent her summers while she grew up, with Maria and Arne and a decidedly protected idyll. A little inland lake, crayfish, a swimming school and wasps.

Now Arne was no more, and the same applied to the crayfish. Now there was only her and her mum left. And the family place. Which was so strongly associated with Arne, the way he would busy himself repairing the house, his fishing and the endless things he would always think up for the evenings. He was a different sort of dad out there. A daughter's dad, one who had time and room for everything that never found a place

54

in their professional home, which she called the house in Rotebro, where she grew up. A house where everything was done in a planned and orderly manner and 'Not just now, Olivia, we'll discuss that later'. At their summer place it was always the opposite.

But now Arne was no longer there. Just her mum, Maria, and that wasn't really the same. For Maria the place seemed to almost be a liability. Something they must take care of all the time so that Arne wouldn't be ashamed if he had seen it. But how could he see it? He's dead, right. He never bothered if the paint on the façade started to peel off. But Maria did. Sometimes Olivia got the impression that there was something neurotic about it. That Maria felt obliged to work away out there to keep something else at bay. Perhaps she should try to talk about it? Perhaps she should…

'Yes?'

Her mobile had rung.

'Hi, it's Ulf.'

'Hi.'

'I've spoken to my dad. About that Stilton guy.'

'Already? Great. Thanks! What did he say.'

'No idea… he said.'

'OK. So he didn't have any idea where Stilton can be found?'

'No, but he was familiar with that case on Nordkoster.'

'Oh, right.'

Then there was silence. Olivia was now leaving the Klaraberg road and driving up the ramp towards Centralbron. What more could she say? Thanks? For what? 'No idea' again?

'But thanks anyway.'

'You're welcome. If you need help with anything you only have to phone.'

Olivia hung up.

* * *

55

Bosques' sister had given Dan Nilsson a lift to Paquera, on the other side of the island. He had taken the ferry across to Puntaneras and then proceeded to San José by taxi. Expensive, but he didn't want to risk missing the plane.

He stepped out of the taxi at Juan Santamaria, the international airport at San José. He didn't have any baggage. It was hot and humid. His thin shirt had sweat rings almost down to his midriff. A bit further away, newly arrived tourists poured out and were enchanted by the heat. Costa Rica! They were here at last.

Nilsson went into the departure hall.

'Which gate is it?'

'Six.'

'Where is the security check?'

'Over there.'

'Thanks.'

He walked towards the security check. He had never travelled this direction before, only come into the country. A long time ago. Now he was on his way out. He tried to stay inside his own bell jar. He simply must. He must not allow himself to think. Not think about more than one phase at a time. Now it was the security phase, then came the gate phase, and after that he would be on board. Once he was there, that was it. Then it wouldn't particularly matter if he started to crack a little, he could cope with that. Upon his arrival, the next phase would start.

The Sweden phase.

* * *

He twisted and turned in his seat on the aircraft.

Just as he had suspected he would, he felt like a deflating balloon on the plane. Hidden corners had become visible and the past was oozing out.

Bit by bit.

When the professionally pleasant serving staff had done their bit, and the lights were finally dimmed inside the plane, he had fallen asleep.

Or so he thought.

But what took place in the dreamlike state inside his brain could hardly be called sleep. More like torture. With ingredients that were painfully tangible.

A beach, a murder, a victim.

Everything revolved around that.

And everything should revolve around that.

* * *

Olivia had now applied herself to the floor drain in the bathroom. With a growing feeling of nausea, and with the help of a toothbrush and a borrowed screwdriver, she had fished up a fat grey-black sausage about twenty centimetres long. A sausage of hairs which had effectively blocked the water lock in the floor drain. She felt even more nauseated when she realised that some of that hair was probably not hers. It must have accumulated over the years. Holding the hair sausage at arm's length, she carried it to the rubbish bin and then tied the plastic bag as soon as she had deposited her burden. She almost felt as if it could come to life.

Now she would open her emails.

Spam. Spam. Spam. And then her mobile rang.

It was her mum.

'You are already up, aren't you?' she asked.

'It's half past eight.'

'I never know with you.'

'What do you want?'

'What time should I pick you up tomorrow?'

'You what?'

'Have you bought masking tape?'

Oh, that meant Tynningö. Yes, of course. Maria had phoned a couple of days earlier and explained that it was time to deal with the sunny side of the house, where the façade got the worst of it. Arne had always paid particular attention to that. They would repaint it over the weekend. She had never asked whether Olivia had any other plans. In Maria's world you didn't have other plans if you were Maria's daughter and Maria had plans.

This weekend they were going to repaint that side of the house.

'Can't make it.'

Olivia quickly flipped through the calendar inside her head searching for an excuse.

'What do you mean, you can't make it? What is it that you can't make?'

A fraction of a second before she would be exposed as a bluff, she caught sight of the file next to her laptop. The beach case.

'I need to go down to Nordkoster this weekend.'

'Nordkoster? What would take you there?'

'It's umm… it's a college thing, an assignment.'

'But can't you do it next weekend?'

'No, it… I've already booked the train ticket.'

'But surely you can…'

'And you know what the assignment is? It's a murder case that dad worked on! Back in the Eighties! Weird isn't it!'

'What's weird?'

'That it's the same case.'

'He worked on lots of cases.'

'Yes, I know, but even so.'

The rest of the conversation didn't take long. Maria seemed to realise that she couldn't force Olivia to go to their summer house. So she asked how Elvis was, and then hung up straight after Olivia had answered.

Olivia quickly opened the railway booking site on her laptop.

* * *

Jelle had kept pretty much to himself all day. Sold a few copies of the magazine. Visited the New Community soup kitchen on Kammakargatan. Got some cheap food. Avoided people. He avoided people as often as he could. He could cope with Vera and perhaps one or two of the other homeless, otherwise he completely avoided contact. As he had done for several years now. Created a bell jar of loneliness. Isolation, physically as well as mentally. Found an inner vacuum where he tried to keep his footing. A vacuum that had been drained of all that had happened in the past. All that had happened, and that nothing could ever change. He had mental problems, and a diagnosis, he was on medicines to keep his psychoses in check. So as to be able to function – more or less. Or survive, he thought, it was more a question of surviving. To manage to survive from when he woke up in the morning, to when he fell asleep in the evening. With as little contact as possible with the rest of the world.

And as few thoughts as possible.

Thoughts about who he had been in the past. In another life, in another universe, before the first stroke of lightning came. The one that wrecked any possibility of a normal life, and created a chain reaction of breakdown and chaos and finally the first psychosis. And the hell that came in its wake. How he became a totally different person. A person who successively and deliberately destroyed all the social nets he had. So as to be able to sink. To let go.

To let go of everything.

That was six years ago, in a formal sense. For Jelle it was far longer ago. For him, every year that had passed had managed to rub out all normal concepts of time. He found himself in a timeless nothing. He fetched magazines, sold magazines, ate sometimes, looked for reasonably safe places to sleep. Places where he would be left in peace. Where nobody would be fighting or singing or dreaming noisily horrendous nightmares. Some time ago he had found an old wooden shack, with part of the roof caved in, it was off the beaten track some way outside the city.

It was a place he could die, when the time came.

Now he was on his way there.

* * *

The TV screen was on the wall in a sparsely furnished room. A rather large screen. Now you could get hold of a forty-two-inch screen for next to nothing. Especially if you weren't fussy about where you bought it. That was how this TV had been obtained, the TV which was now being watched by two youths with hoods on their jackets. One of them zapped a bit feverishly between different channels. Suddenly the other one reacted.

'Hey! Look!'

The zapper had tuned in to a channel where a man was being bombarded with kicks.

'Hell man, it's that bloke in the park! It's our fucking film!'

A couple of seconds later, a female presenter appeared on the screen and introduced a current affairs programme that had replaced something else at short notice.

'That was a short excerpt from one of the controversial film clips showing extreme violence on the Trashkick site. We shall shortly be discussing this.'

She made a gesture with her arm towards the wings.

'Here is a well-known journalist who has written about major social problems for many years: drugs, escort activities, trafficking... Now she is working on a series of articles about violence and youth – Eva Carlsén!'

The woman who entered the studio was dressed in black jeans and a black jacket with a white T-shirt underneath. Her blonde hair was worn up and her reasonably high heels carried a body in good physical shape. She was approaching fifty and knew what she was doing. She made her presence felt without any effort.

Carlsén sat down on a studio armchair.

'Welcome. A few years ago you wrote a book that attracted a lot of attention; it was a report on so-called escort services in Sweden, escort being a euphemism for luxury prostitution, but now you are concentrating on juvenile violence. This is how you introduce your series of articles...'

The presenter held up a newspaper.

'A feeling of anxiety is the mother of evil, and violence is a cry of help from a child who has gone astray. Anxiety is the breeding ground for the meaningless juvenile violence we see today. Anxiety is growing up in a society where you are not needed.'

The presenter lowered the newspaper and looked at Carlsén.

'Strong words. Is the situation really that serious?'

'Yes and no. When I write "the meaningless juvenile violence" I am, of course, referring to a specific violence, the perpetrators are specific individuals, in a limited degree. It is not the case that all young people engage in violence, in general; on the contrary, this is about a fairly small group.'

'*But, nevertheless, we have all been shocked by the films that have been posted online, where homeless people have been brutally beaten up. Who are they, the people that do this?*'

'*They are damaged children, deep down, abused children, children who have never had an opportunity to develop empathy – because they have been let down by the adult world. Now they react to their experience of having been abused and vent their anger on people who they think are even more worthless then they themselves are, in this case the homeless.*'

'Hell, that's fucking rubbish!'

It was the guy in the dark green jacket who reacted. His mate reached out for the remote.

'Hang on! I want to hear this.'

On the screen, the presenter shook her head a little.

'*So who is to blame?*' she asked.

'*We are all to blame. Every one of us who has created a society where young people can end up so far outside all the safety nets that they become inhuman.*'

'*And how can we remedy that, in your opinion? Is it possible to remedy it?*'

'*It's a political issue, it's about how society uses its resources. I can only describe what is happening, why it is happening, and what it leads to.*'

'*Repulsive films on the Internet?*'

'*Among other things.*'

At this point, the youth clicked the remote. When he put it down on the table, a little tattoo could be seen on his lower arm.

Two letters inside a ring: KF.
'What's the bitch called?' his mate asked.
'Carlsén. We've got to push off to Årsta now!'

* * *

Edward Hopper would have painted it if he had still been alive, and Swedish, and had found himself east of Stockholm in a forest area next to Jarla Lake, that night.

Painted that scene.

He would have captured the light from the only narrow lantern, high up on a metal pole, the way the soft yellow light fell upon the long, deserted road, the asphalt, the emptiness, the muted green shadows from the forest, and on the very edge of the field of light the solitary figure, a man, worn-out, tall, slightly stooped, possibly entering the field of light, possibly not... he would have been pleased with the painting.

Or not.

Perhaps he would have been bothered by the way his model suddenly deviated from the road and disappeared up into the forest. And left behind him, to the artist's disappointment, a deserted road.

The model who disappeared couldn't care less which.

He was on his way to his night shack. The shack with the partly caved-in roof behind what had once been a depot for large machines. Where he had some sort of roof to shield him from the rain, walls from the wind, a floor from the worst cold. No lighting, but what would he need that for? He knew what it looked like in here. But what he himself looked like, that was something he had forgotten several years earlier.

He slept here.

At best.

But at the worst times, like tonight, it crept up upon him. That which he did not want to come creeping up. This wasn't about rats or cockroaches, or spiders, animals could crawl however much they wished as far as he was concerned. That which came creeping, came from inside him.

From what had happened long, long ago.

And that was something he couldn't deal with.

He couldn't kill it with a stone or frighten it off with sudden movements. He couldn't even kill it by screaming. Although he tried, tonight too, tried to scream away that which came creeping and knew that it was useless.

You can't kill the past with screams.

Not even with an hour's continuous screaming. You simply destroy your vocal cords. When you have done that then you make use of the very last thing you want to make use of, because though you know it helps, it destroys you at the same time.

You take medicine.

Haldol and Stesolid.

Which kill that which creeps, and silence the screams. And mutilate yet another bit of your dignity.

Then you pass out.

5

The bay had the same shape as it had then. The rocks lay where they always had lain. The beach followed a wide arc along the same thick forest edge. When it was low tide, it was still dry quite a long way out, right down to the sea. In that respect nothing had changed at Hasslevikarna, twenty-three years later. It was still a beautiful and peaceful place. Anybody who came here to enjoy it today could hardly imagine what had happened then.

Just here, on that particular night when there was a spring tide.

* * *

He came out from the arrival hall at Göteborg's Landvetter airport wearing a short leather jacket and black jeans. He had changed in the toilet. He wasn't carrying anything, and went straight to the taxi rank. An immigrant, looking as though he would rather have been in bed, slipped out of the first taxi and opened one of the back doors.

Dan Nilsson climbed in.

'The Central Station.'

He was going to take a train up the coast to Strömstad.

* * *

You could feel it as soon as *Kostervåg* had left the shelter of the harbour. The big red ferry felt the heaving sea. It got worse for every nautical mile they progressed. The whole of the North Sea pushed against land here. When the wind reached nine to ten metres per second, Olivia's stomach started to churn. She never usually became seasick. She had sailed a lot in her parents' boat, mainly in the Stockholm archipelago but even there a strong wind could blow up. The only times she had reacted was when there was a heavy swell with long waves.

Like now.

She made sure she knew where the toilet was. On the left, opposite the canteen. The crossing wouldn't take so very long, so she ought to manage it. She had bought a cup of coffee and a cinnamon bun, which is what you usually did on this type of ferry, and took a seat beside one of the large windows. She was curious to see what the archipelago looked like on the west coast, so different from her own on the east. Here the rocks were low, worn, dark.

Dangerous, she thought, when she saw how the waves broke against a barely visible reef some way out.

But for the skipper this must be everyday fare, she thought. Three return journeys every day in the winter, and at least twenty now. In June. Olivia turned her gaze inwards. The saloon was fairly full, even though this was an early crossing. Islanders who were on their way home from a night job in Strömstad. Summer visitors on their way to their first week's holiday. And just a few day trippers.

Like her.

Well almost.

She was actually going to stay one night on the island. No longer. She had booked a cabin in a little holiday camp in the middle of the island. Rather expensive, it was high season after all. She looked out again. Far away she could make out a dark strip of coast and she realised it must be Norway. So close? she thought, and that same moment her mobile rang. It was Lenni.

'People might think you were dead! You haven't been online in fucking ages! Where the hell are you?'

'I'm on my way to Nordkoster.'

'And where's that?'

Lenni's knowledge of geography was not the best, she could hardly have marked in Göteborg on an empty map. But she did have other talents. Among them what she was now going to share with Olivia. It had all gone a treat with Jakob, they were as good as a couple now and were planning to go off to the big Peace & Love festival together.

'Erik went home with Lollo, there at Strand, but he did ask about you first!'

Oh, nice, Olivia thought, at least she was the first choice.

'So what are you doing down there? On that island. Have you met somebody?'

Olivia explained a bit, not all, since she knew that Lenni only had a limited interest in her college work.

'Hang on, that's the doorbell!' Lenni cut her off. 'It must be Jakob! Keep in touch, Livia! Phone when you get back!'

Lenni hung up just as the ferry was approaching the sound between the Koster islands.

The ferry called at the west jetty on the south-eastern part of Nordkoster. Some ubiquitous goods carrier mopeds with ubiquitous islanders were parked on the quayside. The first deliveries of the day had arrived.

And Olivia was one of them.

She stepped down onto the jetty and felt how it rocked. She came close to losing her balance and it took a few moments before she realised that the jetty was immobile. It was her who was wobbling.

'A rough crossing?'

The woman who asked was approaching Olivia. An elderly grey-haired women wearing a long black raincoat and with a face that had been facing the sea for the greater part of her life.

'A little.'

'I'm Betty Nordeman.'

'Olivia Rönning.'

'You've got no luggage?'

Olivia was holding a sports bag in her hand and thought that was surely a type of luggage. She was only going to stay one night.

'Only this.'

'Have you got a change of clothes in there?'

'No. A change of clothes?'

'You can feel it yourself, the wind is blowing from the sea and it will get worse and if we get rain too then it can be hell here. You haven't planned on sitting inside the cabin all the time, or have you?'

'No, but I do have an extra jumper.'

Betty Nordeman shook her head a little. They never learnt, did they, these mainlanders. Just because the sun shone in Strömstad they would come out here with just swimming trunks and a snorkel and an hour later they would have to rush off to Leffe's and buy lots of rain clothes and wellies and God knows what.

'Shall we move along?'

Betty started to walk and Olivia followed her. She found it hard to keep up. They passed a number of basket-like cages piled on the quay. Olivia pointed.

'Are those lobster traps?'

'Yes.'

'Is there a lot of lobster fishing here?'

'Not like there used to be. Now we're only allowed fourteen traps per fisherman, they've decided, before we could have as many as we wanted. But it's probably just as well, because there are hardly any lobsters left out there.'

'Pity, I like lobster.'

'I don't. The last time I ate lobster was the first time, and since then I've stuck to crabs. It's them that like lobster!'

Betty pointed at a couple of enormous yachts beside the jetty some way away.

'Norwegians. They sail here and buy up every lobster we catch. Soon they'll buy up all of Nordkoster.'

Olivia gave a little laugh. She could imagine that there would be some tension between the Norwegian nouveaux riches and the old islanders. They lived so close to each other.

'But the lobster season doesn't start until September so they'll have to cool it till then... or fly in some from America, like he did once, him Magnuson.'

'Who's he?'

'I'll show you when we go past.'

They walked up through the little gathering of wooden houses down by the water. Some red and black fishing huts. A restaurant, Strandkanten. A couple of shops selling a mixture of archipelago kitsch and old fishing tackle. And then Leffe's Laundry. And Leffe's Fishmongers. Leffe's Kayaks. And Leffe's Veranda.

'This Leffe guy seems to have a finger in every pie.'

'Yes, we call him XL here on the island. Short for Extra Leffe. He grew up on the eastern side of the island. On one occasion he visited Strömstad and got a bad headache, and since then he hasn't left the island. There it is!'

They were now a bit above the harbour. Houses large and small lined the narrow lane. Almost all of them were well tended, with neat façades, properly painted. Mum would approve of this, Olivia thought, and looked in the direction Betty was pointing. At a large, magnificent house, obviously designed specially for its beautiful site on a plot sloping down towards the sea.

'That's Magnuson's house. Bertil Magnuson, you know the man who owns that mining company, he had that built in the Eighties, he had no planning permission or anything, and then afterwards he bought his way out of it.'

'How do you mean?'

'He gave all the local councillors a fancy dinner and flew in a hundred lobsters from America and that problem was soon dealt with. For the people from the mainland, the rules are not the same as for us.'

They continued walking towards the part of the island where there were fewer houses. Betty guided, and Olivia listened.

Betty had the gift of the gab. Olivia had her work cut out to keep track of who had been fishing lobster unlawfully, who had had an affair with somebody else's wife and who hadn't kept their garden in good order.

Crimes great and small.

'And that's where his companion lived, by the way, the one who disappeared.'

'Whose companion?'

Betty looked quickly at Olivia.

'Him, Magnuson, I told you about him earlier.'

'Yeah, right. And who disappeared? Magnuson?'

'No, his companion, I just said. I can't remember his name. Anyway, he disappeared, people thought he'd been kidnapped or murdered, as I recall.'

Olivia stopped in her tracks.

'But, wait a minute! Did that happen here?'

Betty smiled at Olivia's excited expression.

'No, it was somewhere in Africa, and a bloody long time ago.'

But this had fired Olivia's imagination.

'When did he disappear?'

'Sometime in the Eighties it must have been.'

Olivia picked up the scent. Could there be a connection?

'Was that the same year that woman was murdered? At Hasslevikarna?'

Betty came to a sudden halt and turned towards Olivia.

'Is that why you're here? Murder tourism?'

Olivia tried to read Betty. Was it the question that had made her angry, or what? Olivia quickly explained why she was on the island. That she was a student at the Police College and was working on a student assignment about the beach case.

'Is that right? So you're going to join the police, are you?'

Betty scrutinized Olivia with a sceptical look.

'Yes, that's the intention, but I've not finished…'

'Well now, we're all different aren't we?'

Nor was Betty especially interested in hearing about Olivia's studies.

'But no, he didn't disappear the same year as the murder on the beach.'

'When did he disappear?'

'A lot earlier.'

Olivia felt a sting of disappointment. But what had she thought? That she would find some sort of connection between a disappearance and the beach murder as soon as she had set foot on Nordkoster? And, on top of that, a connection that the police had missed over all those years?

They met some families with small children out cycling, and Betty said hello to everyone. And kept on talking.

'But that murder on the beach, nobody here on the island will ever forget that. It was horrific. It hung over us for years and years.'

'Were you here yourself when it happened?'

'Yes, of course. Where else would I have been?'

Betty looked at Olivia as if that was the stupidest question she had ever been asked. So Olivia refrained from mentioning that there was an entire world outside of Nordkoster where Betty could have been. And then there was a long harangue about what Betty had done when the air ambulance arrived and the island was invaded by police and everything.

'And then they interrogated everybody on the island and you can be sure that I told them what I thought had happened.'

'And what did you think?'

'Satanists. Racists. Some sort of -ists that was for sure, that's what I told them.'

'Cyclists?'

Olivia meant it as a joke, but a few seconds passed before Betty twigged. Was she making fun of an old islander?... but then she started laughing. City humour. You had to take it for what it was.

'There're the cabins!'

Betty pointed at a row of small yellow cabins a bit ahead of them. They were well kept too. Newly painted for the high season, set out in the shape of a horseshoe at the edge of a beautiful meadow.

Just behind started a dark forest.

'Now it's my son who runs it. You booked it with him, Axel.'

They got closer to the cabins and Betty got going again. Her hand indicated cabin after cabin.

'Well, we've had all sorts of people staying here I can tell you...'

Olivia looked at the small huts. All of them were numbered with a figure in brass that looked as if it had just been polished. Everything was spick and span at Nordemans.

'Do you remember who was staying here then, when the murder took place?'

Betty made a bit of a face.

'You don't give up do you? But yes, I do actually remember. Some of them anyway.'

Betty pointed at the first in the row of cabins.

'There, for example, a couple of homos stayed there, there was a lot of hush-hush about that, it wasn't like it is today when every Tom, Dick and Harry climbs out of the closet. They said they were birdwatchers, but I didn't see them looking at anything other than themselves.'

Homos. Olivia had hardly heard the word used before. Would two homos have been capable of killing the woman on the beach? If, of course, they were homos, that might have been fake.

'In number two was a family with children, as far as I recall. Yes, that's right. Mum and dad with two kids who ran about frightening the sheep in the meadows. One of the kids got badly cut on the barbed wire and the parents were extremely indignant, they considered the farmer had been irresponsible. But the gods punish some people straight away, that's what I thought.

'Number four was empty, I know that, but there was a Turk staying in number five. He was here a long time, several weeks, he always had this red fez on his head, and he had a harelip and he lisped something awful. But he was nice and polite. Even kissed me on the hand once.'

Betty laughed at the memory. Olivia's head was processing the polite Turk. The woman had dark hair, could she have been Turkish? A Kurd? Honour killing? In the newspapers there had been something about her possibly being from Latin America, but what was that based on? Betty nodded at cabin number six.

'And there were a couple of drug addicts in there, unfortunately. But I won't stand for that sort of thing so I kicked them out. I had to scrub the whole cabin after them! The devils! And I found old syringes and bloody serviettes in the bin.'

Drugs? Olivia had read somewhere that there were traces of Rohypnol in the woman's body. Could there be a connection? She didn't have time to follow that thought through before Betty went on.

'But when I come to think of it, I reckon I threw them out before the murder... yes, I did, because after that they stole a boat and went off to the mainland. To stock up on drugs, if you ask me.'

And there went Olivia's lead too.

'What an incredible memory you have!' she said.

Betty paused for breath and lapped up the praise.

'Well, yes, I suppose I do, but we have a ledger too.'

'But nevertheless!'

'Well, I'm interested in people. That's what I'm like, quite simply.'

Betty looked smugly at Olivia and pointed to a cabin at the end of the row with number ten.

'And that's where the silly woman from Stockholm stayed. She stayed there first, then on a Norwegian yacht in the harbour. She was a real slut, made a show of herself for those poor lobster boys down by the quay so they couldn't keep their eyes off her. But of course the police interrogated her too!'

'To help them with their enquiries?'

'I suppose so, they talked to her here first, and then I heard that they took her to Strömstad and continued there. That's what Gunnar said.'

'Who's he?'

'Gunnar Wernemyr, policeman, but he's retired now.'

'And what was she called, the silly woman?'

'Her name was… let me think, I can't remember but she had the same first name as Kennedy's wife.'

'And what was she called?'

'Don't you know what Kennedy's wife was called? You know who I mean, she got together with that Greek later, Onassis.'

'No?'

'Jackie… Jackie Kennedy. Yes, that's what she was called, the silly woman, Jackie, I can't remember more than that. That's your cabin!'

Betty pointed at one of the yellow cabins and walked up to the door with Olivia.

'The key's hanging on a hook inside. If you need anything, Axel lives there.'

Betty pointed to a house with asbestos-cement cladding on a rise a bit away. Olivia opened the door and put her sports bag inside. Betty remained outside.

'Hope it suits you.'

'It'll be perfect!'

'OK then. We might meet in the harbour this evening, XL is going to play his trombone at the Strandkant restaurant, if you end up there. Bye for now!'

Betty started to walk away. Suddenly Olivia remembered what she had intended to ask all the time but not managed to fit in.

'Fru Nordeman!'

'Call me Betty.'

'Betty… I was wondering, there was a little boy who saw what happened on the beach, wasn't there?'

'That was Ove, the Gardman boy, they lived in a house in the forest there.' Betty pointed towards the dark forest. 'His mother's dead now, and his father is in a home in Strömstad, but Ove still has the house.'

'Is he there now?'

'No, he is out travelling. He's one of those, what do you call it… a marine biologist, but he comes here now and then to look after the house when he's in Sweden.'

'OK, thanks!'

'And Olivia, bear in mind what I said, about the weather, it's going to get worse by the hour, so don't go out on the rocks on the north side or anything like that, not on your own. If you do go there, then perhaps Axel can go with you. It can be dangerous up there if you take the wrong path.'

Betty went off. Olivia remained where she was a minute or two and watched her. Then she glanced up at the cement-tiled house where her son Axel evidently lived. The idea that a guy she didn't know should follow along with her as a bodyguard just because there was a bit of wind, she found that somewhat comical.

* * *

He had bought a suitcase in Strömstad. A suitcase on wheels and with an extendable handle. When he went on board the Koster ferry he looked just like any other tourist.

But he wasn't.

He was a tourist, perhaps, but not just anybody.

He was a man who had struggled with a growing chaos in his chest the whole way from Göteborg and not managed to get it under control until now.

When he went on board the ferry.

Now he knew that it wasn't much further. Now he must be in control of himself. What he was going to do didn't allow for wavering or weakness. He was forced to steel himself.

When the ferry departed, inside him it felt shiny, cold, stripped. Like the rocks they passed. He suddenly thought about Bosques.

They had hugged each other.

* * *

Olivia was lying down on the simple bed in the cabin. She had slept badly on the train. Now she stretched out and inhaled the mouldy smell of the cabin. Perhaps it isn't mouldy, she thought, more like stuffy. She glanced up at the bare walls. Not a painting, no posters, not even one of those old fisherman's floats of green glass. Betty would never be interviewed by one of the glossy magazines. Nor Axel, if it was him who was responsible for the furnishings. She raised the map again. She had bought it before she got on the ferry in Strömstad. A rather detailed map of the north-west side, only that. Coves with funny names, and not far away, on the map, Hasslevikarna.

That was where she was really going.

The site of the murder.

Because that is what the entire journey was about, she knew that. Getting to the site of the murder and seeing what it looked like.

Murder tourist?

If you like. That's what she'd have to be. But she was going to get to that beach. The place where a young woman had been buried and drowned.

With a child in her womb.

Olivia let the map sink down onto her chest and she let her mind wander, wander off to the Hasslevikarna coves and out on to the beach, the sea, the low tide, the darkness, and the naked young woman in the sand, and the little boy in the darkness somewhere, and then the perpetrators, three of them, that's what it had said in the investigation, based on the boy's statement, but how could they be sure of that? A terrified nine-year-old in the middle of the night? Perhaps they weren't sure? Had they just assumed that he had actually seen three men? Or had the police simply just accepted that as a starting point, as they had nothing else to go on? What if there were five? A little sect?

There she was again.

This wasn't especially constructive.

She got up and felt that the time had come.

To be a murder tourist.

What Betty had said about the weather was fairly accurate, apart from the fact that the rain had already hit the island now in the afternoon. The wind coming from the sea had increased in strength by a couple of metres per second, and the temperature had dropped radically.

It was pretty horrible outside.

Olivia could hardly open the door when she went out. It slammed shut behind her as soon as she was out. Her extra jumper helped a little, but the wind pulled her hair across her face so she could hardly see, and the rain poured down. Why the hell hadn't she brought a raincoat with her? She had behaved like an amateur! Or somebody from the mainland, as Betty would have said. Olivia glanced up at Axel's house.

No way. There were limits.

She chose a path that led into the dark forest.

The very overgrown forest. There had been no thinnings here for decades, and nobody had cleared the undergrowth either. Dry, brittle branches, a tangle of brushwood, everything almost black with the odd bit of rusty sheep netting.

But she followed the path. She could just about manage that. The advantage was that there was much less wind in among the trees. Just the rain. At first she had used the map to shield her head until she realised it was a really stupid idea. The map was her only chance of getting to where she wanted to go.

First she was going to see the little boy's house. Ove Gardman. According to Betty it was somewhere around here, in among the trees, which Olivia was beginning to doubt. All around her was just a mass of bushes and fallen trees and netting.

Suddenly there it was in front of her.

A simple black wooden house. Two storeys, in the middle of the forest, in an opening where the trees had long been chopped down. There was a steep edge at the back and no garden. She looked at the house. It seemed to be deserted, and a bit spooky. At any rate under the circumstances that now prevailed. A strong gale and getting darker. She got the shivers. Why had she wanted to see this house? She already knew that the boy, or man as he must be today, presumably thirty-two years old, wasn't there. Betty had told her. She shook her head a little but pulled out her mobile and took a couple of pictures of the house. She could always append them to her assignment report, she thought.

Ove Gardman's house.

She reminded herself to phone him when she got back to the cabin.

It took Olivia almost half an hour to get to the north side of the island. Now she was there, almost anyway, and she was beginning to fathom what Betty had warned her about. Here it was completely exposed to the open sea. The rain beat down from the black clouds. The wind howled round the rocks. Gigantic waves from the North Sea rolled in and crashed over the rocks. It was hard for her to judge how far up they came.

She crouched down behind a large rock and looked out towards the sea. She thought she was in a safe position, but suddenly a super wave came roaring up to the rock and the water reached way up her legs. When she felt how the cold pull tugged at her body, she panicked and screamed.

If she hadn't fallen into a little gully, she would have been pulled into the sea.

But she didn't realise that until much later.

Now she was running.

As fast as her legs could carry her.

Away from the sea up onto dry land.

She ran and ran until she tripped on a flat rock, or an oasis of flat rocks. She landed flat on her stomach. Once down, she hugged the rock, hugged Mother Earth, gasping, with a bleeding forehead from when she fell into the gully.

It was quite a while before she turned round and looked out at the raging sea beyond the small coves, and realised what an idiot she was.

Then her whole body started to shake.

She was soaked to her skin.

* * *

Considering it was a trombone evening with XL, there weren't really very many people in the Strandkanten restaurant, which otherwise had a very good reputation. Perhaps the trombone had put them off. There were a few islanders at the tables, with glasses of beer, XL in one corner with his trombone, and Dan Nilsson was there too.

He was sitting at the table closest to the water. The wind was driving the rain against the window. He had come here directly from the ferry. Not because he was hungry, or thirsty, or to get out of the rain.

He needed to gather strength.

All the strength he could muster.

He knew there was a minimal risk he could be recognised, he used to have a holiday house here many, many years ago. But that was a risk he was forced to take.

Now he was sitting here with a glass of beer in front of him. One of the waitresses had whispered to XL during a break from the trombone: he looks like a policeman that guy by the window, and XL had answered that there was something familiar about his face. But Nilsson didn't hear that. He was somewhere totally different in his thoughts. Further north on the island.

Where he had been before.

A place he was going to visit again, this evening.

And then yet another place.

And when that was done, he was done too.

Or perhaps it was the opposite, not quite clear.

He didn't know.

That was what he was going to find out.

* * *

Besides being soaked to the skin, bleeding from her forehead and half in a state of shock, she had also suffered a minor catastrophe. She had lost the map. Or the super wave had taken it. Now she no longer had a map. She didn't know which way to go. Nordkoster is not a large island, not in the summer sun and the heat of June, but in stormy weather when it's pissing it down and it's getting dark, then the island is big enough to get lost on.

For somebody from the mainland.

Strips of forest, patches of heathland, rocky areas that suddenly appear before you.

Especially if you have never been there before.

Like Olivia.

Here she was, in the middle of nowhere. Totally disoriented. With dark forest in front of her and slippery rocks behind her. And since her otherwise excellent mobile had been immersed in the sea and given up on her, she didn't have many other choices.

Except to start walking.

In one direction or the other.

So she walked, shaking, in one direction or the other.

Several times.

* * *

Dan Nilsson knew exactly where he was going, even though it had now got really dark because of the awful weather. He didn't need a map. He pulled his suitcase along after him on the gravel road, veered off away from the sea and then turned down along the path he knew would be there.

Which led to the place he was going to.

The first place.

* * *

She wasn't normally afraid of the dark. She had slept alone in the house in Rotebro since she was quite young. The same when they'd been out at their holiday house. The opposite really, she found it peaceful and calming when the darkness came down and everything else died out. And she was left by herself.

Alone.

And she was alone now. But under rather different circumstances. Now she was alone in strange surroundings. There was the roar of thunder and the rain was coming down in bucketfuls. She could hardly see more than a metre or two in front of her. Just trees and rocks, and then more of the same. She slipped on moss, tripped over stones, was suddenly rammed by branches in her face, and slid down into deep gullies. And she could hear sounds too. The howling of the wind, that didn't scare her, and nor did the raging sea round about her, she knew what that was. But the other sounds? That sudden muted bellowing that cut through the darkness. Was it sheep? Surely sheep didn't sound like that? And that thin shriek that she had heard between the trees just a moment ago, where did that come from? No children would be outside now, would they? She suddenly heard the shriek again, closer, and then another one. She huddled against a tree trunk and stared into the darkness. Could she see eyes over there? Two eyes? Yellow? A tawny owl? Did they have tawny owls on Nordkoster?

Then she saw the shadow.

A distant stroke of lightning threw a sliver of light into the forest and revealed a shadow that moved between the trees only a few metres away.

It seemed to be a shadow.

And it terrified her.

The sliver of light vanished just as quickly as it had come, and it became all dark again. She didn't know what it was she had seen.

Between the trees.

A human?

* * *

The man who carried his wheeled suitcase through the thick forest was indeed a human. A focused human. The rain had made his blond hair fasten in wet wisps across his face. It didn't bother him. He had been out in worse weather than this. In other parts of the world. With totally different tasks. All the more unpleasant tasks, as far as he was concerned. He had a certain degree of empirical readiness. Would it help him this time? That he didn't know.

He had no experience of this task.

She had admittedly only seen it on the map, and on Google Earth for that matter, but since the rainclouds had decided to suddenly move on over to the mainland and had let a cold moon slip through a crack, she could recognise the outline.

She was looking at the coves at Hasslevikarna.

She had roamed around in total confusion for quite a while. Her clothes were still soaking wet. The cut on her forehead had stopped bleeding but she was shaking all over, and now she had stumbled across this. Which was her original destination. Ages ago.

Now she was shaking for other reasons too.

The weird blue light from that dead heavenly body up there created an eerie mood in the bay. And it was evidently low tide too. The beach seemed to go on forever. It started up by the sand dunes and went far out towards the sea.

She reached one side of the beach and sank down on a large rock and shook her way into a strange state of suggestion.

So this was where it had happened.

That horrible murder.

Here was the beach. Here was the place where the naked woman had been buried.

She ran her hand across the rocks in front of her.

Where had the boy been sitting when he had seen it? At the place where she was sitting just now? Or was it on the other side of the long beach? Where she could make out other rocks. She stood up and looked across to the other side and that was when she saw him.

A man.

He came out of the edge of the forest way over on the other side, with a... what was it? A suitcase on wheels? Olivia crouched down and hid behind the rock. She saw how the man let go of his suitcase on wheels and started to walk across the dry sand down towards the sea. Slowly, further and further towards the sea. Suddenly he stopped, a long way out. Stood completely still and looked up at the moon... and then down towards the sand and up again. The wind tugged at his hair and jacket. Suddenly he squatted down and lowered his head as if in prayer, then he stood up again. Olivia pressed her clenched fists against her mouth. What was the man up to? Just there? Half way out to the sea? Just now when there was a low tide and a full moon?

Who was he?

Was he mad?

It was hard for her to say how long he stood there. It could have been three minutes, it could have been fifteen. She didn't know. Suddenly he turned and walked back up towards the dunes. Just as slowly, back to where he had left his suitcase, turned round again and looked out towards the sea.

Then he disappeared into the forest.

Olivia remained sitting where she was. Long enough to be certain that the man had got some distance away.

Unless of course he had stayed near the edge of the forest.

* * *

He hadn't. He had gone on towards his other place. The next place, rather, the one that was really more important. The first had just been more of a mourning rite. The second was concrete.

It was there he would do something.

He knew, of course, where it was, the green house, but he didn't remember it as having such a thick hedge around the grounds. But that served his purpose. It made it easy to be able to slip in and stay hidden behind the hedge. Nobody would see him from the outside.

He noticed that there were lights on inside the house and that worried him. There were people there. He would have to sneak past, along the side of the hedge, to get right there. Right up to the place that he must get to.

He started to move forwards, cautiously. He held the suitcase in his hand. He took each step as quietly as he could. In the dark it was hard to see where he was putting his feet. When he was almost level with the house, he heard a door open on the other side. He pushed his body into the hedge and got a thick branch in his face. He stood absolutely still. Suddenly he saw a little boy rounding the corner of the house, ten metres away. The boy gave a laugh and pressed himself against the wall. Was he playing hide-and-seek? Nilsson breathed as quietly as he could. If the boy were to turn and look in his direction then he would be discovered. He was too close for anything else.

'Johan!'

A woman was calling. The boy crouched down a little and turned his head slightly, towards the hedge. For a moment Nilsson thought that their eyes had met. The boy didn't move.

'Johan!'

The woman called out louder now. Suddenly the boy detached himself from the wall and started to run again, disappearing behind the other corner of the house. Nilsson remained standing in the hedge until he heard the door slam on the other side. It fell silent. He waited several minutes before he started to move again.

* * *

She would probably have died in the forest. Frozen to death, or some other end that would look good on the newspaper placards, she thought. But she didn't, and it wasn't through her own efforts.

It was thanks to Axel.

When she finally sank down on a rock, utterly exhausted, she heard the voice.

'Have you lost your way?'

A tall, broad-shouldered youth with short hair and intense eyes was standing about a metre away and looking at her wet apparition. He didn't really need an answer to the question. And she didn't answer either.

'Who are you?' she said.

'Axel. My mother said I should take a walk and see where you'd got to. She went past your cabin and you hadn't come back. Have you lost your way?'

That's putting it mildly, she thought, I'm about as fucking lost as you possibly could be on this fucking island.

'Yes,' she said.

'That's quite an achievement.'

'You what?'

'Losing your way on this island, it isn't very large.'

'Thanks.'

Olivia was helped up. Axel looked at her.

'You are completely soaked. Did you have a tumble?'

Have a tumble? Up at Hasslevikarna? Was that what they called it, the islanders? That you have a tumble? When half the fucking North Sea crashes down upon you?

What a bunch of weirdos.

'Can you help me back?'

'Yeah, sure. Take my jacket.'

Axel put his big warm jacket round the frozen Olivia and led her through the big bad forest all the way back to the little yellow cabin, and once there he offered to go and fetch a bit of food.

My hero, Olivia thought, sitting on her bed wrapped in a blanket and with some lukewarm food on the plate in her hand. A person who saves lives.

Who doesn't talk too much, but just gets on with it.

Axel Nordeman.

'Are you one of the lobster boys?'

She had asked him that, not really serious.

'Yes.'

He had answered. And that was it.

Not exactly your Ulf Molin type.

With food and warmth and survival, most things were back to normal with Olivia. Even her mobile. That, too, had dried out with a bit of help from a borrowed hairdryer.

When she had checked her text messages and emails, it suddenly struck her that she had forgotten that she had to phone Ove Gardman again. She had phoned him yesterday, on the night train down to Göteborg, and got an answering machine. Now she was going to try again. She checked the time, it was pushing ten. She phoned and reached the answering machine again. She left a new message and asked him to phone her as soon as he heard it. Then she hung up and started coughing violently.

Pneumonia? went through her head.

* * *

Quite other things went through Nilsson's head. He was squatting down. His suitcase next to him. Far behind him the green house could just be made out. There were no lights on there now.

With an extreme effort he pushed the larger rock aside. He had already moved the smaller one. He looked down into the exposed hole. A deep hole, just as he remembered it. He had dug it himself. A long time ago. To deal with any eventuality.

He glanced at the suitcase.

* * *

Suddenly she was overcome by tiredness. Suddenly her entire body was like a rag doll. All that roaming around getting lost had done her in. She hardly had the energy to pull the bedspread back and creep under the covers. The little bedside lamp spread a warm glow over the room and she felt as if she was drifting away. Slowly… and dad Arne drifted up. He shook his head a little when he looked at her.

'That could have been really nasty.'

'I know. It was stupid.'

'It wasn't like you. You usually know what you're doing.'

'I get that from you.'

Then Arne smiled, and Olivia felt tears running down her cheeks. He looked so thin, like he must have looked at the end, when she didn't see him, when she was in Barcelona, running away.

'Sleep tight.'

Olivia opened her eyes. Was it Arne who had said that? She shook her head a little and felt how hot her face was, her brow. Was she running a temperature? Bound to happen, wasn't it? Here. In a cabin on an island off the west coast that I've only booked for one night. Can you get more wilderness than that? What should I do now?

Axel?

He might not have gone to bed yet, he lived on his own after all, he'd told her. Perhaps he was sitting up there playing video games. A lobster boy? Hardly. But what if he suddenly knocked on the door and asked if the food was OK?

'Yeah, it tasted great.'

'Good. Anything else you need?'

'No, I'm doing fine thanks. But perhaps a thermometer?'

'A thermometer?'

Then one thing would have led to another and when the bedside lamp was about to be turned off they would both be naked and terrible horny.

Thought Olivia, feverishly.

One-eyed Vera had been to a football match. *Situation Sthlm* versus a rehab from Rågsved. The match had ended with *Situation* 2–0 up. Pärt had scored both goals.

He'd dine off that for a long time.

Now he was walking along with Vera and Jelle and enjoying the warm night. The match had been played on the Tanto pitch in the south of the city. Because of some bickering afterwards with the referee and some other hassle after the match, they hadn't moved off until about elevenish. And now it was more like half past eleven.

Pärt was in a buoyant mood, he had after all scored two goals. Vera was in a good mood too, she had found some black nail polish in a skip near Zinken. Jelle was feeling so-so. But that's how he nearly always felt, so nobody took any notice. There they were making their way through the night, two cheerful and one a bit disheartened.

Vera was hungry and suggested they should look in at Dragon House. The Chinese eatery down at Hornstull. She had just got her monthly pension and considered she could treat her less well-off friends. Pärt refused to enter and Jelle didn't like Chinese. So instead they feasted on various sausages with accessories at Abraham's Grill on Hornsgatan. When Pärt had received his generous portion he smiled a little.

'Now is tasty.'

Then they strolled on along Hornsgatan.

'Anyone know how things are with Benseman?'

'No change.'

Suddenly somebody waltzed past them, a very short man without shoulders, a straggly little ponytail and a pointed nose. The man glanced across at Jelle in the midst of his waltzing.

'Hi there, how's things?' said the short man with a decidedly squeaky voice.

'Teeth bothering me.'

'OK then. See you around.'

The short man continued his tripping.

'Who the hell was that?'

Vera looked at the ponytail man.

'The Mink,' said Jelle.

'The Mink? Who's that?'

'A guy from the past.'

'Homeless?'

'No, not as I know of. He's got a place in Kärrtorp.'

'Can't you kip down there then?'

'No.'

Jelle had no intention of kipping down at Mink's place. The conversation they had just had was about the level of the relationship they had.

Nowadays.

And now Jelle knew what was coming.

'You're welcome to kip down in my caravan,' said Vera.

'I know. Thanks.'

'But you don't want to?'

'No.'

'Where would you rather kip down then?'

'It'll sort itself.'

They had had this conversation several times of late, Vera and him. It wasn't about sleeping in Vera's caravan. They both knew that. It was about something Jelle wasn't too keen on, and the simplest way to avoid hurting Vera's feelings was to decline the invitation.

To kip down in the caravan.

That meant no to the other thing too.

For the moment.

Olivia turned over in the bed in the lonely cabin. She slipped in and out of feverish dreams. First she'd be on the beach at Hasslevikarna, then in Barcelona. Suddenly she felt how an icy-cold hand was touching her naked foot on the edge of the bed.

She flew up!

Her elbow knocked the little bedside table and the lamp fell onto the floor. She threw herself up against the wall and stared around the cabin – empty. She pushed the covers a little to one side. Her violent heartbeats made her gasp for air. Had she been dreaming? Of course she'd been dreaming, what else could it have been? She was the only one there. There was nobody else in the cabin.

She sat up on the edge of the bed, picked up the lamp and tried to calm down. Breathe deep breaths, that's what Maria had taught her when she was little on the odd occasion she had a nightmare. She dried her forehead and that was when she heard it. A sound. Like a voice, from outside. From outside the door.

Axel?

Olivia wrapped a blanket around her, went towards the door and opened it – two metres in front of her stood a man carrying a suitcase with wheels. The man from Hasslevikarna. Olivia slammed the door shut, locked it and rushed to the only window. She pulled down the blind while looking around her for some sort of object. Something to hit him with, anything at all!

There was a knock on the door.

Olivia didn't make a sound. She was shaking all over. Could she be heard from Axel's place if she screamed? Probably not, the wind out there would howl louder.

There was another knock.

Olivia hyperventilated and walked slowly towards the door.

Silently.

'My name is Dan Nilsson, I'm sorry to disturb you.'

The voice came through the door. Dan Nilsson?

'What's the matter? What do you want?' said Olivia.

'I can't get a signal on my mobile, and I need to phone for a taxi boat, I saw your light was on and… do you possibly have a mobile I can borrow?'

She did have a mobile. But the man out there didn't need to know that.

'Just a quick call,' he said through the door. 'I can pay for it.'

Pay for a quick call? To order a taxi boat? Olivia didn't know what to do. She could lie and say she didn't have a mobile and send him on his way. Or send him up to Axel's. But at the same time she was beginning to get curious. What had he been doing up at Hasslevikarna? Standing out there on the beach at low tide in the moonlight? Who was he? What would Arne have done?

He would have opened the door.

And Olivia did too. Carefully. Just a little. She held out her mobile through the gap.

'Thank you,' said Nilsson.

He took the mobile, dialled in a number and ordered a taxi boat to come to the west jetty. He would be there in a quarter of an hour.

'Thanks for the loan,' he said.

Olivia got the phone back through the gap again. Nilsson turned and started to walk away.

Then Olivia opened the door fully.

'I saw you up at Hasslevikarna this evening.'

Olivia was standing against the light from the bedside lamp when Nilsson turned round again. He looked at her and blinked, as if in surprise, but she didn't know at what. It only lasted a flash of a second.

'What were you doing there?' he asked.

'I'd got lost and ended up there.'

'A beautiful place.'

'Yes.'

Silence… and what were you doing there? Didn't he understand that that was the underlying question?

Perhaps he did, but it was a question he had no intention whatsoever of answering.

'Good night.'

Nilsson went on his way, with the image of Olivia on his retina.

* * *

The trombone lay in its black case and XL sat next to it, on the quay below the restaurant. It had been a long evening and he had poured quite a lot down his throat. Now he was going to sober up a little. He would open a smoke house tomorrow. Leffe's Smokehouse. Freshly smoked fish for the mainlanders, that would turn a nice profit. The well-built islander next to him was sober. He was on call to man the taxi boat and had just got a booking.

'Who is it?'

'Someone from over there.'

Over there could mean anything from Strömstad to Stockholm.

'How much did you ask for?'

'Two thousand.'

XL did a bit of mental arithmetic and compared it with his smokehouse. The hourly rate did not work out to the smokehouse's advantage.

'Is that him?'

XL nodded upwards. A man with a leather jacket and black jeans was walking towards them.

A man who had done what he had to do.

On Nordkoster Island.

Now he was forced to take another step.

In Stockholm.

* * *

She had finally fallen asleep. With the lamp on, the door locked and the name Dan Nilsson on her lips.

The man from Hasslevikarna.

The rest of the night Olivia was in the grip of feverish nightmares. For hours. Suddenly a frayed bellow pushed up through her throat and out of her wide-open mouth. A terrible bellow. Cold sweat ran out of every pore and her hands clawed at the air. On the windowsill behind her, a spider sat watching the drama taking place in the bed. How the young woman tried to clamber up out of a hole of terror.

In the end she got out.

She remembered the nightmare down to the tiniest detail. She had been buried in the sand. Naked. The tide was low and there was moonlight and it was cold. The sea started to roll in. Closer and closer. The water rushed up towards her head, but it wasn't water, it was a lava stream of thousands of small black crabs that gushed forth towards her naked face and into her open mouth.

That was when the bellow came.

Olivia leapt out of bed and gasped for breath. She pulled up the blanket with one hand, wiped the sweat off her face and stared around in the cabin. Had the entire night been a dream? Had that man really been there? She went up to the door and opened it. She needed air, oxygen, and stepped out into the darkness. The wind had died down a great deal. She felt she needed to pee. She went down the steps and then squatted behind a large bush. It was then she saw it, a little to her left.

The suitcase.

The man's wheeled suitcase lay on the ground.

She went up to it and peered around her in the darkness. She couldn't see anything. Or anybody. She couldn't see Dan Nilsson at any rate. She sank down beside the suitcase. Should she open it?

She unzipped the flap from one side to the other, and cautiously lifted the upper part of the case.

It was completely empty.

* * *

From a distance, it might look rather idyllic, the greyish caravan. Embedded in the nocturnal greenery from the Nothing forest, quite close to the Pampas Marina in Solna, with a weak yellow glow through the oval window.

But on the inside the idyll vanished.

The caravan was very decrepit. At one time the Calor gas stove beside the wall had worked, now it was all rusty and useless. At one time the plexiglass dome on the roof had let in some light, now it was covered with dirt and opaque. At one time the doorway had been covered with long colourful plastic ribbons, now there were only three left, and they only reached halfway to the floor. At one time the caravan had served as a holiday dream for a family with two children from Tumba, now it was One-eyed Vera's.

At first she had cleaned it, often, tried to maintain a decent level of hygiene. But as she found more and more things in skips and insisted on dragging them back, the level sank considerably. Now there were ant paths going back and forth among the junk, and earwigs lurking in various corners.

But rather that than dossing down in tunnels or bicycle sheds.

The walls had been decorated with newspaper articles about the homeless and small posters she had found now and then;

above one bunk hung something that looked like a child's drawing of a harpoon, above the other was a cutting: 'It isn't the people who are outside who should be allowed in, it is the people on the inside who should be thrown out.'

Vera liked that.

Now she was sitting at her worn formica table and painting her nails black.

It wasn't going too well.

It was that time of night when nothing went well. When she kept watch. Vera often kept watch, and waited, kept watch during the hours of dark and cramps. She rarely dared to sleep. When she finally did fall asleep it was more like a form of collapse. She just flopped down, or fell into a sort of hibernation.

This had been going on a long time.

It was about her mental state, as for so many of those around her. A mental state that had been damaged and mutilated long, long ago.

In her case, which was hardly a unique one but did have its personal details, there were three things that had done the most damage. Or caused the worst mutilation. A bunch of keys had damaged her. Physically as well as mentally. The blows from her father's big bunch of keys had left visible white scars on her face and invisible scars inside her.

She had been beaten with the bunch of keys.

More often than she deserved, in her opinion. Blind to the insight that a child never deserved a bunch of keys in the face: she blamed herself for some of the blows. She knew that she had been a difficult child.

What she didn't know, then, was that she was a difficult child in a dysfunctional family, with two parents who couldn't cope with life and vented their frustration on the only person in the vicinity.

Their daughter Vera.

It was the bunch of keys that damaged her.

But it was what happened to her grandmother that mutilated her.

Vera had loved her grandmother, and her grandmother had loved Vera, and for every blow of the keys that landed on Vera's face, her grandmother had shrunk.

Helpless.

And afraid, of her own son.

Until she gave up.

Vera was thirteen when it happened. She went to visit her grandmother's farm in Uppland with her parents. The booze they had with them led to the usual results, and a few hours later her grandmother went out. She just couldn't face watching and hearing the misery of it all. She knew what would come: the bunch of keys. When it did come, Vera managed to get out of the way, this time, and ran to fetch grandmother.

She found her in the barn. Hanging from a thick rope attached to a beam.

Dead.

That was a shock in itself, but it didn't stop there. When she tried to get the attention of her extremely intoxicated parents, they were beyond communication. So she had to do it herself. Take her grandmother down from the beam and lay her on the ground. And cry. For hours, she had sat beside her grandmother's body until her tear ducts had dried up.

That mutilated her.

And that is what made it so hard to get her newly found black nail polish as even as she wanted. It got a bit messy. Partly because Vera's eyes were veiled in tears by the memory of her grandmother, but partly because she was shaking.

That was when she thought about Jelle.

She nearly always did that when it became too painful to keep watch. Thought about him, his eyes, there was something about his eyes that had caught her attention, from the first time they had come across each other, up at the magazine office.

He didn't look, he saw. That's what Vera thought, as if he saw her, saw beyond what was her shabby outside, right into who she was in another world.

Or could have been. If she hadn't lacked the tools and ended up keeping the wrong company, and started down the path to Calvary carved between various institutions and authorities.

It was as if he saw the other Vera. The strong, original one. The one who could fulfill the role of citizen in any modern welfare state she chose.

If there still had been one.

But there wasn't one, Vera thought, they have pared it down to the ground. The 'people's home', the welfare state that had once been created in Sweden was no more. But we did have the postal code lottery!

And then she smiled a little, and saw that the nail of her little finger looked really nicely painted.

6

The man who lay in the bed had had a bit of work done, discreetly, conjuring away a couple of bags under his eyes. His greying hair was short and thick, it was trimmed every fifth day, the rest of his body getting its due in his private gym on the floor below.

He kept his age at arm's length. From the double bed in his bedroom he could see the Cedergren tower, a folly just a couple of plots away. Stocksund's most famous landmark. It had been intended to be a showpiece, and had been started by forest-owner Albert Gotthard Nestor Cedergren.

The man in the bed lived himself on Granhällsvägen, down by the water, in a much smaller building. Only about 420 square metres, with a sea view. But that would have to do. He did, after all, have his little treasure on Nordkoster too.

Now he was lying on his back and being massaged by the bed, a gentle, exclusive massage of his whole body. Even the insides of his thighs got the treatment. A favour that was worth the extra twenty thousand it had cost.

He delighted in the moment.

Today, he was going to meet the King.

Well 'meet' was perhaps a clumsy way of putting it. He was going to be present at a ceremony at the Chamber of Commerce at which the realm's monarch would be the main figure. He himself would be the number two main figure. In fact, the entire ceremony was planned in his honour. He was going to be awarded a medal for running Sweden's most successful company abroad in the previous year, or whatever the citation was.

As the founder and managing director of Magnuson World Mining AB.

MWM.

It was he who was Bertil Magnuson.

'Bertil! What about this?'

Linn Magnuson swept into the room in one of her creations. It was the cerise one again, the one she had worn the other evening. It was very beautiful.

'That's pretty.'

'Do you think so? It isn't too… you know…'

'Provocative?'

'No, but simple? You know who'll be there.'

Bertil did know. More or less. The cream of Stockholm's business community, a few titled bigwigs, a few well-chosen politicians, not at cabinet level but almost. Or perhaps? Perhaps Minister of Finance Borg would nip in for a few minutes, if he was lucky. That always provided a bit of extra glory. Erik would not be able to come, unfortunately. His latest tweet: 'Brussels. Meeting with the top brass in the Commission. Hope to fit in a barber first.'

Erik was always fussy about his appearance.

'What about this then?' Linn asked.

Bertil sat up in bed. Not as a reaction to his wife's latest presentation, an expensive piece she had found at the Weird & Wow boutique on Sibyllegatan, but because he felt he had to.

He had to empty his bladder.

This had been a bit of a problem of late. He had to visit the toilet more frequently than a man in his position had time to do. Only a week ago, he had met a professor of geology who had almost frightened him to death. The man in question told how he had become incontinent at the age of sixty-four.

Bertil was sixty-six.

'I think you should wear that one,' he said.

'Do you think so? Yes, perhaps. It looks lovely.'

'So do you.'

Bertil gave Linn a light kiss on her cheek. He would have given her more than that. She was extremely attractive considering she had passed fifty, and he loved her to distraction, but his bladder steered him past her body and out of the room.

He could feel that he was nervous.

This was a big day for him, in many ways, and even bigger for MWM. His company. Following the news about the award, the last few days had seen a growing amount of criticism of their prospecting activities in the Congo. They were picked on from all sides, there were negative articles in the papers and demonstrations too. About questionable methods and exploitation and infringement of international law and all the other things they could think of.

On the other hand, people had picked on Bertil as long as he could remember. They always picked on you if you were Swedish and were doing well abroad. And MWM was doing very well. The little company that he had started with a colleague had grown into a multinational conglomerate of companies large and small, spread throughout the world.

Now MWM was a big player.

He was a big player.

With a bladder that was a bit too small.

* * *

She had woken in the cabin, long after the check-out time. Axel wasn't bothered. Olivia had blamed her high temperature, the soaked clothes, her 'tumble' as he had called it. Axel still wasn't bothered. When she started to explain that she normally woke up very early, he had asked her if she wanted to stay another night. And she did. On one level, his level. But on another level she knew that she must return home.

That was on the cat level.

Quite a lot of persuasion had been required to get her neighbour to look after Elvis. Her neighbour was a nerd who worked down at Pet Sounds, and he had finally agreed.

Two nights.

Three nights? No way.

'Afraid I can't, I would have like to have stayed,' she said.

'Did you like the island?'

'I like the island a lot. The weather's a bit nasty, but I'd like to come back.'

'That would be nice.'

That's how real lobster boys express themselves, she thought, walking up Badhusgatan in Strömstad and noticing how something in her throat seemed to be swelling. She was on her way to visit a former policeman. Gunnar Wernemyr. The man who – according to Betty Nordeman – had interrogated the silly Jackie from Stockholm. Olivia had found Wernemyr in the Eniro address registry online, and had phoned him before getting on the ferry from Nordkoster. He had been very friendly. He had nothing against meeting a young police student, pensioner that he was. And besides, in less than three seconds he had realised which Jackie from Stockholm Olivia was interested in. It was in connection with the Hasslevikarna murder.

'She was called Jackie Berglund. I remember her very well.'

Just before she turned down on Västra Klevgatan, her mobile rang. It was Åke Gustafsson, her tutor. He was curious.

'How's it going?'

'With the beach case?'

'Yes. Did you get hold of Stilton?'

Stilton? He hadn't been on the agenda at all the last twenty-four hours.

'No. But I spoke to Verner Brost, at the Cold Case Division, he said that Stilton had left the force for personal reasons. Do you know anything about that?'

'No. Or rather yes.'

'No, or rather yes?'

'He left for personal reasons.'

'OK. No, otherwise I haven't found much.'

She thought she could save her Koster experiences for a more considered summary at some later date.

If there ever was to be one.

The Wernemyrs lived in a beautiful old building, on the first floor, with a view of the harbour that estate agents love. Gunnar's wife, Märit, had made some coffee and given Olivia a spoonful of brown liquid to ease her throat.

Now they sat in the couple's green-painted kitchen, which probably hadn't been renovated since the early 1960s. On the windowsill, small china dogs vied for space with photos of grandchildren and pink Mårbacka geraniums. Olivia was always interested in photos. She pointed at one of them.

'Are they your grandchildren?'

'Yes. Ida and Emil. They're our pride and joy,' said Märit. 'They're coming to visit next week and they'll be staying over the midsummer holiday. It will be such fun to look after them again.'

'Now, then, don't exaggerate,' Gunnar smiled. 'You usually think it's rather nice when they go home again too.'

'Yes, it is rather a lot at once. How does your throat feel?'

Märit gave Olivia a sympathetic look.

'A bit better, thanks.'

Olivia sipped some coffee from the dainty china cup with red roses on it. Her grandmother had the same service. And they chatted about today's police training, all three of them. Märit had worked in the police archives in Strömstad.

'Now they've centralised it all,' she said. 'Everything has been put into the central archives down in Göteborg.'

'I suppose that's where the case records are now,' said Gunnar.

'Yes,' said Olivia.

She hoped he wouldn't be too secretive when it came to opening his heart a little about the investigation. It had, after all, happened many years ago.

'So what did you want to know about Jackie Berglund?'

Not so secretive, Olivia thought, and said:

'How many times did you interrogate her?'

'Twice, here at the station. And once out on Nordkoster, to help with enquiries. That was the first,' said Gunnar.

'Why was she brought in here for an interrogation?'

'It was because of the yacht. Do you know about that?'

'Not really...'

'Well, Jackie was evidently a female escort.'

A luxury prostitute, Olivia reflected from the viewpoint of her Rotebro upbringing.

'You know, one of those luxury whores,' said Märit in her Strömstad manner.

Olivia smiled a little. Gunnar went on:

'She was on board a fancy Norwegian yacht with two Norwegians who left the island shortly after the murder. Or tried to leave the island, one of our police boats stopped the yacht some distance from land, checked where it came from and accompanied it back to the island. And because the Norwegians were extremely drunk and Jackie Berglund was clearly under the influence of something other than alcohol, all three of them were brought here so that we could interrogate them when they had sobered up.'

'And you were in charge of the interrogation?'

'Yes.'

'Gunnar was the best interrogator on the west coast.'

Märit said that more as a statement of fact that as a boast.

'And what did you get out of them?' Olivia asked.

'One of the Norwegians said they'd heard on the radio that a storm would blow up the next day so they left the island, they wanted to get to their home harbour. The other one said that they had run out of booze and they were sailing to Norway to get some more.'

Very different versions, Olivia thought.

'And what did Jackie Berglund say?'

'That she had no idea why they sailed off, she just went along with them.'

'She said: "Sailing's not exactly my thing",' said Märit with a Stockholm dialect.

Olivia looked at Märit.

'That's what she said, that Berglund woman, we had a good laugh about it when you came home and told me, do you remember?'

Märit smiled at Gunnar who looked a bit embarrassed. Leaking information from an interrogation to your wife was not exactly according to the rule book. Olivia didn't care.

'But what did they say about the actual murder?' she asked.

'They all said the same about that, none of them had been up by Hasslevikarna, not on the murder evening or before that.'

'Was that true?'

'We don't know, not a hundred per cent, the case was of course never solved. We didn't have anything that could connect them to the site of the murder. Are you related to Arne Rönning, by the way?'

'He's my father. Or was.'

'We read that he had passed away,' said Gunnar. 'I'm sorry.'

Olivia nodded and Märit pulled out a photo album with pictures from Gunnar's police career. In a couple of photos he was standing with Arne and another policeman.

'Is that Tom Stilton?' Olivia wondered.

'Yes.'

'Right... you don't have any idea where he is today? Stilton?'

'No.'

* * *

She had chosen the cerise dress, in the end, after all. She was particularly fond of it. It was simply cut, but pretty. Now she was standing next to her husband at the Chamber of Commerce and smiling. It wasn't just for show. She smiled because she was proud of her husband. Just like she knew he was proud of her. They had never had any problems with keeping a professional balance. He looked after his business, and she looked after hers, and they were both successful. She on a lesser scale, globally, but still successful. She was a career coach, and had been doing very well in recent years. Everybody wanted to have a career and she knew the tricks. She had learnt some of them from Bertil, there were few with his experience, but the greater part of her success was due to her own merits.

She was competent.

So when the Swedish monarch leaned forward and gave her a compliment on the cerise piece it wasn't indirect polite flattery intended for Bertil. It was addressed directly to her.

'Thank you.'

It wasn't the first time they had met. The monarch and Bertil shared an interest in hunting, especially grouse shooting. They had been in the same hunting party a couple of times and were on speaking terms. In as far as anyone was on speaking terms with a king, she thought. But sufficiently 'speaking' for Bertil and his wife to be invited to a couple of small dinners with people in the royal family's closest circles. They were rather formal for Linn's taste, the Queen was no joker, but they were important for Bertil. Contacts were established, and it was never a bad thing if word got about that you had had dinner with the King now and then.

Linn smiled to herself, that was important in Bertil's world, less important in her own. What was more important was to try to bring an end to all the mud that was being slung at MWM just now. Mud that even splashed onto her. On their way into the ceremony there had been a little flock on Västra Trädgårdsgatan with banners which accused MWM of rather nasty things. She saw that this irritated Bertil. He knew that the media would cover this too, and be sure to compare it with his award.

And dirty it a little.

A pity.

She looked around her. Most of the people there were familiar to her. There was a cast of rich business men named Pirre and Tusse and Latte and Pygge and Mygge and similar. She had never really learnt who was who. In her world people had more distinct names. But she knew that these people were important for Bertil. People he went hunting with, sailing with, did business with – and to whom he was often related.

But he refrained from other activities.

She knew her husband well enough to know that.

They were still in love with each other and had a good sex life. Not that frequent, but fully satisfactory when it finally went bang.

'Satisfactory', she thought. What a word for sex. And smiled, just when Bertil looked at her. He was looking good today. A tie in a muted purple, simple black suit, elegant, his hand-sewn Italian number. The only thing she didn't like was the shirt. All blue with a white collar. That was more or less the ugliest item of clothing she could imagine. For several years she had waged quite a campaign against that sort of shirt.

Without success.

Some things were deeper than scars. For Bertil, it was a blue shirt with a white collar. It was a sort of archetypical emblem for him. It signalled a belonging that she herself felt very alien to.

Timeless class.

So he thought.

Absolutely ridiculous, in her opinion. And ugly.

Bertil received his award directly from the King's hand. He bowed slightly here and there, glanced at Linn and gave her a wink. Hope his bladder stays under control, she thought. This is not exactly a good moment to go looking for the toilet.

'Champagne!'

A number of rented white jackets sailed around with trays full of well-chilled Grande Cuvée. Linn and Bertil each took a glass and raised them.

That was when it rang.

Or, rather, vibrated. The mobile in Bertil's pocket.

He withdrew a little with his champagne glass, fished up his mobile answered it.

'Magnuson.'

A dialogue could be heard in the mobile. Fairly short, but – for Magnuson – shocking. An excerpt from a recorded conversation.

'I know that you're prepared to go a long way, Bertil, but murder?'
'Nobody can link us to it.'
'But we know.'
'We don't know anything... if we don't want to.'

The dialogue was cut off.

Bertil lowered the mobile after a couple of seconds, with a decidedly numb arm. He knew exactly when that conversation had taken place and he knew exactly who the voices belonged to.

Nils Wendt and Bertil Magnuson.

The last line had been his own.

'We don't know anything... if we don't want to.'

What he hadn't known, was that the conversation had been recorded.

'A toast! Bertil!'

The King raised his glass to Bertil. With supreme effort he raised his own and forced his mouth into a sort of smile.

A desperate smile.

Linn reacted immediately. His bladder? She quickly took a couple of steps and smiled.

'If the King can excuse us, I must kidnap my husband a few minutes.'

'But of course, of course.'

The King did not stand on ceremony. Especially when faced with a cerise beauty like Linn Magnuson.

So the cerise beauty took her obviously preoccupied husband aside.

'Bladder?' she whispered.

'What? Oh, yes.'

'Come along.'

Just like an efficient wife should behave when her husband goes down, she took command and led him to a not too distant toilet where he sneaked in like a shadow of his old self.

Linn waited outside.

Which was probably lucky, for a very simple reason.

Bertil did not empty his bladder.

He bent down over the toilet bowl and vomited. The dainty sandwiches as well as the champagne and his breakfast toast with marmalade all came up.

The big player had shrunk.

* * *

The passenger on the seat next to her explained how unfortunate it was that the seats were so close together, considering how germs fly hither and thither through the air. Olivia agreed. She also did her best to smother her mouth and nose when she couldn't help releasing a hefty sneeze, and tried to turn away as best she could. And she wasn't very successful. Sometime around Linköping, the passenger moved to another seat.

Olivia remained where she was, on the X2000 express. She had a pain in her chest and felt that her forehead was alarmingly hot. She had spent an hour on her mobile and perhaps another thirty minutes making notes. Then her thoughts had turned to the conversation in Strömstad and to Jackie Berglund... 'Sailing's not exactly my thing.' And what was your thing then, Jackie? she wondered. To be rented out on a fancy yacht to be fucked by Norwegians? While a young woman was buried in the sand fifteen minutes away from your orgies. Or what?

Or what? Suddenly an entirely different thought popped up inside Olivia's feverish head.

What did she know about the drowned woman?

She suddenly realised how much she had been coloured by the fact that nobody knew anything. About the 'poor' victim. And how that had created an image of a helpless young woman who was subjected to horrifyingly evil treatment.

What if it wasn't like that at all?

Nobody knew anything about the victim after all.

Not even her name.

What if she had been rented out too? A call girl.

But she was pregnant!

Calm down now, Olivia, there are limits.

Or are there? At college they had had a lesson about porn sites. About how they were organised, how hard it was to trace them, how hard it was to... pregnant women! Here and there, not infrequently, among the billions of porn films that were churned out, there were special sites for 'Looking for a bit of kinky stuff?' and 'Fucking pregnant women?'

She remembered that she had found that even more repulsive that the rest. Sex with donkeys or dinosaurs, fine, that was just ridiculous. But buying sex with women in the final stage of pregnancy?

There was a market for it, unfortunately.

That was a reality.

What if the victim on the beach had been one of Jackie's mates? Rented out precisely on account of her being pregnant. And then something went wrong on that fancy yacht and ended with the murder.

Then again! ... and now her feverish imagination was in over-drive... then again perhaps one of the Norwegians was the father of the child and she refused to have an abortion? She and Jackie might have had sex with those Norwegians on other occasions and then the victim had got preggers and tried to blackmail the Norwegian and then it all blew up and they killed her?

At that point, her mobile rang.

It was her mum. She wanted to invite Olivia to dinner.

'This evening?'

'Yes. Have you got anything else on?'

'Just now I'm sitting on a train from Göteborg and...'

'When do you arrive?'

'At about five-ish, then I need to...'

'But you don't sound too good? Are you ill?'

'I've got a bit of a...'

'Have you got a fever?'

'Perhaps, I haven't...'

'Is your throat swollen?'

'A bit.'

In five seconds, Maria's worried questions had taken Olivia all the way back to when she was five. She was ill and her mum was worried about her.

'What time?'

'Seven,' said Maria.

* * *

The esplanade on Strandgatan is very beautiful. Seen from the water, it is an impressive mixture of old architecture stretching out along the tree-lined street. Specially if you raise your eyes and look up at the roofs. All those eccentric towers and corners and brickwork. A respectable face to the world.

What hides behind that face is another matter.

The beauty of the street was hardly foremost in Bertil Magnuson's mind as he walked along the quay. At a safe distance from anyone he called Pigge and Mygge and Tusse. His slightly concerned wife had dropped him off at Nybroplan at the beginning of Strandgatan after he had firmly reassured her that everything was okay now. It had just been a bit too much with the ceremony and the king and those chanting demonstrators outside.

'I'm all right now,' he said.

'Are you sure?'

'Yes, I'm sure. I need to think about a contract that we're going to negotiate on Wednesday, I want to walk a little.'

He often did that when he needed to think something through, so Linn dropped him off and drove on.

Bertil was decidedly overwrought as he walked along. He had immediately understood who lay behind that taped conversation on his mobile.

Nils Wendt.

At one time a very close friend. A musketeer. One of the three who stuck together through thick and thin at the Stockholm School of Economics back in the Sixties. The third was Erik Grandén, now a very senior man at the Ministry of Foreign Affairs. The trio had seen themselves as modern versions of Dumas' heroes. They even had the same motto as the musketeers.

That was as far as their imagination would stretch.

But they were convinced that they would astound the world. At any rate, parts of it.

And they succeeded.

Grandén became a political wunderkind and chairman of the youth section of the Moderate Alliance party when he was only

twenty-six. Magnuson himself and Wendt started MWM –
Magnuson Wendt Mining. This soon became a bold and
successful prospecting company in Sweden as well as abroad.

Then things started going a bit wrong.

Not for the company. That expanded, globally and finan-
cially and was floated on the Stock Exchange after a few
years. But things started to go wrong for Wendt. Or the
relationship between Bertil and Wendt. That went wrong.
And it ended with Wendt disappearing from the picture. And
'Wendt' was changed to 'World' – Magnuson World Mining.

And now Wendt was back.

With an extremely unpleasant conversation between him
and Bertil. A conversation that Bertil had had no idea had
been recorded, but which he immediately understood the
scope of. If it were to become public then Bertil Magnuson's
time as a big player was over.

On every level.

He glanced up at Grevegatan. He had been born just
near there, at an impeccable address. He could hear the
Hedvig Eleanora church bells from his nursery. He was born
into an industrial family. His father and uncle had founded
the firm. Adolf and Viktor. The Magnuson Brothers. They
had built up a small but strong mining company, had an
excellent nose for minerals and gone from small local quar-
ries to international mining. Over the years, they had put
the family company on the world map and provided Bertil
with a springboard of a share portfolio out into the business
world.

Bertil had his own ideas. He had bold visions. He helped to
manage the family company but at the same time saw that
there were completely different markets to exploit apart from
the traditional ones. The ones the brothers upheld.

Exotic markets.

Difficult markets.

Which meant wheeling and dealing with all manner of auto-cratic potentates. People with whom the brothers would never have mixed. But times change and fathers and brothers die. As soon as Adolf and Viktor were buried, Bertil started a subsidiary.

With the help of Nils Wendt.

The extremely gifted Wendt. One of the musketeers. A genius when it came to prospecting and mineral analyses and market structures. All the things that Bertil was less good at. Together, they became industrial pioneers in numerous parts of the world. Asia. Australia. And above all: Africa. Until things went wrong and Wendt suddenly vanished, because of something extremely unpleasant that Bertil had repressed since then. Sublimated. Transformed into a non-event.

But Nils Wendt hadn't done that.

Evidently.

Because it must have been Nils who had phoned and played that recorded conversation. There was no other possible explanation.

Bertil was convinced of that.

When he had walked as far at the bridge over to Djurgården, he had silently formulated his first question: what the hell was Wendt after? And his second question: more money? And just as he was about to formulate his third question: where is he?, his mobile rang again.

Bertil held it in front of him, or down by his thigh, people were coming and going all around him, many of them with dogs, it was that sort of pathway. He pressed the answer button and put the phone to his ear.

Without saying anything.

Silence.

'Hello?'

It was Erik Grandén. The busy tweeter who had hoped to find a barber in Brussels. Bertil immediately recognised his voice.

'Hello, Erik.'

'Congratulations on your award!'

'Thank you.'

'How was the king? On good form?'

'Yes.'

'Nice, nice. Having an after-party now?'

'No, I… we'll do that this evening. Did you find a barber?'

'Not yet, the one I wanted was busy. Strange. But I've been tipped off about a salon that I hope I can find time to call in at before the morning plane. I'll be in touch over the weekend! Say hello to Linn!'

'Thanks. Bye.'

Bertil hung up and thought about Erik. Grandén. The third musketeer. A big player too, in his own field. With a gigantic contact web in Sweden as well as abroad.

'Put him on the board.'

It was actually Bertil's mother who had said that, after his father had died, when Bertil described his friend Erik's tentacles which reach out everywhere.

'But he doesn't know anything about mining,' Bertil said.

'You don't either. What you can do is to surround yourself with people who do know. The right people. You are good at that. Put him on the board.'

The second time she said it, Bertil realised that it was an absolutely brilliant idea. Why hadn't he thought of it himself? You don't see the wood for the trees. Erik had been too close, both as a friend and a musketeer. Of course Erik should sit on the board of MWM.

And so it became.

Erik found himself on the board. A bit of a case of helping a friend, on Erik's part, to start with. But since, over the years, he had bought quite a hefty number of shares in the company, he could just as well take a little responsibility for it too. He could always pull a few strings that Bertil couldn't get at. He was, after all, Erik Grandén.

And so it went on, for many years, until Erik had advanced to such a high level in the political world that a post on the board became rather sensitive. In a private company. One which, besides, was subject to rather a lot of criticism in the media.

So he resigned.

Now they dealt with what needed to be dealt with in private. It was less sensitive like that.

It looked from outside as if they were just good friends.

Up till now.

Erik had no idea about the recorded conversation and its origin. If he were to find out about that, then the bonds of the three musketeers would be put under extreme pressure.

On a political level too.

* * *

It was approaching seven in the evening. Jelle had managed to sell three magazines. In four hours. That wasn't many. A hundred and twenty kronor, of which he would get sixty. An hourly rate of fifteen kronor. But he could buy a can of fish-balls. He didn't actually like fishballs that much, it was the lobster sauce he was after. He wasn't especially interested in food in general, never had been, even during periods when he could have treated himself to this or that. For him, food was nourishment. If there was no food, then you had to acquire nourishment some other way. That was possible, too. It wasn't food that was his foremost problem, it was a place to live.

He had his wooden shack by Jarla Lake, but that was begin-ning to get on his nerves. Something had got into the very walls of that place. Something that made its presence felt as soon as he entered. That made it harder and harder to sleep there. The walls have heard too many screams for far too long, he thought, it's time to move.

If 'move' was the right word. You move from a flat or a house, you don't move from a bare shed without any fittings. You leave it.

He was going to leave it.

That's what he was thinking about now. To where? He had kipped down at various places round about town, sometimes at a hostel, but that wasn't his cup of tea. Arguments and drunkenness and people high on drugs and staff who wanted you out of the place by eight in the morning latest. He had given up on that. He must find something else.

'Hi, Jelle! You look like you styled your hair with a hand grenade.'

One-eyed Vera was walking towards him with a big smile, pointing as his tousled hair. She had sold all her thirty magazines at Ringen and now she was here. At the Söder market hall by Medborgarplatsen. A pitch that Jelle had taken over the other day. Benseman wasn't here, after all. A good pitch, he thought. Three magazines today rather contradicted that.

'Hi,' he said.

'How are you doing?'

'So-so… three magazines.'

'I sold thirty.'

'That's good.'

'How long do you plan on standing here?'

'Don't know, I've still got some left.'

'I can buy them.'

Sellers sometimes bought copies off each other, to help a colleague. For the same price as they had bought them. Hoping for better luck themselves. So Vera's offer was perfectly reasonable.

'Thanks, but I…'

'A bit too proud for that, aren't you?'

'Possibly.'

Vera gave a little laugh, and put her arm under Jelle's.

'Pride won't fill your belly.'

'I'm not hungry.'

'You're cold.'

Vera had felt Jelle's hand. And it was actually rather cold, which was a bit strange, it must have been more than 20 C outside. His hand oughtn't to be cold.

'Did you sleep in that shack last night again?'

'Yes.'

'How long can you cope with that?'

'Don't know.'

There was silence. Vera looked at Jelle's face and Jelle looked at the Söder market hall, and the seconds turned into a minute or two. Then Jelle looked at Vera.

'Is it okay if I…'

'Yes.'

They didn't say any more. They didn't have to say any more. Jelle picked up his worn little rucksack, put his bundle inside, and off they went. Side by side, each of them in a world of their own, already moving on in their thoughts. Towards the caravan, and what it would be like there.

And if you walk along absorbed in your own thoughts, you hardly register the fact that a couple of young men in dark hooded jackets are standing over by Björns Trädgård staring at you. You don't even notice if they start to walk in the same direction as you.

* * *

The red terraced house in Rotebro was built in the mid-Sixties. The Rönning family were the second owners, so far. It was a nice compact house, well cared for, situated in a quiet cul-de-sac in an area with the same type of houses everywhere. Olivia had grown up here, as an only child, but the whole place had been crawling with playmates. Now most of them were on their way into adult life and on their way into other residences. In other places. Now it was mostly parents who lived here, on their own.

Like Maria.

Olivia saw her through the kitchen window when she came up the drive. Her mama, the defence lawyer, with her Spanish ancestry, the woman with the quick tongue who was always correct, and whom her papa had loved most of all in the world.

And she had loved him, as Olivia understood. Their home had always had a calm and sensible atmosphere, very rarely any rows. Arguments, disagreements, endless discussions, but never anything nasty. Never anything that could make itself felt inside a child's tummy.

She had always felt safe at home.

And felt seen. At least by Arne, or perhaps most by him. Maria was as she was. Perhaps not a touchy-feely mum, but always there when needed. When you were ill, for example. Like now. Then mama was there, ready to care for her, and with prescriptions and instructions.

It had its advantages.

'What are we going to eat?'

'Garlic chicken special.'

'And what is the special bit?'

'What isn't in the recipe. Drink this,' said Maria.

'What is it?'

'Hot water, ginger, a little honey, and a couple of drops of something secret.'

Olivia smiled a little, and drank it. What was the secret? Did she notice a trace of mint through her runny nose? Perhaps. She felt how the warm soothing drink was gladly welcomed by her mangled throat, and thought: mama Maria.

They had sat down at the white dining table in the well-polished kitchen. Olivia could still be surprised by how her mother had embraced the Scandinavian way of decorating a home. There wasn't the slightest sign of fiery colours. Every-thing was white and sober. As a teenager, she had revolted for a while and made them let her have a strong red colour on the walls in her room. Now it had been changed back to a consider-ably more low-key beige shade.

'So, what was it like on Nordkoster?' Maria asked.

Olivia told her a censored version of her visit to the island, a very censored version. One that excluded everything important, in fact. And then she ate, and drank some good wine. Fever and red wine? Olivia had wondered when Maria poured. But Maria didn't think like that. A bit of red wine was always right.

'Did you and dad ever talk about the Nordkoster case?' said Olivia.

'Not that I recall, but you had only just been born so there wasn't much discussing.'

Did she sound a bit disappointed? No, shame on you Olivia, pull yourself together!

'Are you going to be busy with that all summer?' asked Maria.

Is she worried about the holiday house now? Masking tape and paint scraper?

'I don't think so, I'm just going to check a few things and then write something.'

'What are you going to check?'

Since Arne died, Maria had rarely had a chance to sit at the kitchen table with a good wine and discuss legal cases. In effect, never. So now she took the chance.

'There was a girl on the island when the murder took place, Jackie Berglund, and I'm rather curious about her.'

'Why?'

'Because she and some Norwegian men disappeared from the island straight after the murder, on a boat, and I thought their interrogations lacked in substance.'

'You think they might have known the victim?'

'Perhaps.'

'You mean she might have been on the boat from the beginning?'

'Yes, perhaps. This Jackie was a call girl.'

'Ah…'

'Ah what?' Olivia wondered. What did she mean by that?

'The victim might have been a call girl too,' Maria went on.

'I was thinking along those lines.'

'Then you ought to talk to Eva Carlsén.'

'Who's that?'

'I saw her on a current affairs programme on TV yesterday, she has written a report about escort activities, looking back but also at current times. She seemed to be a very competent woman.'

'Like you,' Olivia thought, and memorised the name Eva Carlsén.

Her stomach was filled to the brim, and she was a little unsteady on her feet, which forced her to take a taxi which Maria would pay for. Now she was feeling much better. In fact so much better that she almost forgot to ask what she had intended from the very first.

'That investigation on Nordkoster was led by a detective called Tom Stilton, do you remember him?'

'Tom, oh yes!'

Maria smiled a little, standing there inside the gate.

'He was very good at squash. We played a few times. He was handsome too, a bit of George Clooney about him. Why do you ask that?'

'I've been trying to get hold of him, it seems that he has left the force.'

'Yes, that's right, I remember that, it was a couple of years before dad died.'

'Do you know why?' asked Olivia.

'Why he left?'

'Yes.'

'No. But I remember that he got divorced at around the same time, Arne told me about it.'

'From Marianne Boglund?'

'Yes, how did you know that?'

'I've met her.'

The taxi driver suddenly got out of his car, presumably as a sign to her to hurry up. Olivia took a quick step towards Maria.

'Bye, mum, and thanks a ton for dinner and medicine and wine and everything!'

Mother and daughter hugged each other.

* * *

It was an ordinary hotel in Stockholm. The Oden, on Karlbergsvägen, mid-range, with ordinary rooms. This particular one consisted of a double bed, some generic graphic works, a TV against a light grey wall. The news programme was just broadcasting a special report in connection with the announcement of the mining company MWM having been named the Company of the Year. Behind the studio reporter there was a picture of the managing director Bertil Magnuson.

The man who sat on the edge of the double bed had just showered. He was half-naked, a towel wrapped around his hips, his hair still wet. He turned up the sound.

'The mining company MWM has been named Swedish Company of the Year Abroad, which has led to strong reactions among environmental and human rights activists in Sweden as well as other countries. Over the years, the mining company has been criticised for its connections to countries with corrupt regimes and dictators. As early as the 1980s, when the company started activities in the then

Zaire, criticism was harsh. The company was accused of having bribed its way to good relations with President Mobutu, which the prize-winning journalist Jan Nyström – among others – was investigating when he was tragically killed in an accident in 1984. But today too MWM's methods are questioned. Our reporter Karin Lindell is now in Eastern Congo.'

The man on the bed leant forward a little. The towel around his hips slipped down to the floor. All his attention was directed at the TV report. A woman reporter appeared on a screen behind the studio reporter. She was standing in front of a fenced-in area.

'Here in the Northern Kivu province in Eastern Congo is one of MWM's complexes for mining coltan, also known as the grey gold. We aren't allowed inside the area, soldiers guard the entrance, but the population in Walikale has told of the horrific working conditions found here.'

'There are rumours of child labour in the actual mining area, is that true?'

'Yes. That, and also physical attacks on the local population. Unfortunately nobody dares be interviewed in front of a camera, they are afraid of reprisals. One woman put it like this: "If you've been raped once, then you're not going to protest again."'

The naked man on the bed reacted. With one hand he gripped the bedspread tightly.

'You called coltan the grey gold, what did you mean by that?'

Karin Lindell held up a bit of grey rock to the camera.

'*This looks like a worthless bit of rock, but it is coltan. The element tantalum can be refined from this, and tantalum is one of the most important components in modern electronics. For example, tantalum is used in circuit cards in computers and mobile telephones the world over. It is thus an extremely valuable mineral, which has been illegally mined and smuggled for many years.*'

'*But MWM's coltan mining in the Congo is hardly illegal surely?*'

'*No. MWM is one of the few companies that still has its old concession to mine, they got that from the earlier dictatorship.*'

'*So what are the critics saying?*'

'*They are against child labour and physical abuse plus the fact that nothing of what they mine actually benefits the Congo. It is all taken out of the country.*'

The studio reporter turned towards the picture of Bertil Magnuson showing in the background.

'*We have the managing director of MWM, Bertil Magnuson, with us via telephone. What are your comments on these reports?*'

'*First, I think there is an unnecessarily hard tone in the report, and it is extremely tendentiously biased. I can't sit here and comment on the facts. I would just like to emphasize that our company is a long-term and responsible player in the raw materials sector, and I am convinced that the economic benefit of responsibly developed natural resources is of great importance for lessening poverty in this region.*'

The man on the bed turned the TV off and picked up the towel from the floor. He was called Nils Wendt. Nothing of what was said in the report was new for him. It had only reinforced his conviction. He would concern himself with Bertil Magnuson a little longer.

One for all.

* * *

Jelle had been in the caravan before, several times, short visits for various reasons. Mainly to keep Vera company when she was feeling bad. But he had never spent the night there. This time he would do so. That, at any rate, was his intention when he got there. There were three sleeping places in the caravan. Two of them were on either side of the table, one went across the end side. That was too short for Jelle, the other two were too narrow for two people beside each other.

But not on top.

Jelle knew what would come. He had thought about it all the way there. He would make love with One-eyed Vera. An idea that had started as an idea already back at Medborgarplatsen. Gradually it had grown into something else, he noticed. Grown to desire.

Or randiness.

Vera had walked by his side. Sat by his side on the underground. Stood close to him on the sixty-six-metre-long escalator at Västra Skogen. Held him under his arm on the way through the Ingenting forest and not said a word the whole time. He assumed that she was thinking the same thing.

She was.

And it did something to her body. It changed temperature and became warm, from within. She knew that she had a good body, still strong, ample, with breasts that had never been suckled and which filled really large cups when she occasionally felt like wearing a bra. That wasn't very often. She wasn't worried about her body. That would see her through. It always had done when it had been needed, which was a very long time ago now. So she longed, and was nervous.

She wanted it to be good.

'There's a bit of the hard stuff in the cupboard there.'

Vera pointed at one of the veneer cupboards behind Jelle. He turned round and opened the hatch. A little bottle of Explorer vodka, half full, or half empty, depending on how you looked at it.

'Do you want some?'

Jelle looked at Vera. She had lit a little copper lamp on the wall. It provided just as little light as was needed.

'No,' she said.

Jelle closed the hatch and looked at Vera.

'Shall we?'

'Yes.'

Vera took off her clothes on the upper part of her body, first, and Jelle sat still, opposite. He looked at her exposed breasts. It was the first time he had seen them, naked, and he felt how his organ stiffened under the table. He hadn't touched a woman's breasts for more than six years. Not even in his thoughts. He had never had any sexual fantasies. Now he was sitting opposite a pair of very large breasts which cast a shadow in the low light on the wall. He started to pull off his shirt.

'It is very cramped here.'

'Yes.'

Vera took her dress off, pushed her knickers down over her thighs and leaned back a little. Now she was completely naked. Jelle had stood up and pulled down what had to be pulled down. He saw that his organ stood at an angle that he had almost forgotten. Vera saw that too, and slightly spread her legs. Jelle leant forward a little, stretched out a hand and ran it along one of Vera's thighs. They both looked at each other.

'Do you want the light off?' she asked.

'No.'

He had nothing to hide. He knew that Vera knew what this was about, who they were, there was nothing uncomfortable about it. If she wanted the lamp on, then he did too. The woman in the light in front of him was the person she was and now he was going to make love to her. When he reached up to her pudenda he felt how wet it was. He rubbed a couple of fingers along her velvety labia and Vera clutched Jelle's organ with her right hand. Then she closed her eyes.

She had all the time in the world.

The young men crouched in the dark some distance away. They knew they were hidden. The weak light from the caravan's oval window hardly reached outside, but it was enough for them to be able to see.

In.

One-eyed Vera lay down on the narrow bunk. She had a cushion under her head. She put one foot on the floor to support her leg and give Jelle enough room to lean over her body. He had no difficulty in getting his shaft in, but he did it carefully, slowly, and heard a short low panting from Vera.

Now they were here.

They were making love.

Their bodies rocked up and down with small rhythmic jerks. The bunk restricted their movements, in a stimulating manner. Jelle had to restrain himself, Vera could keep up.

In the dark outside, a discreet little yellow light marked a mobile camera.

Vera felt when Jelle came, and she felt how she too got there at almost the same second. When he remained inside her, the last tremor went through her body. Then she faded away.

Jelle kept his member inside her, a long time, until it just slipped out by itself. He had banged himself hard against the side wall. He carefully got up and sat on the edge of the bunk. He saw how Vera had fallen asleep, her even breathing, even in a way he didn't recognise. He had seen Vera sleep before, or pass out, he had sat with her many a night.

Here.

In the caravan.

Without staying over.

Nights when she had struggled not to explode. So as not to give in to the manic worms that crawled around in her brain and wanted to get out. He had held her for hours sometimes, spoken quietly about light and darkness, about himself, about anything at all that could keep her afloat. It had often helped. She often passed out in the end with her head on his chest, with uncomfortably uneven breaths.

Now she was breathing very evenly.

Jelle leaned over her face and carefully stroked her small white scars. He knew about the bunch of keys. He had heard that story several times. And each time he had felt that same helpless fury within himself.

To do that to a child!

He pulled a blanket up over Vera's naked body, got up and sat on the other bunk. Somewhat distracted, he pulled on his clothes and sank down stretched out.

He lay there a long while.

Then he got up.

He avoided looking at Vera.

He carefully shut the caravan door. He didn't want to wake her, didn't want to explain what he couldn't explain. Why he went on his way. He just went. With his back to the caravan, right through the forest.

Right through Ingenting forest.

Bertil Magnuson had finally pulled himself together close to the Djurgård Bridge and realised that he must act. How, he hadn't decided. The first thing he did was to turn off his mobile phone. He had considered changing his number, straight away, but realised the risks. Then Wendt might ring his home telephone, in the house, and then Linn might answer. That would not be good.

That would be a catastrophe.

So he settled for turning off his mobile, sticking his head in the sand and hoping it would stop at that.

That one phone call.

Before he went home he paid a quick visit to the head office on Sveavägen. The staff there had bought flowers and champagne. The entire company was involved in his award. Nobody had mentioned the demonstrations at the ceremony. He didn't expect anything else. They were one hundred per cent loyal. If anybody wasn't, then there was soon a replacement.

In his office he had commented by telephone on a TV report about MWM. A crap report. After that comment he had asked his secretary to write a press release which emphasized MWM's appreciation of the award, and how it spurred the company to continue its efforts for Swedish mining abroad. Not least in Africa.

The bull by the horns.

Now he was approaching his house in Stocksund. It was late and he hoped that Linn hadn't gone and invited Tom, Dick and Harry to celebrate. He couldn't face that.

She hadn't.

Linn had put together a little simple dinner-for-two out on the terrace. She knew her husband. They ate their food in relative silence, until Linn put down her knife and fork.

'How are you feeling?'

She looked straight out across the water when she asked.

'Fine. You mean about…'

'No, I mean in general.'

'What makes you ask?'

'Because you're not *here*.'

She knew her husband very well. Bertil had floated off as soon as he got his wine glass in his hand. He didn't usually do that. He had the ability to keep things where they belonged, and here at home he belonged to her. This is where they were private, intimate. In touch with each other.

And now they were not.

'Is it about those demonstrators?'

'Yes.'

Bertil lied, the truth was totally off limits.

'This isn't the first time, why are you so bothered now?'

'It seems to be getting worse.'

Linn had noticed that too. She had also seen the report on TV earlier that evening, about MWM, and it had been decidedly spiteful, with an obviously unbalanced bias.

She thought.

'Is it something you want to talk about? Something we…'

'No. Not now, I'm too tired. Did the King like your dress?'

And that was that.

Then it became private anyway, and intimate. So intimate that, as Linn used to think, it detonated in their double bed. Short, but 'adequate'. And with an unusual intense degree of commitment on Bertil's part. As if he allowed himself to react in bed, Linn thought. That was fine for her, as long as it was only about business problems and not anything else.

When Linn had fallen asleep, Bertil slipped out of bed.

Wrapped in his elegant grey dressing gown he walked silently out onto the terrace, without turning on any lights, pulled out his mobile and lit a little cigarillo. He had stopped smoking many years ago. Today he had suddenly bought a packet on his way home. Without really thinking about it. With slightly unsteady hands he turned his mobile on, waited, and saw that he had received four messages. The first two were congratulations from people who thought it was important to keep Bertil Magnuson on side. The third was silent. Perhaps somebody had changed their mind and decided it wasn't so important to keep him on side. And then came the fourth message. An excerpt from a taped conversation.

'I know that you're prepared to go a long way, Bertil, but murder?'

'Nobody can link us to it.'

'But we know.'

'We don't know anything… if we don't want to. Why are you so agitated?'

'Because an innocent person had been murdered!'

'That's your interpretation.'

'And what is yours?'

'I solved a problem.'

And a couple more sentences. From the same conversation. With the same people. Who talked about a problem that had been solved. Many, many years ago.

And suddenly created a new one today.

A problem that Bertil didn't know how to handle. When a problem turned up, he usually made a phone call and then the problem was dealt with. He had phoned many a potentate around the world and many a problem had been dealt with. This time he didn't have anybody to phone. He was the one who had been phoned.

He hated the situation.

And he hated Nils Wendt.

When he turned round he saw Linn standing in the bedroom window, looking at him.

Quick as a flash, he hid the cigarillo behind his back.

* * *

A sound woke Vera. A sound she didn't recognise, which pierced her sleep and caused her to sit up on her elbow. The bunk next to her was empty. Had the sound come from Jelle? Was he outside peeing or something? Vera got up and wrapped the blanket around her warm naked body. Jelle must have put the blanket there, she thought, after they had made love. Because that is what they had done. Made love. That was how Vera experienced it, and it warmed her wounded soul. It had felt so right, what could have been so wrong. A little smile came to her lips, she wouldn't dream about the bunch of keys tonight, she knew that, and opened the door.

The blow struck her right in her face.

Vera was knocked backwards and fell down against the bunk. Blood gushed out of her mouth and nose. One of the youths was inside the caravan before she could get up, and he hit her again. But Vera was no weakling. She dived to one side and then got to her feet waving her arms wildly, and started to fight. The cramped interior of the caravan made the fight chaotic. The youth hit out and Vera hit out and when the other youth came in with his mobile's camera switched on he realised that he had to help.

To knock the old crone down.

So it became two against Vera, and that was one too many. And since she put up such resistance she got a lot of blows in return. It took almost ten minutes before a powerful blow with the Calor gas cylinder across her nose floored her. After another two minutes she had been kicked uncon- scious. When she finally lay there without moving on the floor, with a naked and bloody body, one of the youths started filming again.

Several kilometres away a man sat alone on the floor of a decrepit wooden shack and wrestled with his wretchedness. Sneaking off like a rat. He knew what Vera would feel like when she woke up and how she would look at him when they met, and he wouldn't have a good explanation. He wouldn't have any explanation at all.

Perhaps it would be for the best if they didn't meet.

Jelle thought.

7

A few solitary leaves from last year fluttered down to the ground in the gentle wind, you could just catch a glimpse of the bay through the trees, and somewhere down there was an opening, a dog-walking area, where the council wanted to put an exercise track.

Just as soon as they got rid of that shabby caravan.

Arvo Pärt came hobbling through the forest, above the bay, he found it rather hard to walk. His muscles were aching after that football match the other evening. But two goals easily outweighed a bit of physical pain, that wasn't why he was on his way to Vera's. It was for another pain. He had suddenly met a man down by the Trekanten Lake, sometime during the night, they had downed a few cans of good beer and suddenly the guy had become furious.

'You're not bloody Arvo Pärt!'

'What the hell do you mean?'

'Arvo Pärt composes music and is famous and why the hell do you say you're called Arvo Pärt? Are you crazy?'

Arvo Pärt, who a long time ago, and rather thoroughly, had repressed the fact that he was called Silon Karp, had at first been extremely angry, then he'd been thumped in the face and finally he'd started crying. Why couldn't he be Arvo Pärt? That's who he was!

Now he was hobbling towards One-eyed Vera's caravan. He knew that he would find consolation there. Vera knew how you put people back together after they'd been treated roughly.

Above all, she knew that he was Arvo Pärt.

'Vera!'

Pärt had knocked twice. Now he called out. You didn't open Vera's door just like that, then she'd be angry.

But this particular morning she could hardly be angry. She couldn't be anything. Pärt realised that immediately when he eventually dared to open the door and saw a naked body lying on the floor in a dried-up pool of blood with a stream of ants all around.

He didn't recognise her face.

Her false teeth lay by the threshold.

* * *

Olivia woke up with a start, alert, and she noticed that her throat was much better. Mama's medicine, she thought. Perhaps that would be something for Maria to do? Alternative medicine? Honey and a bit of hocus-pocus. Instead of being obsessed with the holiday house. And then she was reminded of Eva Carlsén, the woman that Maria had seen on TV and who had written a book about the escort trade.

Carlsén was in the Eniro address directory.

Olivia had suggested they meet, rather than doing it by phone. She didn't like talking on the phone, she was somebody who liked to have a quick word. Besides, she wanted to make some notes. So they met on Skeppsholmen. Carlsén had a meeting out there which would finish at about eleven, and at half past they were sitting on one of the park benches down by the water and looking out to where the *Vasa* had sunk.

'But you came across Jackie Berglund there, then?'

'Yes.'

Carlsén had told a bit about her work on the escort trade. How she had begun with a friend of hers who had suddenly mentioned that she had been a call girl for a few years when she was young, and this had got Carlsén interested. She had soon discovered that the trade was still flourishing to this day. Mainly online. But there was some hidden activity too, more exclusive, and that was where Jackie Berglund came into the picture. She ran one of these hidden escort firms that never features in adverts or even on the Net.

'What's the firm called?'

'Red Velvet.'

'Did she run it herself?'

'Yes, and still does as far as I know. She's a rather enterprising businesswoman.'

'In what way?'

'She has worked her way up. Started as a call girl herself, worked with Milton a while, got in touch with a lot of girls and set up on her own.'

'Criminal?'

'Grey area… escort activities are not in themselves criminal, but if they include sexual services then it would be seen as running a brothel.'

'And it was hers?'

'Presumably, but I never managed to get any proof of that.'

'You tried?'

'Yes, but I got the feeling that she had some very high-up people who protected her.'

'Like?'

'That I don't know. I brought along some of my material, I don't know if there is anything you might want…'

'Very much!'

Carlsén handed over a ring binder and looked at Olivia.

'Why are you so interested in Jackie Berglund?'

'She's mentioned in an old murder case that I'm studying, a student project, a woman who was murdered on Nordkoster.'

'When was that?'

'1987.'

Carlsén reacted visibly.

'You know about that?' Olivia asked.

'Yes, I do indeed, it was terrible, I had a summer cottage there.'

'What, on Nordkoster?'

'Yes.'

'Were you there when it happened?'

'Yes.'

'Really! That's amazing. Tell me! I've been there and met that Betty Nordeman who...'

'The woman with the holiday cabins?'

Carlsén smiled a little.

'Yes! And she was also there then and told me a lot about weird people who had stayed in the cabins and talked about all sorts of things. But tell me!'

Carlsén looked out across the water.

'I was actually there to empty my cottage, I was going to sell it, I was only there for the weekend, then I heard a helicopter in the evening and saw that it was an air ambulance and I thought that somebody had fallen in from some boat or other, but then of course the police came the morning after and they talked with everybody on the island and... yes, it was all rather unpleasant... but you've been assigned that as a student project? Are the police going to start investigating again?'

'No, not at all. It seems to be totally cold as far as they are concerned. I can't even get hold of the guy who was in charge of the investigation. But I became a bit curious about Jackie Berglund.'

'Was she there? When it happened?'

'Yes.'

'What was she doing there?'

Olivia told about how Jackie had been on the island at the time of the murder and that the police had interrogated her but it hadn't led to anything. Carlsén gave a little nod.

'She might have been involved in this and that... I did an interview with her too, a couple of years ago, I can send you the file if you want.'

'Yeah, that'd be fantastic.'

Olivia tore a bit of paper from her block, wrote down her mail address and reached across.

'Thanks. Just be a bit careful,' said Carlsén.

'How do you mean?'

'If you're going to go nosing around Jackie Berglund, she surrounds herself with some very tough types.'

'Okay.'

Carlsén was just getting up.

'And what are you working on? Now?' asked Olivia.

'I'm writing a series of articles about juvenile violence, or as it manifests itself in those online films, youths who beat up homeless people and post the films on Internet sites.'

'I've seen those… nasty.'

'Yes. There was a new one there this morning.'

'Just as repulsive?'

'No, this one was even worse.'

* * *

Jelle had gone over and over his visit to the caravan all night, in his head, and not until around dawn had he finally slept a while. In his shack. Now he was sitting at New Community and trying to shock his body into life with the help of a mediocre cup of coffee, black as pitch. He had decided that he couldn't just sneak off. That wasn't going to work. He would seek out Vera at the Ring, or wherever she might be selling her magazines, and apologise.

He couldn't do much more than that.

Just as he was about to get up, his mobile chirped. Text. He clicked to open it. The spelling was atrocious, but the content was crystal clear and the signature was short: Pärt.

Jelle had a lot of time to think before he reached the outer edge of the Ingenting forest. His imagination had fluttered off to the most distant ice-cold cavities. Some of the way, he had run, now he hurried between the trees and the rocks, panting, and that was when he saw him. Over by the caravan: Rune Forss.

138

The policeman.

He had had dealings with Forss before, and knew exactly what type he was. Now Forss was standing next to the cordoned-off caravan smoking a cigarette. Jelle sneaked in behind a tree and tried to calm down. His heart had fluttered around inside his chest at every possible pace the last thirty minutes, the sweat was running down inside his jacket. Then he saw a hand waving some way away between some bushes.

Pärt.

Jelle went up to Pärt. He had sat there on a rock and had cried himself into a mess. A mix of saliva and snot on his chin. He had taken his jumper off. His naked torso was covered with tattoos of china plates, front and back, with blue and red decoration. He wiped his despairing face with his sweater. Pärt was the one who had found her and called the police, and he had still been there when the police arrived and One-eyed Vera was carried into an ambulance and driven off with sirens sounding.

'She was alive?'

'I think so… yes…'

Jelle stared at the ground and flopped down. She was alive at least. Pärt told him he had been questioned by the police. They had estimated that the assault must have taken place many hours earlier, some time during the night. Jelle realised when it must have happened. When he himself had left the caravan and disappeared.

For no reason.

Sneaked off like a rat.

Suddenly he vomited.

The man who stepped out of the caravan was called Janne Klinga and was a member of Rune Forss' team investigating the assaults on homeless people. AHP as it was known internally. Klinga went up to Forss who stood there smoking.

'Same perpetrators?' he said.

'Maybe, maybe not.'

'If the woman dies, then this will become a murder investigation.'

'Yes… then we can't be called AHP any longer, it would have to be changed to MHP, and I've just got used to the name… that would be irritating.'

Klinga gave him a quick glance. He didn't particularly like Forss.

* * *

On her way home from the meeting with Carlsén, Olivia had phoned Lenni and suggested they should get together. She felt she had neglected her friend too long.

Now she was sitting at Blue Lotus. A little pavement café fairly near where she lived. She drank red tea and thought about Carlsén. They had immediately hit it off with each other, she felt. As happens sometimes, with some women. Quite a different matter than the meeting with that cold Marianne Boglund. Carlsén was open and interested.

The file she had been given lay open in front of her on the little table. Jackie Berglund had a section all for herself. While waiting for Lenni, Olivia started to read.

A great deal of material.

You have climbed up quite high in the world since you 'escorted' those Norwegians on Nordkoster, Olivia thought, when she studied what Jackie's business consisted of today. The selection of female escorts from Red Velvet was comprehensive. Yet, as Eva pointed out in a footnote, probably the most lucrative part of the business wasn't visible. That took place via completely different channels.

With completely different customers.

Customers in high places, Olivia assumed. And where she was now, this particular moment, she would have given a great deal to get a look at Jackie's list of customers. What names would she find there? Any she recognised?

She felt like someone out of the Famous Five.

But there weren't five of her. She was alone, twenty-three years old, a student at the police college and was expected to have grown out of that world. But she knew that she wasn't just making things up. She had a concrete murder case, unsolved, with a concrete corpse and a concrete mystery to solve. A mystery that her own father had wrestled with once upon a time. She was just about to open a chocolate energy bar when Lenni turned up.

'Hi, gorgeous, sorry I'm late!'

Lenni bent down and hugged Olivia. She was wearing a thin yellow and very low-cut summer dress and smelt strongly of Madame. Her favourite perfume. Her long blonde hair was newly washed and her mouth glowed bright red. Lenni always went a bit over the top, but she was the best and most loyal friend Olivia had.

'And what are you doing? Writing a thesis?'

'No, it's that college student project, you know.'

Lenni sighed loudly.

'Aren't you going to finish that soon, feels like you've been working on that for ages.'

'No I haven't, but it is quite a big case so it takes…'

'What are you drinking?'

In her usual style, Lenni cut her off when she thought the subject of conversation was getting boring. Like now. Olivia informed her as to what she had in her cup. Lenni disappeared inside the café to order. When she came out again, Olivia had put away the material about Jackie Berglund and was ready for a total update on Lenni's life.

Which she got. With all the details. Even the ones she didn't want. She got to see pictures of Jakob with clothes, and without, and hear about the crazy boss at Lenni's job. Which for the

141

time being was in a DVD shop. Olivia laughed at Lenni's hilarious and razor-sharp comments on her own life and adventures and those of others. Lenni had a priceless talent for getting Olivia to relax and slowly return to something that resembled the life of an ordinary twenty-three year old. She came close to regretting that she hadn't been with them that evening at the Strand. I must be getting a bit boring, she thought. First, completely absorbed by the Police College, and now by that beach case.

So she and Lenni decided they'd have a DVD evening this evening. Just the two of them. Watch a horror film, drink beer and guzzle cheese puffs. And everything would be like in the old days.

Before Jackie Berglund.

* * *

The roulette ball whirled round slower and slower. Finally landing on the zero. That could demolish any watertight system at all. If there were any such systems.

Some people claimed there were, and even believed it.

But not Abbas, not for a second. Abbas el Fassi was the croupier at the table and had seen most things in the way of systems pass by. Here, at Casino Cosmopol in Stockholm, and at some other casinos around the world. He knew that a system didn't exist that could create a fortune at the roulette table. There was luck, and there was cheating.

Not a system.

But luck, yes there was luck, it could create money at any roulette table anywhere. Especially if you had placed the table's maximum stake on Zero and the ball had landed there. Which it just had. That gave quite a sum to the gambler. In this case a company director who had had the pouches under his eyes cut away, and who was troubled by a big problem.

Bertil Magnuson pulled in the considerable payout and flipped some across to Abbas, as was customary. He pushed some more of his winnings across to the man next to him. Lars Örnhielm, generally known as Latte. One of the friends in Bertil's entourage. With a sunbed tan and an Armani suit. Latte happily received the chips and immediately spread them out any old way across the table. Like a free-range hen, Abbas thought.

Then Bertil's phone vibrated in his pocket.

He had forgotten to turn it off.

Bertil got up while pulling out the mobile, and pushed through away from the vultures behind the players' backs to find a space further away.

But not so far away that Abbas couldn't keep an eye on him, like the professional croupier he was. Who saw nothing, but observed everything. Full focus on the gaming table, but faceted eyes which would have made even a wasp envious.

So he saw how Magnuson, one of his regulars, held his mobile against his ear without uttering a word. But with an expression that revealed quite a lot about what he heard.

It was not something he liked.

Abbas found himself thinking about that conversation, later, when he slipped into the Riche bar. Not because it had been particularly long, but because immediately after that phone call Magnuson had left the casino. And left a small fortune on the table and an evidently confounded crony who hadn't realised that Magnuson had left until he had used all his own chips. Then Latte had understood that he ought to go after him. But before doing that, he attempted to manage Magnuson's capital in the best possible way, and lost it all in fifteen minutes.

A free-range hen.

Then he left.

It was the phone call that Abbas wondered about. Why had Magnuson disappeared straight after that? What was it all about? Business? Perhaps, but Magnuson had been one of his regulars long enough for Abbas to know that he wasn't reckless with money. Not stingy, but not somebody who just threw money around. Now he had just abandoned quite a hefty sum on the table.

And simply left.

Abbas ordered a glass of mineral water in the bar and went and stood a bit to the side. He was an observer, thirty-five years old, of Moroccan extraction, childhood in Marseille. In an earlier life he had supported himself as a street vendor of pirate-copy designer handbags. First in Marseille, then in Venice. Following a dramatic incident with a knife at the Ponte di Rialto, he had moved his business to Sweden. Then quite a lot of police water ran under quite different bridges, which ended with Abbas changing his beliefs and his profession, training as a croupier and becoming fascinated by Sufism.

Now he had a permanent job at Casino Cosmopol.

He was a non-committal sort of person, some people would have said, after a quick glance. Slender-limbed, smoothly shaved. He might occasionally apply a thin line of mascara to accentuate his eyes. Always dressed in nice-fitting clothes, always in discreet colours, perfectly tailored. From some distance they looked as if they had been painted directly onto his body.

'Hi!'

The girl who had had her eye on Abbas for a while was blonde and very sober, and a bit lonely. He looked a bit lonely too, so she thought they could be lonely together.

'How's things?'

Abbas looked at the young girl, about nineteen? Perhaps twenty?

'I am not here,' he said.

'Sorry?'

'I am not here.'

'You are not here?'

'No.'

'It looks as if you are here.'

The girl smiled a little, hesitantly, and Abbas smiled back. His teeth became extra white against his brown face, his quiet voice remarkably penetrating right through the loud bar music.

'That's only what you think,' he said.

At this point the girl made a quick decision. Difficult guys were not her thing, and this one was definitely a difficult guy. He must be taking something, she thought, gave a little nod and went back to her lonely corner.

Abbas watched as she walked away and thought about Jolene Olsäter. She was about the same age and had Down syndrome.

Jolene would have known exactly what he meant.

* * *

The projector lamp went out in the confined room in the police headquarters on Bergsgatan. Rune Forss turned the ceiling light on. He and his AHP group had just looked at a screening of a mobile film that they had downloaded. The film had shown the assault on Vera Larsson in the caravan out in the Ingenting forest.

'No direct images of the perpetrators' faces.'

'No.'

'But the beginning of the film was interesting.'

'When they were having sex?'

'Yes.'

There were four of them in the room, including Janne Klinga. They had all reacted when the mobile camera had filmed through the oval window into the caravan and showed a naked man on top of a woman they assumed was Vera Larsson. The man's face could just be seen in a quick blurred movement. Too quick to show anything that would make him recognisable.

'We've got to get hold of that man.'

The others agreed with Rune Forss. Even though it was unlikely that the man himself had assaulted Vera Larsson, he was nevertheless of considerable interest. He must have been on the scene almost at the same time that the assault took place.

'Send the film to the technical unit and ask them to work on his face, we might be able to get a sharper image of it.'

'Do you think it's another homeless person?' Klinga wondered.

'No idea.'

'Was Vera Larsson a prostitute?'

'Not as far as we are aware,' said Forss. 'But you never can know with those types.'

* * *

Seen from the perspective of a hospital series on TV the whole thing was properly choreographed. The yellow-green light, all the apparatuses, the quiet exchange of medical terms, the handling of small and large instruments by hands in rubber gloves.

An operation just like any other.

Seen from the inside, from the patient's perspective, it looked rather different. For a start, the patient couldn't look out, because her eyes were closed. And secondly there was no awareness of anything because the patient was anaesthetized.

But thirdly, that which we know so little about, there was a sensation of voices and an inner kaleidoscope of pictures, deep down inside where nobody knows where it is, until we are there ourselves.

Vera was in there.

So at the same time that the outer world was fully occupied with her body, and organs, and everything that was damaged, Vera herself was in a completely different place.

Alone.

With a bunch of keys and a hanged body.

And a chalk-white child who sat writing on the palm of her hand with a pen of sorrow… 'is this how it was meant to be' … 'is this how it was meant to be' …

Outside, far outside, lay the large Söder Hospital like a gigantic bunker of stone, white as a skeleton, with rows of lit-up windows. Not far from the car park stood a solitary man, with long hair, in the dark. He was looking at the windows trying to find one to concentrate on.

The one he chose suddenly went dark.

8

A sombre mood had settled over Glasblåsar park that morning, as if the wind had laid a mourning veil over the people.
One-eyed Vera was dead. Their beloved Vera was dead. Her
flame had been extinguished just after midnight as a result of
her ruptured organs. The doctors had done what doctors do,
clinically and professionally; when Vera's heart became a thin
line, the nurses had taken over.

Ad mortem.

Silently, they dropped into the park, one by one, nodded to
each other, gave a little shudder and sank down on the benches.
An editor from *Situation Sthlm* came too. Vera had been one
of their sellers for many years. He said a few moving words
about vulnerability, and about Vera having been a source of
vivid warmth. They all nodded in agreement.

Then they descended into their own memories.

Their beloved Vera was dead. She who never managed to get
there, to life. Who wrestled with those figments of her imagination and those grimy childhood memories and never succeeded
in gaining control herself.

Now she was dead.

Now she would never again stand in the setting sun and
release her sudden hoarse laugh, or throw herself into complicated discussions about the lack of care for those she called 'the
people who have gone astray'.

The sledgehammer was no more.

Jelle had slipped in at the edge of the park, unnoticed. He
sat down on a bench at the far end. A clear indication of his dual
needs: I am here, at a distance, stay away. He didn't know why
he had made his way here. Or he did know. Here were the only
people who knew who Vera Larsson was. The murdered woman
from northern Uppland. There were no others. No others who
cared, or who mourned. Only the people sitting here, on the

benches round about.

A gathering of social casualties, of ragamuffins.

And him.

Who had loved her and seen her fall asleep and caressed her white scar and then left.

Like a cowardly rat.

Jelle got up again.

Finally, he had made up his mind. At first he had wandered around aimlessly hoping to stumble across a stairwell where he could shelter, or an open attic, anywhere he could be left in peace. But in the end he found himself back at his old shack beside Järla Lake. He was safe there. He wouldn't be disturbed there.

He could get really drunk there.

Jelle never got drunk. He hadn't touched spirits for years. Now he had some cash from the magazine and bought a half-bottle of vodka and four strong beers.

That ought to do it.

He sank down on the floor. A couple of thick roots had pushed up the planks and he felt the musty smell of damp soil. He had laid out some brown cardboard and covered that with newspapers here and there, that sufficed, at this time of year. In the winter he got cold as ice as soon as he fell asleep.

He looked at his hands. Emaciated, with thin long fingers. More like claws, he thought, when they grasped the first can of beer.

And the second.

Then he added to that with a few glugs of vodka. When the intoxication started to hit, he had already articulated the question five times, in a low voice.

'Why the hell did I leave?'

And not found an answer. So he had reformulated the question, somewhat louder.

'Why the hell didn't I stay?'

A very similar question, five times again, and the same answer. No idea.

When the third beer and the fifth glug of vodka had settled in his body, he started crying.

Slow heavy tears that laboriously made their way down over his rough skin.

Jelle was crying.

You can cry because you have lost something, or because you haven't been given something. You can cry for many reasons, trivial or deeply tragic, or for no reason at all. You just cry, because a sensation has swept past and lifted up a hatch to the past.

Jelle's crying had an immediate cause. One-eyed Vera. But the tears had deeper sources than that, as he well knew. Sources that were about his divorced wife, about some vanished friends, but above all about the old woman on her deathbed. Mama. Who died six years ago. He had sat beside her deathbed, at the Radium Home. Her body, drugged with morphine, had rested peacefully under the thin covers, the hand he held was like a shrivelled bird's claw. But he had felt how the hand had suddenly contracted a little and seen how his mother's eyelids opened a slight gap into her pupils and heard how some words passed her narrow dried lips. He had leaned much closer to her face, closer than he had been for many, many years, and heard what she said. Every single word. Phrase for phrase.

Then she died.

And now he was lying here crying.

When the intoxication eventually led him into a mist of horrible memories, the first scream came. And when the images of smoke and fire and a bloody harpoon appeared again, he roared out loud.

* * *

He switched without effort between French and Portuguese. French in the left mobile, and Portuguese in the right one. He was sitting in his exclusive director's office on the top floor on Sveavägen with a view of the churchyard with Palme's grave.

An old object of hate in his circles.

Not the grave, but the man who was shot and ended up in the grave.

Olof Palme.

When he heard the news of the murder, Bertil Magnuson was sitting at the Alexandra nightclub with Latte and a couple of other jolly men from the same dark blue soil.

'Champagne!'

Latte had called out, and champagne there was.

All night long.

Now it was twenty-five years later and the murder was still unsolved. Which hardly bothered Bertil. He was negotiating in the Congo. A landowner outside Walikale had demanded economic compensation on a level that was unreasonable. The company's Portuguese local manager had problems. The company's French agent wanted them to agree to the demands, but Bertil didn't want to.

'I'll phone the military commander in Kinshasa.'

He phoned and booked a telephone meeting with yet another shady potentate. Reluctant landowners were a small problem for Bertil Magnuson. It always sorted itself out in the end.

With soft methods or with hard ones.

Unfortunately none of them were applicable to his real problem. The taped conversation.

He had found out that the call from Wendt couldn't be traced. So that path was blocked. Thus he didn't know whether Wendt had rung from abroad, or was in Sweden. But he assumed that Wendt wanted some sort of contact with him. Sooner or later. Otherwise there wouldn't be any point in phoning at all. Would there?

Bertil tried to reason it out.

So he phoned K. Sedovic. A very reliable person. He asked him to check all the hotels and motels and hostels in the Stockholm area to see if there was any trace of Nils Wendt. If he was even in Sweden. A long shot, Bertil knew. And even if Wendt was in Sweden he wouldn't necessarily be staying in a hotel or similar. Above all, not under his own name.

But what else could he do?

* * *

A pretty woman, Olivia thought. She had kept her figure, must have been successful as a female escort in younger years. Lived on her looks and her body. Olivia fast-forwarded the tape. She was sitting at her kitchen table with her laptop and looking at the interview that Eva Carlsén had sent a link to. With Jackie Berglund. It had taken place in a boutique in Östermalm. Weird & Wow on Sybillegatan. A typical boutique of its type, and for the area. Coquettish interior details combined with shockingly expensive designer clothes. A façade boutique, that was what Eva had called it, a façade for Jackie's other business.

Red Velvet.

The interview had been recorded a couple of years earlier. It was Eva who was doing the interviewing, and it was clear that Jackie ran the boutique herself. Olivia searched online and quickly found it. And the same owner: Jackie Berglund.

That would be worth a visit, Olivia thought.

She looked at the rest of the interview. Eva had got Jackie to talk about her background as a female escort. It was nothing she was ashamed of, on the contrary, it had been a way for her to survive. She categorically denied that there had been any sexual services.

'We were like geishas, sophisticated lady companions, we were invited to events and dinners to create a better atmosphere, besides, we made contacts.'

She returned to how she made contacts a couple of times. When Eva tried to establish what sort of contacts this concerned, then Jackie's answers were vague. Not to say dismissive. She thought it was private.

'But were they business contacts?' Eva asked.

'What else would they be?'

'Friend contacts.'

'They were both.'

'Do you still have those contacts today?'

'Some of them.'

And thus it went on. It was clear what Eva was after, clear to Olivia at least. She wanted to establish whether contacts were the same as customers. Not customers in the boutique, but customers in the business that was using the boutique as a façade. Red Velvet.

Jackie's escort service.

But Jackie was much too sharp to fall for that trap. She almost smiled when Eva pressed her a fourth time about her customers. The smile quickly vanished, however, when Eva asked a follow-up question.

'Do you have a register of customers?'

'For the boutique?'

'No.'

'Now I'm not sure what you mean.'

'A register of customers for your other activity, as a supplier of call girls? Via Red Velvet.'

Olivia couldn't believe she had dared ask that question. Her respect for Eva went up a few notches. And evidently nor could Jackie believe how someone had dared ask that question. She looked at Eva with an expression that suddenly came from another world altogether. A forbidden world. A look that reminded Olivia of Eva's warning. A woman with that look wasn't somebody you should go snooping on.

Especially if you were only twenty-three years old, and didn't have anything concrete to go on.

Nothing at all.

And thought you were Sherlock Holmes.

Olivia couldn't help but smile a little, at herself, right into her laptop. Suddenly she came to think about the German police that had created a Trojan that could get inside your laptop and record everything that went on in front of the camera.

She pulled the lid down a little.

It was almost midnight when Jelle woke up in his miserable shack. Slowly, arduously, with eyes that seemed to be glued shut and what felt like a snail in his mouth. One hell of a hangover and covered in vomit, something that he had no memory of. He slowly pushed himself up into a sitting position with his back against the wall. He saw the moonlight filter in between the boards. His brain felt like mashed potato. He sat there a long time and felt something building up. Inside him, a sort of heated fury forged through his chest and up into his head. He found it almost hard to see. Suddenly he jerked into action and stood up. He kicked the door open with considerable violence. The boards flew in all directions. The murder of Vera and his own treachery had taken up position in his body like an iron-bar lever. He banged one hand against the doorpost and stepped out.

Out of the vacuum.

It was well past midnight when he started to climb up the steps. The stone steps to the left of the Katarina garage. Harald Lindberg's steps. From Katarinavägen up to Klevgränd, four flights of steps, in all 119 stone steps up and just as many down again, with a streetlight beside each landing.

It was raining, a heavy lukewarm summer rain, but that didn't bother him.

He had made up his mind that the time had come.

Long ago, back in the Stone Age, he had had an athletic body. Muscular and 192 centimetres tall. There was nothing athletic about him nowadays. He knew that his physical condition was abysmal, that his muscles had almost withered away, that his body had been lying fallow for many years. That he was almost a wreck.

Almost.

Now he was going to change that.

He made his way up the stone steps, step by step, and it took him some time. It took six minutes up to Klevgränd and four minutes down again. And when he started to go up a second time, that was the end.

Absolutely.

He sank down on the first landing and felt how his heart pumped. He could almost hear it through his ribs. How it struggled like a jackhammer and couldn't understand what this person was trying to do, and who he thought he was.

Or what he was capable of.

Not very much. Yet. Just now – nothing. Just now he was sitting, perspiring and panting and trying with great effort to press the right buttons on his mobile. In the end he managed it. In the end he found the film online.

The murder of Vera.

The film began by showing the back of a man who was copulating with a woman beneath him. Him and Vera. He started the film again. Could you see his face? Doubtful. But nevertheless. He knew that Forss and his henchmen would closely examine every frame. The man in the caravan must be of considerable interest to them. What would happen if they could identify him? At the scene of a murder? And Forss of all people?

Jelle didn't like the idea. He didn't like Forss. A piece of shit. But Forss could cause an awful lot of hassle if he thought that Jelle was involved in the murder of Vera.

And that could happen soon.

Jelle let the film roll on a little. When they started to beat up Vera, he clicked away and looked down over Katarinavägen. What cowardly bastards, he thought, they waited until I'd left. They didn't dare come near when I was still there. They wanted to get at Vera when she was on her own.

Poor Vera.

He shook his head a little and rubbed his eyes. What feelings had he actually had for Vera? Before what happened had actually happened?

Sorrow.

From the very first second he met her and saw how her eyes clung, leechlike, onto his as if he was a rope ladder to life. And he wasn't. He had climbed down quite a long way the last few years. Not all the way down, admittedly, not to where Vera was, but he wasn't many rungs above her.

Now she was dead and he was sitting here. Absolutely knackered. On some stone steps close to Slussen, and thinking about her, and how he had left her on her own in the caravan and walked away. Now he was going to do some walking here. Up and down the steps. Night after night, until he was fit enough to be able to do what he felt he was obliged to do.

Deal with the men who had murdered Vera.

* * *

It was as Bertil Magnuson expected. K. Sedovic had given his report: no Nils Wendt at any hotel in Stockholm. But where could he be hanging out? If he was even in Stockholm? He hardly had any contacts left from the old days, Bertil had already checked that, discreetly. Wendt was not in anybody's address book nowadays.

So what now?

Bertil got up and crossed to the window. The cars rolled past down on Sveavägen. You couldn't hear them. A few years earlier they had installed exclusive windows with insulating glass on the entire street side of the building. A sensible investment, Bertil thought, and then another thought came into his head.

Or idea, rather.

A sudden realisation.

About where Nils Wendt might well be found with his repulsive recording.

The boy with wavy blond hair took it easy. The skateboard had a crack down the middle. He had found it in a skip the day before and repaired it as best he could. The wheels were worn and he was on a steep hill so he took it easy. Tarmac. Then there was a long straight stretch towards the high rise buildings with their gaudy colours, Flemingsberg, with small groves of trees in front. Here and there, a playground. On almost every balcony, a satellite dish stuck out. A lot of people here wanted to watch TV channels from other countries.

The boy looked towards one of the blue buildings, up at the seventh floor.

She sat beside a formica table in the kitchen, smoking, turned towards a little gap where she had opened the window. She didn't want smoke in her flat. She would have liked to have stopped smoking altogether. She'd been wanting to do that for years, but it was the only bad habit she had and she knew that the sum of all bad habits was constant. If she stopped smoking she would only start with something else.

Something worse.

She was called Ovette Andersson and was the mother of Acke, a boy with wavy blond hair just over ten years old.

Ovette was forty-two.

She blew out some smoke through the gap and turned towards the clock on the wall, spontaneously. The clock had stopped. It had been stopped a long time. New batteries, new tights, new bed sheets, new existence, she thought. The list was overwhelmingly long. And at the very top was a pair of new soccer boots for Acke. He would get them as soon as she could afford it, she had promised him that. After the rent and all the rest had been paid. And all the rest included some big debts which the bailiffs were collecting and instalments to pay for some cosmetic surgery. She had enlarged her breasts some years ago, and borrowed money to do it. Now she had to look after every penny.

'Hi!'

Acke put his cracked skateboard down and went straight to the fridge to get some cold water. He loved cold water. Ovette always put a couple of litres in a jar in the fridge so it would be waiting for him when he came home.

They lived in a two-room flat. Two rooms and a kitchen and a bathroom in one of the high rise blocks. Acke went to Annerstad School down in the local centre. Now it was the summer holidays. Ovette pulled Acke towards her.

'I think I'll have to work this evening.'

'I know.'

'I might be rather late.'

'I know.'

'Have you got your soccer training?'

'Yeah.'

Acke was lying, but Ovette didn't know that.

'Don't forget your key.'

'No.'

Acke had had his own key as long as he remembered. He looked after himself for a large part of the day. The part when his mum was in the city working. Then he usually played soccer until it got too dark and then he went home and heated up what his mum had prepared. It always tasted good. Then he played his video games.

Unless he was doing something else.

* * *

Olivia was in a hurry and in fact she hated hypermarkets. Especially the ones she had never been in before. She hated wandering about more or less totally lost in narrow aisles with overfull shelves trying to find a little can of vongole, and in the end be forced to seek out some sort of staff person in a semi-uniform.

'What did you say it was called, did you say...?'

'Vongole.'

'Is that a vegetable?'

But she didn't have time to choose a shop today. She had just fetched her car from its MOT test in Lännersta and had turned in to shop at the huge ICA Maxi in Nacka. Now she was rushing from the car park towards the glassed-in entrance and realised that she probably didn't have a five-kronor coin so she would have to settle for a plastic basket. She had a fifty-kronor note in her pocket but there wasn't time to change that. A few metres in front of the entrance stood a tall thin man with a magazine in his hand. One of those homeless people who earned a meagre living by selling *Situation Stockholm*. The man had some scabs on his face, his long hair was matted and shone with grease, and judging by his clothes he had spent the last few weeks very close to the ground. Olivia glanced at the man. It said 'Jelle' on the ID-card around his neck. She passed by quickly. Sometimes she bought a magazine, but not today. Not when she was in such a hurry. She continued through the rotating doors and got a few metres inside the lobby – then she stopped abruptly. Slowly, she turned round and looked at the man standing out there for a moment. Without really knowing why, she walked out again, went and stood a couple of metres away from the man and looked at him. He turned towards her and moved forward a step or two.

'*Situation Stockholm*?'

Olivia dug into her pocket, got hold of the fifty-kronor note and held it up while scanning the man's face. He took the note and handed over change and a magazine.

'Thanks.'

Olivia took the magazine and put together her question in her mouth.

'Are you Tom Stilton?'

'What of it? Yes?'

'It says "Jelle" on that.'

'Tom Jesper Stilton.'

'Okay.'

'What of it?'

Olivia quickly walked past the man and in through the revolving doors again. She stopped at the same place as before, caught up with her shocked breathing, and turned round. The man outside was just putting his magazines in a shabby backpack and starting to leave. Olivia reacted. Slowly. She walked out again, and went after the man. He was walking quite fast. She had to almost half run the last bit to catch up with him. The man didn't stop. Olivia cut in front of him.

'What's the matter? D'you want some more magazines?' he said.

'No. My name is Olivia Rönning and I'm a student at the Police College. I want to talk to you. About the beach case. The one on Nordkoster.'

The man's weatherworn face didn't show any reaction at all. He just turned round and walked straight out into the street. A car had to brake suddenly and the driver with his hair backcombed made an obscene gesture. The man continued to walk. Olivia stayed where she was. A long time. Such a long time that she saw him disappear round a concrete corner some way away, and she stood so still and erect that an elderly gentleman felt obliged to hesitantly address her.

'Are you feeling all right?'

Olivia was feeling everything other than all right.

She sank down in her car and tried to pull herself together. The car was in the big car park beside the hypermarket where she had just met the man who had been in charge of the murder investigation on Nordkoster for sixteen years.

Former Detective Chief Inspector Tom Stilton.

'Jelle'?

How the hell could he get from Jesper to Jelle?

According to her tutor one of the best murder investigators in Sweden, with one of the most rapid careers in Swedish police history. And today he was selling *Situation Sthlm*. Someone who slept rough. In dreadful physical condition. So dreadful that Olivia had had to make a big effort to convince herself that it really was him.

But it was.

She had seen quite a number of pictures of Stilton when she had ploughed through the newspaper articles at the National Library about the beach case, and seen an old photo of him at Gunnar's in Strömstad. She had been somewhat fascinated by his intense expression, and noted that he looked attractive as well as distinct.

He didn't any more.

His physical decline had drained his appearance of all personality. Even his eyes seemed to have died. His thin body unwillingly supported a long-haired head which definitely did not match.

Yet it was Stilton.

She had reacted instinctively, at first, when she passed him, a fleeting sensation had swept past and formed an image when she stopped inside the doors: Tom Stilton? It isn't possible. It is… and then she had gone out again and studied his face.

Nose. Eyebrows. The clearly visible scar under one corner of his mouth.

It was him.

And now he had disappeared.

Olivia twisted a little in her seat. Next to her lay a notebook with a large number of written questions and thoughts about the beach case. All written down, ready to be answered by the man who had been in charge of the murder investigation.

Tom Stilton.

A shabby rough sleeper.

The rough sleeper himself was now sitting beside Järla Lake. His backpack still on his back. He sat here sometimes, not so far from his wooden shack. Some thick bushes, some water trickling under an old wooden bridge, relative silence.

He pulled a branch off a bush next to him, stripped the leaves off and stretched it down as far as he could reach. Far down where he stirred it around in the murky water.

He was disturbed.

Not because he had been recognised, he had to live with that. He was indeed Tom Jesper Stilton and had no plans to change his name. But because of what she had said, the girl who had cut in front of him and looked confounded.

Olivia Rönning.

He knew the name. Very well.

'I want to talk to you. About the beach case. The one on Nordkoster.'

There are eternities, and there are eternities. And there are aeons. An eternity of eternities. That was approximately the distance that Stilton felt to his former life. Yet just one phrase was needed for that aeon to shrink to the size of a tick and begin its greedy penetration.

The beach case.

It sounded so trifling, he thought. A beach and a case. So harmless. But he himself had never called it the beach case. He thought it degraded one of the most repulsive murders he had investigated. It sounded like a newspaper headline. He himself had always referred to the case as Nordkoster. Concrete. What a policeman would say.

And unsolved.

And as for why was Olivia Rönning was interested in Nordkoster, that wasn't his problem. She came from another world. But she had planted a tick in his mental body. She had made an incision in what he was now, and let the past in, and that disturbed him. He didn't want to be disturbed. Not by the past, and definitely not by what had disturbed him sufficiently for almost eighteen years.

Jelle pulled the branch up out of the water.

* * *

The light summer rain poured down on the demonstrators who had gathered together on the pavement opposite MWM's head office on Sveavägen. Their banners with various slogans: LEAVE THE CONGO NOW!, PLUNDERERS!, STOP CHILD LABOUR! A little group of policemen stood some way away.

Over by Olof Palmes gata an elderly man was leaning against a façade. He watched the demonstrators, registered their banners and read one of their pamphlets.

MWM's coltan mining destroys irreplaceable natural habitats. In the face of greed, gorillas are threatened with extinction when their food sources disappear! They are also killed and sold as bushmeat! Stop MWM's unscrupulous rape of nature!

The pamphlet was illustrated with horrible pictures of dead gorillas, fastened to poles like bleeding Christ figures.

The man lowered the pamphlet. He slowly raised his eyes to look up at the façade across the street, right up to the very top floor, where the head office lay. Where the owner and managing director Bertil Magnuson had his office. The man's gaze fastened on that. He knew that Bertil was in the room. He had seen him arrive in the brightly polished Jaguar and sneak in through the entrance.

You have aged, Bertil, Nils Wendt thought. He felt the pocket with the cassette tape.

* * *

In the city there was still a bit of the working day left, although it was gradually coming to an end. For Ovette Andersson, the working day had only just begun. Her workplace, the pavement area between Riksbanken and the Academy of Fine Arts, was in effect active day and night. The cars had already started to crawl along on the lookout for what the Law on Prostitution termed 'sex-sellers'. As opposed to 'sex-buyers'. As if it was about a formal business transaction with sex products.

It wasn't long before the first car crept up beside Ovette and the window was lowered. When the formalities had been dealt with, and Ovette climbed into the car, she pushed away the last thought of Acke. He was doing his soccer training. He was having a good time. He would soon get some new soccer boots. She pulled the car door shut.

* * *

It was almost seven in the evening when Olivia stepped into her flat. Elvis lay stretched out like a Playboy centrefold on the hall mat with his legs spread in all directions: he demanded tender attention. Olivia lifted him up and sank her face into her beloved cat's soft fur. He smelt faintly of the food he had eaten that morning. Now he took up position across her shoulder, his favourite place, and started to chew a little on her hair.

With the cat on her shoulders she took a cold juice out of the fridge and sank down at the kitchen table. On the way home from Nacka, she had sorted the experience with Stilton. She had found him, at last, and he was a rough sleeper. Fine. She assumed there were reasons for that and they were not her concern. But he was still an important source for the beach case. A totally uninterested source, obviously, but...? Sure, she could drop the case, it was not a compulsory assignment after all, but that wasn't really how she was made.

The opposite.

The meeting with Stilton had given the case a new dimension, for her, and her easily courted imagination. Had Stilton's fall from a feted detective chief inspector to a physical wreck anything to do with the beach case? Had he come across something six years earlier that led to his leaving the police force? Even though he left for private reasons?

'Not only.'

Åke Gustafsson had admitted that when she'd phoned him again and pressed him a little.

'What else was it then?'

'There was a conflict about an investigation.'

'The beach case?'

'I don't know, I'd started at the college then, I only heard about it in passing.'

'So it was also a reason for his leaving?'

'Possibly.'

Olivia's imagination didn't need more than that. 'Possibly.' That he had left the force because there had been a conflict around something that might have been connected with the beach case? Or another case that had some link? What was Stilton doing when he left the force? Could she find out?

She made up her mind. She wasn't going to drop Stilton. She'd hunt him down whatever it took. Or in more concrete terms, she would go to the editorial office of *Situation Sthlm* and find out all she could about Stilton.

And then contact him again.

Somewhat better prepared.

* * *

Those stone steps were where they met again. It was late, just after one in the morning, by chance. Stilton was on the way down for the fourth time when Mink was on the way up.

They met on the second landing.

'Hi there.'

'Toothache?'

'Sit down.'

Stilton pointed to a step. Mink reacted immediately. Both at the rather sharp tone and the fact that Stilton didn't just walk on. Did he want to talk? Mink looked at the step Stilton had pointed to and wondered when the most recent dog poo had landed there. He sat down. Stilton sat next to him. So close that Mink couldn't help but notice a not entirely pleasant smell of rubbish and ammonia.

And a great deal of sweat.

'How are you doing, Tom?' he asked with his squeaky voice.

'They've killed Vera.'

'Was she the one in the caravan?'

'Yes.'

'Did you know her?'

'Yes.'

'Do you know who did it?'

'No, do you?'

'Why should I know?'

'In the old days, you knew before most people as soon as there was some shit going on. Have you lost your touch?'

A comment like that would have led to a headbutt and a broken nose for in theory anyone except Stilton. You didn't headbutt Stilton. So Mink swallowed and observed the tall rough sleeper with the strong odour next to him. Some years ago the roles had been decidedly switched. When Mink had been a few notches further down on the social scale and Stilton definitely a few notches higher up.

Now things were as they were. Mink gave his ponytail a little tug.

'Do you want some assistance?'

'Yes,' said Stilton.

'OK. And what are you going to do? If you get hold of them?'

'Say hello from Vera.'

Stilton got up. Two steps down, he turned and looked back up.

'I'll be here at night, at around this time. Get in touch.'

He continued on his way down. Mink remained sitting. Rather surprised. There was something new about Stilton, changed, something in the way he moved, and in his gaze.

It was firm again.

Back in place.

The last few years it had slipped away as soon as you tried to catch it. Now it had landed right in Mink's eyes and not deviated a millimetre.

Jelle had Tom Stilton's gaze again.

What had happened?

Stilton himself was satisfied with the meeting on the stone steps. He knew Mink, and was well aware of his capabilities. One of Mink's few talents was to snap up information. A comment here, an overheard conversation there, being always on the move in totally different circles and catching tiny scraps which he put together into a pattern. A name. An event. Under different circumstances, he could have become a brilliant current-affairs analyst.

Under rather different circumstances.

But Mink had made good use of his talent. Not least since he first came in contact with the then Detective Chief Inspector Tom Stilton. Stilton had quickly understood how he could utilize Mink's absorbing ability and unscrupulous snitching.

'I don't snitch!'

'Sorry.'

'Do you see me as some miserable snitch?'

Stilton could still recall the conversation. Mink had been furiously indignant.

'I see you as an informant. How do you see yourself?' said Stilton.

'Informant is OK. Two professionals who exchange experiences is better.'

'And what is your profession?'

'A tightrope walker.'

At this point Stilton realised that Mink was perhaps a rather more complex snitch than the others he made use of, and perhaps worth taking a bit of little extra care of.

A tightrope walker.

An hour or so later, Stilton made his way through the Ingenting forest carrying a cardboard box, the sort removal men use. He had forgotten the meeting with Mink. He was totally concentrated upon the dirty grey caravan. On being able to cope with an encounter with it. He had made up his mind to move there.

For the time being.

He knew that the police had finished there and that the council wanted to get rid of the caravan. But Vera's murder clogged up the paperwork a little. So the caravan was still there.

And as long as it was there, Stilton was going to live in it.

If he could manage that.

It wasn't that easy. First. Just seeing the bunk where they had made love put him off balance. But he put the cardboard box down on the floor and sat on the bunk on the opposite side. It was at least dry inside. A lamp, mattresses, with a new tube and a bit of maintenance he would surely get the Calor gas burners to work again. He couldn't give a shit about the ant tracks. He looked around. The police had taken most of what Vera had kept in the caravan. Including a drawing of a harpoon that he had once done. Here, at this table, when Vera wanted to know what his childhood had been like.

'Involved a harpoon?'

'Roughly.'

He had told her a little about Rödlöga, a cluster of islets in the outer archipelago north of Stockholm. About growing up with a granny with personal memories of the seal hunts in former days and of plundering wrecked ships. And Vera had hung on his every word.

'It sounds like a good childhood. Right?'

'It was good.'

She didn't need to know any more than that. Nobody else knew any more, except Mette and Mårten Olsäter, and his ex-wife. But it stopped with them.

Not even Abbas el Fassi knew.

Now, Rune Forss would presumably be sitting in some neon yellow police room and looking at a drawing of a harpoon and wondering if it had any connection with Vera Larsson's murder. Stilton smiled somewhere inside. Forss was an idiot. He would never solve Vera's murder. He would tick off his hours and put his reports together and then he would squeeze his fat fingers into a bowling ball.

That was where he put his commitment.

Stilton stretched out on the berth and then sat up again.

It wasn't that easy to just take over her caravan. She was still there, he could feel it. And see it. There were still traces of the blood that had been wiped off the floor. He got up and smashed a hand into the wall.

And looked at the traces of blood again.

He had never thought in terms of vengeance. As a murder investigator he had always kept his distance in relation to victim as well as perpetrator. At the very most, he had on a few occasions been moved by how it could affect close family members. Ordinary people going about their lives who suddenly were struck by a lightning bolt straight to the heart. He could still remember once one early morning when he had to wake a single mother and tell her that her only son had confessed to murdering three people.

'My son?'

'You have a son called Lage Svensson?'

'Yes. What did you say he'd done?'

That sort of conversation. It could stick in Stilton's mind for a while.

But never revenge.

Until now. With Vera. This was different.

He sank down on the bunk again and looked up at the filthy ceiling. There was a smattering from the rain falling on the half-broken plexiglass dome. He slowly started to let in some of what he usually kept out.

How had he ended up here?

With ant tracks and a wiped-up pool of blood and a body – his – that was more than halfway to becoming a total wreck?

In a caravan?

He knew what had set it off six years ago, he would never forget that. His mother's last words. But, nevertheless, he was still amazed at how fast it had happened. To let go of things.

How easy it had been once he had made up his mind. How quickly he had drained himself. Deliberately. Let go of everything that he could let go of, and a bit more besides, and actively striven to sink. And he'd noticed how easily one thing led to another. How there was nothing to prevent him from abstaining. From turning himself off. From cutting away. How easy it had been to slide into a life where he was totally without responsibility, totally vegetative.

Into a vacuum.

He had reflected inside this – his vacuum – many times, cut away from everybody else's existence. He had reflected upon primary elements such as life and death, about the very meaning of life. He had seen things in outline, tried to find an anchor, a purpose, something on which to hang his life. But he hadn't found anything. Not a single nail. Not even a drawing pin. The fall from a position in normal accepted life, down to a hole among those who were despised, had simply left him empty handed.

Mentally as well as physically.

For a time he had tried to see his existence as a form of freedom. Free from social obligations, from responsibility, from everything.

A free man!

Self-deception like some of the homeless people devoted themselves to. He pretty soon abandoned that. He was not a free man, and he knew it.

He was, however, a man in his own right.

A wreck in a caravan, a lot of people would think. With good reason. But a wreck who had learnt that a person who stands right at the bottom at least has solid ground under his feet. And that was more than a lot of people could boast of. Other more high-flying people.

Stilton sat up. Would it be like this in Vera's caravan too? A hell of a lot of brooding? That was what he wanted to get away from in the wooden shack. He dug a little in his backpack and fished out a little bottle of pills which he put on the table.

An escape bottle.

Very early on in his falling journey he had learnt how you solve certain problems. You flee from them. You fill a glass with water, take a couple of Stesolids and you have an escape dose.

It isn't harder than that.

'You're like Ben the Fibber.'

'Who?'

Stilton remembered the conversation. He had been sitting with an old jailbird in Mosebacke Square and feeling pretty bad, and in the end he had fished out his bottle of pills and then the guy had looked at him and shaken his head.

'You're like Ben the Fibber.'

'Who?'

'He was always running away, as soon as things got difficult, he swallowed something white and lay down on the floor and just soaked up Tom Waits, in those days he was still a bar drunk, but what did that help? He died on that same floor thirty years later and a week went by before anyone reacted. Tom Waits didn't. That's what it looks like. You run away, and if you run far enough then nobody will find you until the stench leaks out through the letterbox. What's the point of that?'

Stilton hadn't said a word. Why should he answer a question like that? He didn't even have answers for himself. If you have lost it, then you have lost it, and then you flee to manage to survive.

Stilton pulled the bottle of pills towards him.

Why should he give a damn about Ben the Fibber?

* * *

Little Acke wasn't at his football practice, as Ovette thought. Far from it.

And far from home too.

He had been fetched by some older boys and now he sat half-crouched against a rock wall. His eyes were riveted on what was happening not far away. This was the second time he was with them. Here. In a gigantic underground cavern that had originally been intended for a sewage works, somewhere in the Årsta area.

Deep, deep underground.

They had rigged up coloured spotlights at the front. The lamps shone across the rock facing in shades of blue and green and red. The sounds from what they were doing could be clearly heard over where Acke was. They weren't nice sounds. He reacted instinctively by putting his hands over his ears, but he quickly took them down again. He knew you weren't meant to cover your ears.

Acke was frightened.

He pulled out a lighter and clicked it a few times.

Soon it would be his turn.

He thought about the money. If it went well he would get a bit of money, that's what they'd promised. If it didn't go well, he wouldn't get anything. He wanted the money. He knew how things were at home. There was never any money, except for things they absolutely must have. Never for anything else. Something that his mum and him could do together. Like many of his mates did with their parents. The big theme park or something like that. There was never any money for that.

His mum said.

Acke wanted to give the money to her. He had already worked out how he'd explain it. He'd found one of those scratch lottery tickets and it had given a win of 100 kronor.

That was what he would get if it went well this evening.

He would give it to his mum.

A couple of steel reflections hit his eyes.

9

The two figures were crouching behind a parked van.

It was just after twelve, in the middle of the day, in the middle of a district with small houses in Bromma. A father had just passed on the pavement opposite wheeling a buggy in front of him. The headphones from his mobile were pressed into his ears and the conversation was about work. Taking paternity leave was one thing, but dropping his work was quite another. Luckily, nowadays you could combine the two. So with nearly all his attention on his work and a lot less focus on the baby in the pram, they rolled past and disappeared.

The two figures looked at each other.

The street was empty again.

They quickly nipped in through the hedge at the back of the house. The garden was full of apple trees and large lilac bushes that hid their presence quite well. They broke in through the kitchen door quietly and effectively, and vanished inside.

Half an hour later a taxi stopped outside a small yellow house in Bromma. Eva Carlsén climbed out. She looked towards her house and reminded herself that she must get a new tiled roof. And new drainpipes. That was her job now. Before, it had been her husband, Anders, who looked after such things. After their divorce she had to deal with it all.

All the practical things.

Keeping the house in good condition and looking after the garden.

And all the other stuff.

She walked in through the gate. Suddenly the anger seared like a razor blade through her heart. Quickly and effectively it slit open the wound again. Abandoned! Dropped! Dumped! They swelled up with such force that she simply had to come to a halt. She almost lost her balance. Hell! she thought. She hated it. Not having control of herself. She was a person with logical thoughts and she hated things she couldn't control. She took a few deep breaths to calm herself down. He isn't worth it, she thought. Like a mantra.

She continued towards the house.

Two pairs of eyes followed her, from the gate and right up to the front door. When she disappeared out of their vision, they slipped away from the curtains.

Eva opened her handbag to pull out the door key. Suddenly she saw something move in the neighbour's house. Monika, of course she would be standing there spying. Monika had always liked Anders. Very much. She had laughed at his jokes across the fence with a glow in her eyes. She could hardly manage to hide her malicious pleasure when she heard about the divorce.

Eve got the key out, put it in the lock and opened the door. Now she would throw herself into the shower. Wash away all those destructive feelings so that she could focus on what she ought to be focusing on. Her series of articles. She took a couple of steps into the hall and turned towards the coat hooks to hang up her thin jacket.

Suddenly she was knocked down.

From behind.

* * *

The sellers' meeting was just coming to an end and everybody wanted to start on their way into town to start flogging their copies. Olivia had to step to one side in the doorway and let out an illustrious flock of homeless people with bundles of magazines in their hands, and chattering away for all they were worth. Last of all came Muriel tripping along. She had fired herself up with a whole constellation of drugs at breakfast and felt fantastic. She didn't have any magazines. She wasn't a seller. You had to fill certain criteria to be allowed to sell *Situation Sthlm*. Among them, that you were entitled to welfare benefits as a citizen of the country. Or had established contacts with the social services, probation officers or psychiatric services. Muriel didn't have any of that. She was just happy when she wasn't a wreck. In between she tried to get hold of drugs. Now she was the last to come tripping out and that gave Olivia a chance to slip in. She went straight up to the reception and asked for Jelle.

'Jelle? No, I don't know where he is, he wasn't at the meeting today.'

The man in reception looked at Olivia.

'Does he live anywhere?' she asked.

'No, he's homeless.'

'But he usually turns up here, right?'

'Yes, when he collects magazines.'

'Does he have a mobile?'

'I think so, unless it's been nicked.'

'Have you got a number for him?'

'I don't want to hand that out.'

'Why not?'

'Because I don't know if he wants me to.'

Olivia respected that. Even a homeless person has the right to some integrity. She gave her own mobile number and asked the guy to give it to Stilton if he turned up.

'You could ask in the mobile-phone shop at Hornstull.'

That was Bo Fast speaking. He was sitting in a corner and had overheard the conversation. Olivia turned towards Fast.

'He's a bit matey with the people who work there,' he said.

'OK, right. Thanks.'

'Have you ever met Jelle?'

'Once.'

'He's a bit special…'

'In what way d'you mean?'

'Special.'

OK, Olivia thought, he's special. Compared to what? Other homeless people? His past? What did he mean? She would have liked to have asked rather a lot but she didn't exactly see Bo Fast as a fast-flowing source of information. She would have to wait until Stilton got in touch with her, if he ever did.

Which she doubted.

* * *

The ambulance medics put a mask over Eva Carlsén's mouth and carried her into the ambulance. With some promptness. She was bleeding heavily from the back of her head. If her neighbour, Monika, hadn't seen the door open in the middle of the day and got curious, it might have ended very nastily. The ambulance disappeared with sirens on just as a policeman pulled out a pen and notebook and turned towards Monika.

No, she hadn't seen any unknown people in the district, no special cars, and no, she hadn't heard anything unusual either.

The police officers inside the house made some more usual discoveries. The entire house seemed to have been searched. Emptied drawers and wardrobes where they had raked out the entire contents, knocked-over chests of drawers and broken china.

Pure destruction.

'Break-in?' One policeman said to the other.

* * *

Stilton needed some more magazines. He had sold all of the copies he had bought the day before, including the copy Olivia Rönning had bought. Now he bought another ten, across the counter.

'Jelle!'

'Yes?'

It was the guy in the reception who was calling out.

'A girl was here asking about your mobile number…'

'Oh yeah?'

'She left a mobile number…'

Stilton was given a piece of paper with a number and he saw that it said 'Olivia Rönning' under it. He went across to the round table and sat down. On the wall behind him hung a large number of photos with black frames, of homeless people who had died the last year. About one a month had died, and three new ones came instead.

Vera's photo had just been put up.

Stilton rubbed the paper with the number on between his fingers. Furious. He didn't like it when people pestered him. When he wasn't allowed to be left in peace. When they tried to get inside his vacuum. Especially people outside the circle of homeless people. Like Olivia Rönning.

He looked at the paper again. He had two choices. Ring her now and get it over with. Answer her damned questions and disappear. Or not give a fuck about ringing. Then there'd be a risk that she would start nosing around and find Vera's caravan and come barging in there. He definitely didn't want that.

He phoned her.

'Olivia! This is Jelle. Tom Stilton. Phone me.'

Stilton hung up. He wasn't going to waste his pay-as-you-go card on Rönning. Five seconds later, his mobile rang.

'Hi! This is Olivia! Great that you got in touch!'

'I'm in a hurry.'

'OK, but listen, I… can't we meet? Just briefly? I can come…'

'What are your bloody questions?'

'They are… shall I list them now?'

Stilton didn't answer so Olivia had to immediately gabble them. Luckily she had her notebook right next to her and she started listing her questions. Quickly, now she had the chance, she didn't know when she'd have contact with him again next time. Or if there even was going to be a next time. 'Was the woman on the beach anaesthetized when she was drowned? Where were the rest of her clothes, did you find them? Did you get a DNA sample from the fetus? Were you sure there were only three people on the beach besides the victim? How could you tell she was of Latin American origin?'

Olivia managed to rattle off another two questions before Stilton abruptly hung up.

In the middle of a sentence.

Olivia sat in her open car with a silent mobile in her hand and a stinging expletive on her lips.

'Fucking asshole!'

'Who? Me?'

A pedestrian passed by the car just then and thought Olivia's exclamation was directed at him.

'You're bloody well parked on a zebra crossing!'

And she was. She had braked her car as soon as Stilton phoning and was still parked on the crossing and saw the pedestrian give her the finger before he walked on.

'Have a nice day!' Olivia called out after him and revved her engine.

Absolutely furious.

Who the hell did Stilton think he was? A damned rough sleeper who treated her like shit! And thought that he could get away with it?

She made a totally illegal U-turn and zoomed off.

The shop was simply called MOBILE TELEPHONES and lay on Långholmsgatan, just opposite the exit from the underground station at Hornstull. A dirty shop window with some mobile phones on display, a few alarm clocks and some other bits and pieces. Olivia went up the two stone steps to the shop door and opened it. A dirty grey curtain was folded back over the entrance. The shop itself had a floor area of about four square metres surrounded by glass display cases filled with mobile phones. Hundreds of them. Of every make, in every colour and all of them second-hand. On a few shelves behind the counter were yellow and blue plastic containers with more heaps of mobiles. Second-hand. And in a narrow passage at the far end was a cubbyhole where they repaired even more second-hand mobiles.

Not exactly your huge electronics store.

'Hi, I'm looking for Tom Stilton, d'you know where I can get hold of him?'

Olivia had turned towards the man in front of the glass display cases. She tried to look like she absolutely didn't feel.

Friendly, calm, trying to find a friend.

'Stilton? Don't know who that is...'

'Well, Jelle then, he calls himself Jelle?'

'Oh, right, Jelle? Is he called Stilton?'

'Yep.'

'Well, would you believe it, isn't that some stinky cheese?'

'Right.'

'And he's called the same as a stinky cheese?'

'Evidently. Do you know where he hangs out?'

'Now?'

'Yes?'

'No. He comes by now and then, when they've nicked his mobile, they're like ravens the way they nick things from one another, but that was a few days ago.'

'Oh, right...'

'But you can ask Wejle, he sells magazines over there, by the entrance to the underground, he might know where Jelle is.'

'And what does Wejle look like?'

'You can't miss him.'

The shop-owner was right. You couldn't miss Wejle. Outside the underground. Apart from the fact that he sold *Situation*

Sthlm with a strong penetrating voice, his appearance was also such that it quite obviously distinguished him from the stream of travellers on their way to the underground. His slouch hat, for example, with feathers from birds that were very endangered. The moustache, very closely related to Åke Gustafsson's eyebrows. And of course his eyes, dark, intense and genuinely friendly.

'Jelle, my dear lady, you don't put Jelle where you place him.'

Olivia interpreted this as meaning that Jelle was rather fickle.

'But where has he been hanging out recently?'

'That is hidden from us.'

'Sorry?'

'Jelle moves quietly at night, we don't really know where, you can be sitting on a bench out in Jakobsberg with him, pondering the right of minks to exist or not, and suddenly he's gone. Like a seal hunter, he melts into the rocks.'

Olivia realised that Wejle presumably had many qualities as a salesman, but not as an informant. She bought one of his magazines that she already had a copy of and went back to her car.

Then he phoned.

It took Olivia a while to find. She did admittedly live surprisingly close herself, almost round the corner, so it wasn't the address that was the problem. Bondegatan 25A. But where the dustbin room lay. Inside the doors and iron-gridded gates with their codes. Stilton had given the necessary number combinations but it still took some time.

Especially when in the middle of a cement corridor she met a man wearing short trousers with wide braces, round his neck a cervical collar that hadn't been washed since it had been put there. And on top of that the man had weird red spectacles and seemed half drunk.

'And where do you think you're going then? Bibblan!' he said.

'Bibblan?'

'She's doing her washing today, don't come and do yours too, you'll end up in the tumble dryer!'

'I'm looking for the dustbin room.'

'Are you going to kip down there?'

'No.'

'Good. Cause I've put down a ring of rat poison.'

'Are there rats in the dustbin room?'

'Beavers, some folks might call them, beasts as long as half a metre, not a place for a young thing like you.'

'Where's the dustbin room?'

'There.'

The cervical collar pointed down the corridor and Olivia slipped past. Towards the rats.

'Are there rats here?'

Olivia had asked that question the very same moment Stilton had pushed open the heavy steel door.

'No.'

He disappeared into the darkness. Olivia pushed the door open a bit more and stepped in after him.

'Close the door.'

Olivia wasn't sure she should do that. The door was her escape route after all. But she did close it. That was when she noticed the stench. A stench that some dustbin rooms are spared, dustbin rooms where the ventilation works like it ought to. It wasn't working here.

The stench was frightful.

Olivia held a hand over her nose and mouth and tried to accustom her eyes to the dark. It wasn't total darkness, in the middle of the floor a little tea light had been lit. With its help she could see Stilton's outline against a wall. He was sitting on the cement floor.

'You've got the tea light, that's your time,' he said.

'My time?'

'Until it goes out.'

Stilton's voice was calm and brief. He had decided to behave himself. Olivia had decided to get answers to her questions.

Then she would leave.

Then she would never again set her foot anywhere near Tom Stilton.

The stinky cheese.

'Yes, well, it was those questions about…'

'The woman on the beach was not anaesthetized. The amount of Rohypnol in her body was enough to keep her calm but not to anaesthetize her. So she was conscious when they buried her. Her coat was the only item of clothing we found. We assumed that the perpetrator had taken the rest of the clothes with him but missed the coat in the dark. The only thing of value we found in the coat was a little earring.'

'There was nothing about that in…'

'We took a blood sample from the fetus. It was sent later to England for DNA analysis so we could determine a possible paternity if anyone turned up. And they didn't. We weren't sure if there were only three people on the beach besides the victim. The witness was nine years old and terrified and saw the event from about a hundred metres away, in the dark, but we had nothing else to go on. We could never confirm that information in the investigation. The woman was probably of Latin American extraction but we could never ascertain that. Ove Gardman lived close to the beach, he ran to his parents and after about forty-five minutes the air ambulance arrived. Any more questions?'

Olivia stared in Stilton's direction in the dark. The tea light fluttered a little. He had answered every single question she had rattled off on her mobile, in exactly the order she had asked them. Who the hell was this man?

But she tried to be concrete.

'Why was that earring of value?'

'Because the victim didn't have any holes in her ears.'

'And it was that sort of earring?'

'Yes. Have you finished?'

'No, I would very much like to know what your theories were,' she said.

'We had a lot.'

'Such as?'

'Drugs, that the woman was a drugs courier, working for a cartel that was active on the west coast in those days, that something had gone wrong during a delivery. We interrogated a drug addict who had been on the island before the murder took place but that didn't lead anywhere. Illegal immigration, that the woman hadn't been able to pay her smugglers. Trafficking, that the woman was a prostitute and had tried to flee from her pimp and was murdered. We couldn't find proof for any theory. The biggest problem was that the woman could never be identified.'

'And nobody reported her missing?'

'No.'

'But there must have been a father to the child?'

'Yes, but he might not have known about it. The child. Or he might have been one of the perpetrators.'

That thought hadn't occurred to Olivia.

'Were there any theories about some sect?' she asked.

'Sect?'

'Yes, that there might be one, about the rise and fall of the tide and the moon, and...'

'We never went into that.'

'OK. But what about the actual place then, Nordkoster? That's a very difficult place to get to and from. Not an ideal place for a murder.'

'And what does an ideal place for a murder look like?'

'One where you can quickly get away if you have planned a very advanced murder.'

Stilton was silent for a few moments.

'The place confounded us.'

At that moment the tea light fluttered out.

'Your time is up.'

'Jackie Berglund,' said Olivia.

Now it was pitch black in the dustbin room. Neither of them could see the other. You could only hear breaths. Is this when the beavers come out? Olivia wondered.

'What about Jackie Berglund?'

Stilton gave her a few seconds in the dark.

'I've got the impression that she was involved in some way, she was an escort girl then, and that the victim might also have been, or at least knew Jackie... and there was a link between them, did you think along those lines?'

Stilton didn't answer immediately. His thoughts were in a slightly different place: Jackie Berglund, and the fact that the girl across from him in the dark had touched upon his own ideas, at some time in the past.

But he answered:

'No, have you finished now?'

Olivia was far from finished, but she had understood that Stilton was, and she got up.

Probably it was the dark that did it, the relative anonymity, but at the same time that she was feeling her way to the metal door she asked a question. Behind her, in the dark.

'Why are you a rough sleeper?'

'I'm homeless.'

'And why are you homeless?'

'Because I haven't got anywhere to live.'

Nothing more was forthcoming. Olivia reached the door and pressed the handle. She was just about to open it when she heard him, behind her.

'You.'

'Yes?'

'Your dad was in the investigation.'

'I know.'

'Why don't you ask him?'

'He died four years ago.'

Olivia pushed the door open and stepped out.

So he didn't know that her dad was dead, she thought, on her way to the car. How long had he been a rough sleeper? Ever since he had left the force? Six years? But surely you can't end up so far down just like that? It must take some time? Had he simply cut off all contact with the people he had worked with?

Weird.

Whatever, she had got some answers to her questions and would probably never have any more to do with Stilton. Now she would just put together everything she had found out and come to some sort of conclusion. Then she would hand it in to Åke Gustafsson.

But that thing with the earring.

The woman on the beach had had an earring in her coat pocket.

But no holes in her ears.

Where did the earring come from?

Olivia decided to delay her summary a little while longer.

Stilton had lit a new tea light in the dustbin room. He was going to remain sitting there until he was certain she had disappeared. Then he would presumably be rid of her. He was fully aware that he had given her far too much information. Confidential. Far too many details. But he couldn't give a damn about that. His relation to his police past was cold as ice. At some time he might explain why, to somebody.

But to whom, that he had no idea.

But he had very deliberately not mentioned a rather important detail to Olivia. The child in the murdered woman's womb had survived, following an emergency caesarean by the helicopter doctor. A piece of information that had never been made public to protect the child.

And then he thought about Arne Rönning. So he was dead? Sad. Arne had been a good police officer. And a good man. For a few years they had had quite close personal contact. They had trusted each other, liked each other, shared some secrets.

And now he was dead.

And his daughter had suddenly turned up.

Stilton looked at his thin hands. They were shaking slightly. This entire dive deep into the Nordkoster murder had raked up things in the wrong places. And then Arne's death on top of that. He pulled out his little Stesolid bottle and twisted the top off… and changed his mind.

He would resist the temptation.

He would not become like Ben the Fibber.

He would find a couple of murderers.

He blew out the tea light and got up. He was going to go to the stone steps.

* * *

It was quite a nasty wound. It the blow had struck her just a little higher up it might well have crushed the base of her skull.

That's what the doctor told Eva Carlsén.

As it was some stitches, a firm bandage and some painkillers had sufficed. The doctor, a woman from Tunisia, was just as empathetic as Carlsén needed. Not because of the wound – that would heal – but for the actual assault. That affected her much deeper. The violation. Strangers in her own home who had been through all her private things. It was repulsive.

Thieves? A simple break-in?

But what valuable things did she have at home? Paintings? Camera? Computer? No cash, she knew that. Or perhaps they weren't thieves? Were they people who were out to get her, her specifically? Who had been waiting in the house for her to turn up? So that they could attack her?

Adolescent violence?

That programme on TV?

First, she went home, a bit dozy because of the painkillers, then she looked through the whole house and could see that nothing had been stolen. Just vandalised.

And she could feel that.

Then she went to the police station in Solna.

On her way to the station she cursed herself for not getting her contact details removed from Eniro. She should not be listed on that, bearing in mind the work she did.

She would get her name removed.

* * *

Dusk had settled over Stockholm, the city traffic had thinned out. People had left the large offices on Sveavägen a couple of hours earlier. The only person still there was in the managing director's office on the top floor. Bertil Magnuson. He was trying to keep calm with the help of a drink. Whisky. Not a good way in the long term, but temporarily, just for the moment, and not in large quantities. He would soon go home and he knew that Linn would have her radar turned on. The slightest deviation from normal would get her to bite.

No, not bite – now he was being unfair. She wasn't like that. People bit you in his other world. Or perhaps stabbed would be a better word. It could come from the right or the left. They took no prisoners and they could kill if it served their purpose. That was a part of his business culture. And sometimes you killed somebody even though you didn't really want to, but you had no choice. Like he had done too, indirectly. Unfortunately it wasn't completely watertight. There was one person who had leaked.

Nils Wendt.

He took a big gulp, lit a cigarillo and looked out over Sveavägen. Across to the graveyard around Adolf Fredrik's Church. He thought about his own death. He had read in an American magazine that nowadays there were air-conditioned coffins available. Interesting. The idea of an air-conditioned coffin appealed to him, perhaps with an inbuilt massage motor that kept the corpse in good condition? He smiled a little.

But the grave?

Where should that be? They had a family grave at Norra graveyard, but he didn't want to go there. He wanted a place of his own. A mausoleum. A monument to one of Sweden's great industrialists.

Or like the Wallenberg family. Secret grave sites on the family's own property. He was more of a self-made man, although his father and uncle had grafted him. With various traits.

He was Bertil Magnuson.

So far, the whisky had done its job.

Raised him up to where he deserved to be.

No, he would just have to deal with that creep Nils.

* * *

Olivia had bought a tub of Indian food from Shanti. A take-away, but tasty, quick and well spiced. She indulged in a short slumber on the sofa after her meal. With Elvis on her tummy. Then things started to spin around inside her head again. She started to recapitulate her meeting in the dustbin room. Some time I'm going to tell mum about this, she thought. The meeting in the dustbin room where rats as large as beavers crept around along the walls and the stench, the scene wouldn't have been out of place in a film by… she couldn't think of a good comparison so she started again with the dustbin room.

When she had rewound every single word in her head there was one moment that particularly struck her. It was when she had told him of her little hypothesis about Jackie Berglund and asked whether Stilton had thought along the same lines. At that point there had been a little break in the dialogue. Silence, many seconds longer than during the earlier part of the exchange. At that point Stilton hadn't said anything straight away. Like he'd done all the time before. At that point he had stopped to think.

Olivia imagined.

And why had he done that?

Because there *was* something with Jackie!

She pushed a rather insulted Elvis onto the floor and picked up the folder she had been given by Eva Carlsén. It was admittedly almost nine in the evening, but it was summer and not dark yet and she could always apologise.

'I'm so sorry to disturb you so late.'

'That's OK, come in.'

'Thanks.'

Eva invited Olivia in with a gesture into the hall. Just as Olivia passed the folder across, she saw the back of Eva's head was bandaged.

'Goodness! What have you done?'

'Had a break-in and been knocked down and just come home from the hospital and the police and… the whole works.'

'Gosh! Sorry! Then I won't…'

'It's quite all right, I'm feeling OK now.'

'But, what on earth…! A break-in? Here?'

'Yes.'

Eva walked into the living room with Olivia behind her. A couple of low lamps spread a calm soft glow across the sofa and armchairs. Most of the mess from the break-in had been tidied up. Eva made a gesture in the direction of an armchair and Olivia sank down into it.

'But what did they steal?'

'Nothing.'

'Really, but then why? What…'

'I think it was some people who were out to scare me.'

'Because… you mean because of what you're writing?'

'Yes.'

'That's creepy… those guys who beat up homeless people?'

'Murder. The woman in the caravan died.'

'I saw that.'

'We'll see if I end up on Trashkick,' Eva smiled. 'Would you like something? I'm just making some coffee.'

'Thanks, that'd be nice.'

Eva went towards the kitchen.

'Can I give you a hand?' Olivia asked.

'No, it's fine.'

Olivia looked about her in the living room which had been furnished in a personal style. Bold colours, lovely rugs, floor-to-ceiling bookshelves all along the walls. Wonder if she's read them all, Olivia thought. Her eye fell on a shelf with photographs. True to character, she became curious. She got up and went up to the shelf: a very old wedding photo, probably Eva's mum and dad. Then a considerably newer wedding photo with Eva and a well-built man, and next to that a photo with a much younger Eva and a handsome young man next to her.

'Milk in your coffee? Sugar?

Eva's voice could be heard from the kitchen.

'Please, milk.'

Eva came in with two cups in her hands. Olivia went up to her and took one of the cups. Eva gestured towards the sofa.

'Sit down.'

Olivia sank down on the soft sofa, put the cup on the table and nodded towards Eva's wedding photo.

'Is that your husband?

'Was. We're divorced.'

Eva sat down in an armchair and talked a little about her ex. A successful athlete many years ago. They had got to know each other when she studied at the College of Journalism. Now they were divorced, since about a year ago. He had met a new woman and the divorce had been very difficult.

'He behaved like a real bastard, quite simply,' she said.

'What a shame.'

'Yes. I can't exactly say I've had any luck with men in my life, it has mainly been sorrow and grief!'

Eva smiled over her cup of coffee. Olivia wondered why she had the wedding photo on display if he was such a bastard? Personally, she would have put it away, from the off. She nodded towards the photos again.

'And that nice-looking young guy you're holding, was that the first sorrow?'

'No, that's my brother, Sverker, he died from an overdose. Now that's enough about me.'

Eva suddenly adopted a totally different tone.

'Oh, I'm sorry, I didn't mean to… sorry.'

Eva looked at Olivia. Her face was peculiarly strict, for a few seconds, then she sank back into the armchair and gave a little smile again.

'I'm the one who should apologise, the thing is… my head feels as if it's about to explode and it has been hell today, sorry, how are you getting on? Did you get anything from the material?'

'Yes, but there was something I want to ask you, do you know who Jackie Berglund worked for in 1987, when she was a female escort?'

'Yes, it was a fairly well-known guy, Carl Videung, he ran Gold Card. I think it says that in the folder.'

'Oh? Then I missed it, what was Gold Card?'

'An escort firm, and Jackie Berglund was one of the escorts.'

'OK, thanks. Carl Videung, what a strange name.'

'Especially for a pornography baron.'

'Is that what he was?'

'In those days. Are you still looking into Jackie?'

'Yes.'

'You remember what I said?'

'About her? That I should be careful.'

'Yes.'

* * *

Jackie Berglund stood beside a panorama window on Norr Mälarstrand and looked out across the water. She loved her flat, six rooms, top floor, with a fantastic view all the way to the heights of Söder. The only thing that disturbed her was the willow tree on the other side of the street. That hid the view, considerably. She thought that something ought to be done about it.

She turned round and went into the large living room. A trendy interior designer had been given a free rein a year or so before, and had achieved a miracle, a mixture of cold and warm and stuffed animals. Entirely in Jackie's taste. She filled her little glass with a dry martini and put a CD on, a tango, she loved tango. Now and then she had men in her flat who she danced with, rarely someone who could tango. Some day I'm going to find a tango man, she thought, a mysterious man with ever-ready genitals and a limited vocabulary.

She was looking forward to that.

Just as she was on her way to a new martini she heard the phone. Not the one closest to her, the one in her study. She looked at the clock, almost half past midnight. That was when they rang.

Often.

The clients.

'Jackie Berglund.'

'Hi Jackie, this is Latte!'

'Hi.'

'Jackie, we have a little party going on and we could do with a bit of assistance.'

Regular clients, like Lars Örnhielm, knew how to express themselves on Jackie's telephone line. Not too clearly. Not the wrong choice of words.

'How many do you need?'

'Seven or eight. High class!'

'Preferences?'

'Nothing special, but you know, nice with a happy ending.'

'OK. Where?'

'I'll text you.'

Jackie hung up and smiled a little. Happy ending, that was something they'd taken from the menu of the Asian girls when they wanted to know if they should end with a top massage.

Latte needed some sweet girls who could deliver a happy ending.

No problem.

* * *

Acke came home that night in a battered condition. A decidedly battered condition. The ten-year-old walked between the high-rise blocks in Flemingsberg, on the dark side, away from the streetlights, with his skateboard under his arm, limping. The pain had come from the blows. Repeated blows. On places that you couldn't see outside his clothes. He felt extremely lonely, limping along there, and those thoughts came into his head again. About his dad. The dad who didn't exist. That mum never talked about. But he must be somewhere. All children must have a dad, mustn't they?

He pushed those thoughts away and clasped the key around his neck. He knew that his mum was in town and working, and he knew what she was working on.

Or as.

An older boy at school had enlightened him after football some time ago.

'Prossy! Your mum's a prossy!'

Acke didn't know what 'prossy' meant. As soon as he got home he went online and checked it.

Alone at home.

Then he fetched the jug of cold water that his mum had put in the fridge before she went into town and drank almost the whole of it. Then he went to bed.

And thought about his mum.

That perhaps he could help her with money so that she wouldn't have to be what they called her.

Cars passed by now and then in the mist on their way to or from Waxholm. It was early morning in Bogesandsland and nobody paid any attention to the grey Volvo. It was parked on a discreet gravelled area not very far from the beautiful castle, surrounded by forest. In among the swathes of mist a group of wild pigs were grubbing for food.

Nils Wendt sat in the driving seat and looked at his face in the rear-view mirror. He had woken up at about three in the morning in his hotel room. At five o'clock he had got into his hire car and left the city, driving towards Waxholm. He wanted to get away from people. He looked at his face in the mirror. Haggard, he thought, you look haggard, Nils.

But he was going to cope with this.

There wasn't much more to do now. This morning he had thought out the final pieces of the puzzle he was building. His harassment of Bertil had led to a plan. A plan that started to acquire form when he saw the strongly critical TV news report about MWM's activities in the Congo.

Just as ruthless as before.

Then he had seen the demonstrators and read the pamphlets and clicked his way through lots of posts on various Facebook groups, 'Rape-free mobile phones!' for example, and understood how indignant the feelings were.

That was when his plan fell into place.

He would strike where it would be felt the most.

By a quarter past nine Bertil had solved the problem with the landowner in Walikale. Not personally, of course, but his good friend the military commander. He had sent a group of security police to the landowner and explained that on account of the troubles in the area they might have to order an evacuation. Just as a security measure. The landowner was no fool. He asked if there was any way to avoid a compulsory evacuation. The police explained that the Swedish company MWM had offered to be responsible for security on condition that they could use some of the ground for mineral prospecting. That would mean that the troubles would be kept under control.

Done.

Bertil reminded his secretary to phone the company's top manager in Kinshasa and make sure that an adequate gift was sent to the military commander.

'He is very fond of topaz.'

So when Bertil went and stood beside the window and felt the strong rays of the morning sun he was in a comparatively good mood. Walikale had been dealt with. He was still thinking about the Congo when he automatically pulled his vibrating mobile phone out of his pocket and clicked to answer.

'This is Nils Wendt.'

Although the voice Bertil had heard on the tape recording was many years younger, it was without doubt the same voice on the phone now. But not recorded.

It was Nils Wendt.

Bertil felt how his blood surged. He hated that man. A little insect that could cause a catastrophe. But he tried to restrain himself.

'Hello, Nils, are you in town?'

'Where can we meet?'

'Why should we meet?'

'Shall I ring off?'

'No! Wait! You want to meet?'

'Don't you?'

'All right.'

'Where?'

Bertil feverishly flicked through places his head and looked out of the window.

The graveyard at Adolf Fredrik's Church.
'Whereabouts there?'
'At Palme's grave.'
'23.00.'
The call was ended.

* * *

Ovette Andersson came out of the main entrance, alone, it was just after ten o'clock. She had followed along with Acke, against his will, to see the teachers in charge of after-school leisure activities. She wanted to talk to somebody there about his bruises. A couple of times recently he had come home and had bruises all over his body. Large yellowy-blue bruises. At first he had tried to hide it, they hardly ever saw each other in the mornings, but Ovette had happened to open the door when he was getting undressed one evening and had seen them.

'Whatever have you done!'
'What?'
'You've got bruises all over your body.'
'It's football.'
'That's how you get such big bruises?'
'Yes.'

And then Acke had slipped into bed. Ovette had sat in the kitchen and lit a cigarette by the window. Football?

Her son's bruises had been on her mind since then. A couple of nights later, when she came home after her night shift, she had sneaked into his room and carefully lifted the covers and looked at them again.

Yellowy-blue bruises all over. And large scabs.

It was then she decided to talk to the teachers at the school leisure centre.

'No, he isn't being bullied.'

Acke's teacher looked rather surprised.

'But he's got bruises all over his body,' said Ovette.

'What does he say himself?'

'That it's the football.'

'And isn't it that then?'

'Not that sort of bruises. Everywhere!'

'Well. I don't know. He certainly isn't being bullied, not here. We have a special programme to prevent bullying and violence and we would have noticed if there was anything going on here.'

And Ovette had to be satisfied with that.

Who else could she talk to? She didn't have a social network. No neighbours she mixed with. The people she mixed with worked on the street and weren't particularly interested in other people's children. That was a bit of a minefield.

Ovette left the school and suddenly felt infinitely alone. And desperate. The whole of her hopeless existence played out before her eyes. Her inability to get out of the prostitution swamp. Her marked body. Everything. And now she saw her only child being hurt and she had nobody she could turn to. Not a single telephone number for anybody who could listen, and console, or help her. There was only her and Acke in the whole empty world.

She stopped beside a street lamp and lit a cigarette. Her chapped hands shook. Not from the cool breeze, but from something much colder, something that came from inside. Came from a dark sinkhole in her chest which seemed to get bigger with every breath and be just waiting for her to let go. If there had been a secret door out of life, she would have crept through it.

That was when she remembered him.

A guy who might be able to help her.

They had grown up together in Kärrtorp. Lived in the same block of flats and had a bit of contact over the years. It had been a long time ago, but still. Whenever they did come across each other, it was always easy. They shared a past, had the same origins, knew each other's weaknesses but didn't care.

She could talk to him.

Mink.

* * *

It took a while for Olivia to trace him, but when his name turned up at the Rådan Retirement House in Silverdal, her efforts were rewarded.

And she was surprised.

The retirement home was very close to the Police College.

A small world, Olivia thought, when she steered her car on the familiar roads and parked outside the home. She could almost see the college through the trees. In some strange way, the entire college environment felt extremely distant. And yet it wasn't at all long since she had been sitting on a bench over there and had chosen a case having no idea at all where it would lead her.

Just this minute it was leading her up to the second floor and out onto a little terrace where a man was sitting hunched over in a wheelchair.

Former pornography baron Carl Videung.

Now almost ninety years old, she had discovered. No close relations, and pleased by any distraction while he lingered out his days. Whoever it might be.

Now it was Olivia Rönning. She quickly realised that Videung was extremely hard of hearing and also had some speech impairments. So she had to express herself concisely, clearly and loudly.

'Jackie Berglund!'

Yes, after a while, two cups of coffee and some ginger biscuits later, the name turned up inside Videung's head.

'She was a call girl.'

Olivia managed to decipher.

'Do you remember any other call girls?'

More coffee, more ginger biscuits, and then a nod from Videung.

'Who, then?'

Now more coffee wasn't helping, and the biscuits were finished. The man in the wheelchair just looked at Olivia and smiled, a long time. Is he sitting and judging me, Olivia wondered. Whether I would do as a call girl? A dirty old man? Now the old man made a gesture that seemed to indicate that he wanted to write something. Olivia quickly produced a pen and a notebook and handed them over to Videung. He couldn't hold the pad himself. Olivia had to push it down onto his thin knee and hold it in that position. He started to write. With handwriting that seemed close to ninety years old but was at least legible.

'Miriam Wixell.'

'One of the call girls was called Miriam Wixell?'

Videung nodded and let out a very long fart. Olivia twisted her head away slightly from the rotten odour and closed the notebook.

'Do you remember if any of the girls were of foreign extraction?'

Videung smiled a little and nodded and held up one finger.

'One of them?'

Videung nodded again.

'Do you remember where she came from?'

Videung shook his head.

'Did she have black hair?'

Videung turned towards the window and pointed at a Saintpaulia in a plant pot on the sill. Olivia looked at the flower.

Bright blue.

'Was her hair blue?'

Videung nodded and smiled again. Blue hair, Olivia thought. Then it must have been dyed? Did you dye your hair blue if it was black? Perhaps. What did she know about how call girls in the Eighties dyed their hair?

Nothing.

She got up and thanked Videung and slipped away from the veranda to avoid yet another trombone from the former porn baron's brown eye.

She did at least have a name.

Miriam Wixell.

* * *

Ovette had chosen a table deep inside the café. She didn't want to bump into any of her colleagues from work. She sat with her back to the entrance with a cup of coffee in front of her. You weren't allowed to smoke in here. Her hands moved restlessly across the table. Moving sugar cubes and cutlery and wondering if he would turn up.

'Hi there, Vettan!'

He always called her Vettan. Mink had come.

He walked up to her table, swept away the little ponytail on his neck, and sat down. In the best of moods. He had just gone past a betting shop and had backed a winner. Four hundred kronor paid straight out. The money was burning a hole in his pocket.

'How much did you win?'

'Four thousand!'

Mink always added at least one extra nought. Except when it came to his age. Then he made a deduction. He was forty-one, but could readily say he was between twenty-six and thirty-five, depending on the company. When he tried 'just over twenty' with a girl from the north that was perhaps a bit risky. But she was new in town and looking for fun so she swallowed it all, even though she thought he looked a bit older.

'This town has a price,' he said, and made New York look like a suburb of Stockholm.

But Ovette was not from the north, and she knew how old Mink was, so he didn't need to pretend.

'Thanks for coming.'

'Mink always comes.'

He smiled, and thought he was a master of innuendo. Not many others thought the same. Most people kept Mink at a distance, after a while, when they had seen through his rather hollow figure and heard of his exceptional escapades one time too many. Like that he had solved the Olof Palme murder, or discovered Roxette. That's when most people dropped out. What they often missed was that Mink had a big heart, hidden deep under a front of semi-desperate jargon. A heart that this very moment beat heavily when he saw the pictures Ovette showed on her mobile. Pictures of an almost naked boy with a body that looked as if it had been beaten black and blue and was covered with scabs.

'I took this when he was asleep.'

'What's happened?'

'No idea, at the school leisure centre they claimed that nothing had happened there, and Acke himself says it's from football.'

'You don't get knocked about like that in football, I played for Bajen for many years, OK you could get bashed a bit in the penalty area, I was a centre, but never so that you'd look like that.'

'No.'

'Jesus, he looks as if he's been beaten up!'

'Yes.'

Ovette dried her eyes quickly. Mink looked at her and took her hand in his.

'Do you want me to have a chat with him?'

Ovette nodded.

Mink decided to have a chat with young Acke.

Football?

No way.

* * *

It was almost closing time. The boutiques on Sibyllegatan were starting to turn down the lights. In Weird & Wow the lights were still on. Jackie Berglund always stayed open an extra hour. She knew her customers and this meant they could always drop in at the last minute and snap up an item of clothing or a furnishing detail to brighten up the evening's party. At this particular moment an elderly gentleman from posh Östermalm was after something with which to appease his wife. He had missed an anniversary the day before and things had turned a bit sour, as he said.

'Turned sour.'

Now he was fingering a pair of earrings hanging among other designer labels.

'What do you take for these?'

'For you I take seven hundred.'

'And for others?'

'Five hundred.'

That's how they carried on, Jackie and her circle of more or less affluent customers, joking in a moronic manner.

But everything for business.

'Do you think she would like these?' asked the man.

'Women have a weakness for earrings.'

'Do they?'

'Yes.'

Since the elderly man didn't have a clue as to what women had a weakness for, he took Jackie's word on trust and left the boutique with a pair of earrings in a beautiful pink box. When the shop door closed, Jackie's mobile rang.

It was Carl Videung.

With a decidedly clear voice and impeccable hearing he informed Jackie about a visit he had received earlier in the day. A young woman from the Police College had asked about his escort services in former days. He had acted half-dead so that he could find out what she was after.

'Can't help being a bit curious when I smell coppers,' he said.

'Well, what did she want then?'

'Don't know, but she asked about you.'

'Me?'

'Yes. And who else was working at the same time as you.'

'At Gold Card?'

'Yes.'

'And what did you say?'

'I gave her Miriam Wixell.'

'Why did you do that?'

'Because Miriam pulled out when she did, that wasn't a nice thing to do, don't you remember?'

'Yes. So what?'

'So I thought that the fancy Miriam might be a little embarrassed if police trainees start poking their noses into her past.'

'You're nasty.'

'I hope so.'

'What did you say about me?'

'Nothing. I'm not that nasty.'

And thus the conversation ended. As far as Videung was concerned. For Jackie it replayed a while inside her head. Why was a girl going around asking about her time as a female escort? And who was she?'

'What was she called?'

'Olivia Rönning.'

That's what Videung had answered when Jackie rang him back.

Olivia Rönning?

* * *

Olivia sat at home on the sofa and looked in *Nordisk Kriminalkrönika* from 2006. Descriptions from the police themselves of various criminal cases during the previous year. She had borrowed it from the college library on her way home from Rådan. For a very special reason. She wanted to see if there were any criminal cases during 2005 that might possibly have involved Tom Stilton. And led to a conflict. The one that Åke Gustafsson believed had happened.

A lot of things had happened in the criminal arena in 2005. Various cases and incidents caught her interest. Among them an article about the spectacular escape from the Hall high security prison, the one involving the Malexander murderer Tony Olsson. So it took her a while to reach page seventy-one.

It was there she found it.

A brutal murder of a young woman in Stockholm. Jill Engberg. With details that made Olivia very tense. Jill was a female escort, and pregnant, and the case was unsolved. The murder was in 2005. The same year that Stilton left the police force. Did he work on that case? It didn't mention him in the article, which was written by Rune Forss. Wasn't he the guy on TV who was dealing with the assaults on the homeless, Olivia wondered, just as she phoned Åke Gustafsson.

She had got up speed.

'Did Stilton work on the investigation of Jill Engberg? 2005?'

'I don't know,' answered Gustafsson.

She lost some momentum. But it didn't slow down her imagination. Jill was a pregnant female escort. Jackie was a female escort sixteen years earlier. The murdered girl on the beach was pregnant. Jackie had been on the island. Was there any connection between Jill and Jackie? Did Jill work for Jackie? In Red Velvet? Had Stilton come across such links and steered in the direction of the beach case? Was that why he was so strangely quiet for a while in the dustbin room?

She took a deep breath. She had been under the impression that the meeting in the dustbin room was the last contact she need have with Tom Stilton. A deep breath later, she phoned him again.

'Did you work on the murder of Jill Engberg in 2005?'

'Yes, for a while, ' he answered, and then hung up.

Which was something Olivia was beginning to get used to. He might well phone her in ten minutes and want to meet in some cosy spot and sit in the dark and the stench and play twenty questions.

Among the beavers.

But he didn't.

* * *

Stilton sat in the editorial office of *Situation Sthlm*, almost alone. A girl was busy in reception. He had borrowed one of the magazine's computers and gone online and started to look at the films from the Trashkick site. The first two weren't there any longer but the rest were. Three of them. An assault under Väster Bridge of a homeless immigrant, Julio Hernandez, the next to last with Benseman and then One-eyed Vera. After her murder, nothing else had been posted.

Stilton forced himself to look at the films. Carefully. With attention to detail. Looked all over the screen to see anything besides what was in focus. That's probably why he discovered it. On the film from Väster Bridge. He cursed not being able to zoom in. Freeze an image and click on it to get a close up. But he could stop the film. And when he leaned towards the screen he could see it quite clearly. On his lower arm. Of one of the attackers. A tattoo. Two letters, KF, with a ring round them.

Stilton leaned back and raised his eyes. They landed on Vera's photo on the wall in its black frame. At the very end of the row of other dead people. Stilton pulled his notebook towards him and wrote 'KF' with a ring round it.

Then he looked at the photo of Vera again.

* * *

The late screening of *Black Swan* had just finished and people were pouring out of the Grand Cinema on Sveavägen. A lot of them going in the direction of Kungsgatan. It was a lovely light evening with a pleasantly lukewarm breeze. A breeze that swept in over the graveyard around Adolf Fredrik's Church and caused the flowers on the graves to sway. In here it was a bit darker. At least in some places. Beside Palme's grave it was half-dark. Seen from Sveavägen, the four persons who were just meeting there were hardly visible.

Two of them were Bertil Magnuson and Nils Wendt.

The two others had been called in at very short notice, via K. Sedovic. The man that Bertil always contacted when anything slightly uncomfortable had to be dealt with. He assumed that such could be the case this evening.

And Wendt assumed the same.

He knew who Bertil was. And he wasn't a man who came underdressed to a meeting like this. So Wendt hadn't reacted when the two extra men appeared. Nor did he react when Bertil explained in a friendly tone that his two 'advisors' were going to check that Wendt didn't have a recorder on him.

'Perhaps you understand why.'

Wendt did. He let the advisors do their job. He didn't have a tape recorder on him. Not this time. But he did have a cassette tape, with a recording of a conversation, which one of the gorillas handed over to Bertil. He held it up in front of Wendt.

'The conversation?'

'Yes. Or rather a copy of it. Listen by all means,' said Wendt.

Bertil looked at the cassette.

'Is the rest of the conversation on it?'

'Yes, the whole of it.'

'And where's the original?'

'Somewhere I expect to return to by the first of July at the latest. If I don't do so, the tape will be sent to the police.'

Bertil gave a little smile.

'Life insurance?'

'Yes.'

Bertil looked across the graveyard. He nodded to his advisors that they could withdraw a little, which they did. Wendt looked at Bertil. He knew that Bertil knew that Wendt was a person who never left anything to chance. All of their business cooperation had built upon that. Bertil could react impulsively, but never Wendt. He had a belt and braces and an extra safety belt in every situation. If he claimed that he had arranged for the original, which was in some unknown location, to be sent to the police if he didn't return before the first of July, then that is what would happen. He knew that Bertil would assume the same.

Which he did too. He turned towards Wendt again.

'You've grown old,' he said.

'You too.'

'One for all, do you remember that?'

'Yes.'

'What happened to that?'

'It disappeared in Zaire,' said Wendt.

'Not only that. You disappeared with almost two million.'

'Were you surprised?'

'I was furious.'

'I can understand that. Are you still married to Linn?'

'Yes.'

'Does she know about this?'

'No.'

The men looked at each other. Bertil twisted towards the churchyard. The mild evening breeze stroked along between the grave stones. Wendt kept his gaze firmly on Bertil's face.

'Do you have any children?' he asked.

'No, do you?'

If they had stood somewhere not quite so dark perhaps Bertil would have seen the slight fluttering, for a second or so, of Wendt's eyelids, but now he didn't notice them.

'No, I don't have any children.'

The dialogue ended in silence after a couple of seconds. Bertil looked out of the corner of his eye at his advisors. He still didn't understand what was going on. What was Wendt after?

'So, what do you want?' he said and turned towards Wendt.

'Within three days you should issue a statement where you declare that MWM will immediately cease all coltan mining in the Congo. In addition, economic compensation is to be given to all the inhabitants of the Walikale area who have been affected by your exploitation.'

Bertil looked at Wendt. For a second the thought crossed his mind that he was dealing with a mentally ill person. But he wasn't. Ill, absolutely, but not mentally ill. Just completely stark raving mad.

'Are you serious?'

'Do I usually joke?'

No, Nils Wendt never joked. He was one of the driest people Bertil had met, and even though many years had passed since they knew each other, he could see in Wendt's face and eyes that he hadn't become any funnier over the years.

He was deadly serious.

'So you mean that if I don't do what you say then that conversation will end up with the police?'

He had to say it aloud to fully understand the meaning.

'Yes,' answered Wendt. 'And you will be well aware of the consequences, no doubt.'

And Bertil was. He wasn't a fool. The consequences of the taped conversation being made public were something he had envisaged already when he heard the first short excerpt on his mobile. The consequences would be catastrophic.

On all levels.

On all the levels that Wendt naturally understood.

'Good luck!'

Wendt started to walk away.

'Nils!'

Wendt turned his head and looked back.

'Seriously, what's this about... really?'

'Revenge.'

'Revenge? For what?'

'Nordkoster.'

Wendt continued walking.

The advisors, who were standing off on one side, reacted a little and looked towards Bertil. He had his gaze directed at the ground, not far from Palme's grave.

'Is there anything else you want help with?'

One of them asked.

Bertil raised his head and saw Wendt's back some way away among the gravestones.

'Yes.'

* * *

Stilton sat on the third landing of the stone steps and talked with Mink on his mobile.

'Two letters. K and F. With a ring round them'

'A tattoo?' Mink asked.

'Looked like it, could have been drawn with a pen too, I don't know.'

'Which arm?'

'Looked like his right arm, but it was hard to tell, so I can't say a hundred per cent.'

'OK.'

'Have you heard anything otherwise?'

'Not yet.'

'See you.'

Stilton hung up and started to walk again. He was on his way up the steps, towards Klevgränd, for the fifth time that night. He had lowered his step time by several minutes and felt that his lungs were keeping up. He wasn't panting as much as before and he sweated considerably less.

He was on his way.

11

Linn Magnuson was stressed. She was stuck in a traffic jam on her way in from Stocksund. In a little less than half an hour she would be standing on the podium at the Swedish Association of Local Authorities and Regions to talk about 'Good leadership' in front of a large number of intermediate managers from all over the country. Luckily she knew exactly what she would talk about. Clarity, communication, and dealing with relationships. Three points that she was completely at home with.

Dealing with relationships, she thought, lucky that it's about working relationships and not private life. She didn't feel that she was much of an expert at that just now. The relationship between her and Bertil was swaying. She didn't know why. It wasn't her, it was him. He had come home in the middle of the night, round about three, she thought it was, and gone straight out onto the terrace and sat in the dark. That wasn't in itself so unusual. He often had telephone meetings at the weirdest times and would come home after that. What was unusual was that he had sat on the terrace with a little bottle of mineral water. That had never happened before, as far as Linn could remember. That he had sat on the terrace in the middle of the night with a mineral water. Never. If he had something with him it was always a little glass with something brown-coloured in it. Whisky, calvados, cognac. Never water. And in a close relationship like theirs, it was that sort of seemingly insignificant deviation that got you thinking.

Speculating.

The company? Another woman? His bladder? Had he undergone an examination in secret and discovered he had cancer?

Something was not as it should be.

That hadn't been as it should be for a long time.

When she was going to ask him in the morning, he had already gone. Not just gone, he had never been to bed.

She left the queue and accelerated past the university.

* * *

'A student essay?'

'Yes.'

Olivia had arranged a meeting with Miriam Wixell under slightly false pretences. She had claimed that she was in her third term at the police college, which was true, and had been asked to write about so-called escort activities. 'A really important essay.' She had deliberately adopted a naive approach. Pretended she was something of an innocent and hardly knew anything at all. She had found Wixell's name when one of the teachers had given her an old file about Gold Card, and Wixell was the only person she could find.

'What do you want to know?'

That's what Wixell had asked her on the phone.

'Well, it's more about how you thought. I'm twenty-three myself and I'm trying to think what it was like for people like you. How you became a female escort. What was the attraction?'

After further empty phrases she had hooked Wixell.

Now they were sitting at an outdoor café on Birger Jarlsgatan. The sharp sun reached down between the high buildings and had led Wixell to put on a pair of sunglasses. Olivia dutifully pulled out a small notebook and looked at her.

'You write about food?'

'Yes, on a freelance basis. Mainly travel magazines.'

'How exciting. But doesn't it make you fat?'

'What do you mean?'

'Well, you would have to eat lots of food that you're going to write about.'

214

'It's not so bad.'

Wixell gave a little smile. She had agreed to an interview and a free lunch. She quickly described her time as a female escort. It hadn't been long. When she had been asked to do things she wasn't prepared to do, then she had dropped out.

'You mean like sex, that sort of thing?'

Said Olivia with the widest eyes she could manage.

'That sort of thing.'

'But there were a lot of you working for Gold Card, right?'

'Yes.'

'Were you only Swedish girls, or what?'

'I can't remember.'

'Do you remember any of the others?'

'Why do you ask that?'

'Well, perhaps I can get in touch with someone else too.'

'I can't remember who the others were.'

'OK...'

Olivia noticed that Wixell became a little wary. But there was still more to ask.

'Do you remember if there was anyone with blue hair?' she asked.

'Yes, I do!'

Wixell laughed suddenly. The memory of somebody with blue hair was evidently amusing.

'It was a blonde girl from Kärrtorp, Ovette I think she was called, she thought it would be sexy. With blue hair!'

'But it wasn't?'

'No, it was just ugly.'

'I can imagine. Was there anyone who looked a bit Latin American too? Anyone you remember?'

'Yeah... she... I can't remember her name, but there was a really pretty girl who looked like that.'

'Dark? With black hair?'

'Yes... yes? Is it someone you know?'

'No, it was someone who was described in that investigation and I wondered whether it might be someone who wasn't Swedish and that there weren't many immigrants in those days, I thought.'

'Oh right? But there were some?'

Wixell suddenly felt that she couldn't really grasp what this young girl was doing. She thanked her for the lunch and left. Rather abruptly. Olivia still had a question left but she never had time to ask it:

'Did that dark-haired girl hang around with Jackie Berglund?'

Olivia got up too and started to walk. In the direction of Stureplan. A mild wind was blowing from Nybroviken bay. Lightly dressed pedestrians streamed in every direction. Olivia went with the flow. Somewhere near the East Restaurant a thought came into her mind.

She was only a couple of blocks away.

From the boutique.

Weird & Wow.

There it was.

Jackie Berglund's boutique on Sibyllegatan. Olivia looked at the shop for a while, from the other side of the street. She heard Eva Carlsén's words ringing in her ears: don't go nosing around Jackie Berglund.

I'm not going nosing. I'm just going to visit her boutique and look at what's for sale. I'm a completely unknown person who will be entering as a customer. What's the harm in that? Olivia reflected.

And stepped into the boutique.

The first thing she reacted to was the smell. She breathed in a heavy dose of half-sweet perfume.

The second thing was the boutique's wares. They were nowhere near her sort of thing. Ornaments and bits and pieces that she would never think of having at home, and clothes that certainly wouldn't suit her. With price tags that were really ridiculous, she thought, and leaned towards a dress. When she looked up, Jackie Berglund stood there right in front of her. Well made-up, dark hair, slightly above average height. Her intense blue eyes observed the young woman. Olivia suddenly remembered what those eyes had looked like when Eva Carlsén had asked about Red Velvet.

'Can I help you?'

Olivia couldn't think clearly, and didn't know what to answer.

'No, I'm just looking.'

'Are you interested in home furnishing?'

'No.'

Not a wise answer. Olivia immediately regretted her words.

'You might like to look at the dresses here, new ones and vintage too,' said Jackie.

'Yes, right… umm…no, I don't think they're really my style.'

But she would have realised that the second I walked in, Olivia thought. She pottered around a few moments. Picked up some earrings and touched an old gramophone horn from the 1930s. Then she felt it was time to slip out.

'But thank you very much!'

Olivia left the boutique.

That was when Jackie put two and two together. Or thought she had done. She phoned Carl Videung.

'That Olivia Rönning who visited you, and asked about me, what did she look like?'

'Dark hair.'

'A bit of a squint?'

'Yes.'

Jackie hung up and keyed in a new number.

* * *

Mink was not a morning person, more like a night person. The night was when Mink was in his element. It was then that he moved between the circles he did move in, and made sure he picked up something here which he could sell there. It might be a tip-off, or a white bag, or just a dog: last night he had rescued a tired Alsatian dog from an overdose victim in Kungsträdgården and taken him to a nurse in the suburbs, in Bandhagen, who had then broken down. She knew that her boyfriend did drugs, but she thought he had it under control. And he hadn't.

The Alsatian was called Mona.

That too, Mink thought, and wondered if there was some political connection. Had the dog been named after the famous Social Democratic politician Mona Sahlin? He was sitting on the regional train on his way to Flemingsberg and had decided to have a talk with Acke.

At the school recreation centre.

Mink was not exactly a strategic genius.

Acke wasn't at the school centre.

Mink asked the kids outside the building and soon discovered that nobody knew where Acke was.

'Are you Acke's dad?'

'No, I'm his mentor.'

That was what Mink said. Mentor? Rather neat, he thought. Of course, he wasn't entirely sure what it really implied, but it was somebody who knew a bit more than anybody else and Mink knew most things.

So mentor felt good.

On his way back to the station he suddenly caught sight of Acke. Or at least he saw a boy on his own who was kicking a football against a fence further down the street, and from the pictures on Vettan's mobile he thought the boy could be Acke. Besides, he had seen Acke a few times with Vettan when he was younger.

'Hi there, Acke!'

Acke turned round. Mink approached him with a smile.

'Can I take a shot with the ball?'

Acke rolled the football across to the short man with the ponytail. He soon ducked when Mink kicked the ball – it veered off in all the directions that Mink hadn't intended.

'Perfect!'

Mink smiled. Acke looked if he could see the vanished ball.

'D'you like football?' said Mink.

'Yes.'

'Me too. Do you know who Zlatan is?'

Acke could hardly credit this weird guy. Who Zlatan was? Is the guy crazy?

'Yes, of course. He plays for Milan.'

'And before that he played for Spain and Holland, you know I worked with Zlatan early in his career, as his mentor, when he was in Malmö football club, I was the one who got him into Europe.'

'Yeah, right…'

'I suppose you could say I opened the E4 for Zlatan.'

Acke was ten years old and here was an adult man who talked about Zlatan and he couldn't really follow what he was talking about.

'Do you know Zlatan?'

'You bet I do, if there's anybody Zlatan rings if things go wrong, then it's me. We're buddies! Anyway, hello, my name is Mink.'

'Hi.'

'I know your mum, Ovette. Do you want a hamburger?'

Acke gobbled down a double cheeseburger at the Flemingsberg Kebab & Grill in the centre. Mink sat opposite him. He wondered how he should go about this. Ten year olds were not exactly his field, so he dived straight in.

'Your mum says you've got lots of bruises and you blame football. I think you're lying.'

At first Acke thought of getting up and leaving. Had his mum told this guy about his bruises? Why had she done that?

'What's it got to do with you?'

'That you're lying?'

'I'm not lying!'

'I've played top football for many years, that's why I came into contact with Zlatan, I know what sort of injuries you can get on the field. Your bruises are not football injuries, you'll have to think up something better.'

'Mum believes me.'

'Do you like lying to her?'

'No.'

'Then why do you do it?'

Acke squirmed in his seat. He didn't like lying to his mum but he didn't dare tell her the truth.

'OK Acke, let's say like this, you can go on lying to Ovette, that's fine by me, I used to lie to my mum, lots of times, but between us – you and me – those aren't football injuries, are they?'

'No.'

'Been in a fight?'

'Sort of.'

'You can tell me,' said Mink.

Acke hesitated a second or two. Then he pulled up his sleeve a bit.

'This is what I am.'

Mink looked at the exposed arm. It said KF with a ring around on his arm. Drawn with a marker pen.

'What does that mean?'

Ten minutes later Mink left the hamburger bar to make a call. Acke waited inside.

Mink phoned Stilton.

'Kid Fighters?'

'Yes,' said Mink. 'That's what they call themselves, the slightly older boys get tattoos with KF on their arms, with a ring round.

'Where do they hang out?'

'He wasn't exactly sure, somewhere in Årsta, underground.'

'The same place every time?'

'Yes.'

'And they're there every evening?'

'He thought so.'

'Do you have any contact with UE?'

'I think so. A number…'

Stilton knew that Mink never dropped a contact. A large part of his survival depended on that.

Mink followed Acke home. It felt best that way. When Ovette let them in, she got a big hug. From Acke, who immediately ran in to fetch his football clothes.

'Are you going to play now?

'Yes!'

Ovette looked at Mink who looked at Acke and got a wink back. Acke disappeared outside.

'Is he going to football?' Ovette asked.

She looked slightly worried.

'Yes.'

Mink stepped uninvited into the kitchen.

'But what did he say? Did you get anything out of him?' Ovette wondered.

'They weren't football injuries. Are you going to work tonight?'

'No.'

Ovette sank down opposite Mink. The cold light from the neon tube above the sink showed her face with unsentimental honesty. And that face had not worn well. For the first time,

Mink saw what a tough life Vettan lived. In a purely physical sense. He had always met her before when she had make-up on, even at the café in town, now she had nothing on her face that could hide what it meant to earn her living the way she did.

'Must you carry on with that shit?'

'The street?'

'Yes.'

Ovette opened the little airing window and lit a cigarette. Mink knew her very well, from the old days, and he knew some things about her life. Some but not all. He didn't know why she sold herself on the street, but he assumed it was about money. Survival, and a never-ending illusion that tonight would be the last night. Or the next to last. Or just one more night and then that's it.

But that night never arrived.

'What else could I do?'

'Get a job? Anything at all?'

'Like you?'

Mink smiled a little and shrugged his shoulders. He was not exactly a brilliant role model when it came to that side of reality. He hadn't had a job in that sense since he was in charge of the Katarina lift one season when he was young. Up and down for nine hours and then straight out into the bustle.

'Have you got some coffee?'

'Yes.'

While Ovette made a couple of cups of filter coffee, Mink tried to tell her as kindly as he could about Acke's bruises. Without Ovette being hit too hard.

* * *

Stilton had been helped by Mink many years earlier to get into touch with UE, on police business. It was about a suspected infringement of an underground military area. UE stood for

Urban Exploration, a loosely formed group of individuals who devoted their time to mapping underground places in urban environments. Tunnel systems. Abandoned factories. Rock shelters and air raid shelters. Abandoned environments, often forbidden to enter.

The activities of UE were not entirely legal.

Mink had sent a text message with the phone number of his UE contact and Stilton had rung up and asked for a meeting. He said he was going to do a report for *Situation Sthlm* about weird and hidden environments in the Greater Stockholm region. The guy knew about the magazine and liked it.

So it worked.

Their activities not being entirely legal, not surprisingly the two guys who turned up had hidden their faces with balaclava helmets when they met. Stilton had nothing against that. The meeting place had also been chosen with discretion in mind. A van parked down in Hammarby docks. One of the guys sat behind the wheel. The other one sat in the back. Stilton sat on the passenger seat. His general appearance wasn't a problem, seeing as he was writing for *Situation Sthlm*, and neither of the guys reacted.

'What do you want to know?'

Stilton explained what the report was going to be about. To show how incredibly many hidden spaces there were under a city like Stockholm, and that UE presumably were those that knew most about this, and were most familiar with the spaces themselves. Flattery and white lies. One of the guys laughed a little and wondered if it was about showing places where rough sleepers could find somewhere to sleep. Stilton joined in with the laughter and said that was a risk they must take. Then the two guys looked at each other, after which they pulled their balaclavas off, and one of them was a girl.

Well now, that was a little lesson about preconceived notions, Stilton thought.

'Have you got a map?' the girl asked.

Stilton had come equipped with a map. He pulled it out and opened it flat.

The girl and the guy devoted the next half hour to pointing out every manner of weird space hidden under the ground in the city region. Stilton acted sometimes fascinated, sometimes surprised. And it perhaps wasn't all acting. He was actually genuinely surprised about some of the places. Both over the fact that they existed, and that this young couple knew about them. He came very close to being impressed.

'Incredible,' he said, more than once.

But after half an hour he felt it was time. He said that one of his homeless mates claimed that there was a really fantastic underground space in the Årsta area that hardly anyone knew about.

'Do you?'

The girl and the guy smiled at each other. What they didn't know about Stockholm's underground spaces wasn't worth knowing… and so on…

'There is a space there,' said the guy. 'It's called Wine and Spirits.'

The girl pulled the map towards her and pointed out the place.

'There.'

'Large?' Stilton asked.

'Gigantic. It was meant to be some sort of water treatment or sewage works in the beginning, but now it is just entirely empty. It reaches down several storeys underground.'

'Have you been there?'

The couple looked at each other again. How much should they tell?

'I won't put in your names or take any pictures, nobody knows I've talked to you, it's OK,' said Stilton.

They weighed it over for a few seconds.

'We have been there,' said the girl.

'How do you get down? Is it difficult?'

'Yes and no,' said the guy.

'What do you mean?'

'You can either get in through the grid gates at the front and then down a very long tunnel through the rocks, it's an old cable tunnel, and then there's a steel door into the main cavern, that's usually sealed… that is the simple way,' said the guy.

'And the hard one?'

The girl looked at the guy behind the wheel who looked at Stilton. Now they were talking secrets.

'There is a narrow shaft, you can access it via a manhole on the street… here…'

The guy pointed at the map again.

'There's a narrow metal ladder attached to the wall under the grid, you have to climb down about fifteen metres in the shaft, then you come to an iron door and inside that is a passage…'

'Which leads to the cavern?'

'Yes, but it is…'

The guy became silent.

'It is…?'

'It's a damn narrow passage.'

'And long,' said the girl. 'And pitch black.'

'OK.'

Stilton nodded. The girl folded up the map. The guy looked at Stilton.

'You're not going to try to get in that way?'

'Absolutely not.'

'Good, you'd never get through.'

Mink phoned when Stilton was on his way from Hammarby docks.

'Did you get hold of them?'

'Yes.'

'Did they know anything?'

'Yes.'

'So there is a rock shelter there, in Årsta?'

'Yes.'

'OK, now we know.'

'We?' thought Stilton, Mink was sounding a bit like in the old days. Did he think they were a team?

'So what are you going to do?' asked Mink.

'Check it out.'

Stilton hung up.

He would climb down the narrow shaft under the manhole with the help of the metal ladder on the wall. Fifteen metres down there would be an iron hatch in the rock wall. If he was lucky, it would be open. If he had even more luck, he would be able to squeeze through the hatch and crawl in. On his stomach. In a pitch black passage. It wouldn't be possible to turn in the passage. If he couldn't go forward any more, he would have to push himself back again.

If he didn't get stuck.

That was one of his recurrent nightmares. Getting stuck. In various places in every dream, but always with the same scenario: he lay there stuck, jammed in, a locked position, and knew he would never get loose. That he would just fade away in a vice of terror.

Now he was going to put himself in precisely such a nightmare situation. Voluntarily. He would slither along inside an unknown rock passage that wasn't much wider than a human body.

If he got stuck, he would be stuck for good.

Very slowly he started to climb down the metal ladder in the narrow shaft. Fat black spiders crept along the walls. Halfway down it occurred to him that the hatch might not be open. A sort of forbidden hope that he quickly pushed aside.

The hatch was open.

Or half open. Stilton pushed it further as much as he could with one foot, and managed to get the upper part of his body in through the hatch. He looked ahead, which was rather pointless. There was just a black hole that went in a few metres, and after that only black. When he lit his torch he saw that the passage bent slightly and disappeared.

He pushed his entire body through the opening and gasped. It was much narrower than he had anticipated. He lay on his stomach in the passage with his arms stretched out ahead and realised what a crazy idea it was. Then he thought about Vera. He turned the torch off and started to shuffle along.

He had to push with his toes to move forward. If he raised his head he hit the rock. If he lowered it too far he scraped his chin. It was extremely slow, but he moved forward. A decimetre at a time shuffling in the black passage. He felt the sweat running down his neck. It took a while before he reached the bend he had seen. There, he would have to make a decision. If the bend was too sharp he would never get through. The risk of getting stuck was too great.

The risk of living his nightmare was maximal.

Now he was at the bend.

He turned on the torch and saw the rat's yellow eyes little more than a metre in front of him. It didn't really bother him. If you have lived as a rough sleeper for a few years you get to be very familiar with *rattus norvegicus*. Often the only company available. The rat probably felt something similar because it turned round after a second or so and disappeared past the bend.

Stilton shuffled after it. Into the bend. Halfway through he stopped. The angle was too sharp, which Stilton unfortunately discovered too late, when he had already got the greater part of his body into the bend. He wasn't going to get through. What was a lot worse, existentially speaking, was that he wasn't going be able to go back either. His body had jammed in the bend.

He was stuck.

Like in a vice.

* * *

He had parked his grey Jaguar not far from the Maritime Museum. The front of the car pointing towards the Djurgård Canal. It was almost the only car there. He had nevertheless looked around before he pulled out Wendt's cassette. An old cassette tape. Why hadn't he copied it onto a CD, he wondered. Typical Nils. Luckily the exclusive car had a player for cassettes too.

Now he took the cassette out of the player and held it in his hand. He had listened to the entire taped conversation, even though he remembered every word.

He had tormented himself.

Very slowly, he pulled the narrow plastic tape out of the cassette. Bit by bit, until he had the whole tangle in his hand. Not that it helped very much to destroy the tape. The original tape was still somewhere. Somewhere unknown. With exactly the same conversation, and the same disastrous information. A tape that he must get hold of, one way or another. Preferably within three days. The idea of doing what Wendt demanded, going along with his ultimatum, that was not something he would consider. It wasn't part of his plan.

Yet.

But he was enough of a realist to realise that there was a risk it would end up there. In his plan. When the three days had run out.

What would he do then? If Wendt made the conversation public? What could his lawyers do? Claim that it was a forgery? But a voice analysis would of course reveal that it was him. And Linn? She would immediately recognise his voice.

Bertil lit a cigarillo. He had got through almost a whole

packet today. He glanced at his face in the rear-view mirror. He looked just as worn out as Wendt had done. Unshaven, grey skin. Hadn't slept last night, no breakfast, some spiteful comments about cancelled meetings, and then Linn. He knew that she was sensitive to any change in his behaviour and would be wondering what was going on, and that she would ask some very difficult questions as soon as she got the chance. Questions that he couldn't answer without lying. And it wasn't that easy to lie to Linn.

He was under a great deal of pressure.

'You sound a bit stressed?'

'Oh really? Well, yes, rather a lot on just now.'

Erik Grandén suddenly phoned. He had got home from Brussels and insisted on a light dinner and since Bertil wanted to avoid close contact with Linn as long as possible, a dinner there would be.

'The Theatre Grill at half seven?'

'That'll do nicely.'

'Will you bring Linn?'

'No.'

Bertil hung up on Grandén. He looked at the tangle of tape in his hand, looked out across the Djurgård canal and felt a clump forming in his throat. A warm clump. He swallowed, and swallowed, and then he gave in.

One could call the interior at the Theatre Grill intimate. Muted dark red wallpaper, small gold-framed pictures and dimmed lighting playing on the walls. Erik Grandén liked it here. Right in the city centre. This was where he wanted to be. He had just looked in at the Bukowski auction showrooms on Arsenalgatan. The viewing was for the coming Modern Art auction and Grandén had come across an early Baertling that he was charmed by. He might put in a bid. Baertling had suddenly become bankable again.

He had manoeuvred his tall gangly body into a small sofa cubicle opposite his 'old boy' Bertil Magnuson. Not that they had ever been boys together, but in their circles people liked to be part of the 'old boys' club'. Now they were sitting here and toying with a sole meunière and a couple of glasses of chilled wine, one of the best. Wine was Grandén's field. He had invested a considerable sum in a number of rare bottles that he kept in a special store at the Opera Cellar restaurant.

'Skål!'

'Skål!'

Bertil was quiet. That suited Grandén nicely. He liked to hear his own voice. He expressed himself well, his words were chosen carefully, he had had plenty of training in the public eye.

And he liked being there too.

When he started talking about his 'possible' future appointment at the highest level in Europe it was like hearing an election speech for his own election.

'I say "possible" because nothing is certain until it is certain, as Sarkozy usually says. Incidentally, we have the same barber in Paris. But I would be rather surprised if this didn't come about. Who else would they choose?'

Bertil knew that the question was rhetorical so he took another bite of sole.

'But enough about me, how are things going for MWM? I understand that there have been a few splashes in the pond, in connection with the award.'

'Yes.'

'The Congo?'

'Yes.'

'I read that stuff about child labour, it doesn't look good that.'

'No.'

'Perhaps you should make a donation?'

'To?'

'A children's hospital, in Walikale, pay for the construction and the equipment, plough a few million into the local health care, that would certainly make things look a lot better.'

'Perhaps. The problem is the actual mining, we can't get at the land we want.'

'Have you moved too fast?'

Bertil smiled a little. Erik was phenomenal at seeming to be an outsider. In every situation where there were 'a few hitches'.

'You know exactly how quickly we've been moving, Erik, you saw all the planning yourself, didn't you?'

'We don't need to go into that.'

Grandén didn't like to be reminded that he still had his fingers in the jam jar. Officially, he had licked them clean a long time ago.

'Is that why you seem a bit off?' he asked.

'No.'

Suddenly Bertil came close, very close, to saying too much. It might have been the wine, lack of sleep, the pressure, or just the need to unburden himself. Just relax a little, with an old musketeer.

But he stopped himself.

He wouldn't have had a chance to explain. The taped conversation. And even if he could, if he actually were to confess to his old friend the reason for the conversation, then he knew how Erik would react. What he knew was that Erik was the same type of person as him, through and through. Cast in the same egocentric steel mould. If he were to hear about the conversation it is highly likely he would have signalled to the waiter for the bill, thanked his old friend for a long and profitable friendship and then disappeared from Bertil's life.

For good.

So he steered the conversation towards Erik's favourite subject instead.

'What actually is this appointment that's coming up?'

'Confidential. But if it falls into place then you're going to be saying "Skål!" to one of Europe's most powerful men next time we sit here.'

Erik Grandén pulled in his lower lip a little. An organic movement that was his way of indicating maximal subtext.

In Bertil's eyes, he just looked affected.

* * *

He assumed he must have passed out for a while. How long? That he didn't know. When he came to, he felt a cold draught through the narrow passage. Something must have been opened at the other end, the end that he was aiming for, and had created a cold draught. It was probably the cold that had caused his body to shrink a few millimetres and loosen. Just a little. But enough so that by manically pushing with his feet he could get through the bend and lie outstretched again.

He breathed out, several minutes, and could only note that it would be impossible to slither backwards. If he was going to get out of here, there was only one way. One direction, and that was deeper in.

He started to slither again.

And slither.

And because his sense of time had disappeared long ago, he had no idea how long he slithered, but suddenly he was there. Almost at the edge of the end of the passage. He slithered the last little bit and looked out.

Into an enormous cavern hewn out of the rock.

What he saw there, he would never forget.

First it was the light. Or lights. Many stands hung with spotlights that spread a flashing rotating red and green light over the whole cavern. A strong light. It took a while for Stilton's eyes to adjust.

Then he saw the cages.

Two of them. Rectangular. Three metres wide and two metres high. Set up in the middle of the cavern. Built of steel frames with grey metal netting between.

And inside the cages, the boys.

Two in each cage, around ten or eleven years old. Naked, except for a pair of small shorts in black leather. In an almost reckless fight with each other. Without gloves. Bleeding a bit here and there on their bodies.

And the spectators.

Several rows around the cages. Spurring them on. Shouting. Cheering. Their hands full of banknotes that changed owner several times during the course of the fight.

Cage fighting.

With betting.

If he hadn't been forewarned through Acke's story, it would have taken a long time for him to understand what he was seeing.

It was bad enough anyway.

Even though he had used one of *Situation Sthlm*'s computers a couple of hours earlier and searched for 'cage fighting' and read a lot of extremely frightening information. How it had started in England many years ago. Parents who let their children fight in metal cages. To 'train themselves' as one father had put it. He had seen a video on YouTube where two eight year olds fought inside a steel cage at Greenlands Labour Club in Preston. It had almost made him sick to watch it.

But he continued to click.

Methodically, he had sought out more and more obscure information. How cage fighting had spread to other countries and escalated year by year. With more money and betting involved, and parallel with the spread it had moved further and further from public view. Eventually it ended up entirely underground.

Hidden from the everyday world, but well known to those who enjoyed seeing children fighting each other in cages. Like under-age gladiators.

How the hell could that be kept secret, Stilton wondered.

And how could they get the children to take part?

He understood that when he read a text that explained that the child who won a fight rose a step on a special ranking list. The one at the top of the list after ten fights won money. The world was crawling with poor children. Homeless children. Kidnapped children. Children without anyone who cared about them. Children who might have a chance to get somewhere by fighting in cages.

Or children who simply wanted to try to win a bit of money to help their mum.

Repulsive, Stilton thought. He read about how fights were often arranged by youths who themselves had started in the cages. And how they had a special tattoo which indicated who they were.

Two letters: KF. With a ring round them.

Like one of the people who beat up the rough sleeper at Västerbron.

Kid fighters, according to Acke.

That was why he was down here.

He found it hard to keep looking at the cages. One of the young boys had been knocked down and lay bleeding on the floor of the cage. A metal hatch was lifted slightly and the boy was dragged out. Like a carcass. The other boy danced around inside the cage while the spectators whistled and cheered and then became silent. A new fight was about to begin.

That was when he sneezed.

Not just once, but four times. The dust in the passage had lodged in his nose. By the fourth sneeze he had been discovered.

Four of them pulled him out of the opening and one knocked him down. In the fall, he hit his head against the rock wall. He was dragged into a smaller cavern, out of sight of the spectators. There they pulled his clothes off him. There were still four of them. Two slightly younger, two slightly older. He was lifted up and thrown against the cold granite wall. Blood from his head wound ran down over his shoulders. One of the younger assailants pulled out a spray can and wrote TRASHKICK across his naked back.

Another one pulled out a mobile phone.

One of the disadvantages of mobiles is that you can phone someone by mistake when the phone is in your pocket. An advantage is that you can easily get at the last number you phoned. That was what happened when Mink's mobile received a call. A call-back from someone who had been alert and focused during the last conversation but who now was in a totally different state. So different that Mink could only hear a weak wheezing. But the number on the display showed who it came from: Stilton.

Mink quickly worked out where he must be.

More or less.

Årsta is large if you don't know where to start looking, so it took a while for Mink to find nothing. In the end he phoned Vettan and spoke to Acke and got Acke to give him a more detailed description of where in Årsta it was. Approximately. It helped, a little. Mink got a good impression of the area. Good enough that he eventually could find Stilton. Huddled up against a grey rock face. Naked and bloody. His clothes thrown around him. He was holding his mobile in his hand. Mink could see that Stilton had been badly beaten up. But he was alive. And communicating. He managed to get his trousers and jacket on.

'You need to go to hospital.'

'No!'

Stilton hated hospitals. Mink considered forcing him. He decided not to, and phoned for a taxi.

The first that arrived immediately turned back when the driver saw the two of them. The second taxi stopped and the driver suggested that they should phone for an ambulance. Then left. The third taxi had just taken someone to a nearby address not far away when Mink waved it down. By then, Mink had learnt his lesson and put Stilton out of sight. Behind some bushes. He quickly explained to the taxi driver that his mate had been beaten up and needed to be bandaged up a little and before the driver could reply Mink pushed two five-hundred-crown notes through the window.

The day's winnings.

'I drove a taxi for many years, so I know what it's like some-times, drunks and shit, but this is OK, we're going to Wiboms väg in Solna, a thousand crowns without the meter, not bad for a short drive, eh?'

Olivia sat in her kitchen and was eating an ice cream. With her laptop open. Suddenly she dropped the ice cream on the floor and stared at the screen, all eyes. She had gone into the Trashkick site out of pure curiosity. First she'd seen a naked man being beaten up, in a rock shelter somewhere, rather dark images, and then the body was thrown out somewhere and landed beside a stone wall.

'Stilton?'

At first she felt like the ice cream she had just been eating. Ice cold, inside. Then she keyed in Stilton's number.

And waited.

Elvis quickly lapped up the melting ice cream on the floor.

Would he answer? He did, in the end, although it wasn't him. It was an unfamiliar voice that answered on his mobile.

'Hello, this is Mink answering Stilton's mobile.'

Mink? Was that one of the people who had beaten him up? Pinched his mobile? Why didn't he answer himself?

'Hi, my name is Olivia Rönning and… is Tom there? Stilton?'

'Yes.'

'Where?'

'In Vera's caravan. What do you want?'

Vera's caravan? That Vera? The one who'd been murdered?

'How is he? I saw online that he'd been beaten up and…'

'He's OK. Do you know him?'

'Yes.'

White lie, a bit, Olivia thought. But I'll make it even whiter.

'He's helping me with a job at the moment. Where is Vera's caravan?'

Mink needed help with the wounded Stilton. Above all he needed bandages and plasters. Olivia could get that. So he told her how to find Vera's caravan and asked her to hurry.

Olivia found her first-aid kit and threw herself into her car. It wasn't entirely clear to her why she was doing this. Sympathy for the beaten-up Stilton?

Presumably.

But mainly pure impulse.

Stilton pointed to the cupboard where it was kept. Vera had used it herself a few times when she'd had cuts and sores of one sort or another. Mink took out a glass jar with some yellowy-brown wax-like content. The hand-written label said 'Healing resin' and the contents were listed.

'Resin, sheep fat, beeswax, alum extract…'

He read from the label on the jar.

'Just rub it on.'

Stilton sat half-naked on the bunk with a bloody towel around the top of his head where there was a big gash that had been caused when he was thrown against the wall of the cavern. He pointed at his other wounds. The visible ones, where the bleeding had stopped. Mink looked at the weird mixture in the jar.

'Do you have faith in this stuff?'

'Vera did. She'd got the recipe from her grandmother, before she hung herself.'

'Oh, hell, goes to show.'

Show what? Stilton wondered. Mink started to rub on the ointment.

When Olivia got close to the caravan and cautiously looked in through the window she met with a really strange sight in the weak light of the lantern. A thin little figure with a pointed nose and a ponytail was crouching in front of an unclothed Stilton. The little guy was putting on some yellowy-brown goo from an old glass jar. For a moment Olivia considered rewinding, getting back in her car and buying more ice cream.

Knock, knock!

Mink opened the door.

'Olivia?'

'Yes.'

Mink stepped back into the caravan with the jar in his hand and continued to apply the ointment to Stilton's chest. Olivia climbed the two steps up into the caravan and went inside. She put her first-aid kit down. Stilton looked at her.

'Hello, Tom.'

Stilton didn't answer.

On the way to Ingenting forest, Olivia had caught up with her impulse. Why did she want to go to the caravan? And above all, what would Stilton think about it? Did he know she was going to come? He ought to have realised when that Mink guy told her where the caravan was, surely? Or was he too dazed to twig what was happening? Wasn't it really an extreme infringement of his privacy to just come here? They had only met in that dustbin room. She looked at Stilton who kept his gaze directed towards the floor. Was he furious?

'What's happened?' she asked. 'Have you been…?'

'Drop it.'

Stilton cut her off without looking up. Olivia didn't know whether she ought to leave. Or sit down. She sat down. Stilton gave her a quick look and then sank down onto the bunk. He was in so much more pain than what could be seen. He needed to lie down. Mink pulled a blanket over him.

'Have you got any painkillers here?' he asked.

'No. Wait, yes, there.'

Stilton pointed at his backpack. Mink opened it and got a new little bottle out.

'What's this?'

'Stesolid.'

'That's not a painkiller, that's a…'

'Two pills and water.'

'OK.'

Olivia looked around quickly, saw a plastic bottle with water and poured some into an unwashed glass. There weren't any others. Mink took the glass and helped Stilton to swallow two pills while he whispered to Olivia:

'Stesolid is a sedative, it's not a painkiller.'

Olivia nodded. They both looked at Stilton. He had closed his eyes. Olivia sank down a little on the other bunk. Mink sat on the floor with his back leaning against the door. Olivia glanced around the inside of the caravan.

'Does he live here?'

'Evidently.'

'You don't know? You don't know him?'

'I know him, he lives a bit here and a bit there, just now he's living here.'

'Were you the one who found him?'

'Yes. '

'Are you homeless too?'

'No, definitely not. I live in Kärrtorp, a studio flat, I own it, it must be worth at least five million today.'

'Oh, right, are you an artist?'

'A tightrope-walking artist!'

'What does that mean?'

'It means I'm involved in all sorts of things. Capital, derivatives, in and out, and in between I do a lot with art, Picasso, Chagall, Dickens.'

'Wasn't Dickens an author?'

'Mainly, absolutely, but he did some etchings when he was young, heavyweight stuff, not well known, but good!'

At this point Stilton opened his eyes slightly and glared at Mink for a moment.

'I've got to go out into the bushes for a moment.'

Mink disappeared. When he shut the door behind him, Stilton opened his eyes properly. Olivia looked at him.

'Is that a mate of yours? Mink?'

'He's an old snitch. Soon you'll hear how he solved the Palme murder. Why did you come here?'

Olivia didn't really know what to say. The first-aid kit? But that was just an excuse.

'I don't really know. Do you want me to leave?'

Stilton didn't answer.

'Do you want me to?'

'I want to be left in peace. From the beach case. You phoned and wondered if I worked on the Jill case. I did, and I found links to Jackie Berglund. Jill worked for her, in Red Velvet, and bearing in mind the murder and Jill's pregnancy I looked into the beach case again. It didn't lead anywhere. Are we done with each other now?'

Olivia looked at Stilton. She realised that she ought to leave. But there was something she wanted to tell him and this might be the last opportunity.

'I was on Nordkoster a week or so ago, up by the Hasslevikarna coves, and met a very strange man. On the beach. Can I tell you about it?'

Stilton looked at Olivia.

Outside the caravan Mink stood in the dark and inhaled something that broadened his mind. He was always ready to rethink his options. There had been a period when he had a private pipeline from Colombia straight into his nose, but when the doctors had to replace the cartilage in his nose with some fancy laminate, he understood that it was time cut down his consumption and he turned to less potent habits.

He looked up at the oval window out of the corner of his eye, into the caravan, and saw Olivia talking for all she was worth.

Pretty girl, he thought. Wonder how those two know each other?

The pretty girl had poured out another glass of water for Stilton. She had finished her story. Stilton hadn't said a word. She handed over the glass while putting her hand on the wall of the caravan again.

'Is this where Vera Larsson lived?'

'Yes.'

'Is this where she was…'

'Drop it.'

Again.

Then Mink came in, with a totally unmotivated but very characteristic smile which he flashed at Stilton on the bunk.

'Feeling better?'

'Are you?'

Mink gave a little laugh. Caught out a bit there, but so what? Hadn't he helped the former cop in an extremely precarious situation?

'I'm feeling tip-top!'

'Good. Can you leave now?' said Stilton.

He closed his eyes again.

Side by side, they walked away from the caravan. A thoughtful Olivia next to a short, spaced-out snitch whose facial expressions seem to stretch in every direction.

'Yes, you know, got my finger in lots of pies, you have to spread your…'

'Have you known Stilton a long time?'

'Yonks. I mean, he was a cop before and we were a bit of a team for many a year. I can tell you that without me he wouldn't have collected nearly as many scalps, in fact a lot of them would still be on their original heads, if you get my meaning. You always need somebody who can hammer in that final nail in the coffin and that's me in a nutshell. Incidentally, I solved the Palme murder.'

'Oh yes?'

Olivia steeled herself. Every metre that separated her from her car felt like having to traverse a bog. Until it finally occurred to her that he would of course ask for a lift. How the hell could she get out of that? In the middle of the Ingenting forest.

'Yes, you know, I served it up on a plate to the murder squad. But did they act? No. I mean it was so fucking crystal clear that the man's wife shot him! He'd been having a lot on the side, and she had got fed up with it and BANG! Nobody saw the shots! Did they?'

And now they had reached the Mustang.

The crucial point.

Mink just stared at the car.

'Is that yours?'

'Yes.'

'Wow, that's a fancy machine! What… hell, it's a Thunderbird!'

'Mustang.'

'Yeah, right. You'll give me a ride, right? You know we can go past Kärrtorp and I can stock up on some stuff, there's a bed waiting and, well, Mink is well hung!'

That was the last straw for Olivia. She looked down at him. He was a head shorter than her, had a wide smile and no shoulders. She stepped closer to him.

'You? Sorry, but I wouldn't touch you with a bargepole even if someone was pointing a loaded gun at my head… you are a pathetic little shit, get it? Take the tube!'

She got into her car, revved up and shot off with a spray of gravel in her wake.

* * *

Down in the rock shelter in Årsta there was a rush of activity. Stilton's appearance had scared the organisers. Did more people know where they hung out? The rock shelter had been quickly emptied of spectators. Now they were moving all the lighting and other electronic equipment out. Cages were being dismantled.

These premises were useless now.

'Where shall we take it?'

The guy who asked had a black hooded jacket and was called Liam. His mate, Isse, who had a dark green hooded jacket was just going past carrying a large metal box. On his lower arm the KF tattoo could be seen.

'I don't know, they're talking about it now!'

Isse nodded backwards towards a rock wall where four older boys were having a discussion with a large map between them. Liam turned back and pulled his mobile out. He was going to see how many visitors the new film had already notched up on their site.

The film with the naked rough sleeper.

* * *

Olivia was still furious when she arrived back home and went into the building. 'Mink is well hung!' Her head was still partly back there in the forest when she reached out to turn the light on in the stairwell and was slapped hard across her cheek. Before she could scream, a hand was pressed over her mouth and an arm around her waist and she was dragged into the lift. A very old lift, for two people, with one of those concertina iron doors. It was pitch black in the stairwell. She couldn't see anything. But she could feel how yet another person pushed their way into the far too cramped lift. The hand was still pressed over her mouth. The iron doors were pulled shut with a crash and the lift started to move slowly upwards. Olivia was terrified. She had no idea what was happening. The bodies that were pressing against her were hard. She assumed they were men. She could feel the raw sweat and sour breath pushing up into her nose. None of them could move. They stood there like packed meat in the dark.

Suddenly the lift stopped between two floors.

Silence… Olivia got cramp in her stomach.

'I'm taking my hand away now. If you scream then I'll wring your neck.'

The rough voice came from behind. Olivia felt the man's breath on her neck. The hand over her mouth twisted her head back and forth a few times. Then it was moved from her mouth. Olivia violently gulped in some air.

'Why are you interested in Jackie Berglund?'

Now the voice from the side. A lighter voice, a man's voice, about ten centimetres from her left cheek.

Jackie Berglund.

That was what this was about.

Then Olivia felt real terror.

She had moral courage, sure, but she wasn't a Lisbeth Salander. Far from it. What were they going to do? Ought she to scream out? And get her neck wrung?

'Jackie doesn't like people poking their noses into her business,' said the light voice.

'OK.'

'You're not going to go snooping around?'

'No.'

'Good.'

A rough hand was pressed over her mouth again. The men's bodies pushed hard against her. She struggled to breathe through her nose. Tears ran down her cheeks. The men's breath settled over her face. A long time. Suddenly the lift started to move down again, all the way to the ground floor. The iron door was abruptly opened and the men pushed their way out. Olivia fell back against the inside wall of the lift. She saw two large figures disappear out onto the street. The door slammed shut behind them.

Olivia slipped slowly down to the floor of the lift while her stomach did somersaults. Her knees banged together. She was on the edge. Suddenly she started to scream. A high-pitched scream, and she screamed until the light in the stairwell was turned on and a neighbour from the first floor came running down and found her.

The neighbour helped her up the stairs. Olivia said that two men had frightened her in the entrance lobby. She didn't say why, and thanked the neighbour for his help. He went down again while Olivia turned towards her flat door – it was slightly ajar. Had they been up in the flat too? The fucking bastards! Olivia pushed the door open and stepped inside quickly, locked the door behind her and sank down in the hall. Her hands were still shaking when she pulled out her mobile. Her first reflex was to phone the police. But what would she say? She couldn't get her head round this just now, so instead she keyed in Lenni's number instead. An answering machine started up, and Olivia hung up. Ought she to ring her mother? She lowered her mobile and looked up. She wasn't shaking so much now. Her stomach had settled down. From the hall floor she could see into the living room, and suddenly she noticed that a window was half open. It hadn't been when she left the flat earlier. Or had it? She got up and suddenly thought about Elvis.

'Elvis!'

She quickly searched the little flat. No Elvis. The window? She lived on the second floor and sometimes Elvis had got out onto the window ledge. Once or twice in the spring he had even managed to somehow get down onto a neighbour's window ledge and eventually down into the yard. She closed the window and ran down to the yard. With a little torch.

A small back garden, with a few trees and benches and plenty of opportunity for an agile cat to get into the neighbouring back gardens.

'Elvis!'

No cat.

Bertil Magnuson had stretched out on a sofa in his big office, awake, with a glowing cigarillo in his hand. He had come here straight from the Theatre Grill, restless and nervous, phoned Linn and – to his relief – found himself talking to her answering machine. He had quickly explained that he had to have a conference call with Sydney at three in the morning and would probably sleep at the office. That happened now and then. Just down the corridor they had a comfortable bedroom for such occasions. But Bertil wasn't going to use that. He wasn't going to sleep at all. He just wanted to be alone. A few hours earlier he had come to a decision. And what made him do it was a couple of sentences from the graveyard the previous evening.

'Are you still married to Linn?'

'Yes.'

'Does she know about this?'

'No.'

Was that a veiled threat? Was Nils contemplating getting in touch with Linn and letting her listen to the tape? Could he be such a bastard? Regardless, Bertil couldn't take that risk. So he made a decision instead.

And now he needed to be left alone.

Then Latte phoned.

He had phoned several times during the evening. Bertil hadn't felt up to answering. Now he did, to stop him phoning again.

'Where are you? There's one hell of a party we've got going here!' Latte shouted into his mobile.

The Cub League was having a party. They consisted of eighteen mature men with lots of connections to one another. Via family, business empires or boarding schools. And all with an absolute faith in the discretion of the others in the league.

'We've booked the entire club!'

'Latte, I'm not…'

'And Jackie has delivered some really top of the line merchandise! No one older than twenty four! With happy ending in the contract! You must come, Bibbe!'

'I'm not in the mood, Latte.'

'But you will be! We must bloody well celebrate the Company of the Year! I've got hold of a gang of dwarves who serve wearing ballet dresses and Nippe has flown in five kilos of Iranian caviar! Of course you must come!'

'No!'

'What's the matter?'

'Nothing, I'm simply not in the mood. Say hi to the others!'

Bertil hung up and turned his mobile off. He knew that Latte would try again and then Nippe and the rest of the 'old boys' would try too. When they'd made up their mind to have a party, then a party there would be. There wasn't much that could get in the way. They were never short of money. Nor of bizarre ideas. Bertil had been to some parties in a variety of incredible settings. A year or two ago they had held a party in an enormous barn out on the Östgöta plain. A barn full of unbelievably expensive luxury cars and artificial lawns with fountains and a mobile bar that moved through the barn on a special steel rail. And in every car there was a half-naked young woman in the driving seat, hired from Jackie Berglund to be ready to cater to the whims of the old boys' network, whatever they may be.

And Bertil was most definitely not in that sort of mood now.

He was not going to go to any party.

Whatever the circumstances.

Not tonight.

12

Nature had exploded this spring and early summer. It had been extremely hot and sunny. It was almost too quick for comfort, but there was a positive side to it: Lake Mälaren soon reached bathing temperature. At least most parts of the lake. And at least for some people. But not for Lena Holmstad. She still thought the water was a bit too cold for swimming. She sat on a rocky promontory that had been warmed up by the sun, listening to an audiobook with the help of small headphones. A coffee cup next to her. She took a gulp and felt satisfied. She had been a clever mum. Fixed a picnic basket and cycled out with her two sons to their favourite spot on Kärsön.

This would be the first swim of the season.

And she had even baked the cakes herself.

She ought to take a photo of the basket and put it on Facebook, she thought. So that all her friends could see what a super mum she was.

Lena fumbled for her mobile. Suddenly the elder boy, Daniel, came running up. With blue lips and dripping wet. He wanted his diving mask and snorkel. Lena took her headphones off, pointed at the beach bag and tried to point out to her son that he perhaps ought to warm up a bit in the sun before throwing himself into the water again.

'But I am warm!'

'But you're shivering, pet!'

'Pah!'

'Where's Simon?'

Lena looked out towards the water. Where was he, her youngest? She'd seen him only a few moments ago. She felt the panic rising. Fast. She couldn't see little Simon. She got up quickly and knocked over her cup, spilling coffee on her mobile.

'Look what you've done!'

Daniel picked up her coffee-saturated mobile.

'He's over there,' he said.

Then she caught sight of him. A little bobbing head that swam in a life jacket, just off to the left. Down below the rocks. A bit too far away, Lena thought.

'Simon! Swim over here again! It's too deep for you there!'

'It isn't deep at all,' the five-year-old called back. 'Look! I can stand here!'

Simon carefully stood up so as not to lose his balance. The water only reached up to his waist. Daniel came up to Lena.

'Can he stand there? That's really weird.'

And it was. Lena knew that it was quite deep there. Sometimes people jumped in from those rocks above. And Daniel knew that too.

'I'll swim across to him! Stay where you are, Simon! I'm coming!'

Daniel threw himself into the water with his diving mask and snorkel and started to swim towards his little brother. Lena observed her sons and felt how her pulse was returning to normal. What had she been thinking? He did have a life jacket on after all. It had only been a few seconds. Amazing that you can get so silly over the years. As soon as you've given birth to your first child, it starts.

The thought of a catastrophe.

Daniel had almost reached his little brother. Simon was getting a bit cold and was trying to keep warm by wrapping his arms around his chest.

'Simon! What are you standing on?' Daniel called out.

'A stone, I think. It's a bit slippery, but large. Is mum angry?'

'No.'

Daniel reached his brother.

'She was just a bit worried,' he said. 'I'll have a look, then we can swim back.'

Daniel put his head under the surface and started breathing through the snorkel. He loved snorkelling. Even if it wasn't as fantastic here as in Thailand. In the rather murky water he could just make out his brother's feet standing on... what? Daniel swam closer to be able to see better. When he was right up close he could see it.

Lena was standing on the shore. She was thinking of going back to her audiobook. Suddenly she saw Daniel's head shoot up out of the water and shout out.

'Mum! There's a car down here! He's standing on the roof of a car. And there's a bloke inside!'

* * *

It was almost eleven o'clock. She had slept as if she'd been knocked out for just over eight hours. Lying across the bed, fully dressed. She hated waking up dressed. She tore her clothes off and was just going into the shower when things caught up with her.

'Elvis?'

There was no Elvis in the flat. She looked down into the yard.

No cat.

She had her shower and let the lukewarm water rinse away some of the night's experiences. Some, a lot still remained. Both from the caravan and the lift. Had those bastards in the lift anything to do with Elvis? Had they left the window open just so that the cat would slip out? What ought she to do?

She phoned the police and reported that her cat had disappeared. It had an identity chip in its ear but no collar. The policeman who she spoke to was fairly sympathetic and promised to get in touch directly if anything came in.

'Thank you.'

She didn't mention the bastards in the lift. She didn't really know how she could explain it without explaining what she herself was doing. Spying on an elegant boutique-owner in

Östermalm. On account of a student project about an un-solved murder on Nordkoster in 1987.

Not exactly crystal clear.

She would, however, drive out to Stilton to see how he was getting on. She had a feeling that he was much worse than he had let on the previous evening. Besides, perhaps she should tell him about the lift. At least he knew who Jackie Berglund was.

Olivia squeezed some fish paste onto a bit of crisp bread, and gobbled this on her way to the car. She felt a little better as soon as she came out into the sun. She lowered the car roof, sank down into the front seat, put her headphones on, started the straight-four and swept off.

Towards Ingenting forest.

The special sensation of driving an open car in the sun and wind did her good. The speed and the wind blew away some of the night's unpleasantness. She was slowly getting back into better balance. Perhaps she should buy something to take with her? It didn't seem to be the world's best stocked caravan out there. She stopped at a 7-Eleven to buy some sandwiches and pastries. When she got out of the car and passed the front she noticed a strange smell. From the engine compartment. A smell that was unfamiliar. Don't say that something's got burnt now, a belt or some other shit, not today, not after that night, that's something I absolutely do not need, she thought, and opened the bonnet.

Five seconds later she vomited. Right on the street.

The remains of her beloved Elvis lay burnt on one side of the engine block. The heat during the drive from Söder out to Solna had transformed the cat to a piece of smouldering black meat.

* * *

A crane was just lifting the grey car out of the sea by the rocks on Kärsön. Water poured out of the open driver's door. The corpse had already been taken out by divers and put into a blue bag on a stretcher. The entire area had been cordoned off. Crime scene technicians were checking tyre tracks from the slope to the rocks.

And some other stuff.

The woman who lifted up one of the police tapes and approached the stretcher had been called in an hour earlier. By the County Police Commissioner herself. A couple of other murder investigations in combination with the summer holidays meant that they were short of investigators this particular day, so Mette Olsäter from the National Crime Squad had been summoned. Besides, Commissioner Carin Götblad had long since had her eye on Olsäter. She knew that the case would be in safe hands. Mette's track record was long and unblemished. This would be something like her fifteenth murder investigation.

It soon became clear that this was a case of murder or manslaughter. There was a possibility that the man in the car had himself driven down the slope and out across the rocks to drown himself. Until he was put on the stretcher and the forensic doctor noted that he had a rather large hole on the back of his head. Large enough to make it impossible to drive a car. They had also found blood on a granite rock face not far from the slope.

Possibly from the man in the car.

Mette established that a person or persons had come with the car to the place. Possibly the man was already dead then, or he died there. The blood on the rock face and the forensic doctor would show that. Then he was put behind the steering wheel, and a person or persons pushed the car down the slope and it ended up where it did.

So far it was fairly clear.

Hypothetically.

What was less clear was the man's identity. He had no personal belongings on him. Mette asked the doctor to pull down the zip so she could see the man's face again. She studied it. Quite a long time, and flipped through her photographic memory. She almost got there. Not quite, no name, but a vague feeling from the past.

* * *

'Do you think he was alive when I started?'

'Impossible to say…'

The police woman in front of Olivia handed her another serviette. Olivia had gradually got over the first shock. Now she was crying because she couldn't stop. The police had been called to 7-Eleven by the shop owner and had seen what had happened. With the help of a chap from the shop they had collected the remains of Elvis and put them into a plastic bag. They had put Olivia in a police car and driven to the station. There she had eventually managed to tell them. About the men who had threatened her in a lift. About the open door to her flat, the missing cat, and about what connected them. Then she had been asked to describe the men. But it wasn't a particularly detailed description. She had hardly seen them, in the dark. There wasn't much more that could be done, by the police, just now.

'Where's the car?' she asked.

'It's here, in the station yard, we drove it here. But perhaps it would be best if…'

'Can you drive it home for me?'

Which they did. Perhaps because Olivia was a future colleague. She didn't want to go with them.

She didn't want to sit in the car.

* * *

Mette Olsäter stood in the Forensic Medicine department in Solna with a pathologist. In front of them lay a naked body. An hour earlier, Mette's memory had caught up with the past and found the right picture. The picture of a man who had disappeared a long time ago and whom she herself had been tasked with trying to trace.

Nils Wendt.

It must be him, she thought. Some years older here on the slab. Drowned and with a hole on the back of his head. But with a physiognomy that in other respects made her very certain.

This is going to be interesting, she thought, and studied the naked corpse.

'There are several external characteristics that can help you with identification.'

The pathologist looked at Mette.

'An old gold filling in his upper jaw, scar from when his appendix was removed, another scar here by his eyebrow, and this too...'

The pathologist pointed at a large angular birthmark on the outside of the man's left thigh. Mette leaned closer to the corpse, to the thigh, the mark. She thought she recognised it. But from where? She couldn't immediately place it.

'When did he die?'

'Preliminary estimate?'

'Yes.'

'Within the last twenty-four hours.'

'And the wound on the back of his head, could he have got that from falling on the rocks out there?'

'Possibly. I'll have to get back to you on that.'

Mette Olsäter rapidly put together a small team. A couple of old hands together with a couple of younger talents who hadn't gone off on holiday yet. The team was installed in a central command room on Polhemsgatan.

And started to work.

Methodically.

They had people out looking for witnesses in the Kärsön area. Others were looking for close relatives of Nils Wendt. They had found a sister who lived in Geneva. She hadn't heard from her brother since he disappeared in the Eighties, but she confirmed the description they could give her. The scar on his eyebrow was from their childhood. She had pushed her brother into a bookcase.

That was all they had so far. Now they must collect all the reports together as soon as possible. Not least from their technicians.

They were busy working on the car.

Mette gave the younger members of the group, Lisa Hedqvist and Bosse Thyrén, a briefing about how Wendt disappeared in 1984. The disappearance happened just after a Swedish journalist, Jan Nyström, had been found dead in a car. That too had been dumped in a lake, outside Kinshasa in what was then Zaire.

'Rather remarkable,' said Mette.

'That the methods are similar?' Lisa wondered.

'Yes. Anyhow, they classified the event in Zaire as an accident, locally, but we strongly suspected that it was murder. And at the same time Wendt disappeared from Kinshasa, and there was speculation as to whether he too was involved in the event.'

'With the journalist?'

'Yes. The journalist was writing an article about Wendt's company, MWM. But it was never made clear.'

Lisa Hedqvist's mobile rang. She answered, made a note and hung up.

'The divers have found a mobile in the water, roughly where the car was,' she said. 'It might have fallen out of the open driver's door?'

'Does it still work?' Mette asked.

'Not yet, it's on the way to the technical department.'

'Good.'

Mette turned towards Bosse Thyrén.

'Perhaps you could try to get hold of Wendt's ex-partner, he lived with a woman before he disappeared.'

'Back in the Eighties?'

'Yes. Hansson I think she was called, I'll check that.'

Bosse Thyrén nodded and left. An older colleague came up to Mette.

'We did a quick check of the Stockholm hotels, there was no Nils Wendt booked in anywhere.'

'OK. Contact the credit card companies and see if they have anything. And the airlines.'

The group left the room. They all had their tasks. Mette remained there alone.

She started thinking about the motive.

* * *

Olivia struggled to hold herself together.

First she washed the cat dishes and put them in a cupboard in the kitchen. Then she took out the cat litter. Then she collected together all the bobbles and balls that Elvis used to play with. At that point she was close to breaking down. She put it all in a plastic bag and wasn't sure whether to throw it away. Not yet, she thought, not yet. She put the bag on the window sill and looked out.

For a long time, not moving.

She felt how the worry grew in her chest, the stinging sensation in her stomach, how it became hard to breathe. For every new question, the pressure increased. Was he alive when she started to drive? Had she done it with her car? Did I kill Elvis? Questions that would pain her for a long time to come.

She knew that.

Deep inside, she knew whose fault it all was. It wasn't hers. It wasn't her who had put Elvis under the bonnet. It was the bastards who'd been sent by Jackie Berglund.

She hated that woman!

And noticed that it helped a little. To direct her hate and despair towards an actual person. An old luxury whore!

She left the window, wrapped herself in a blanket, held a cup of hot tea in her hand, went into the bedroom and sank down against the headboard. On the bedspread, she had laid out all the photos of Elvis that she could find. There were quite a lot. She touched them. One by one, and it lessened the shock a little. Then the thought hit her.

Hard.

What would they kill next time?

And she continued.

Her?

It was time to drop this.

Enough was enough. Now she would abandon the beach case. There were limits, and that limit was Elvis.

Olivia sat up on the bed and put the cup down. Just as well to get it over with, she thought. That extremely tough telephone call that she must make. Just as well to do it before I break down totally.

The call to her mum.

'Oh dear, dear!'

'Yes, I know, it's really hard to face,' said Olivia.

'But how could you leave a window open when he's alone at home?'

'I don't know, I just forgot it, he has sneaked out before, and…'

'But then he's been down in the yard, hasn't he?'

'Yes.'

'And you've had a look down there? A proper look?'

'Yes.'

'Have you reported it to the police?'

'Yes.'

'Good. It really is a pity, darling, but I'm sure he'll come back soon! Cats can stay away for many days!'

Olivia burst into tears the second she ended the conversation. She just couldn't hold herself together any longer. She had managed to tell her mum the only reasonable version she could think of. That Elvis had disappeared. It just felt simply impossible to tell her what had really happened, and it would have led to thousands of follow-up questions concentrated in a single one.

'Did you kill him with your car?'

She didn't want to hear that question. Not from mum. She couldn't cope with that. So it ended up with a big fat white lie and they would both have to live with that. Elvis would be a missing cat and she would mourn losing him.

A sort of family secret.

She huddled up with all the cat photos around her on the bed and sobbed in sorrow.

13

MISSING COMPANY DIRECTOR FOUND MURDERED

The news about the murder of Nils Wendt hit the headlines.
At the time of his disappearance he was a partner with Bertil
Magnuson in their jointly owned company Magnuson Wendt
Mining. There had been speculation that the disappearance
had been caused by a conflict between the two major owners.
Even whether Magnuson himself was involved in Wendt's
disappearance. But nothing was clarified.

Then.

Perhaps it would be now.

And naturally there were new speculations today. As to
whether the murder could be linked to today's MWM. And
where Nils Wendt had been all these years. After all, he had
been missing since 1984.

And was suddenly found murdered.

In Stockholm.

* * *

Bertil Magnuson had sunk down on a cane armchair in one
of the sitting areas in the Sturebadet spa. He had just spent
twenty minutes in the steam room and felt nice and tender.
On the glass table beside him lay a pile of newspapers. All
with some amount, large or small, of coverage on the Nils
Wendt murder. Bertil scrutinized every article, to see if there
was any mention at all in any paper about where Wendt had
been living before he turned up in Stockholm. But he couldn't
find anything. Not even any speculation. What Wendt had
done between 1984 and today was still unknown. Nobody
knew where he had been living.

Bertil ran his hands along his towelling dressing gown. He had a glass of cold mineral water by his side, misted up, he was pondering his situation. He had just got rid of an acute three-day problem and got a first of July problem instead. A bit more time. But still. Time went quickly when the trigger was cocked.

Suddenly, Erik Grandén came in, he too was wearing a white towelling dressing gown.

'Hi Bertil. I heard that you'd be here.'

'Are you going to the sauna?'

Grandén looked around and could see that they were alone. Even so, he lowered his well modulated voice.

'I read about Nils.'

'Yes.'

'Murdered?'

'Evidently.'

Grandén sank down on the cane armchair next to Bertil. Even sitting, he was almost a head taller. He looked down at Bertil.

'But isn't it extremely, how should I say, unpleasant?'

'For whom?'

'For whom? What do you mean?'

'You have hardly missed him, surely?'

'No, but we were old friends after all, a long time ago, one for all.'

'That was a very long time ago, Erik.'

'Yes indeed, but nevertheless? Don't you feel anything?'

'Oh yes.'

But not in the way you think, ran through Bertil's mind.

'And why was he suddenly here? In Stockholm?' said Grandén.

'No idea.'

'Could it have anything to do with us? With the company?'

'Why should it?'

'I don't know, but in my present situation it would be extremely unsuitable if people started digging into the past.'

'And find out that you were on the board?'

'Any of my association with MWM. Even though there is nothing at all amiss, it can happen so easily that one thing can spill over into another.'

'I don't think this is going to spill onto you, Erik.'

'Nice to hear.'

Grandén got up, took off his towelling dress gown and exposed a trim body which was almost as white as the towelling. At the base of his spine he had a very small blue-yellow tattoo.

'What's that?' Bertil asked.

'A budgerigar. Jussi. He flew away when I was seven. I'm going to the steam room now.'

'Do that.'

Grandén vanished in the direction of the steam room. When the door closed behind him, Bertil's mobile rang.

It was Mette Olsäter.

* * *

Stilton had struggled to ignore it. For quite a long time. But after yet another night of throbbing internal pains he had given up and made his way to Pelarbacken. A clinic run by Christian lay workers from Ersta Diakoni, and which was focused on the homeless.

There they established that Stilton was suffering from a few different things. However nothing so serious that it required a hospital bed. They weren't keen on taking up a bed unless it was absolutely necessary. His inner organs hadn't been damaged. The outer wounds were patched up. It was with a certain degree of surprise that the young doctor poked – with a rather long instrument – in the weird yellowy-brown goo that was smeared over most of the wounds.

'What is this?'

'Healing resin.'

'Resin?'

'Yes.'

'Right, yes? Remarkable.'

'What?'

'Well, there has been a decidedly rapid healing of the edges of the wounds.'

'Yes?'

What did he think? That only doctors knew anything about medicines?

'Can you buy this anywhere?'

'No.'

Stilton got a new and clean bandage for his head. He left the clinic with a prescription that he didn't intend going to the chemist's with. Out on the street, the images came back into his head. The images of bleeding cheered-on boys fighting in cages. Revolting images. He pushed the images out of his mind and thought about Mink. That little Jack-of-all-trades had actually saved his life. More or less. If he had been left lying on the ground out in Årsta the rest of the night he would have been really deep in the shit. Mink got him home, put the ointment on his wounds and covered him with a blanket.

Hope he got a lift home, Stilton thought.

'Did he get a lift home?'

'Who?'

'Mink? The other night?'

Olivia had phoned when Stilton was standing in the Stockholm City Mission centre on Fleminggatan. He was trying on some new clothes. The old ones were rather covered in blood.

'No,' she said.

'Why not?'

'How are you feeling?'

'Why didn't he get a lift?'

'He wanted to walk.'

Nonsense, Stilton thought. More likely they had fallen out as soon as they left the caravan. He knew what Mink could be like, and the little he had seen of Rönning told him that it wasn't exactly her thing.

'What do you want?' he asked. 'I thought we were done with each other.'

'Do you remember when I told you in the caravan about when I was on Nordkoster, about a man who turned up there, first up by the beach and then at my cabin?'

'Yes. And?'

Olivia told of what she had seen on a news site just ten minutes earlier. Something that had really given her quite a jolt. When she had finished, Stilton said:

'You must tell that to the person in charge of the investigation.'

* * *

The person who was in charge of the investigation sat opposite the murdered man Nils Wendt's former partner Bertil Magnuson in the lobby on Sveavägen, on the second floor. Magnuson had given her ten minutes. Then he was forced to rush to a meeting, he claimed. Mette Olsäter jumped straight in.

'Have you and Wendt had any contact recently?'

'No. Should we have?'

'He has evidently been in Stockholm and you share a past. Magnuson Wendt Mining.'

'We haven't had any contact. I am extremely shocked, as you will understand, all these years I've thought that he... well...'

'He?'

'Well all sorts of ideas have crossed my mind, that he killed himself, or something happened to him, mugged perhaps, or he just disappeared.'

'Yes.'

'Do you know why he suddenly turned up?'

'No. Do you?'

'No.'

Mette observed the man in front of her. A secretary looked out and gave a little wave to Magnuson. He made his apologies and explained that, when he had time, he would of course help in every way that he could.

'We did, after all, like you said, share a past.'

* * *

From the information office at the police headquarters, Olivia found out who was in charge of the investigation of the murder of Nils Wendt. When she tried to get in touch with Mette Olsäter, she met with a brick wall. No telephone numbers could be given to her. There was, however, a number and an office you could contact if you had any tips.

Olivia wasn't interested in that. She phoned Stilton again.

'I can't get hold of the person in charge of the investigation.'

'Who is it?'

'Mette Olsäter.'

'Oh, I see.'

Stilton pondered a few seconds. He knew that what Olivia wanted to say was something that Mette Olsäter needed to know. As soon as possible.

'Where are you now?' he said.

'At home.'

'Pick me up at Kammakargatan 46 in two hours.'

'I haven't got a car.'

'What?'

'It's… there's something wrong with the engine.'

'OK, meet me at the terminal for the Värmdö buses then, down at Slussen.'

It was already beginning to get a bit dark when they got off the 448 bus and started to walk through a district with lovely old houses. The sign at the bus stop had said Fösabacken. This was not an area that Olivia was familiar with at all.

'In here.'

Stilton nodded with his bandaged head. They walked down a little road with bushes on either side, a road leading down to the sea approach to Stockholm. Suddenly Stilton stopped beside a privet hedge.

'It's there.'

He pointed across the road towards a large old house which had seen better days. It was painted yellow and green. Olivia looked at the house.

'Does she live there?'

'Yes, as far as I know.'

Olivia was slightly confounded. A victim of her own stereo-type understanding of how and where senior detective chief inspectors should live. Anywhere but in a dilapidated old mansion like this. Stilton looked at her.

'Aren't you going to go in then?'

'Aren't you coming too?'

'No.'

Stilton wasn't going with her. Not all the way. Olivia would have to do this herself.

'I'll wait here.'

Why, that he wasn't going to explain to her.

Olivia took a few steps up to the big wooden gate and went in. Somewhat surprised, she passed all manner of weird small constructions in the large plot. They looked like play-houses that had run wild, with ropes hanging from them and large-meshed nets and plank paths. And all sorts of coloured lamps here and there. From a circus that had closed down? she wondered. Beside a large children's swing, a couple of half-naked children played. Neither of them reacted to Olivia's presence. Rather hesitantly she climbed the old fan-shaped wooden steps up to the front door, and rang the bell.

There was a slight delay. It was a large house. In the end, Mette Olsäter opened the door. She had been working since early morning, got the investigation into Wendt's murder up and running and divided the group so that they could work day and night. She would do the night shift tomorrow. Now she looked out through the door with a dismayed expression on her face. It took a few seconds, before she could get everything in place in her head. The young girl who had asked about Tom. Olivia Rönning? That's it, and what did she want now? Asking about Tom again?

'Hello?' she said.

'Hello, they wouldn't give me your phone number at the police headquarters so I asked Tom Stilton and he took me here and…'

'Is Tom here?'

'Yes, he…'

When Olivia turned slightly out towards the road, Mette followed the turn. She caught a glimpse of a figure just down the road.

No more was necessary.

'Come in!'

With a couple of rapid steps she had passed Olivia. Her well-built body moved surprisingly quickly across the garden and out through the gate. Before Stilton had covered many metres she had caught up with him. Now she stood in front of him. Silent. Stilton looked away. He had a habit of doing that. Mette stayed where she was, like Vera used to. After a while she put an arm under Stilton's, turned him round and started to walk towards the gate again.

They walked along like an old couple. A tall bandaged man looking the worse for wear and a voluminous – to put it mildly – woman with a few drops of sweat on her upper lip. In through the gate. At that point Stilton stopped.

'Who's there?'

'Jimi's playing computer games with the kids, they're upstairs, Jolene's asleep. Mårten's in the kitchen.'

Olivia had heeded Mette's words and stepped inside. Into the hall, or whatever one could call it. A fairly cluttered area where she had to step over this and that to make her way to the room where the light was on. What sort of room it was, Olivia found it hard to think of the correct word. But it was large. She was after all in what had once been quite a stylish mansion. With beautiful wooden panelling on the walls and ceilings with white stucco details and strange objects here and there.

They weren't strange to the people who had collected them, during innumerable journeys around the world. Philippine bridal crowns decorated with tiny feather-clad monkey skulls. Multi-coloured textiles from the ghettos of Cape Town. Large tubes with ground bones which sounded like spirit voices when you lifted them. Objects that one of them had taken a fancy to and thought there would be room for in the huge house. It didn't really matter where. Here, for example, in this room.

Olivia gaped at it all.

Is this how people lived? Could you live like this? The distance to her parents' prim terraced house in sober white out in Rotebro must be a couple of light years, at least.

She carefully navigated through the room and heard a light clatter from further in. She made her way towards the clatter, via a couple of other exotically furnished rooms which reinforced Olivia's feeling of… well, she didn't really know what. But there was something in the room which embraced her. Which combined the fascination with something else that she was unable to put into words.

She ended up in the kitchen.

An enormous kitchen, by her standards. Filled with strong aromas that coiled their way into her nostrils. Beside a modern gas cooker stood a plump man with straggly grey hair and an apron with a chequered pattern. He was sixty-seven and just turned towards her.

'Hello! And who are you?'

'Olivia Rönning. Mette said I should go in, she is…'

'Welcome! I'm Mårten. We're just about to eat, are you hungry?'

Mette closed the front door behind Stilton and then went ahead of him through the hall. Stilton hesitated a moment or two. There was a large gilt-framed mirror on the wall. He happened to look into it and gave a start. He hadn't seen his face for almost four years. He never looked in shop windows, in toilets he always avoided the mirrors. He didn't want to see himself. Now he couldn't avoid it. He studied his face in the mirror. It wasn't his.

'Tom.'

Mette stood further down the hall and looked at him.

'Shall we go in?'

'Smells good, doesn't it?'

Mårten pointed with a ladle towards a large casserole dish on the cooker. Olivia was standing next to him.

'Yes, what is it?'

'Well now. I was aiming for soup, but I'm not sure, we'll have to taste it.'

Then Mette and Stilton walked in. It took Mårten a few seconds, seconds that Stilton registered, but then he smiled.

'Hello Tom.'

Stilton nodded.

'Would you like something to eat?'

'No.'

Mette was fully aware of the extremely delicate situation. She knew that Tom could leave the house the very second that things tensed up, so she quickly turned to Olivia.

'You wanted to see me?'

'Yes.'

'She's Olivia Rönning,' said Mårten.

'I know, we've met.'

Mette turned towards Olivia.

'Arne's daughter, aren't you?'

Olivia nodded.

'Is it about him?'

'No, it's about that Nils Wendt, who was found murdered yesterday. I've met him.'

Mette gave a start.

'Where? When?'

'On Nordkoster, last week.'

Olivia quickly told about her meeting with the man on Nordkoster. She had recognised him from the portrait of Nils Wendt that a newspaper had published today. Admittedly a very old portrait, but sufficiently similar for Olivia to be quite certain who she had seen.

'It must have been him. He said his name was Dan Nilsson,' she said.

Mette was absolutely certain, for a very concrete reason.

'He used the same name when he rented his car here.'

'Oh really? But what was he doing there? On Nordkoster? Up by the Hasslevikarna coves?'

'I don't know, but he had links to the island, he had a summer cottage there many years ago, before he disappeared.'

'When did he disappear?'

'In the mid-Eighties,' said Mette.

'Then it must be him that she talked about.'

'Who?'

270

'A woman that I rented a cabin from, Betty Nordeman, she talked about somebody who disappeared and perhaps was murdered and who knew that person who was in the papers today, Magnuson?'

'Bertil Magnuson. They were business partners, and they had summer houses on the island, both of them.'

On the surface, Mette was fully focused on Olivia Rönning and her information, but out of the corner of her eye she was checking every detail of Tom. His face, his eyes, his body language. He was still sitting there. She had told Jimi and the grandchildren not to come down, and hoped for God's sake that Mårten had enough subtle intuition and wouldn't suddenly think of bringing Tom into the conversation.

'But you, Tom, how did you and Olivia come into contact with each other?'

That was Mårten. Suddenly. What had happened to the subtle intuition? A sudden silence around the table. Mette avoided looking at Tom so as not to put any pressure on him.

'We met in a dustbin room,' said Olivia.

Her voice was steady and distinct. It was up to each of them to decide whether it was meant as a humorous comment or an intuitive way of saving Stilton. Or quiet simply as actual information. Mårten chose that interpretation.

'A dustbin room? What were you doing there?'

'I had asked her to come.'

Stilton looked Mårten straight in the eye when he said that.

'Oh Jesus. Do you live in a dustbin room?'

'No, in a caravan. How's Kerouac?'

The iron cramp suddenly loosened its grip in Mette's chest.

'Not too bad, I think he has arthritis.'

'Why?'

'Because he has difficulty moving his legs.'

Olivia looked from Stilton to Mårten.

'Who's Kerouac?'

'It's my mate,' said Mårten.

'It's a spider.'

Stilton smiled when he said that, at the same time that his eyes met Mette's gaze, and what passed between them during a few endless seconds wiped away years of despair in Mette.

Tom was communicating again.

'But there was something else.'

Olivia turned towards Mette while Mårten got up and started to hand out some funny-looking plates.

'What?'

'He had a suitcase with him on the beach, one of those with wheels that you can pull behind you, and he had it with him at the cabin too. Then when I woke up and peeped out it lay there below the steps, and then I opened it and it was completely empty.'

Mette had now reached out and picked up a little notebook and she wrote a few words in it. Two of them were 'Empty suitcase?'

'Do you think that Wendt could have been involved in that murder on the beach, of that woman? 1987?' said Olivia.

'Hardly, he disappeared three years before the murder took place.'

Mette pushed the notebook away.

'But he could of course have returned to the island with-out anybody knowing about it, and then disappeared again? Couldn't he?'

Both Mette and Stilton smiled a little. One of them inwardly and the other more obviously. That was Mette.

'You've learnt something at the breakfast table.'

Olivia, too, smiled a little and looked down at what Mårten possibly thought was soup. It looked good. Everybody tucked in, although Stilton only took one spoonful while the others took five. His stomach was still suffering the after-effects of the beating. Mette hadn't yet dared ask about the bandage around his head.

They ate.

The soup contained meat and vegetables and strong spices and they drank some red wine with it, while Mette told about Wendt's earlier life. How he and Bertil Magnuson had started the then Magnuson Wendt Mining company and quickly become successful internationally.

'By dealing with a shitload of dictators in Africa to exploit their natural resources! They didn't give a fuck about apartheid and Mobutu and you name it!'

Mårten had suddenly exploded. He hated both the old and the new MWM. He had spent a large part of his left-radical years demonstrating and printing pamphlets about the company's ruthless exploitation of impoverished countries and the environmental pollution that resulted.

'The bastards!'

'Mårten.'

Mette laid a hand on her indignant husband's arm. He was after all of an age when a stroke could result from the next outburst. Mårten shrugged his shoulders slightly and looked at Olivia.

'Do you want to have a look at Kerouac?'

Olivia looked at Mette and Stilton out of the corner of her eye but didn't get much support. Mårten was already on his way out of the kitchen. She got up and followed him. When Mårten turned round in the door to see if Olivia was with him, he got a special look from Mette.

He left the room.

Stilton knew exactly what it meant. The look. He nodded towards the cellar under the kitchen floor.

'Does he still smoke?'

'No.'

Mette's answer was so quick and short that Stilton understood. End of that. He couldn't care less. He never had done. He knew that Mårten used to smoke a joint now and then down in his music room. And Mette knew that he knew and that they were the only people in the world who knew. Apart from the joint-smoker himself.

And thus it would remain.

Mette and Stilton looked at each other. After a few seconds Stilton felt he must ask what he had wanted to ask ever since she caught up with him out on the road.

'How are things with Abbas?'

'Fine. He misses you.'

Silence again. Stilton traced the edge of his water glass with a finger. He had said no to wine. Now he was thinking about Abbas and he found it rather painful.

'You can say hello from me,' he said.

'Yes, I will.'

And then Mette dared ask.

'What have you done to your head?'

She nodded towards Stilton's bandage and he didn't feel like evading the issue so he told her about the beating-up in Årsta.

'Unconscious?'

And about the cage fighting.

'Children fighting in cages!'

And about his private hunt for the people who murdered Vera Larsson and their link with the cage fighting. When he had finished, Mette was noticeably agitated.

'But that's just dreadful! We must put a stop to it! Have you told the people in charge of the case?'

'Rune Forss?'

'Yes.'

They looked at each other for a few seconds.

'But for Christ's sake, Tom, that was more than six years ago.'

'Do you think I've forgotten?'

'No, I don't think that, or I don't know, but if you want to help us find the people who killed the woman in the caravan then I think you must swallow that and talk to Forss! Now! There are children getting hurt! Otherwise I'll do it!'

Stilton didn't answer. He could, however, hear how heavy bass tones from the cellar were beginning to come up through the kitchen floor.

* * *

Linn sat alone down in the beautiful yacht. A Bavaria 31 Cruiser. It was moored at their private jetty in the sound quite near the Stocksund Bridge. She liked sitting there in the evenings. The boat rocking a little with the waves, and she could look out over the water. On the other side lay Bockholmen with its lovely old inn. On the right she could see the cars driving over the bridge. A bit further up she saw the Cedergren Tower sticking up above the trees and just now she saw Bertil up by the house, on his way down to the jetty with a little glass in his hand. With something brown in it.

Good.

'Have you eaten?' she asked.

'Yes.'

Bertil sat down on a wooden bollard next to the yacht. He sipped his drink and looked at Linn.

'I am sorry.'

'For?'

'A bit of everything, I have been rather absent lately…'

'Yes. Is your bladder better?'

Bladder? He hadn't felt anything down there for a while…

'It seems to have settled down,' he said.

'That's good. Have you heard anything about Nils' murder?'

'No. Or rather, yes, the police were in touch.'

'With you?'

'Yes.'

'What did they want?'

'They wanted to know if Nils had been in touch with me.'

'Really? What… but he hadn't, surely?'

'No. I haven't heard a sound from him… since he walked out of the office in Kinshasa.'

'Twenty-seven years ago,' said Linn.

'Yes.'

'And now he's been murdered. Disappeared for twenty-seven years and then suddenly murdered, here, in Stockholm. It is strange, isn't it?'

'Unfathomable.'

'And where has he been all those years?'

'Nobody knows.'

And if anybody did know, Bertil would have given his right hand to get in touch with them. That question had been at the top of his agenda for a long time. Where the hell had Wendt holed up? The tape was in some unknown location, which could be anywhere at all on earth. A rather large area to search.

Bertil leaned back slightly and downed his drink.

'Have you started smoking again?'

The question came out of the blue and Bertil had no time to duck.

'Yes.'

'Why?'

'Why not?'

Linn immediately noticed the piercing undertone. He was ready to attack if she were to go on. She dropped it.

Perhaps he had been more affected by the murder of Nils than he wanted to show.

* * *

'There he is!'

Mårten pointed at the whitewashed stone wall in the cellar. Olivia followed his finger and saw how a large cellar spider crawled out of a crack in the wall.

'Is that Kerouac?'

'Yes. A genuine cellar spider, not an ordinary house spider, he is eight years old.'

'Oh, right.'

Olivia looked at Kerouac's subcutaneous nerves which were vibrating slightly. The spider that might possibly be suffering from arthritis. She noticed how it moved rather carefully across the wall, with long black legs and a body that was just over one centimetre in diameter.

'He loves music, but he is fussy about it, it took me a few years to learn his taste, I'll show you!'

Mårten moved his finger along the other wall. It was covered from floor to ceiling with vinyl records, large and small. Mårten was an aficionado. A vinyl fan with one of Sweden's most original collections. Now he pulled out a 45-rpm by Little Gerhard, an old rock king from a forgotten age, and placed the B-side on a gramophone.

One of those with an arm and a needle.

It didn't take many chords before Kerouac had stopped his slow crawl across the wall. When Little Gerhard's voice reached full volume, the spider changed direction and crept towards the crack again.

'But now look at this!'

Mårten was like an enthralled child. He quickly pulled out a CD from the much smaller collection on the short wall. He lifted the needle off the vinyl record and pushed the CD into a modern player.

'Watch this now! And listen!'

It was Gram Parsons. A country guy who had left some immortal traces behind him when he died from an overdose.

Now the sound of 'Return of the Grievous Angel' flowed out of Mårten's well-rigged stereo system. Olivia stared at Kerouac. Suddenly the spider had stopped, some way away from the crack. It twisted its fat black body almost 180 degrees and started to move out across the wall again.

'Pretty obvious, isn't it?'

Mårten looked at Olivia and smiled. She wasn't really sure whether she had ended up in a lunatic asylum or in Detective Chief Inspector Mette Olsäter's house. She nodded and asked if Mårten was a potter.

'No, that's Mette's.'

Olivia had nodded towards the door where they had just passed a room with a large kiln. She turned towards Mårten.

'And what do you do then? What area do you work in?'

'I'm a pensioner.'

'Yes, right, and before you became a pensioner?'

Stilton and Mette stood in the hall when Mårten and Olivia came up from the cellar. Mette glanced at them, leaned a little towards Stilton and lowered her voice.

'You know you've always got a place to sleep here.'

'Thanks.'

'And think about what I said.'

'About?'

'Rune Forss. You or me.'

Stilton didn't answer her. Mårten and Olivia came up. Stilton nodded goodbye to Mårten and went out through the front door. Mette gave Olivia a small hug and whispered:

'Thanks for bringing Tom with you.'

'It was him who brought me.'

'Without you, he would never have come here.'

Olivia smiled a little. Mette gave her her card, with her phone number. Olivia thanked her and followed after Stilton.

When Mette had closed the door, she turned and looked at Mårten. He pulled her towards him. He knew exactly how tense the situation had been. He stroked her hair.

'Tom was communicating,' he said.

'Yes.'

Both sat in silence on the bus into the city. Occupied with their own thoughts. Stilton mainly thinking about the meeting with the Olsäters. It was the first time he had met them for almost four years. He was amazed at how easy it had been. How little they had needed to say. How quickly it felt natural.

The next step was Abbas.

Then he thought about that face in the mirror in the hall. That wasn't his. That had been a shock.

Olivia thought about the dilapidated mansion.

In the cellar. About Kerouac. You must be a bit weird if you socialise with a spider? Yes, she thought, you must. Definitely. Or perhaps more of an original? Mårten was a man with a fascinating background, she thought. Down in the cellar he had told her a little about it. He had been a child psychologist before he retired. For many years he had struggled hard to introduce new ideas in Sweden, and had partly succeeded. For a long period he had also worked with Skå-Gustav Jonsson and participated in a number of projects for vulnerable children. And been a political left-wing activist.

She liked Mårten.

And Mette.

And their remarkable, cosy house.

'You fell out with Mink,' Stilton suddenly said.

'Fell out…' Olivia looked out through the bus window. 'He made a pass at me,' she said.

Stilton nodded slightly.

'He suffers from inferio-mega,' he said.

'What's that?'

279

'Megalomania undermined by an inferiority complex. God on clay feet.'

'OK. I think he's creepy.'

Stilton gave a little smile.

They separated at the Slussen bus terminal. Olivia was going to walk home to Skånegatan. Stilton was going to the Katarina garage.

'Aren't you going to the caravan?'

'No.'

'What are you going to do there? At Kararina garage?'

Stilton didn't answer.

'I can walk that way, via Mosebacke.'

Stilton had to put up with that. During the short walk to the Katarina garage, Olivia spoke about her visit to Jackie Berglund's boutique and the bastards in the lift. She deliberately didn't mention the cat.

When she had finished, Stilton looked her straight in the eye.

'Are you going to drop that now?'

'Yes.'

'Good.'

For ten seconds. Then she couldn't help asking.

'What made you leave the police force? Was it connected with the death of Jill Engberg?'

'No.'

They stopped beside the wooden steps up to Mosebacke. Suddenly Stilton went off. Towards the steps on the other side of the garage. The stone steps.

Olivia watched him go.

The MHP-team sat in a partially blacked-out room on Bergsgatan and watched a film that had been downloaded from Trashkick. A film in which Tom Stilton had his clothes ripped off until he was naked, was sprayed across his back, beaten up and thrown against a rock face. It was decidedly quiet in the room when the film ended. Everyone knew who Stilton was. Or had been. Now they saw a beaten-up wreck. Forss turned a light on and broke the silence.

'That was roughly what one might expect,' he said.

'What?'

Klinga looked at Forss.

'Stilton lost it completely in 2005, broke down in the middle of an investigation, about Jill Engberg, a prossy. I had to take over the case. He just disappeared. Resigned and disappeared. And now he has ended up there.'

Forss nodded towards the screen, got up and took his jacket off the hook.

'But we ought to interrogate him, surely?' said Klinga. 'He has evidently been badly beaten up too.'

'Absolutely. When we find him. See you tomorrow.'

* * *

Mårten and Mette had gone to bed. Their son Jimi could take care of the dishes. They were both exhausted and they turned the bedside lamps off straight away, but didn't fall asleep. Mårten turned slightly towards Mette.

'You didn't think I was very subtle, did you?'

'No.'

'On the contrary, I was reading Tom all the time, when you and Olivia were talking about Koster, he was there, present, he listened, took part, but I saw that he'd never break into the conversation by himself, so I invited him in.'

'You took a risk.'

'No.'

Mette smiled a little and kissed Mårten on the neck, gently. Mårten regretted that he hadn't swallowed a Viagra a couple of hours ago. They each turned in a different direction.

He thought about sex.

She thought about an empty suitcase on Nordkoster.

* * *

Olivia thought about her cat. She lay in bed and missed the warm animal by her feet. His purring, his bumping against her legs. The white mask on the wall looked down at her. The moonlight glistened in the white teeth. Now it's just you and me, she thought, and you're a bloody wooden mask! Olivia jumped out of bed, lifted down the wooden mask, threw it in under her bed and crept in under the covers again. Voodoo? she suddenly thought. Now he's lying under the bed and staring up and cooking up something nasty. But voodoo is Haitian, the mask is from Africa and Elvis is dead.

And Kerouac is a fucking spider!

14

Joyously happy! I'm joyously happy!

Not.

Olivia stood naked in front of the bathroom mirror and studied her young aged face. Twenty-three yesterday and at least fifty today, she thought. Swollen and patchy looking, with eyes marbled with thin red streaks. She wrapped herself in her white dressing gown and felt how her breasts were tender and her tummy was tight. That's just all I need, she thought, and crawled into bed again.

* * *

Up on the roof of one of the police buildings on Bergsgatan there are a number of exercise areas, cages shaped like wedges of cake. That's where remand prisoners are taken to get some fresh air. This particular morning they were all empty, except one. A little grey sparrow sat on the cement floor. In comparison there was all the more activity in C-building.

'The suitcase was empty?'

'Yes,' said Mette.

'Where is it now?'

'She gave it to the guy who runs the cabin camp, Axel Nordeman.'

Mette sat right at the back of the room. Various members of her team were reporting back. The tone in the room was low-key but intense. The information about the suitcase was interesting. Everything about Nils Wendt's visit to Nordkoster was interesting. Why was he there? Who did he meet? Why did he leave an empty suitcase behind? Mette had sent a couple of police officers to the island before she went to bed the previous evening. They would get hold of the suitcase and knock on some doors.

'Do we know when he came to Nordkoster?' Lisa Hedqvist wondered.

'Not yet, we'll get a report from the guys there sometime today. But we do know where Olivia saw him the first time, up there near the Hasslevikarna coves on the north side of the island, she didn't know exactly when, she had got lost herself, but she reckoned it was sometime around nine in the evening.'

'Then he visited her in her cabin about an hour later, is that right?'

'More like a couple of hours, sometime before midnight,' Mette said. 'What we know more precisely is that he took a boat taxi from the West Jetty at almost exactly midnight and was taken to Strömstad. That's where the tracks end.'

'Not quite.'

Bosse Thyrén got up. He had done a thorough job since Mette phoned him the evening before.

'Dan Nilsson booked a ticket for the 04.35 train from Strömstad on Monday morning, then he took the express from Göteborg at 07.45 and arrived at the Central Station in Stockholm at 10.50. I've checked the railway booking system. At Central he rented a car from Avis at about a quarter past eleven and just before twelve he checked in at the Hotel Oden on Karlbergsvägen. As Dan Nilsson. The technicians are going through the room there.'

'Excellent, Bosse.'

Mette turned round.

'Have we heard any more about his mobile?'

'No, but we have had a report from the pathologist. The blood on the granite rocks near the murder scene did come from Nils Wendt. There were fragments of skin too. The blood on the ground near the tyre tracks came from him too.'

'So the damage to his skull can thus be linked to the granite rocks?'

'It seems so.'

'But did that kill him? Or did he drown?'

Lisa looked down at the pathologist's report.

'He was alive when the car rolled into the water. Presumably unconscious. He died from drowning.'

'OK, so we know that.'

Mette got up.

'Well done, everybody… now we must focus on determining his movements from when he checked in at the hotel to the time the body was discovered. He must have been seen on more occasions than when he checked in, he must have eaten at a restaurant somewhere, perhaps used the same bank card as when he rented the car, he might have used the hotel's phone…'

'No he didn't, I've checked that,' said Lisa.

'Good.'

Mette walked towards the door. Everyone in the room started moving.

* * *

Just a few buildings away in the same block, sat Rune Forss in a similar room with Janne Klinga. The MHP investigation had been upgraded to a murder enquiry on account of Vera Larsson. The team had been reinforced with a couple of officers and some extra resources had been put at Forss' disposal.

He had sent some of his team out into the city and talked with some of the homeless people who had been beaten up before Vera Larsson was murdered. One of them was still in hospital, a big northerner who couldn't remember anything of what happened. They couldn't do much more at present.

In Forss' opinion.

He sat and browsed through *Strike*, a bowling magazine; Klinga was going through the technical report from the caravan.

'We'll see if that film leads to anything,' said Klinga.

'When they're shagging in the caravan?'

'Yes.'

The man who had engaged in sexual intercourse with Vera Larsson was still unidentified. Suddenly there was a knock on the door.

'Come in!'

Stilton stepped in with a bandage round his head. Forss lowered his magazine and looked at him. Stilton kept his eyes on Klinga.

'Hello, I'm Tom Stilton.'

'Hello.'

Janne Klinga stepped forward and held out his hand.

'Janne Klinga,' he said as they shook hands.

'So you're homeless nowadays?' said Forss.

Stilton didn't react. He had prepared himself fairly well, mentally. He knew it would be like this. It didn't bother him. He looked at Janne Klinga.

'Are you in charge of the investigation into Vera Larsson's murder?'

'No, it's…'

'Do you know who beat you up?' Forss asked.

He looked at Stilton, who still kept his gaze fastened on Janne Klinga.

'I believe Vera Larsson was murdered by a couple of Kid Fighters,' said Stilton.

There was silence in the room for a few moments.

'Kid Fighters,' said Klinga.

Stilton told them what he knew. About cage fighting, exactly where it took place, who took part in it and who he thought arranged it.

And which symbols some of them had tattooed on their arms.

'Two letters with a ring round them, KF, you can catch a glimpse on one of the films on Trashkick. Have you seen that too?' he asked.

'No.'

Klinga glanced at Forss.

'KF stands for Kid Fighters,' said Stilton.

He started to walk towards the door.

'How did you find out all this?' said Klinga.

'The tip came from a young boy in Flemingsberg, Acke Andersson.'

He left the room without even once having looked at Rune Forss.

A few moments later, Forss and Klinga were on their way to the staff canteen. Forss was extremely sceptical about Stilton's information.

'Cage fighting? Kids fighting in cages? Here? In Sweden? We'd have bloody well heard about it. It sounds totally daft.'

Klinga didn't answer. Forss implied that Stilton might have been a victim of his own psychoses again and hallucinated a completely implausible story.

'Or what do you think? "Kid Fighters"? Could there be anything in it?'

'Don't know,' said Klinga.

He wasn't as convinced as to the implausibility of Stilton's information. He decided to look through the downloaded Trashkick films to see if he could find that tattoo.

Later, on his own.

* * *

Ovette Andersson was walking on her own along Karlavägen. Black stiletto heels, a tight black skirt and short leather jacket. She had just finished with a customer in a private garage on Banérgatan and been dropped off where she had been picked up. This wasn't her usual patch. But there had been rumours of plain-clothes police on Mäster Samuelsgatan so she had changed venues.

She re-applied her lipstick and turned down Sibyllegatan, on her way to the underground station. Suddenly she caught sight of a familiar face in a shop on the other side of the street.

In Weird & Wow.

Ovette came to a halt.

So that was what it looked like, her shop. Her posh façade outwards. A huge step from sucking someone off with coke running out of her nose, she thought. It was the first time she had passed Jackie Berglund's boutique. This wasn't an area she hung around in, not nowadays at any rate. There had been a time when Ovette actually was pretty much at home in Östermalm, even though it might be hard to believe now.

It was before Acke.

Weird & Wow, she thought. A clever name. But then of course she had always been smart. Jackie, smart and calculating. Ovette crossed the street and stopped in front of the shop window. She could see the charming woman inside again. That very same moment, Jackie turned round and looked Ovette right in the eye. Ovette returned the look without flinching. Once upon a time they had been workmates, escort girls in the same stable, Gold Card. Her and Jackie and Miriam Wixell, at the end of the Eighties. Miriam had stopped when there was talk of sexual services. Ovette and Jackie had kept on.

The money was good.

Jackie was the smart one of the three. The one who always took the chance to get to know the clientele they served. Ovette just hung along and snorted coke with her customers now and then. Without any ulterior motives. When Gold Card closed down, Jackie took over the business from Carl Videung and renamed it Red Velvet. An exclusive escort firm for a small closed world. Ovette followed along with Jackie to the new firm, worked a few years for her and then she got preggers.

With a customer.

That was not good.

Jackie demanded that she should have an abortion. Ovette refused. It was the first time she was pregnant and would probably be the last. She wanted the baby. It ended with Jackie throwing her out onto the street, literally. And there she had to support herself as best she could with a newborn baby.

Acke.

The son of a customer, only Ovette and Jackie knew who it was. Not even the customer knew.

Now they were standing there glaring at each other, straight through a shop window on Sibyllegatan. The street whore and the luxury prostitute. Finally, Jackie looked away.

Did she look a little bit afraid? Ovette wondered. She stayed where she was a few moments and saw Jackie was tidying things inside the shop, well aware of Ovette's presence outside.

She's afraid of me, Ovette thought. Because I know, and could make use of that knowledge. But I'd never do that because I'm not like you, Jackie Berglund. That's a difference between us. A difference that means that I'm on the street and you're there inside. But it's worth it. Ovette held her head rather high when she continued along towards the underground station.

Jackie tidied things in her boutique, a little maniacally. She was angry and upset. What was she doing here? Ovette Andersson? How the hell did she dare? Finally she turned back towards the window. Ovette had gone. Jackie thought about her. Ovette, the lively one, with the joyful eyes, in those days. She who had the idea of dying her hair blue and made Carl furious. She wasn't that smart, Ovette, or strategic. Which was a good thing, Jackie thought. Ovette knew too much about some customers. But she had kept her mouth shut.

All those years.

She must be afraid of me. She knows who I am and what happens if somebody threatens me. It must have been a coincidence that she walked past here.

Jackie continued to tidy in her boutique, and managed to suppress the unpleasant sight through the window. After a while she could just shrug her shoulders. A little scrubber from Kärrtorp landed with a son. What a comedown. When she could have had an abortion and worked her way up to a totally different level. Some people make daft decisions in life, she thought, while at the same time opening the door for one of her regular customers.

Linn Magnuson.

* * *

Rune Forss had just finished his second cup of coffee in the staff canteen when he caught sight of Mette Olsäter. She was coming towards his table. Janne Klinga had already left.

'Has Tom Stilton been in touch?' Mette asked when she came up to him.

'What do you mean in touch?

'Has he talked to you today?'

'Yes.'

'About cage fighting and Kid Fighters?'

'Yes?'

'Fine. Goodbye!'

Mette started to walk away.

'Olsäter!'

Mette turned round.

'Has he told you about that too?' said Forss.

'Yes. Yesterday.'

'Do you believe that stuff?'

'Why shouldn't I believe it?'

'Because he… You saw the condition he was in?'

'What has that got to do with the information?'

Mette and Forss looked at each other for a couple of seconds. Neither liked the other. When Forss lifted up his cup, Mette went off. Forss followed her with his gaze.

Was the National Crime Squad going to start interfering with his investigation?

* * *

Olivia half lay on her bed with the white laptop balanced on her outstretched legs and a tub of Ben & Jerry ice cream in her hand. She could knock back a whole tub at a single sitting and then skip dinner.

Not exactly low GI, but oh it tasted good!

She had spent a couple of hours on the Internet. Acquainting herself with Nils Wendt's earlier life. In those days he was an active company director and partner of Bertil Magnuson. She didn't think that this was breaking her promise of dropping the beach case. There was, after all, no connection between that and Wendt's murder. So for the time being she called it research. About Magnuson Wendt Mining, first and foremost, the company that later became Magnuson World Mining, and which already back then, before Wendt disappeared, had been severely criticized from various directions. Not least for their contacts with dictatorships.

Roughly what Mårten Olsäter had been on about when he had his little outburst at the dining table.

Her thoughts slipped over to the big old mansion out on Värmdö. She thought about the previous evening. It was an experience that rather shook her up. She recapitulated some of the conversation at the dining table in her head. And what had happened down in the cellar, or rather music room, with Mårten. She tried to grasp the hidden undertones that existed between Stilton and the Olsäters. It was difficult. If she got a chance, she would ask Mette or Mårten what sort of relationship they had. Stilton and the Olsäters. Ask them what they knew about what had happened to Stilton.

She was convinced that they knew more than her.

Suddenly she had found her way to a photo of a young Nils Wendt on the screen. Next to an equally young Bertil Magnuson. The photo was from an article from 1984. It described how the two men had just signed an agreement with President Mobutu in what was then called Zaire. The agreement would earn millions for MWM. They both smiled straight into the camera. At their feet lay a dead lion.

Magnuson was proudly holding a rifle in his hand.

Repulsive, Olivia thought. That very moment, her mobile rang. She checked the display, it wasn't a number she recognised.

'Olivia Rönning.'

'Hello, this is Ove Gardman, I've just checked my Swedish mobile and you have left a couple of messages, you wanted to get in touch with me?'

'Yes, absolutely!'

Olivia pushed her laptop to one side with fingers sticky from the ice cream, and sat up properly. Ove Gardman. The boy witness from Nordkoster!

'What's it about?' Gardman asked.

'Yes, well, it's about an old murder investigation that I'm studying, about what happened at the Hasslevikarna coves, 1987, that you witnessed, if I've correctly understood?'

'Yes, that's right. But how weird.'

'What?'

'No, I was talking about that only a week ago, or so, with a man in Mal Pais.'

'Where is that?'

'In Costa Rica.'

'And you were talking about the murder on the beach?'

'Yes?'

'Who were you talking to?'

'He was called Dan Nilsson.'

Olivia kicked away the last vestiges of her promise about the beach case and tried to keep her voice as stable as possible.

'Are you in Sweden now?'

'Yes.'

'When did you come home?' she said.

'Last night.'

'So you haven't heard about the murder of Nils Wendt?'

'Who's that?'

'Dan Nilsson. He used that name, but he was called Nils Wendt.'

'And he's been murdered?'

'Yes. Yesterday. Here in Stockholm.'

'Oh gosh.'

Olivia let Gardman digest that. She had more to ask, but it was Gardman himself who went on.

'Ugh, he did seem so... really unpleasant, I was at his place there and...'

At this point Gardman became silent and Olivia sneaked in.

'How did you meet?'

'Well, I'm a marine biologist and was in San José to help with a large water reservation that they're planning, out on the Nicoya peninsula, and then I travelled across to the ocean side for a couple of days to see the place and that was when I met him, he was a guide in a rainforest reservation just outside Mal Pais.'

'Did he live there, in Mal Pais?'

'Yep... we had some contact in the reservation there, I don't suppose he got many Swedish visitors and so he invited me to his home for dinner.'

'And that was when you started talking about the murder on Nordkoster?'

'Yes, we drank quite a lot of wine and then somehow we realised that we both had a connection with the island, he used to have a summer house here many years ago, and then I told him about that evening when I saw... er, that thing, up at Hasslevikarna.'

'And how did he react?'

'Well, he... it was a bit strange, because he became extremely interested, and wanted to hear lots of details, but I was only nine years old then and of course it's more than twenty years ago, so I didn't remember so very much.'

'But he was extremely curious?'

'In some way, yes. Then he left Mal Pais. I came back the next evening to fetch something, I'd forgotten my cap there, and he'd gone, a couple of young lads were running around playing with the cap, but they didn't know where he was, just that he had left, evidently.'

'He went to Nordkoster.'

'Did he?'

'Yes.'

'And now he's dead?'

'Unfortunately. May I ask you, where are you now?'

'At home. On Nordkoster.'

'You've no plans to come up to Stockholm?'

'Not just now.'

'OK.'

Olivia thanked Gardman. In fact for much more than he realised. She hung up and immediately keyed in Stilton's number.

Stilton was standing outside the Söderhallarna shopping centre selling *Situation Stockholm*. It wasn't going well. Two copies in one hour. Not because there weren't many people around but because virtually every one of them had a mobile pressed to their ear or a couple of wires hanging from their ears down to a mobile in their hand. We're probably in the process of mutating, Stilton thought. A new race. *Homo digitalis*, an online version of Neanderthal man. Then his own mobile rang.

'It's Olivia! D'you know what I've just found out about Nordkoster?'

'You weren't going to carry on with that? You said that you…'

'Nils Wendt met the boy witness Ove Gardman just over a week ago! In Costa Rica!'

Stilton fell silent. For quite a while.

'That is rather strange,' he finally said.

'Yes, isn't it?'

An excited Olivia quickly described how Gardman had told Wendt about the beach murder and how Wendt just after that had left and gone home to Sweden. To Nordkoster. After having kept away more than twenty-seven years.

'Why did he do that?' she said.

Why did Gardman's story about the beach murder trigger that reaction from Wendt? After all, he disappeared three years before the murder took place. Did he have some other connection with the woman on the beach? She was probably of Latin American extraction?

'Olivia…' Stilton attempted.

'Had they met in Costa Rica? Had she been sent to Nordkoster to fetch something that Wendt had hidden in his summer house?'

'Olivia!'

'Was she tortured in the water to confess what she was looking for? By people who had been tipped off that she would turn up and had followed her? Had she…'

'Olivia!'

'Yes?'

Stilton had tired of Olivia's conspiracy theories.

'You must talk to Mette again.'

'OK? Sure, absolutely!'

'And stick to facts. To Gardman and Wendt. She can do the rest herself.'

'OK. Are you coming along?'

He would go along. Besides, he had taken off his bandage and put a big plaster on the back of his head. A bit more discreet. They would go to a restaurant. Olivia had got hold of Mette who was just going to her car. Mårten and Jolene were at some dance performance or other in the city and would come home late. She herself would stop at a little restaurant in Saltsjö-Duvnäs and have a quick dinner.

'Stazione,' Mette said.

'Where is it?'

'In a red station building, the station's called Saltsjö-Duvnäs, on the Saltsjö local line.'

Now they were sitting there, in the evening sun, on a wooden platform at the back of the beautiful station building, at a little round table just a couple of metres from the trains that came and went right in front of them. A strangely continental atmosphere. The restaurant was a family place, enormously popular with the locals, good food and lots of guests, which meant they had been shown to a table out here on the platform side. Fine with them. It suited their purpose perfectly. There was nobody sitting close to them who could hear. Especially not when Mette noticeably raised her voice a couple of times.

'In Costa Rica?'

At last she had the answer to what she had spent quite a lot of time on twenty-seven years ago. At last she knew where Nils Wendt had hidden all those years.

'In Mal Pais,' said Olivia, 'on the Nicoya peninsula.'

'Incredible!'

Olivia was rather proud of generating such a reaction from the hardened detective. She looked very pleased when Mette immediately phoned Lisa Hedqvist and asked her to contact Ove Gardman and question him about Costa Rica. The information about where Wendt had been hanging out was of far more interest to Mette than his possible connection with the beach case. Admittedly, the period for prosecution hadn't actually expired yet, but she had a decidedly more topical murder investigation to take care of. Besides, she felt that the beach case was still Tom's.

She turned her mobile off and looked at Stilton.

'We need to make a visit.'

'Mal Pais?'

'Yes. Wendt's home. There could be material there which could help us in the investigation, perhaps a motive for the murder, perhaps an explanation for why he disappeared. But it can be rather awkward.'

'Why?' Olivia wondered.

'Because I don't feel comfortable with the Costa Rican police, their efficiency is not exactly a hundred per cent, a lot of bureaucracy.'

'So?'

Olivia saw how Mette and Stilton exchanged a glance which very quickly turned into a consensus.

Then they asked for the bill.

It wasn't often that Mette had cause to visit Casino Cosmopol. The big woman attracted quite a few glances when she strode into one of the gambling rooms. Above all from Abbas. He had clocked her already in the door. It only needed a quick look between them and he understood that it was soon time for another croupier to take over.

Stilton and Olivia stood leaning against Mette's car not far from the casino. On the way in from Stazione, Olivia had been given a short description of the person they were about to contact. Abbas el Fassi. A former bag-seller, now a croupier with a good reputation. He had done some undercover missions for both Mette and Stilton over the years.

Which had worked better and better each time and convinced them both that Abbas could be relied upon one hundred per cent when it came to tasks that needed to be done a little on the side.

Like this one.

Where they didn't want to involve the local police and have to plough through their bureaucracy to get the permission that would be necessary to do this the official way.

So it would have to be the other way.

The Abbas way.

Olivia looked at Stilton.

'Always?'

Stilton had just told her a little about Abbas. About his past. Without going into details. Above all not about what led to Abbas being pulled up out of a semi-criminal swamp with the help of Stilton and finding himself under probation in Mette and Mårten's home. Where he ended up being regarded as one of the family. Largely thanks to Jolene. She was seven years old when Abbas made his appearance, and it was her who eventually broke through Abbas' extremely hard outer shield and got him to dare. Both to accept the family's care and love, and to express his own. A rather enormous step for an orphan boy from Marseilles. Still to this day, Abbas was regarded as a member of the Olsäter family.

And he himself watched over Jolene like a hawk.

And carried a knife.

'Always,' said Stilton.

He had rounded off by implying that Abbas was extremely fond of knives. He always carried a most special knife on him that he had made himself.

'But what if he loses it?'

'He has five.'

Mette and Abbas came out of the casino and headed for the car. Stilton had prepared himself for the meeting with Abbas. It was quite a long time since they last met. Under circumstances that Stilton didn't like to have to think about.

Now they met again.

But it went as it often did with Abbas. A couple of quick looks, a nod, and it was all done. When Abbas slipped into the seat next to Mette, Stilton felt how he had missed him.

Mette had suggested that they should drive to Abbas's home. On Dalagatan. Without thinking about the roadworks for the new underground line. Or the area in which they creating a large cavern which in the future would become a commuter station on Vanadisvägen but for the time being occupied a whole block round where Abbas lived. More than once he'd been sitting in his flat and felt the underground explosions make the whole building vibrate, and looked out at the poor Matteus Church opposite where God had to struggle to keep the bricks in place.

Now they were all sitting in his living room. Mette told him why they had come. A visit to where Wendt had been living in Mal Pais in Costa Rica and a search of his home. Mette would see that there would be some degree of cooperation with the local police via her own channels. Abbas would have to take care of the main task himself.

As he saw fit.

Mette would cover the costs.

Then she went through all the known details in the case so far, and Abbas absorbed it. In silence.

When Mette had had her say, dealing with the issues connected with her own murder enquiry, Stilton pitched in with yet another request.

'If you're going there, you could also see if you can find any connection between Wendt and the woman who was murdered on Nordkoster in 1987. They might have met in Costa Rica, she might have travelled to Nordkoster to fetch something that Wendt had hidden at his summer house, OK?'

Olivia was slightly startled by this. She noted how Stilton, without even a glance at her, had pinched one of her 'conspiracy theories' and made it his own. That's what he's like, she thought. I'll remember that.

Now they were waiting for Abbas' answer.

Olivia had sat quietly the whole time. She felt how the three others had a very special chemistry, which stretched long into the past. There was a fundamental respect in the tone between them. She had also noted how Stilton and Abbas had occasionally looked at each other. Quick glances, as if there was something unsaid between them.

What was it?

'I'll go.'

Abbas didn't say any more than that. But he did, however, ask if anyone wanted some tea. Mette wanted to go home and Stilton wanted to leave and they both said no thank you, and were on their way to the hall when Olivia said yes, she would like some tea.

'That would be nice.'

Olivia didn't really know why she said it, but there was something about Abbas. She had been fascinated by him the moment he had slipped into the car and down onto the seat in a single lithe movement. And there was a scent. Not perfume, something else, that she didn't recognise at all. Now he came in with a silver tray with tea and cups on it.

Olivia looked at the room she was sitting in. A very attractive room. Painted white, sparsely furnished, with a few beautiful etchings on one wall, a thin sober textile hanging covered another wall, no TV, a slightly worn wooden floor. She wondered whether Abbas was a bit of a pedant.

He was, on some levels.

As for the other levels, very few people knew about those.

Olivia looked at Abbas. He stood next to a low discreet bookcase, filled with very slim books. His white short-armed sweater hung comfortably above a pair of well-cut grey chinos. Where does he keep it? Olivia wondered. The knife? That he always carried on him, according to Stilton. Always. Her eyes looked over Abbas' body. He's hardly wearing any clothes. Has he put it down somewhere?

'You have curious eyes.'

Abbas turned round with a little cup of tea in his hand. Olivia felt caught out. She didn't want Abbas to misinterpret her look.

'Stilton says that you always carry a knife.'

Abbas's reaction was minimal, but evident. And negative. Why had Stilton told Olivia about his knife? Unnecessary. The knife was a part of Abbas' hidden character. It was not something public. Not even this young girl ought to have access to that information.

'Sometimes Stilton talks a lot.'

'But is it true? Do you have it on you now?'

'No. Sugar?'

'A little, yes please.'

Abbas turned round again. Olivia sank back on the low armchair and just that very same moment something hit the wooden frame right next to her – a long thin black knife trembled only a couple of centimetres from her shoulder. Olivia jerked to one side and stared at Abbas who was walking towards her with a cup in his hand.

'It isn't a knife, it's a stripped Black Circus, 260 grams. Shall we talk a little about the beach case?'

'Absolutely.'

Olivia took hold of the cup of tea and started to talk. A little too fast and strained. The knife was still stuck in the armchair. At the back of her head, the question was: where the hell had he had the knife?

* * *

Ove Gardman sat in the kitchen in his old family home on Nordkoster. He looked out through the window. A little earlier, he had talked to a woman police officer in Stockholm and told her what he knew about Wendt and Mal Pais. The can of ravioli had been eaten. Not in itself a culinary experience, but it had done the job and satisfied his hunger. Tomorrow he would go shopping and buy some proper food.

He looked around in the old family house.

He had stopped off quickly at his two-room flat in Göteborg before going on to Strömstad, visiting his old dad at the retirement home and travelling across to Nordkoster.

'Home to Nordkoster', since that was where he belonged.

It was as simple as that.

Now his mum and dad no longer lived in the house, and it made the place a bit sad. And empty. His mother Astrid had died three years ago and Bengt had recently had a stroke. Now he was partially paralysed on the right side of his body. An unpleasant handicap for an old weather-beaten lobster fisherman who all his life had defied the sea with his amazing constitution.

Ove sighed a little. He got up from the kitchen table, put his plate in the sink and thought about Costa Rica. It had been a fantastic journey, instructive, and strange.

And it got even stranger when he got home and rang that Olivia Rönning. Dan Nilsson murdered. A missing businessman who was really called Nils Wendt. Who had gone to Nordkoster straight after their meeting in Mal Pais. And then been murdered. What had he done here? On the island? Weird. Unpleasant. Was it connected with what I told him about the woman on the beach? Ove wondered.

He went up to the front door and turned the latch. He never usually did that. You didn't really need to here on Nordkoster, but he did it anyway. Then he went up to his childhood room.

He stood in the doorway and looked into the room. It had hardly been touched since he moved to Göteborg to study at university. The old wallpaper with the shell motif, entirely in accordance with the wishes of the young Ove, had passed its best-before date many years ago and needed painting over.

He crouched down. The linoleum on the floor had fulfilled its function. There would certainly be a wooden floor under it that he could paint or sand down and oil. He tried to pull up the corner of the lino to see what was underneath, but couldn't loosen it. A chisel, perhaps? He went out to the big tool cupboard in the hall, his father Bengt's pride. Everything was there sorted and hung up in perfect order.

Ove smiled to himself when he opened the cupboard and saw it. His own old box of treasures. A wooden box he had made in the carpentry class at school, and that he filled with things he found on the beach. Amazing that it had survived. And here of all places? In Bengt's beloved tool cupboard. He lifted out the box with the powerdrill and carefully picked up his old box.

He took the box into the bedroom and opened it on the bed. Everything was still there, just like he remembered it: the bird's skull that he and mum found up by the Skum coves. Bits of birds' eggs. Beautiful stones and bits of wood, and pieces of glass that had been worn down by the sea. Some odder things too, things that had washed up on the beach. Half a coconut, for example, and all the shells. Whelk and cockle shells, oyster shells and fan mussels. Shells that he and Iris had found the summer they were nine years old and in love. And the hairslide he had found later in the summer. Iris' hairslide. He had found it in the seaweed on the beach and was going to give it back to her, but she had moved home for the summer and the year after he had forgotten about the hairslide and Iris.

Ove took it out of the box.

Just think, there was even a little strand of hair from Iris on it. After all those years. But? Ove held the slide under the light from the table lamp. Hadn't she had blond hair? These hairs were much darker. Almost black. How strange.

Ove started to think about it. When had he found it? Really? The hairslide? Was it the same evening as… yes, damn it, it was! Suddenly his memory was crystal clear! He had found the hairslide in the seaweed next to the new footprints in the sand, and then… then he had heard those voices further along the beach and he'd hidden behind the rocks!

That night there was a spring tide.

Abbas pulled the knife out from the armchair frame. Olivia had drunk her tea and left. He had followed her to the door. There was no more to it. Now he keyed in a number on his mobile and waited. He got an answer. In one of his two mother tongues, French, he expressed his wishes to somebody at the other end.

'How long will it take?' he asked.

'Two days. Where shall we meet?'

'In San José, Costa Rica. I'll text you.'

He hung up.

15

Three people were making their way down the corridor at the National Crime Squad. They were all newly awakened, yet alert and ready.

Mette had summoned her team especially early, at 06.30 they were all in the room. Ten minutes later she had told them about the information she had received from Olivia the day before. To this was added Lisa Hedqvist's conversation with Gardman the previous evening. It didn't really contain anything new. But now they knew where Wendt had been living before he came to Sweden. A large map of Costa Rica was put on the board. Mette pointed out Mal Pais on the Nicoya peninsula.

'I have sent a personal contact out there.'

Nobody reacted. They all knew that Mette knew what she was doing.

Bosse Thyrén walked up to the board. Mette had phoned him when she left Abbas' flat the previous evening and given him the necessary information to get going.

'I have mapped out Wendt's route,' said Bosse. 'He checked in at the airport in San José in Costa Rica under the same name that he used to rent the car here, Dan Nilsson.'

'When was that?'

'Friday, 10th of June, at 23.10 local time.'

Bosse wrote this on the board.

'What passport was he using?'

'We're working on that. The plane flew to London via Miami, arrived 06.10, and then he took a plane to Landvetter, Göteborg, on Sunday 12th of June at 10.35.'

'Still as Dan Nilsson?'

'Yes. From Landvetter airport he took a taxi to the central station and bearing in mind his sighting in Nordkoster later that evening we can assume he went directly to Strömstad and took a boat across.'

'Yes. Thanks, Bosse. Did you get any sleep at all?'

'No. But it's OK.'

Mette gave him an appreciative look.

Bosse's information was quickly put together with his earlier mapping of Wendt's movements after he left Nordkoster. Now they had a pattern of movements that stretched from San José in Costa Rica to the Oden hotel on Karlbergsvägen. Via Nordkoster.

'The technicians have been in touch about Wendt's mobile, they've got it to work.'

One of the older investigators came up to Mette with a plastic folder.

'Have you read it?'

'Yes.'

'Anything of value?'

'Yes, I would say so.'

A slight understatement, Mette noted when she quickly looked at the report. Among other things it contained a detailed list of calls.

With dates and exact times.

* * *

Ove Gardman had phoned Olivia late the previous evening and told her about the hairslide he had found. A slide with a black hair in it. Might that be of interest?

It might.

Gardman has also received an urgent request to stand in for somebody at a lecture on marine biology in Stockholm the next day, and he intended taking the morning train up.

'The lobby bar at the Royal Viking. Next to the Central Station. How would that suit you?' Olivia suggested.

'Fine.'

Gardman strolled into the bar with washed-out blue jeans and a black T-shirt. Tanned, and with sun-bleached hair. Olivia examined the guy who'd come in and wondered if he was single. Then she stopped looking. Gardman went up to the bar and ordered an espresso. When he'd got his coffee he turned round, looked at his watch and caught sight of a dark-haired girl over by the panorama window. He took a gulp of his coffee and waited. Another gulp later Olivia raised her head and had another look at the guy at the bar again.

'Olivia Rönning?' said Gardman.

Olivia was caught off balance, but nodded. Gardman went up to her.

'Ove Gardman,' he said.

'Hello.'

Gardman sat down next to her.

'How young you are,' he said.

'Oh really? How do you mean?'

'Well, you know, when you hear a voice on the phone you get an idea of what the person looks like and... I thought you were older.'

'I'm twenty-three. Have you got the hairslide with you?'

'Yes.'

Gardman pulled out a little transparent plastic bag with a hairslide in it. Olivia examined the slide and Gardman told her where he'd found it.

How.

And above all when.

'Just before you heard the voices?'

'Yes. It was in the seaweed next to some new footprints in the sand and I followed those footprints with my eye and then I saw them, the people there, and heard them, and that was when I hid.'

'Gosh, what a memory!'

'Well it was an extremely special event, I don't think I'd have remembered in such detail if I hadn't found the hairslide.'

'Can I keep it for a while?'

Olivia lifted the plastic bag and looked at Gardman.

'Sure, absolutely. By the way, Axel, Nordeman that is, asked me to give you his regards. He ferried me across to Strömstad this morning.'

'Thanks.'

Gardman glanced at his watch.

'Oh hell, I must push off.'

Already? Olivia thought. Gardman got up and looked at her.

'The lecture starts in half an hour. It was great to meet you! Be sure to get in touch if this has been of any help.'

'Of course, I'll do that.'

Gardman nodded and walked away. Olivia followed him with her gaze. Why didn't I suggest that we could go for a beer before he travelled home? she thought.

Lenni would have asked him.

* * *

The young police inspector Janne Klinga had – with some difficulty – discovered where Stilton hung out. In a caravan in the Ingenting forest. Not the exact location. So he had walked around for a while among the dog owners and early-morning sun worshippers before he caught sight of it. Now he knocked on the door. Stilton glanced out through the window, disappeared, and opened the door. Klinga nodded to him.

'Am I disturbing you?'

'What do you want?'

'I think there's something in what you told us yesterday. About Kid Fighters.'

'Does Rune Forss think so too?'

'No.'

'Come in.'

Klinga went inside and looked around.

'Did you live here before too?' he said.

'When?'

'When Vera Larsson lived here?'

'No.'

Stilton wasn't going to open up. He was on his guard. Perhaps this was just a way for Forss to cause trouble, he couldn't know. He knew nothing about Janne Klinga.

'Does Forss know that you're here?'

'No... can't we keep this between us?'

Stilton looked at the young policeman. Perhaps he was a decent guy who just happened to have ended up with a bad boss? He waved towards one of the bunks. Klinga sat down.

'Why have you come here?'

'Because I think you're on the right track. We've downloaded those Trashkick films and I looked through them last night and saw that tattoo on one of the guys doing the assault. KF with a ring round it. Just like you said.'

Stilton remained silent.

'Then I looked up cage fighting and found quite a few things, mainly in England, young boys fighting in cages, but it seemed to be often with the parents present.'

'There was no sign of parents when I saw it.'

'Out in Årsta?'

'Yes.'

'I was there this morning, in that rock shelter, it was completely empty.'

'They got scared when I turned up, and they moved all the stuff.'

'Presumably. There were quite a lot of traces of activity there, bits of tape, screws, a smashed red light bulb and lots of junkie shit. But we can't link that to cage fighting specifically.'

'No.'

'But I've got some people watching the place.'

'Behind Forss' back?'

'I said that it was where you were beaten up and that it was perhaps worth keeping an eye open out there.'

'And he bought that?'

'Yes. I think he'd been talking to someone from the National Crime Squad, and I suppose he wanted to show them he's doing something.'

Stilton grasped immediately who had spoken to Forss. She doesn't waste any time, he thought.

'And I've been in touch with our youth group. They didn't know anything about it but they'd bear it in mind.'

'Good.'

By now, Stilton was no longer so cautious. He believed Janne Klinga. Enough at any rate to pull out a map of Stockholm and unfold it between them.

'You see the crosses?' he said.

'Yes.'

'Those are the places where the assaults occurred, and the murder. I've tried to see if there's a geographic connection.'

'And is there?'

'Not for the actual assaults, but three of the people who were beaten up, including Vera Larsson, were at the Söderhallarna selling magazines before they were assaulted. That's the cross here.'

'He didn't mention that Vera hadn't actually stood there that evening, it was he who had stood there, but she came along and they walked off together.'

'So what's your theory?' Klinga asked.

'It isn't a theory, it's a hypothesis. The guys who beat up people perhaps pick their victims at Söderhallarna and then follow after them.'

'The other two who were beaten up, what about them? We've had five in all, didn't they stand there?'

'I haven't got hold of one of those, the other hadn't been standing there. He stood at the Ring on Götgatan.'

'That's not very far from Medborgarplatsen.'

'No. Besides, he went past Söderhallarna before he went to the Ring.'

'So we ought to keep a bit of a watch on Söderhallarna?'

'Perhaps, it's not my decision.'

No, Klinga thought. It's up to me or Forss. He found himself wishing that Forss had been a bit more like Stilton.

Decisive.

Klinga got up.

'If you find out anything else, then could you contact me directly? I'm going to do this a bit on the quiet.'

And it was quite clear who he didn't want to hear about it.

'Here's my card if you want to get hold of me,' said Klinga.

Stilton took the card.

'And like I said, this is just between…'

'Sure.'

Klinga nodded and went towards the door. Halfway out, he looked back.

'There was one more thing. On another of those films, the one taken here at the caravan, when Vera Larsson was beaten up, just before that they filmed through a window… it must have been that one, and then you see a naked man having sex with her on this bunk.'

'Yes?'

'Do you have any idea who it was?'

'It was me.'

Klinga gave a bit of a start. Stilton looked him right in the eye.

'But that's just between us.'

Klinga nodded and stepped out and very nearly walked straight into a decidedly excited Olivia Rönning. She cast a glance at Klinga, stepped in and pulled the door shut behind her.

'Who was that out there?'

'Somebody from the council.'

'Oh right. Well, do you know what I've got here?'

Olivia held up Gardman's little plastic bag with the hairslide.

'A hairslide,' said Stilton.

'From the Hasslevikarna coves! Found the same evening that the murder happened, by Ove Gardman, next to the footprints of either the victim or one of the perpetrators!'

Stilton looked at the bag.

'And why didn't he give it to us? Back then? In 1987?'

'I don't know. He was nine years old and had no idea it might be of any value. For him it was simply a beach find.'

Stilton reached out for the bag.

'There's a hair in the slide,' said Olivia. 'Black.'

Now Stilton knew exactly where the Scud missile Rönning was heading.

'DNA?'

'Yes.'

'Why?' said Stilton.

'Well if it's the victim's hair then it's of no interest, but if it isn't?'

'Then perhaps it could be from one of the perpetrators?'

'Yes.'

'Someone with a hairslide?'

'One of them could have been a woman.'

'There is no information about there having been another woman there.'

'Says who? Says a terrified nine year old who was hiding quite a long way away, it was night, he saw some dark figures and heard a woman scream, he thought that there were three or four people there, he didn't have a chance to see if there was more than *one* woman there. Did he?'

'You're back to Jackie Berglund again, are you?'

'I didn't say that.'

But she thought it. And felt it. As soon as Stilton mentioned the name it churned up a pulsating fury inside her head.

She suddenly had some very personal reasons to go after Jackie Berglund.

A lift and a cat.

Above all a cat.

But that had nothing to do with Stilton.

He gave Olivia a sideways look. He knew that there was a lot of sense in Olivia's reasoning.

'You'll have to talk to the cold-case guys.'

'They're not interested.'

'Why not?'

'The case is not "accessible" according to Verner Brost.'

They both looked at each other. Stilton turned his gaze away.

'But your ex-wife works at the SKL lab...?' said the missile.

'And how the hell do you know that?'

'Because I'm Arne's daughter.'

Stilton smiled a little. Slightly sadly, Olivia thought. Had Dad and him been close friends?

She'd ask him about that when the occasion arose.

* * *

The room was a typical interrogation room, designed with one aim in mind. On one side of the table sat Mette Olsäter with a couple of sheets of A4 paper in front of her. On the other side the managing director of MWM, Bertil Magnuson. Today with a dark-grey suit, wine-red tie and a lawyer. A woman who had been summoned at short notice to the police headquarters by Magnuson to be present at the interrogation. He had no idea what it was about, but he was a man who took precautions.

'The interrogation will be taped,' said Mette.

Magnuson glanced at his lawyer. She gave a little nod. Mette pressed the 'Record' button and started by describing the time and place and who was there.

Then the interrogation got under way.

'When we met the day before yesterday you denied having had any contact with the murdered Nils Wendt recently. Your last contact was approximately twenty-seven years ago, is that correct?'

'Yes.'

Magnuson had been fetched in a police car from Sveavägen and driven the short distance to the police headquarters at Polhemsgatan. He was remarkably calm. Mette registered a very distinct male perfume and a slight whiff of cigarillo. She put on a pair of reading spectacles and studied the piece of paper in front of her.

'On Monday, 13th June, at 11.23 in the morning, Nils Wendt phoned from his mobile to a mobile with this number.'

Mette held up a piece of paper for Magnuson to look at.

'Is it correct that this is your mobile number?'

'Yes.'

'The conversation lasted eleven seconds. The same evening, at 19.32, another call came from Wendt's mobile to the same number. That conversation lasted nineteen seconds. The following evening, on Tuesday the 14th, came the next conversation and that lasted about the same time, twenty seconds. Four days later, on Saturday, 15th June, at 15.45, came yet another call to the same mobile, from Nils Wendt. That conversation was a bit longer, it lasted just over one minute.'

Mette took her reading spectacles off and looked at the man in front of her.

'What were those conversations about?'

'They weren't conversations. I received calls on those occasions you have named, I answered, got no reply, there was silence at the other end and then the call was cut off. I assumed it was an anonymous caller who was trying to convey some sort of threat to me, or frighten me, there has been some ill-feeling against our company of late, perhaps you know about that?'

'Yes. The last call was longer?'

'Yes, that... well, to be honest I got angry, it was the fourth time somebody phoned and didn't say anything so I myself said some well-chosen words about what I thought of that type of cowardly way of trying to intimidate, and then I hung up.'

'So you had no idea that it was Nils Wendt who phoned?'

'No. How could I? The man has been missing for twenty-seven years.'

'Do you know where he has been?'

'No idea. Do you?'

'He was living in Mal Pais in Costa Rica. You have never had any contact with him there?'

'No. I thought he was dead.'

Magnuson prayed to the gods that his facial expression didn't reveal what was going on in his brain. Mal Pais? Costa Rica? That must be the 'unknown place' with the original tape recording!

'I would appreciate it if you don't leave Stockholm in the coming days.'

'Am I subject to travel restrictions?' Magnuson wondered.

'No, you definitely are not,' said his lawyer suddenly.

Magnuson couldn't help but smile. That smile vanished quickly when he saw Mette's gaze. If he had been able to read her thoughts, it would probably have vanished even quicker.

Mette was convinced that he was lying.

* * *

There was a time, not so very long ago, when the district around Nytorget square was full of all manner of small shops with all manner of weird goods for sale. And often with proprietors who were just as weird. But like a shadow of the ethnological demise most of them were swept away when new residents with different requirements took over the district and transformed it into a catwalk for hipsters. Now only a handful of the original shops were still holding out. Just. And they were mainly regarded as curios and picturesque elements in the street scene. One of them was a little shop selling old books, and run by Ronny Redlös. It was just opposite the building on Katarina Bangata where Nacka Skoglund used to live. It was there when Nacka was born, during his lifetime and when he died, and it was still there today.

Ronny had taken over the place from his mother.

The shop itself looked the same as most other antiquarian booksellers that have survived. Chock-full of books. With shelves from floor to ceiling, and piles of books on tables and stands. 'A glorious mess of treasures' as it said on the little sign in the window. Ronny himself had a well-used armchair beside one wall, with a standard lamp from the First World War leaning over it. Now he was sitting there with a book on his lap. *Klas the Cat in the Wild West*, about a popular albeit somewhat eccentric Swedish cartoon character.

'Beckett in cartoon format!' said Ronny.

He closed the book and looked at the man who was sitting on a simple stool across the room. The man was homeless and was called Tom Stilton. Ronny often had visits from homeless people. He had a big heart and a degree of solvency which enabled him to buy the books that had been found in skips or dustbin rooms, or wherever else they'd been found. Ronny never asked. He paid a bit for each book and helped a homeless person. Quite often, he then threw the books into a skip somewhere or other, and then a week or two later he would be looking at the same books again.

It went on like that.

'I need to borrow an overcoat,' said Stilton.

He had known Ronny for many years. Not only in his capacity as a homeless person. The first time they met, Stilton had been on duty with the Arlanda Airport Police and had been obliged to take into custody a couple of Ronny's fellow travellers on a flight from Iceland. Ronny had arranged a little group trip to the Penis Museum in Reykjavik and two of his mates had drunk a little bit too much of the hard stuff on their way home.

But not Ronny.

He didn't drink alcohol, at least not more than once a year. On that occasion he drank till he dropped. That was the day his girlfriend disappeared under the ice in Hammarby docks and drowned. That day, the anniversary of her death, Ronny went down to the quay where she had jumped out onto the ice and drank until he was completely incapacitated. A ritual that his mates were very familiar with, and were careful not to disturb. They kept their distance until Ronny was completely drunk. Then they transported him home to the bookshop and tipped him into his bed in the inner room.

'You need an overcoat?' said Ronny.

'Yes.'

'Funeral?'

'No.'

'I've only got a black one.'

'That'll do fine.'

'You've shaved.'

'Yes.'

Stilton had shaved, and even cut some of his hair. Not too neatly, but enough so that it wouldn't hang down on all sides. Now he needed an overcoat, so that he would look reasonably respectable. And a bit of money.

'How much do you need?'

'Enough for a train ticket. To Linköping.'

'What are you going to do there?'

'Help a young girl with something.'

'How young a girl?'

'Twenty-three.'

'I see, then she won't be familiar with *The Wild Detectives*.'

'What's that?'

'Masturbation on a high literary level. Just a moment!'

Ronny disappeared into a cubby hole and returned with his black overcoat and a 500-kronor note. Stilton tried the coat on. It was a bit too short but it would have to do.

'How's Benseman?'

'Poorly,' answered Stilton.

'Are his eyes OK?'

'I think so.'

Benseman and Ronny Redlös had quite another relation than that between Stilton and Ronny. Benseman had read widely, Stilton hadn't. On the other hand, Stilton wasn't an alcoholic.

'I heard that you've had a bit of contact with Abbas again,' said Ronny.

'How did you hear that?'

'Can you take this with you for him?'

Ronny held out a thin book with paper covers.

'He has waited for this for almost a year, I only got hold of it the other day, *In Honour of Friends*, Sufi poems translated by Eric Hermelin, the baron.'

Stilton took the book and read the front cover: *Shaikh'Attar, From Tazkiratú-Awliyã I*, and shoved the book into his inner pocket.

To repay a favour.

He had just got an overcoat and 500 kronor.

* * *

Marianne Boglund was on her way towards her whitewashed terraced house on the edge of Linköping, approaching the gate. It was almost seven in the evening and out of the corner of her eye she saw a figure leaning against a lamp post on the other side of the street. The light from the street light shone down upon a thin man with his hands in a rather too short black overcoat. Marianne hesitated for a moment and looked at the man who held up his hand in a greeting. It can't be, she thought. Although she already knew who it was.

'Tom?'

Stilton crossed the street without taking his eyes off Marianne. He stopped about two metres in front of her. Marianne didn't stand on ceremony.

'You look dreadful.'

'You should have seen me this morning.'

'No thanks. How are you?'

'Fine. You mean...'

'Yes.'

'Fine... or better.'

They looked at each other a second or two. Neither of them felt like delving into Stilton's health status. Especially not Marianne. And especially not out on the street outside her home.

'What do you want?'

'I need help.'

'With money?'

'Money?'

Stilton looked at Marianne in a way that made her wish she'd bitten her tongue. She had spoken very insensitively.

'I need help with this.'

Stilton pulled out a little plastic bag with the hairslide from Nordkoster.

'What is it?'

'A hairslide, with a hair in it. I need help with DNA. Can we walk a little?'

Stilton pointed down the street. Marianne turned slightly towards the terraced house and saw how a man moved through a half-lit kitchen. Had he seen them?

319

'It won't take long.'

Stilton started to walk. Marianne stayed where she was. Just typical Tom, turning up as an unannounced wreck of a man and simply assuming that he is in command.

Again.

'Tom.'

Stilton twisted round slightly.

'Whatever you want, this is the wrong way to go about it.'

Stilton came to a halt. He looked at Marianne, lowered his head a little and then straightened up again.

'Sorry. I'm out of practice.'

'Yes, it shows.'

'The social rules. I'm sorry. I really do need your help. You decide. We can talk here or later or…'

'Why do you need DNA?'

'To be able to compare with DNA from the beach case. On Nordkoster.'

Stilton knew that would hook her, and it did. Marianne had lived with Stilton during the entire investigation of the beach case. She knew very well how committed he had been and what it had cost him. And her. And now he was there again. In a physical condition that tore rather hard at a part of her soul, but which she pushed back. For many reasons.

'Tell me.'

Marianne had started to walk without thinking about it. She fell in beside Stilton when he started to tell the story. How the hairslide had been found on the beach the same evening that the murder happened. How it had ended up in a little boy's box of beach finds where he had suddenly discovered it a day or so ago and then given it to a young police student. Olivia Rönning.

'Rönning?'

'Yes.'

'The daughter of…'

'Yes.'

'And now you want to check if they match, the hairslide and the DNA from the victim on Koster?'

'Yes. Can you do it?'

'No.'

'Can't do it or won't do it?'

'Take care of yourself.'

Marianne turned round and started to walk towards the terrace house again. Stilton watched as she walked away. Would she turn round? She didn't. She never had done. When it was decided, it was decided, no loose ends. He knew that.

But he had tried.

'Who was that?'

Marianne had been thinking about how she should answer that question all the way to the front door. She knew that Tord had seen them through the kitchen window. Seen them walk off down the street. She knew that this would demand special treatment.

'Tom Stilton.'

'Really? Him? What was he doing here?'

'He wanted some help with some DNA.'

'Hasn't he left the police force?'

'Yes.'

Marianne hung up her overcoat, on her own hook. Everyone in the family had a hook of their own. The children had theirs and Tord had his. The children were Tord's from his previous marriage, Emilie and Jacob. She loved them. And Tord's devotion to order, even in the hall. He was like that. Everything in its place, and no experimenting in bed. He was an administrator in charge of Linköping's sports grounds. He was in good physical condition, in good mental balance, well-mannered... in many ways like a younger Stilton.

In many ways not.

The ways that had led her to throw herself head first into a morass of passion and chaos and finally, after eighteen years, led her to give up. And leave Stilton.

'He wanted some private help,' she said.

Tord still stood there by the threshold. She knew that he knew. On one level or another. What she and Stilton had had between them, she and Tord didn't have. And that was enough to make Tord wonder. A little uncertain, she didn't think it was jealousy. Their relationship was too stable for that. But he was wondering.

'What do you mean, private?'

'Does it matter?'

She felt that she was being a bit too defensive. That was stupid. She had nothing to defend. Nothing at all. Or did she? Had the meeting with Stilton affected her in a way that she hadn't been prepared for? His dreadful physical condition? His focus? His total lack of emotion at the situation? Confronting her outside her own home? Possibly, but that was definitely not something that would reach her husband.

'Tord, Tom decided to seek me out, I haven't spoken to him for six years, he's involved in something that I don't care about, but I was obliged to hear him out.'

'Why?

'He's gone now.'

'OK. Well, I was just curious, you were on your way in and then the two of you went off. Shall we have a stir-fry for dinner?'

Stilton was sitting alone in the station café in Linköping. That was an environment in which he felt fairly comfortable. Mediocre coffee, no disapproving looks, you went in and drank your coffee and went out again. He was thinking about Marianne. And about himself. What had he expected? Six years had passed since they had last had contact with each other. Six years of uninterrupted decline, on his part. In all respects. And her? She looked exactly the same as she did six years ago. At any rate in the half-light of that residential area. For some people, life just goes on, he thought, for others it slows down and for some it ceases completely. For him, things had started to move again. Slowly, jerkily, but more forwards than downwards.

That alone.

He really hoped that Marianne looked after what she had, whatever it was. She was worth it. In his really healthy moments he found himself thinking about how his behaviour during their last year together must have pained her. His worsening mental problems. How his abrupt changes of mood had slowly undermined what they had built up together, and in the end it all collapsed.

And now these healthy moments were no longer so healthy.

Stilton got up. He couldn't remain sitting. He felt how the pressure in his chest spread out towards his arms and he had left his Stesolid pills in the caravan. Then his mobile rang.

'Jelle.'

'Hi, Tom, it's Marianne.'

She was talking rather quietly.

'How did you get hold of my number?' said Stilton.

'Olivia Rönning is on Eniro, which you aren't, so I texted her and asked for your number. Is the hairslide DNA urgent?'

'Yes.'

'Come over and give it to me.'

'OK. Why have you changed your mind?'

Marianne ended the call.

* * *

Olivia was rather curious as to why Marianne Boglund wanted Stilton's mobile number. Surely they didn't have any contact? Or had he become interested anyway? In the hairslide? A bit perhaps, there in the caravan, enough to ask her if he could keep it. Jesus, she thought. He worked on this case for God knows how many years. Without solving it. Of course he's bound to be interested. But would he really get in touch with his ex-wife? She remembered her meeting with Marianne Boglund at the college. The chilly distance she showed when Olivia asked about Stilton. Almost dismissive. And now she had asked for his phone number. Wonder why they got divorced? she thought. Was that also connected with the beach case?

Presumably it was thoughts like this churning over in her mind that led her to get on the bus out to Kummelnäs peninsula on Värmdö. Out to that dilapidated old mansion. Out to the Olsäters. She felt that there lots of answers out there that she wanted. Besides, she felt something more indefinable. Something to do with the house itself, the atmosphere, the mood out there. Something that she found herself almost longing to be part of again.

Without knowing why.

Mårten Olsäter was down in the music room. The cave-room. That was his hiding place. He loved his big uninhibited family and all their acquaintances and non-acquaintances who were always invading the house and needed food and entertainment and it was almost always Mårten who had to take charge of things. In the kitchen. He loved it.

But he needed to crawl away now and then.

That was why he had built up his cave-room down here, many years ago, and explained to everybody up above that down here was private. Then he had explained, in due course over the years, to children and grandchildren, what he meant by private.

A space that was his alone.

Nobody entered who wasn't invited.

And considering what Mårten otherwise meant to his family, his wishes were respected. He got what he wanted.

A little cave-room in the cellar.

Here he could return to the past and sink into nostalgia and sentimentality. Here he could take a little dip into sorrow about everything that demanded sorrow. His private sorrow. About everything and everyone that had left a track of despair in the course of his life. And there were quite a lot of tracks.

They tend to have accumulated by the time you become a pensioner.

He handled that sorrow with care.

And on a few occasions he indulged in a wee sip, without Mette knowing. Less often now, in recent years, but now and then. To get in touch with what Abbas sought in Sufism. That which was round the corner.

That was never wrong.

On really good nights it happened that he sang duets with himself.

Then Kerouac crawled into the crack.

When Olivia suddenly found herself standing in front of the big wooden door and ringing the bell, she still didn't really know why she was there.

She just was there.

'Hello!' said Mårten.

He opened the door wearing what a girl in Olivia's genera-tion would hardly recognise as Mah Jong clothes. An echo from the Sixties in Sweden. Unisex, velour. A bit of orange, a bit of red and a bit of anything at all, softly hanging around Mårten's generous girth. He held a plate in his hand, a plate that Mette had made on her potter's wheel.

'Hi. I'm… is Mette here?'

'No. Will you settle for me? Come in!'

Mårten vanished inside and Olivia followed him in. This time nobody had been banished to the upper reaches. The house was crawling with children and grandchildren. One of the children, Janis, lived in a smaller house in the grounds, with her husband

and one child, and regarded her parental home as her own. A couple of other children, or grandchildren, Olivia assumed, rushed around in specially sewn-up fancy-dress costumes and squirted their water pistols. Mårten quickly waved Olivia over to a door across the hall. She just managed to duck away from some sprays of water before reaching the door. Mårten closed it behind her.

'A bit chaotic here,' he smiled.

'Is it always like this?'

'Chaotic?'

'Well, I mean, so many people here?'

'Always. We have five children and nine grandchildren. Plus Ellen.'

'Who's that?'

'My mother. She is ninety-two and lives in the attic. I've just made some tortellini for her. Come along!'

Mårten took Olivia up some decidedly winding stairs, right up to the top of the house, to the attic.

'We've furnished a room for her up here.'

Mårten opened the door to a light and beautiful little room, tastefully furnished. Totally different from the environment a couple of floors lower down. A white iron bed, a little table and a rocking chair. In the rocking chair sat a very old woman with chalk-white hair busying herself with a narrow, narrow piece of knitting which coiled several metres on the floor.

Ellen.

Olivia looked at the long narrow piece of knitting.

'She thinks she is knitting a poem,' Mårten whispered, 'each stitch is a stanza.'

He turned towards Ellen.

'This is Olivia.'

Ellen looked up from her knitting and gave a little smile.

'Very good,' she said.

Mårten went up to her and stroked her gently on the cheek.

'Mama is a little demented,' he whispered to Olivia.

Ellen went on knitting. Mårten put the plate down next to her.

'I'll ask Janis to come up and help you, mama.'

Ellen nodded. Mårten twisted round towards Olivia.

'Would you like some wine?'

They ended up in one of the rooms downstairs. With a door that shut out most of the noise from the children.

And drank wine.

Olivia rarely drank wine. It was mainly if she was a guest somewhere, like at Maria's.

Otherwise she stuck to beer. So after a couple of glasses of something that Mårten called an extremely keenly priced red wine, Olivia started to talk a little more than she had intended. Whether it was the setting or the wine or, quite simply, Mårten, she didn't really know, but she talked about very private things. In a way she never had done with her mother, Maria. She talked about herself. About Arne. About losing her father and not being there when he died. About her never-ending guilty conscience for that.

'Mum thinks that I want to become a police officer to soothe my guilty conscience,' she said.

'I don't think so.'

Mårten had listened, hardly said anything, for a long time. He was a good listener. Many years with noisy people had trained his ear for emotional situations and drilled his empathetic ability.

'Why don't you think so?'

'We rarely do things to satisfy a guilt complex, but we do, however, often think we do it. Or blame it, because we don't really know why we make our choices.'

'So why did I want to join the police then?'

'Perhaps because your dad was a policeman, but not because he died when you weren't there. There's a difference. One is inheritance and environment, the other is guilt. I don't believe in the guilt bit.'

Nor do I, not really, Olivia thought. It's only mum who does.

'Have you been thinking about Tom then?'

Mårten changed direction. Perhaps because he felt that Olivia would feel better for it.

'Why do you wonder that?'

'Isn't that why you came here?'

At this point, Olivia wondered whether Mårten was a sort of medium. If she had ended up in the hands of a paranormal phenomenon. He was spot on.

'Yes, I have been thinking about him, quite a lot, and there are lots of things I can't put together.'

'How he ended up as a rough sleeper?'

'Homeless.'

'Semantics,' Mårten smiled.

'Yes, but, he was a detective chief inspector, a good one as I understand, and must have had a pretty good social net too, not least you, and still he ends up there. A homeless person. Without being a drug addict or something like that.'

'What is "something like that"?'

'I don't know, but it must be an enormous step from the person he was to the person he is.'

'Yes and no. In part he is the same as he was, on certain levels, on others not.'

'Was it the divorce?'

'That contributed, but by then he had already started to slide.'

Mårten sipped his wine. He pondered for a moment as to how far he should take this. He wasn't going to reveal things about Tom in the wrong way, or in a way that perhaps could be misunderstood.

So he chose a middle road.

'Tom came to a point where he just let go. Psychologically there is a terminology for this, but we'll skip that, in concrete terms he was in a situation where he didn't want to hang on.'

'Hang on to what?'

'To what we can call a normality.'

'Why didn't he want to do that?'

'Several reasons, his mental problems, the divorce and…'

'He's got mental problems?'

'He had, psychoses. I don't know if he has them now. When you came here, it was the first time we'd seen him for I think nearly four years.'

'Why did he have psychoses?'

'A psychosis can be triggered by lots of things, people are vulnerable to a greater or lesser degree. Sometimes it only needs a long period of stress, if you are extremely vulnerable. Overwork, or that something extreme suddenly takes place, that can trigger it.'

'Was it something extreme with Tom?'

'Yes.'

'What?'

'He'll have to tell you himself, if and when he wants to.'

'OK, but what did you do? Couldn't you do anything?'

'We did what we could, so we thought. Talked with him, many times, when he still could socialise, invited him to live here when he was thrown out of his flat, but then he slipped out of our hands, didn't turn up when we had decided to meet, couldn't be reached, and in the end he was more or less gone. We knew that Tom was a person who couldn't be budged once he had made up his mind about something, so we let him go.'

'Let him go?'

'You can't hold on to a person who isn't there.'

'But wasn't it dreadful?'

'It was dreadful, especially for Mette, she suffered for several years, and still does. But after your visit here, it got a

bit better, he was communicating again, it was extremely…
overwhelming. For both her and me.'

Mårten filled the wine glasses, sipped his own and smiled
a little. Olivia looked at him and knew where she wanted the
conversation to go although she hadn't really got it on the
admitted it to herself yet.

'So how's Kerouac feeling?' she said.

'Fine! Or good, he's got that problem with his legs, but you
can hardly get a Zimmer frame for a spider, can you?'

'No.'

'Do you have any pets?'

That was the direction Olivia had been aiming at. That was
where she wanted to land. With somebody she could tell about it.
Somebody who was far enough away and yet closer than anybody else. Just now.

'I had a cat and I killed it with my car.'

She said, just to get it said, the most painful part.

'You ran over it?'

'No.'

And then Olivia told him, as clearly as she was capable, from
the moment she saw the open window, via the moment she
started the engine, to the moment she lifted up the bonnet.

Then she cried.

Mårten let her cry. He understood that this was a sorrow
that she would take with her to her own cave-room and dip
into now and then. That would never disappear. But just now
she had formulated it and that was a part of the healing. He
stroked her dark hair and gave her a cloth handkerchief. She
dried her eyes.

'Thank you.'

Then the door was wrenched open.

'Hi! Hiii!'

It was Jolene who crashed into the room and gave Olivia
a big hug right across the table. It was the first time they had met

and Olivia was rather taken by surprise. Mette came in just after her. Mårten quickly poured a glass of wine for her too.

'I want to draw you!' said Jolene to Olivia.

'Me?'

'Only you!'

Jolene had already taken a drawing pad from a shelf and was now kneeling down in front of Olivia. An Olivia who quickly dried her eyes with the handkerchief again and tried to look natural.

Then Stilton phoned. On Olivia's mobile.

'Marianne's going to help,' he said.

'She's going to do the DNA?'

'Do an analysis, yes.'

'Take that away!' said Jolene and pointed at the mobile.

Mårten bent down and whispered something to Jolene who crouched over her drawing pad. Olivia got up and went to one side.

'When is she going to do it?'

'She's doing it now,' said Stilton.

'But how has she… have you been there? In Linköping?'

'Yes.'

At this point she felt a warm feeling for Stilton surge up inside her.

'Thank you', was all she managed to say just as Stilton ended the call. Olivia turned round and saw how Mette looked at her.

'Was that Tom?

'Yes.'

Olivia rapidly and excitedly told the story of the hairslide and that they were now testing for a match, and what that might mean for the beach case. To her surprise Mette was not especially interested.

'But it's really interesting!' said Olivia.

'For him.'

'Tom?'

'Yes. And good that he is working on something.'

'But isn't it interesting for you?'

'Not just now.'

'Why not?'

'Because I'm putting all my effort into solving the murder of Nils Wendt. It has happened now, whereas that happened twenty-four years ago. That's one reason. The other is that it's Tom's case.'

Mette raised her wine glass.

'And so it will remain.'

On the way home, that phrase echoed inside Olivia's head. Did she mean that Stilton was going to take up his old case again? He wasn't even in the police force. He was a homeless person. How would he be able to get at his old case? With her help? Was that what she had meant? 'Without you, he would never have come here', she remembered Mette saying. In the hall that last time. And she remembered very well how Stilton had unhesitatingly nicked her own hypothesis about Wendt's link to the beach victim, when they were at Abbas' place. Was Stilton getting back into his old case again? With her help?

Although her head was full of thoughts and questions, she was extremely wary when she approached the front door of the block of flats where she lived. She'd probably never again open that door without being all tensed up.

Especially after Stilton's call.

And the DNA test.

Which had steered her directly back to that woman again, back to Jackie Berglund.

Whom she hated.

16

There are a large number of low-activity volcanoes in Costa Rica, and some active ones. Like Arenal. When it is active it is a spectacular natural phenomenon. Especially at night, the magma which makes its way down in the ready-cut gullies and embraces the mountain like glowing octopus tentacles. And the smoke, straight up in the sky and dramatically grey-black. If you see such an eruption from a little oval airplane window, then that alone is good value for the price of the journey.

Abbas el Fassi was totally uninterested in volcanoes. But he was afraid of flying.

Extremely afraid.

He didn't know why. There was no rational explanation for it. But every time he was ten thousand metres up in the air only surrounded by a thin metal shell, he found himself on the verge of panic. On the verge; he could control it. He had to, but since he was no friend of drug-based or alcoholic anaesthetics it was an ordeal.

Every time.

It was only his natural brown skin colour that prevented him from looking like a newly dug-up corpse when he reached the Arrivals hall in San José and was met by a young man smoking a cigarette and holding a sign which said: ABASEL. FAS.

'That's me,' said Abbas.

He spoke good Spanish. They were soon in the man's little yellow-green car outside. Not until then, sunk down behind the wheel, did the man turn to Abbas.

'Monsieur Garcia. Police constable. We're going to Mal Pais.'

'Afterwards. First we are going to Calle 34 in San José, do you know where that is?'

'Yes, but I had orders that we should drive directly to…'

'I'm changing that order.'

Garcia looked at Abbas. Abbas looked back. He had a really hellish flight in his body, from Stockholm via London and Miami to San José. He was near the edge. As Garcia could see.

'Calle 34 it is.'

Garcia stopped outside a dilapidated building in a – as he had tried to explain to Abbas in the car on the way there – not particularly hospitable area.

'It won't take long,' said Abbas.

He disappeared in through a shabby door.

Garcia lit another cigarette.

Abbas slowly lifted the lid off the little box and revealed two narrow black knives. Specially made, by his main supplier in Marseilles. A thin pale guy who came when Abbas called and who supplied things that Abbas couldn't transport through the airports' security controls around the world. So the pale man had to make them on the spot. Regardless of where that spot was.

Just now it was Calle 34 in San José, in Costa Rica.

They had known each other a long time.

So the pale guy wasn't offended when Abbas asked for a couple of special tools that he knew the pale guy had with him. With the help of a little microscope he added the final touch to the edges of the blade.

For balance.

Something that could be a matter of life or death.

'Thank you.'

They took the ferry across to the Nicoya peninsula and drove without stopping to Mal Pais, their conversation consisting of only a few words. Abbas found out what instructions Garcia had got from the Swedish police, that is from Mette. He was to drive the Swedish 'representative' and otherwise keep a low profile. On one occasion, Garcia asked what the visit was about.

'A missing Swede.'

He was told no more.

The yellow-green car churned up quite a cloud of dust behind it. It was very rarely as dry as this on the roads along the coast.

'Mal Pais!' said Garcia.

They approached an area that looked like all the other areas they had passed. A few houses along a narrow dried-up road, only a stone's throw from the sea. No type of centre, or even a crossroads, just a dusty road right through. The car came to a halt and Abbas climbed out.

'Wait in the car,' he said.

Abbas did the rounds. With a little plastic folder in his hand with two photos in it. One of the victim on Nordkoster and one of Dan Nilsson.

Alias Nils Wendt.

The rounds of Mal Pais were soon done. It was straight down one way, and then back again. No bars. A couple of restaurants some way up the mountainside, closed, a few small hotels and a beach. When he had walked there and back without meeting a soul, he went down to the beach. There he met with a couple of little boys who were playing at monitor lizards, scrabbling along in the sand and making small strange noises. Abbas knew that little boys had big ears and big eyes, when they wanted, at least he had had when he himself was little. It had helped him to survive in the slum districts in Marseilles. He sank down next to the boys and showed them the picture of Dan Nilsson.

'The big Swede!' said one of the boys straight away.

'Do you know where the big Swede lives?'

'Yes.'

The sun went quickly to bed in the ocean and left Mal Pais in cloying darkness. If he hadn't had the little boys with him, he wouldn't have discovered the simple wooden building in among the trees.

Now it was no problem.

'There!'

Abbas looked towards the beautiful wooden house.

'Does the big Swede live there?'

'Yes. But he isn't there.'

'I know. He has gone to Sweden.'

'Who are you?'

'I'm his cousin, he wanted me to fetch some things for him that he forgot.'

Manual Garcia had followed after Abbas and the boys with the car. Now he got out and came up to them.

'Is this his house?'

'Yes. Come along.'

Abbas gave the little boys a hundred colones each and thanked them for their help. The boys stayed where they were.

'You can go now.'

The boys didn't move. Abbas gave them another hundred colones. Then they thanked him and ran off. Abbas and Garcia went in through the gate and up to the house. Abbas assumed it would be locked. It was. He looked at Garcia.

'I forgot my map in the car,' he said.

Garcia smiled a little. Is that how he wanted it? No problem. Garcia went back to the car and waited a minute or two. When he saw a light turned on in the house, he went back. Abbas opened the front door, from the inside, he had pushed in a little pane at the back and managed to open a window. The fast-descending dark gave enough cover for that sort of break-in. Besides, the animals had started to make themselves heard. Every possible sort of call. From birds, from apes, from the throats of other primates unknown to Abbas. The dry silence of an hour ago had turned into a humid rainforest cacophony.

'What are you looking for?' Garcia asked.

'Documents.'

Garcia lit a cigarette and sat down in an armchair.

And lit another cigarette.

And yet another.

Abbas was a thorough man. Centimetre by centimetre he went through the big Swede's house. He didn't even miss the little stone slab under the double bed which hid a pistol. He left it where it was.

Pistols weren't one of his tools.

When the packet of cigarettes was empty, and Abbas was on his third round of the kitchen, Garcia got up.

'I'm going to buy some cigarettes, do you want anything?'

'No.'

Garcia went out through the gate, got in his car and drove off. He vanished out of Mal Pais with a cloud of dust after him, on his way to Santa Teresa. When the dust had settled, a dark van drove out from one of the narrow tracks down towards the sea. The van stopped between some trees. Three men climbed out of the van.

Big men.

Of a type that the drug dealers in Stockholm would drool over.

Protected by the dark, they moved towards the big Swede's garden. They looked at the house where the lights were on inside. One of them pulled out a mobile and took a couple of pictures of the man who was moving around inside the house.

The other two went round to the back.

Abbas sat on a bamboo chair in the living room. He hadn't found anything of value. Nothing that could help Mette. No papers, no letters. No links to the murder of Nils Wendt in Stockholm. And nothing at all that was connected with the victim on Nordkoster, as Stilton had hoped for. The house was clean, except for the pistol under the bed. Abbas leaned back and closed his eyes. The long flight had taken its toll, physically. Mentally, he was inside his mantra, his way of recharging to be able to focus. So he didn't notice the steps that slipped in through the back door, silently, the door that he himself had used. The very next second he did. He nimbly slipped out of the chair, shadow-like, and floated into the bedroom. The steps got closer. Garcia? Already? He heard the steps come into the room where he had just been sitting. Two? Sounded like it. Then there was silence again. Did they know he was here? Probably. The lights were on inside the house. He must have been visible from outside. Abbas kept close to the wooden wall. It could be neighbours. It could be people who had seen the lights on and wondered what he was doing in the house. It could be completely different people too. With completely different aims. Why couldn't he hear anything? Abbas considered. The people outside knew that he was somewhere in the house and in the house there weren't that many places he could be. The little kitchen was fully visible from the living room. They could see that he wasn't there. So they must realise that he was where he was. Here. He breathed as silently as possible. Why didn't they come in? Should he wait for them? Silently... in the end he made a decision and stepped out into the door opening. Two very brutally sculpted men with just as brutal pistols stood two metres in front of him with the muzzles of their guns pointed at his body. Calm.

'Who are you looking for?' said Abbas.

The men glanced at each other: he speaks Spanish. The man on the right pointed with his pistol towards the chair where Abbas had just been sitting.

'Sit down.'

Abbas looked at the muzzles, went across to the chair and sat down. The men were presumably Costa Ricans, he thought. Malevolent Costa Ricans. Robbers?

'What's this about?' he said.

'You're in the wrong house,' said the man on the left.

'Is it yours?'

'What are you doing here?'

'Cleaning.'

'That was a stupid answer. Try again.'

'I'm looking for a missing monitor lizard,' said Abbas.

The man glanced at each other. Bothersome type. One of them pulled out a thin rope.

'Get up.'

That was a movement that was second nature to Abbas. Get up from a chair, crouching slightly forward, head bent over chest, and – in that movement – act. Neither of the men saw the movement but one of them felt the thin knife go through his throat and out through his carotid artery. The other got a squirt of warm blood straight in one eye. He took an involuntary step to the side and got a knife deep into his shoulder. His pistol went flying across the floor.

Abbas picked it up.

'JUAN!'

The man with the knife in his shoulder called towards the door. Abbas glanced in the same direction.

The third man out there heard the shout from inside the house. He was on his way to the gate when Garcia's headlights caught him. He crouched down in the ditch next to the gate. The yellow-green car braked to a halt in front of the house and Garcia climbed out with a cigarette in his mouth.

Hope that weird Swede is finished by now, he thought.

He was.

When Garcia stepped into the living room, two men lay on the floor. He immediately recognised them, from 'Wanted' descriptions and innumerable reports within the Costa Rican police. Two exceedingly notorious men. One of them lay in a large pool of blood on the floor and was presumably dead. The other sat leaning against a wall holding an arm against his bleeding right shoulder. The weird Swede stood beside the other wall and was wiping clean a couple of long narrow knives.

'A break-in,' said the Swede. 'I'm going to walk to Santa Teresa.'

Abbas knew about the third man. He knew that the third man was somewhere out there in the dark behind him, or he assumed he was anyway. He also knew that it was a long walk on what was now a very dark and empty road in to Santa Teresa. He assumed that the third man had understood what had happened with the first and the second. Not least after Garcia had rushed out, pulled out his mobile and with an almost falsetto voice, informed half the police force on Nicoya.

'Mal Pais!'

The third man must have heard that too.

Abbas was extremely focused as he walked along. With his back to the third man. Metre after metre, through silent dark curves, towards a distant light from Santa Teresa. He knew that he risked getting a bullet in his back. No black knives would help against that. At the same time, it seemed that the third man had been on some sort of mission, together with the throat and the other guy. They weren't robbers. Why should three robbers enter a house that from the gate signalled nada? When there were considerably more interesting houses on the surrounding slopes? More hidden by rainforest, more affluent?

The trio was after something specific.

In the murdered Nils Wendt's house.

What?

The bar was called Good Vibrations Bar. A copyright rip-off that The Beach Boys would just have to put up with. California was quite some way away. But the American surfers here perhaps felt nostalgic when they slipped into the decidedly shabby drinking den in Santa Teresa.

Abbas sat at one end of a long smoky bar counter. Alone, with a GT in front of him. This time only. An alcoholic drink. He had walked in the dark with muscles and senses on full alert and small movements on his body where the knives were hidden. And he'd got this far. Without a bullet in the back. Now he felt like a drink. Against better judgement, said a little corner of his brain. But the rest said it was OK.

He assumed that the third guy was out there.

In the dark.

Abbas sipped his drink. Igeno, the bartender, had mixed it to perfection. Abbas turned round and looked at the other people drinking in the bar. Tanned and even more tanned and some badly sunburned men with torsos that were a major part of their identity. And women. Local women and tourists. Some of them presumably guides, some surfing enthusiasts, all in conversation with one torso or another. Abbas' gaze wandered away from the bar room and in across the counter and ended up on the wall opposite. A couple of really long shelves with bottles, more or less flavoured liquor, all with a single purpose.

That was when he saw it.

The cockroach.

A great big one. With long antennae and strong yellow-brown wings folded over its body. It was crawling across an opening in the bottle shelf. A plank wall that was covered with pinned-up tourist photos and picture postcards. Suddenly, Igeno caught sight of it too, and of Abbas' gaze that followed it. With a little smile he crushed the cockroach with the palm of his hand. Right over a photo. A photo in which Nils Wendt had his arm around a young woman.

Abbas put his drink down with a slight crash on the counter. He pulled out a piece of paper from his back pocket and tried to compare the picture on it with the photo under the crushed cockroach.

'Can you take that away?'

Abbas pointed at the cockroach. Igeno swept it away from the wall.

'Don't you like cockroaches?'

'No, they spoil the view.'

Igeno smiled. Abbas did not. He quickly noted that the young woman that Nils Wendt was holding was identical to the victim on Nordkoster. The woman who had been drowned in the Hasslevikarna coves. He finished his drink. 'See if you can find any connection between Wendt and the woman who was murdered on Nordkoster,' Stilton had said.

And there was.

'Another one?'

Igeno was beside Abbas again.

'No thank you. Do you know who the people are in that photo there?'

Abbas pointed and Igeno turned round and pointed too.

'That's the big Swede, Dan Nilsson, the woman there I don't know who she is.'

'Do you know anybody who might know?'

'No, hang on, perhaps Bosques...'

'Who's that?'

'He used to own the bar, he was the guy who put those up.' Igeno nodded towards the photos on the wall.

'Where can I get hold of Bosques?'

'In his house. He never leaves his house.'

'And where is that?'

'In Cabuya.'

'Is that far away?'

Igeno pulled out a small map and pointed out the village where Bosques had his house. At this point, Abbas considered going back to Mal Pais and asking Garcia to drive him to the village. Two things caused him to choose another alternative. The first was the third, the man who presumably was hiding somewhere outside the bar. The second was the police. It was likely that Wendt's house was now crawling with local police patrols by now. Some of them might want to ask some questions that Abbas didn't want to answer.

So he looked at Igeno who was smiling a little.

'You want to go to Cabuya?'

'Yes.'

Igeno made a phone call and a couple of minutes later one of his sons turned up outside the bar with a quad. Abbas asked if he could borrow the photo on the wall. He could. He went out and sat behind the son on his quad and let his faceted eyes scour the area. Although it was fairly dark and there wasn't much light from the bar, he saw the shadow. Or a glimpse of it. Behind a fairly large palm some way away.

The third man.

'OK, let's go.'

Abbas patted Igeno's son on his shoulder and the quad set off. When Abbas turned his head he saw that the third man was moving back towards Mal Pais with surprising speed. To fetch a car, Abbas assumed. He realised that it wouldn't take very long to catch up with the quad considering that there was only one road. In one direction.

Towards Cabuya.

Igeno's son wondered if he should wait, but Abbas sent him off. This could take some time. Just making his way to Bosques' house took time. There was a lot you had to climb over and past before you reached the veranda.

Bosques sat there. In his white clothes, half-shaved, on a chair by the wall. With a glass of rum in his hand and a naked light bulb hanging some way away. Not turned on. The concert of the crickets in the jungle around them didn't disturb his ears. Nor did the weak rush that could be heard from a small waterfall in among the greenery. He observed a very small insect that was making its way along his brown hand.

Then he looked at Abbas.

'Who are you?'

'My name is Abbas el Fassi, I'm from Sweden.'

'Do you know the big Swede?'

'Yes. Can I come up?'

Bosques looked at Abbas who was standing somewhat below the veranda. He didn't look like a Swede. Or a Scandinavian. He didn't look a bit like the big Swede.

'What do you want?'

'To talk to you, Bosques, about life.'

'Come on up.'

Abbas climbed up onto the veranda and Bosques kicked a stool in his direction. Abbas sat down on the stool.

'Is it Dan Nilsson you call the big Swede?' Abbas asked.

'Yes. Have you met him?'

'No. He's dead.'

Bosques expression was not easy to interpret in the dark by the wall. What Abbas did see was that he took a gulp from his glass and that the glass was not exactly steady on its way down.

'When did he die?'

'A few days ago. He was murdered.'

'By you?'

Bit of a strange question, Abbas thought. But he was on the other side of the world in some pit of a village in a rainforest with a man whom he didn't know. He also didn't know what sort of relation he had to Nils Wendt. The big Swede, as Bosques called him.

'No. I work for the Swedish police.'

'Have you got any ID?'

Bosques had been around a few years.

'No.'

'So why should I believe you?'

Yes, why should he? Abbas thought.

'Have you got a computer?' he said.

'Yes.'

'Can you get online?'

Bosques looked at Abbas with cold eyes. So cold that they pierced the dark. He got up and went inside. Abbas remained where he was. After a minute or two, Bosques came out with a laptop and sat down on his chair again. He carefully pushed his mobile modem into the computer socket and opened it.

'Search for Nils Wendt, murder, Stockholm.'

'Who is Nils Wendt?'

'That's Dan Nilsson's real name. It's spelt with a W and DT at the end.

The blue glow from the laptop reflected from Bosques' face. His fingers played on the keyboard. Then he waited, and looked at the screen, and even though he couldn't understand a word of what stood there, he did recognise the picture on the front of a newspaper. The picture of Dan Nilsson, the big Swede. A twenty-seven-year-old picture. Roughly what Nilsson looked like when he turned up in Mal Pais the first time.

Under the photo it said: 'Nils Wendt'.

'Murdered?'

'Yes.'

Bosques closed the computer and put it on the wooden floor in front of him. He fished out a half-full bottle of rum from the dark and poured some into his glass. Quite a lot.

'It's rum. Do you want some?'

'No,' said Abbas.

Bosques emptied the glass in one gulp, lowered it to his lap and wiped his eyes with his other hand.

'He was a friend.'

Abbas nodded. He gestured with his hand as a token of sympathy. Murdered friends demand respect.

'How long had you known him?' he asked.

'A long time.'

A rather vague measure of time. Abbas was after something more precise. A time that he could link to the picture of the woman from the photo in the bar.

'Can you turn that on?'

Abbas pointed to the light bulb across the room. Bosques twisted round a little and reached an old black Bakelite switch on the wall. The light almost blinded Abbas for a couple of seconds. Then he pulled out the picture.

'I borrowed a photo in Santa Teresa, Nilsson's standing with a woman on the... here.'

Abbas handed over the photo. Bosques took it.

'Do you know who she is?'

'Adelita.'

A name! At last!

'Just Adelita, or...?'

'Adelita Rivera. From Mexico.'

At this point, Abbas weighed it up. Should he also tell that Adelita Rivera had been murdered too? Drowned on a beach in Sweden. She might have been a friend of Bosques too? Two murdered friends and almost no rum left.

He refrained.

'How well did Dan Nilsson know this Adelita Rivera?'

'She was pregnant with his child.'

Abbas kept his gaze fixed on Bosques' eyes. A lot of the situation built upon it. That neither of them fell to one side. But inwardly he knew what this would mean at home. For Tom. Nils Wendt was the father of the victim's child!

'Can you tell me a little about Adelita,' Abbas wondered.

'She was a very beautiful woman?'

And then Bosques told of what he knew about Adelita and Abbas tried to memorise every single detail. He knew what it would be worth to Tom.

'Then she went away,' said Bosques.

'When was that?'

'Many years ago. I don't know where she went. She never came back. The big Swede became sad. He drove down to Mexico to look for her but she had disappeared. Then he went home to Sweden.'

'But that was very recently, wasn't it?'

'Yes. Was he murdered in your home country?'

'Yes. And we don't know why or who did it. I'm here to see if I can find anything that can help us,' said Abbas.

'Find the murderer?'

'Yes, and a motive for the murder.'

'He left a bag with me when he went off.'

'He did?'

Abbas had all his senses on full alert.

'What was in it?'

'I don't know. If he didn't come back before the 1st of July I was to give it to the police.'

'I am the police.'

'You don't have any ID.'

'It's not necessary.'

Before Bosques could blink with his thin eyelids, a long black knife struck the electric wire on the wall. After a few seconds of spluttering, the light bulb in the ceiling went out. Abbas looked at Bosques in the dark.

'I've got one more.'

'OK.'

Bosques got up and went inside again. Quicker than last time he came out with a leather bag in his hand and lifted it across to Abbas.

The third man had parked his dark van at a safe distance from Bosques' house and then sneaked up as close as he dared. Not close enough to see with the naked eye, but with the help of his green infra binoculars he had no difficulty seeing what Abbas lifted up out of the little bag on the veranda.

A little envelope, a plastic folder and a cassette tape.

Abbas put the objects back in again. He immediately realised that it was the bag that the gorillas were after in Wendt's house in Mal Pais. He wasn't going to go through the bag's contents now. Besides, he had himself extinguished the only light on the veranda. He raised the bag a little.

'I will have to take this with me.'

'I understand.'

The black knife had increased Bosques' understanding remarkably.

'Do you have a toilet?'

Abbas got up and Bosques pointed to a door a bit inside the other room. Abbas loosened his knife from the wall and disappeared into the toilet with the bag in his hand. He wasn't going to let go of that. Bosques remained sitting in his chair. The world is a strange place, he thought. And the big Swede is dead.

He fished out a small bottle from his trouser pocket and started to put some clear nail polish on his nails in the dark.

Abbas came out again and took his farewell of Bosques, who wished him good luck. Somewhat reluctantly, Abbas received a hug, unexpectedly. Then Bosques went back inside.

Abbas went down towards the road and started to walk. His mind was filled with thoughts. He had got a name for the woman that Tom had been trying to find for more than twenty years. Adelita Rivera. A Mexican. Who was pregnant with the child of the murdered Nils Wendt.

Strange.

A hundred or so metres away from Bosques' house, where the road was at its narrowest, and the moonlight at its faintest, he suddenly got a pistol against his neck. Far too close for him to be able to use the knives. The third man, he thought. That same moment, the bag was wrenched from his grip. When he twisted round he met with a powerful blow to the back of his head. He lost his balance and fell into the greenery at the side of the road. He lay there and saw a big black van roar out of the forest and vanish down the road.

Then he too vanished somewhere.

The van continued to roar through Cabuya and right across half of the Nicoya peninsula. Not far from the airport in Tambur, it stopped at the roadside. The third man turned on the ceiling light in the driver's compartment and opened the leather bag.

It was full of toilet paper.

Abbas came to his senses by the side of the road. He put his hand on his head and felt quite a large lump up there. It was very tender too. But it was worth it. He had given the third man what he wanted. The leather bag.

What had been in the bag was however inside Abbas' sweater.

He was going to keep it there until he reached Sweden.

The third man was still sitting in his van. He had struggled with himself and had had a mental block for quite a while. Now he realised that there wasn't much he could do. He had been tricked, and by now the knifeman would certainly have got back to the police in Mal Pais. He pulled out his mobile, clicked his way to the photo he had taken through the window of Wendt's house, wrote a short text under it and sent off a picture message.

It reached K. Sedovic in Sweden, who immediately forwarded the message to a man who was sitting on a very roomy veranda not far from the Stocksund Bridge. His wife was inside the house, taking a shower. He read the short text on the mobile, which described the contents of the bag that was later filled with toilet paper: a little envelope, a plastic folder and a cassette tape. An original tape, he thought. With a recorded conversation which made all the difference to Bertil Magnuson.

He looked at the accompanying photo.

At the knifeman Abbas el Fassi.

The croupier?

From the Casino Cosmopol?

What was he doing in Costa Rica?

And what the hell did he want the original tape for?

17

Olivia had slept badly.

She had been out on Tynningö Island over the midsummer holiday. With her mother and a couple of her acquaintances. Of course she could have been celebrating out on Möja with Lenni and a gang of mates, but she chose Tynningö. The sorrow after Elvis swept over her in waves and she had a need to be on her own. Or rather to be with people who would not expect her to be in a festive mood. Yesterday, her mum and she had been there on their own and had painted half of the side of the house that caught the full sun. So that Arne wouldn't have to be ashamed, as Maria had said. Then they had shared perhaps a little too much wine. And she paid for that during the night. She had woken at about three and not been able to get back to sleep until seven. Half an hour before the alarm clock was to go off.

Now she had gobbled down a couple of rice cakes and was on her way to the shower in her dressing gown when the door-bell rang.

She opened. Stilton stood there on the landing in a black over-coat that was a bit too short.

'Hello,' he said.

'Hello! Have you cut your hair?'

'Marianne's been in touch, there was no match.'

Olivia saw how a neighbour slipped by with a sweeping glance at the man beside her door. She stepped to one side and gestured to Stilton to come in. Then Olivia closed the door.

'No match?'

'No.'

Olivia went ahead of him into the kitchen. Stilton followed her without taking off his overcoat.

'So the hair didn't come from the victim?'

'No.'

'It could come from one of the perpetrators.'

'Possibly.'

'Jackie Berglund,' said Olivia.

'Drop it.'

'But why not? Why couldn't it be hers? She has dark hair, she was on the island when the murder took place and she had a bloody useless explanation for why she vanished shortly afterwards. Didn't she?'

'I'll use your shower,' said Stilton.

Olivia didn't know what to say, so she pointed towards the bathroom door across the hall. She was still speechless when he disappeared inside. Using somebody else's shower is decidedly intimate, for some people, for others it's neither here nor there. For Olivia it took a while to accept the thought of Stilton standing in there and rinsing off whatever it was he was rinsing off.

Then she started to think about Jackie Berglund.

Black thoughts.

'Forget Jackie Berglund,' said Stilton.

'Why should I?'

He had taken a long cool shower, thought about Olivia's fixation about Jackie Berglund and decided to let her in on some things. Olivia had got dressed and was giving him coffee at the kitchen table.

'It was like this,' he started. 'In 2005 a young pregnant girl called Jill Engberg was murdered and I was in put in charge of the investigation.'

'I already know that.'

'I'm only starting from the beginning. Jill was a call girl. We soon established that she worked for Jackie Berglund in Red Velvet. The circumstances surrounding the murder made us believe that Jill's murderer could be one of Jackie's customers. I pushed that line pretty hard, but it came to a halt.'

'What sort of halt?'

'Some things happened.'

'Like what?'

Stilton became silent and Olivia waited.

'What happened?' she finally said.

'Well several things happened, at the same time. I had a breakdown and ended up in a psychosis, for one, was on sick leave a while, and when I came back I'd been removed from the case.'

'Why?'

'Officially because I wasn't considered as being in a condition to handle a murder enquiry just then, which might have been true.'

'And unofficially?'

'There were people who, I believe, wanted me away from the Jill case.'

'Because...'

'Because I'd got too close to Jackie Berglund's escort business.'

'Her customers, you mean?'

'Yes.'

'Who took over the case?'

'Rune Forss. A policeman who...'

'I know who he is,' said Olivia. 'But he didn't solve the murder of Jill. I read about that in a...'

'No, he didn't solve it.'

'But you must certainly have been struck by the same thought as me? When you were working on the Jill case?'

'That there were similarities with Nordkoster?'

'Yes.'

'Sure, I was... Jill was pregnant too,' Stilton went on, 'like the victim on the beach, and Jackie cropped up in both investigations, perhaps the victim was a call girl? We didn't know anything about her after all. So my idea was that there might have been a link, that it might have been the same perpetrator with the same motive.'

'And what would that be?'

'Murder a prostitute who had blackmailed him on account of the pregnancy. That was why I took DNA from Jill's fetus and compared it with the DNA from the beach woman's child. There was no match.'

'That doesn't exclude Jackie Berglund from being involved.'

'No, and I had a hypothesis about her that I followed quite a while, she had been on Nordkoster with two Norwegians on a luxury yacht, and I thought that they might have been a quartet from the beginning, with the victim being the fourth person, and then something went wrong between them and three of them murdered the fourth.'

'But?'

'It didn't lead anywhere, I couldn't prove that any of them had been on the beach, or had any contact with the victim, as to whose identity we had no clue.'

'Now perhaps you can show that Jackie had been on the beach?'

'Via the hairslide?'

'Yes.'

Stilton looked at Olivia. She didn't give up, he became all the more impressed by her tenacity, curiosity, her ability to…

'The earring?'

Olivia interrupted Stilton's thoughts.

'You said that you found an earring in the victim's coat pocket, on the beach, which presumably wasn't hers. Isn't that right? You thought it was a bit strange.'

'Yes.'

'Were there fingerprints on it?'

'Only the victim's. Do you want to see it?'

'Have *you* got it?'

'Yes, in the caravan.'

Stilton pulled out the big cardboard box from under one of the bunks in the caravan. Olivia sat on the other one. He opened the box and lifted up a plastic bag with a small beautiful earring in it.

'This is what it looks like.'

Stilton handed the earring across to Olivia.

'Why have you got it here?' she asked.

'It ended up among my things when I gathered everything together at the office when I was removed from the case, it lay in a drawer I emptied.'

Olivia held the earring in her hand. It was a rather special design. Almost like a rosette which became a heart, with a little pearl hanging at the bottom, and a blue stone in the middle. Very beautiful. They reminded her of something. Surely she had seen a similar earring before?

Not so very long ago?

'Can I borrow this until tomorrow?'

'Why?'

'Because... I've seen something similar quite recently.'

In a shop? she suddenly thought.

A shop on Sibyllegatan?

* * *

Mette Olsäter sat with some of her team in the investigation room at Polhemsgatan. A couple of them had celebrated the Midsummer holiday, a couple of others had kept on working. Now they had listened to Mette's interrogation of Bertil Magnuson. For the third time. They all felt the same: he's lying about the telephone calls. Partly it was an empirical feeling. Experienced interrogators who could weigh every sliding nuance in the tone of the person being interrogated. But also something more concrete. Why should Nils Wendt phone Bertil Magnuson four times and not say anything? As Magnuson claimed. Wendt must have understood that Magnuson would not in his wildest imagination ever think that it was Nils Wendt, missing for twenty-seven years, who wasn't saying a word on the other end. And what then would be the point of the calls? On Wendt's part?

'He wasn't silent.'

'No.'

'So what did he say?'

'Something that Magnuson didn't want to reveal.'

'And what could that be about?'

'The past.'

At this point, Mette cut in on her colleagues' reasoning. She assumed that Wendt really had been missing for twenty-seven years and suddenly turned up in Stockholm and phoned his former business partner. And the only thing that connected them today was yesterday.

'So if we hypothetically say that Magnuson is behind the murder of Wendt, then the motive must lie in those four conversations,' she said.

'Blackmail?'

'Perhaps.'

'And what did Wendt have that he could blackmail Magnuson with? Today?' Lisa wondered.

'Something that happened then.'

'And who can know about it? Besides Magnuson?'

'Wendt's sister in Geneva?'

'Doubtful.'

'His ex-wife?' Bosse wondered.

'Or Erik Grandén,' said Mette.

'The politician?'

'He was on the board of Magnuson Wendt Mining when Wendt disappeared.'

'Shall I get in touch with him?' Lisa wondered.

'Yes, do.'

Olivia sat on the underground train. The whole way in to town from the caravan, she had been pondering Stilton's information.

She wasn't sure what he had meant. More than that it wasn't a good idea to get too close to Jackie Berglund. When he himself had done so, it ended with him being removed from the case. But she wasn't a police officer. Yet. She wasn't part of any official investigation. Nobody could remove her. Threaten, absolutely, and kill her cat under the bonnet of a car. But no more. She was free to do what she wanted, she thought.

And she wanted to do just that.

Get close to Jackie Berglund, cat murderer. Try to get something from Jackie that you could use for a DNA test. To see if it was Jackie's hair that Gardman had found on the beach.

And how could that be arranged?

She could hardly walk into Jackie's boutique again. She must have help. Then she had an idea. Which would necessitate her doing something repulsive.

Exceedingly repulsive.

* * *

It was a shabby two-room flat on Söderarmsvägen in Kärrtorp, on the second floor. No name on the door, almost no furniture in the rooms. Wearing only underwear, Mink stood beside the window sticking steel needles in his flesh. It didn't happen often. Almost never. He was on less heavy stuff nowadays. But sometimes he had to have a real blowout. He looked around him in the pad. He was still really pissed off about what happened out at the caravan. 'Not even with a bargepole.' That fucking bitch blew him off like he was a nobody. A loser, someone you could imagine standing in their back garden jerking off into a flowerpot.

It felt fucking awful.

But what do you need to support a fallen ego? In less than ten minutes, Mink was out on the track again. His fluttering brain had already constructed several explanations for the humiliation. From the fact that the girl had had absolutely no clue as to whom she was talking to – Mink the Man – to that she was an idiot quite simply. Besides, she was cross-eyed. A pathetic cunt who thought she could get the better of Mink!

Now it felt much better.

When the doorbell rang, he was right back on the level of his own ego again. His legs almost trotted away by themselves. High? So what? He was a guy on the move. A trickster who had his entire toolbox under control. He almost wrenched open the door.

The pathetic cunt?

Mink stared at Olivia.

'Hello,' she said.

Mink continued to stare.

'I just wanted to apologize,' she went on. 'I was dreadfully rude the other evening, quite out of order, out by the caravan, and I really didn't mean it, but I was so shocked over what they had done to Stilton, and it was nothing personal, I promise.

I was just bloody stupid. Really. Sorry.'

'What the fuck d'you want?'

Olivia thought she had already expressed that very clearly, so she went on according to plan.

'Is this the flat you own? Worth five million?'

'At least.'

She had thought through her strategy very carefully. She had a pretty good idea how this joke of a man should be handled. You just had to find an opening.

'I'm sort of looking for a flat, she said. How many rooms are there?'

Mink turned round and went inside the flat. He left the door open and Olivia took that as a form of invitation. And stepped in. Into the virtually empty two-room flat. Shabby. With wallpaper partly hanging loose. Five million? At least?

'Stilton sends his regards by the way, he…'

Mink had disappeared. Sneaked out through the bedroom window? she thought. Suddenly he turned up again.

'Are you still here?'

He had wrapped himself in some form of dressing gown and held a carton of milk in his hand which he drank from.

'What the fuck d'you want?'

It wasn't going to be that easy.

So Olivia dived straight in.

'I need help. I must get hold of some DNA material from a person that I don't dare let see me, and then I remembered what you had told me.'

'What the fuck was that?'

'How you had helped Stilton with lots of difficult cases, a bit like his right hand, weren't you?'

'Yeah, that's right.'

'And then I thought that perhaps you've some experience of this, you seem to know about most things?'

Mink gulped down some more milk.

'But perhaps you don't do this sort of thing any longer?' said Olivia.

'I do most things.'

He's taken the bait, Olivia thought. Now I'll pull the line in.

'Would you dare do something like this?'

'What d'you mean, dare? What the fuck d'you mean? What fucking thing is it?'

Ah, well and truly hooked.

Olivia came walking along from the underground station at Östermalmstorg with an exceedingly merry gentleman by her side, Mink the Man, a man who was afraid of nothing.

'Some years ago I was on my way up K2, you know the fourth summit of the Himalayas, it was Göran Kropp and me and some sherpas, ice-cold winds, minus 32... pretty tough.'

'Did you get to the top?'

'They got up. I was forced to take care of an Englishman who had broken his foot, I carried him on my back all the way down to base camp. He was nobility, by the way, I've got a standing invitation to visit his mansion in New Hampshire.'

'Isn't that in the US?'

'What did you say the name of the shop was?'

'Weird & Wow. It's over there, on Sibyllegatan.'

Olivia stopped some distance from the shop. She described what Jackie looked like and what she needed.

'A hair, like, that's what you want?'

'Or saliva.'

'Or a contact lens, that's how we nailed the guy in Halmstad, he had vacuumed the entire flat after he'd killed his wife and then we found a contact lens in the bag from the vacuum cleaner and took DNA from it and then we had him.'

'I don't know if Jackie Berglund uses contact lenses.'

'Then I'll have to improvise.'

Mink skipped off towards Weird & Wow.

His idea of improvisation is subject to discussion. He went right into the shop, saw Jackie Berglund stand with her back to him next to a dressing table with a female customer and went straight up to her and pulled out a little wisp of hair. Jackie screamed, turning round towards Mink who then looked extremely surprised.

'But WHAT THE FUCK? Sorry! I thought it was that bitch Nettan!'

'Who?'

Mink waved his arms around as druggies tend to do. It came naturally to him.

'Fucking sorry! My apologies lady! She's got the same hair colour and she nicked a bag of coke and ran this way! Has she been in here?'

'Get out!'

Jackie grabbed Mink's jacket and dragged him to the door. Mink wasn't slow to slip out. With one fist tightly holding a wisp of hair. Jackie turned to the slightly shocked customer.

'Junkies! They hang out over in Humlegård Park and come past sometimes and try to steal and make a mess. I'm so sorry about that.'

'It's all right. Did he steal anything?'

'No.'

Which could be up for debate.

Erik Grandén was just going through his diary for the next few days. Seven countries in as many days. He loved travelling. Flying. Always being on the move. Not strictly an essential part of his job at the Foreign Ministry, but nobody had objected so far. He was always accessible via Twitter. Then Lisa Hedqvist phoned, and wanted to meet him.

'Can't be fitted in.'

He really didn't have time for a meeting. His arrogant tone made it clear that he had much more important things to do than talk with young woman police officers. So Lisa would have to do it over the phone.

'It's about the company called Magnuson Wendt Mining.'

'What about it?'

'You were on the board...'

'Then. It's twenty-seven years ago. Do you know that?'

'Yes. Was there a controversy within the board at that time?'

'Concerning what?'

'I don't know, were there differences between Nils Wendt and Bertil Magnuson?'

'No.'

'None at all?'

'None that I know about.'

'But you do know that Nils Wendt has just been murdered here in Stockholm?'

'That was an extremely stupid question. Are we done now?'

'For the time being.'

Lisa Hedqvist hung up.

Grandén was still holding his phone in his hand.

He didn't like this.

* * *

It had been a lot easier that she had expected. All the way to the caravan she had massaged a battery of arguments and tried to think up every possible objection so she could parry it, and then he simply said:

'OK.'

'OK?'

'Where is it?'

'Here!'

Olivia handed over the little plastic bag with Jackie Berglund's pulled-out wisp of hair. Stilton put it in his pocket. Olivia didn't dare ask why he just said that. OK? Was it because he was on board? Or was he just being kind to her? Why should he?

'That's really great!' she said, nevertheless. 'When do you think that she...'

'Don't know.'

Stilton had no idea whether his ex-wife would help again. He didn't even know if she was interested. When Olivia had left, he phoned her.

She was interested.

'You want me to match the wisp of hair against that hair from the hairslide?'

'Yes. It could be from one of the perpetrators.'

'Does Mette know about this?' said Marianne.

'Not yet.'

'Who's paying for it?'

Stilton had thought about that too. He knew how expensive it was to do an analysis. He had already stretched it once. Begged. To do it again was really pushing it.

So he didn't answer.

'OK,' said Marianne. 'I'll be in touch.'

'Thanks.'

Stilton hung up. Really it was Rönning who ought to fork out for this, he thought. She's the one who's so keen. Couldn't she sell that broken Mustang?

He had more important things to do.

He phoned Mink.

* * *

Bertil was on his way home in the grey Jaguar. He was tense and nervous. He still wasn't clear what that croupier was doing. Abbas el Fassi. He had found out his full name and address and asked K. Sedovic to keep an eye on his flat on Dalagatan. If he should turn up there. He had also made sure he had people out at Arlanda airport. If he should turn up there. Presumably he was on his way back to Sweden. With the original cassette. What was he going to do with it? Did he know Nils? Would he continue with some sort of blackmail? Or was he connected with the police? But, damn it, the man was a croupier! He had worked at Cosmopol almost every time they'd been there and gambled. Bertil couldn't understand it at all, and that made him tense and nervous.

One thing was positive. The original cassette would probably soon be in Sweden. It wasn't still in Costa Rica and wouldn't end up with the police there. It was just a question of making sure it didn't end up with the police here.

Then Erik Grandén phoned.

'Have the police talked to you?'

'About what?'

'The murder of Nils? I got a call from a nosey woman who wanted to know if there'd been any controversy between you and Nils when I was on the board.'

'What do you mean, controversy?'

'That's what I wondered too! Why are the police interested in this?'

'I don't know.'

'Unpleasant.'

'What did you say?'

'No.'

'That there wasn't any controversy?'

'Well there wasn't any controversy. Not that I can remember.'

'None at all.'

'No, sometimes you can't help wondering what level the Swedish police has sunk to.'

Bertil ended the conversation.

* * *

Acke Andersson sat in the big shopping mall in Flemingsberg with the man who was a friend of his mum: Mink, and one of Mink's mates. A man with a big plaster on the back of his head. They ate hamburgers. Or rather, Mink and him ate. The other man drank a milkshake, vanilla.

It was the other man who wanted to meet him.

'I don't know that much,' said Acke.

'But do you know who arranges it? Who they are?' Stilton asked.

'No.'

'But how do you know when you're going to fight?'

'Text.'

'They text you?'

'Yes.'

'Have you got their number?'

'What?'

'The people who text you, you've got a mobile, surely you can see who's texting you?'

'No.'

Stilton gave up. He had asked Mink to fix a meeting with Acke to try to find out if Acke knew any more about the cage fighting. Names. Addresses. He didn't. He got a text and then he made his way there or was fetched by somebody.

'Who fetches you?'

'Guys.'

'Do you know what they're called?'

'No.'

Stilton gave up even more and sucked in the last of his milkshake.

Not that far from the hamburger place stood Liam and Isse with their hooded jackets. They had fetched Acke and taken him to the cage fighting once or twice. Now they were thinking of fetching him again. Suddenly they saw him talking with the bloke they'd filmed in a caravan when he was fucking one of their trashkicks. And who had spied on their latest cage fighting and been beaten up.

A homeless bloke.

Why the fuck was Acke talking with him?

'Perhaps he isn't homeless? Perhaps he's a cop?'

'An undercover cop?'

'Yeah?'

All three left the hamburger joint. Mink and Stilton went towards the railway station. Acke ran off in another direction, without noticing that Liam and Isse followed him. They caught up with him over by the empty football pitch.

'Acke!'

Acke stopped. He recognised the guys. They had fetched him once for the cage fighting. Were they planning a new one? Even though he didn't want to any more. How could he explain that?

'Hi,' he said.

'Who were you with at that burger place?' asked Liam.

'You what?'

'Just now. We saw you. Who were they?'

'A mate of my mum's, and a mate of his.'

'The bloke with the plaster?'

'Yes.'

'What have you told him?'

'About what? I haven't said anything!'

'The bloke with the plaster got into the cage fighting ring last time. How did he find out about it then?' said Liam.

'I dunno.'

'We don't like boys who snitch.'

'I haven't...'

'Shut it!' said Isse.

'But I promise! I haven't...'

A hand slapped hard across Acke's face. Before he could turn away, another slap. Liam and Isse grabbed hold of Acke's jacket, had a look about them and then dragged the boy, bleeding, off. Acke looked back to see where the grown-ups had gone, terrified.

The grown-ups were standing on a platform far away.

18

The phone call came in the middle of the night, just after three o'clock. It took a while for Stilton to clamber up to the surface and answer. It was Abbas. He was between two planes and was very brief. The contents was: the murdered woman on the beach was called Adelita Rivera, was from Mexico and was pregnant with Nils Wendt's child.

Then he hung up.

Stilton sat there a long time in his underwear on the bunk and stared at the mobile in his hand. To him, the information from Abbas was simply incredible. After twenty-three years he had got what he never got before: a name for the victim and a father for the child.

Adelita Rivera and Nils Wendt.

She was murdered almost twenty-four years ago, and he just the previous week.

When he had worked through this unfathomable message many minutes, perhaps even half an hour, he started to think about Olivia. Should he phone her and tell her everything? Just like it was? Or what? What time was it? He looked at his mobile again. Half past three. A bit too early.

He put the mobile aside and lowered his gaze to the floor. An ant path wound its way past not far from his feet. The ants never stopped coming and going. He observed them, one line in each direction right next to each other. No ant deviated from the path. They all went in the same direction as the others. No ant turned back and went in the opposite direction. Or stopped.

He stopped looking at the ants.

A Mexican woman and Nils Wendt.

He still pondered this unfathomable news. Tried to think clearly. Look for connections, links. Facts. Hypotheses. He noticed how he started to reacquire a little of what had lain fallow for many years. He was starting to function again.

On a primitive level. Put things together and take them apart. Analyse.

Not like in the old days, far from it. If he'd been a Porsche then, he was a Skoda now. Without wheels. But nevertheless.

He wasn't still stuck in the vacuum.

* * *

Ovette Andersson stood in Gallerian, the big shopping mall next to Hamngatan, and waited. There was a light shower outside. They had said ten o'clock and now it was almost half past. Her blond hair was damp.

'Sorry!'

Mink came trotting along and raised his arm as an apology. Ovette nodded. They started to walk towards Norrmalmstorg. An unusual-looking couple in that rather posh setting at that time of day, just before lunch, with a stream of affluent shoppers and men in business suits on the street. Mink looked at Ovette. She had some make-up on, but it didn't help much. Her whole face was pained with worry and dried tears.

Acke was missing.

'How so?'

'He wasn't in the flat when I came home, I didn't work that late last night and then he wasn't there when I came home. He wasn't in bed. He wasn't anywhere. And he hadn't been in bed either, and his food was still in the fridge, as if he hadn't been home at all!'

'I met him yesterday.'

'You did?'

'I was out there talking to him at the kebab place in the centre and he was like his usual self, then he went off and I came back into town. Isn't he at the school leisure centre?'

'No. I phoned them. What on earth is he doing?'

Mink, of course, had no idea, but he could sense that Vettan was on the edge. He put an arm around her shoulders. He was at least a head shorter, so it wasn't an entirely natural movement.

'That's life. Kids. He'll be doing something.'

'But I thought about what you told me and if it's something like that, if he's mixed up in that?'

'Those fights?'

'Yes.'

'I don't think so, I'm pretty sure he won't do that any more.'

'How can you know that?'

'Never mind, but contact the cops if you're worried.'

'The cops?'

'Yeah?'

Mink knew what Vettan was thinking. A worn-out whore. She wouldn't exactly be given first priority. But even so. She could get some help there. That's what they were for. They both stopped when they came to Kungsträdgårdsgatan.

'But I'll ask around a bit,' said Mink.

'Thanks.'

* * *

The rain spattered against the dirty plexiglass dome on the roof. Stilton sat on a bunk and put some more of Vera's resin on the wounds on his chest. The jar was almost empty. He could hardly get hold of any more. Both Vera and her grandmother were out of reach. He glanced at a little photo of Vera on a shelf in the caravan. He had asked if he could have a copy of her seller's ID and they'd given him one. With her picture on it. He often thought about her. He didn't used to do that, when she was alive. Then he thought about completely different people. The ones who had been important to him before and that he had let go. Abbas, Mårten and Mette. It always boiled down to

369

three. Occasionally Marianne flashed past. But that was too big, too messy, too sad. It took too much of what little strength he survived on.

He looked down into the jar, almost nothing left. Then there was a knock on the door. Stilton kept on rubbing in the ointment, just now he wasn't interested in visitors. He became interested a couple of seconds later. When his wife's face appeared outside one of the windows. Their eyes met, for quite a long time.

'Come in.'

Marianne opened the door and looked in. She was wearing a simple straight coat, light green, and had an umbrella in one hand. Her other hand was holding a grey briefcase.

'Hello, Tom.'

'How did you find me?'

'Rönning. Can I come in?'

Stilton gestured and Marianne climbed in. He had put newspapers down on the more-or-less cleaned floor where the bloodstains had been. He hoped that no weird insects would crawl over them. Not just now. He put the ointment jar aside and gestured towards the bunk opposite.

This didn't feel that brilliant.

Marianne folded the umbrella and looked about her. Did he really live like this? In utter dereliction? Is it possible? She kept herself in check and glanced at the window.

'Pretty curtains.'

'You think so?'

'Yes... no.'

Marianne smiled and opened her coat a little. She carefully sat down on a bunk and glanced around her again.

'Is this your caravan?'

'No.'

'No, right... no, I see...'

Marianne nodded towards one of Vera's dresses hanging over by the rusty Calor gas cooker.

'Is it hers?'

'Yes.'

'Is she nice?'

'She was murdered. How did it go?'

Straight in, as usual. To get away. Always the same. Yet he did seem focused. There was a little of the old look she saw in his eyes. The look that when he was at his best had struck her rather hard, emotionally. A very long time ago.

'There was a match.'

'Is that true?'

'The hair from that hairslide on the beach came from the same woman as that wisp of hair you gave me. Who is she?'

'Jackie Berglund.'

'*The* Jackie Berglund?'

'Yes.'

Marianne had still been married to Stilton in 2005. When he was in charge of the investigation into the murder of Jill Engberg and when via that had got close to her employer Jackie Berglund. He had talked about various hypotheses concerning Jackie; they had talked about them at home, in the kitchen, in the bathroom, in bed. Until he had his first psychosis and ended up on a psychiatric ward. The psychosis had nothing to do with his work, even though the tough workload had partly paved the way for it. Marianne knew exactly what had triggered the psychosis. Nobody else knew, as far as she was aware, and she suffered with him. Then they took away the Jill case from him. Six months later the marriage broke up too.

Not overnight. It wasn't a decision made in haste. It was a result of Tom's mental condition. He kept her at a distance, rejected her. Deliberately. More and more, he didn't want any help from her, didn't want her to see him, touch him. In the end he achieved what he was after. Marianne couldn't stand it any longer, couldn't support somebody who didn't want supporting.

So they went their separate ways.

And he ended up in a caravan.

And now he sat here.

'So it means that Jackie Berglund presumably was on the beach the same evening that the murder took place...' said Stilton, more or less to himself.

Which she had denied during the interrogation.

He savoured that quite amazing piece of information.

'Evidently,' said Marianne.

'Olivia,' Stilton said calmly.

'Is it her who got all this going?'

'Yes.'

'And what do we do now? With the DNA match?'

'Don't know.'

'You can hardly work on this, can you?'

And why couldn't I, he thought at first. Slightly aggressively. Until he saw how Marianne glanced at the ointment jar with its strange goo and at a couple of copies of *Situation Sthlm* on the table and then at him again.

'No,' he said. 'We'll need Mette's help.'

'How are things with her?'

'Fine.'

'And Mårten?'

'Fine.'

And then he was there again, Marianne thought. Introvert and almost silent.

'How come you're up here in Stockholm?' Stilton asked.

'I'm giving a lecture at the police headquarters.'

'Oh, right.'

'Did someone hit you?'

'Yes.'

Stilton hoped that Marianne did not go looking for clips on Trashkick. The likelihood that she would recognise his body on top of Vera was considerable.

Copulating.

He didn't want her to see that, for some reason.

'Thanks for helping,' he said.

'You're welcome.'

It became rather quiet. Stilton looked at Marianne and she didn't look away. There was something endlessly sad about the whole situation, they felt that, both of them. She knew who he had been, and he wasn't that any longer. He knew that too.

He was somebody else.

'You are extremely beautiful, Marianne, you know that.'

'Thank you.'

'Is everything OK with you?'

'Yes. And you?'

'No.'

She had hardly needed to ask. She stretched a hand across the formica table and laid it on top of Stilton's veined hand.

He let it stay there.

As soon as Marianne had left the caravan, Stilton phoned Olivia. First he told her about Abbas' call between two flights and got a long and justified reaction.

'Adelita Rivera?'

'Yes.'

'From Mexico?'

'Yes.'

'And Nils Wendt was the father of the child?'

'According to Abbas. We'll hear more when he gets back.'

'Incredible! Isn't it?'

'Yes.'

In many ways, Stilton thought. Then he told her about Marianne's DNA match. And got an even bigger reaction.

'Jackie Berglund's?'

'Yes.'

When the news had sunk in a little and the excited Olivia was going on about how they had perhaps solved the entire beach case, Stilton felt obliged to point out that the hairslide *could* have fallen onto the beach at some completely different time than the murder. Earlier in the day, for example. Ove Gardman never saw Jackie lose it just then. Just when he was there and found it.

'But, Jesus, must you be so negative all the time?'

'On the contrary, if you want to be a good police officer then you must learn to never commit yourself to just one hypothesis if there are alternatives, it can come back at you like a boomerang in court.'

Stilton proposed that they should contact Mette Olsäter.

'Because?'

'Because neither of us can interrogate Jackie.'

Mette met up with Stilton and Olivia not far from the entrance to police headquarters on Polhemsgatan. She was fully booked and couldn't go into town. Stilton had reluctantly accepted the meeting place. It was far too near buildings and people with whom he had a wounded past.

But the ball lay in Mette's court.

In many respects.

She was in the middle of the Wendt murder and was just waiting for Abbas to land so that she could get hold of the material he had under his jumper. As he had put it. When he had told her about what happened in Costa Rica, a slightly tidied up version, she realised that the material could contain important keys to her investigation. Motive, perhaps. And in the best case, a murderer.

Or several.

So she was a little stressed.

But she was also an experienced and wise detective. She quickly realised that the DNA match that Stilton and Olivia had got from the beach case ought to be decidedly awkward for Jackie Berglund. She realised just as quickly that the two people standing in front of her couldn't, themselves, do anything about it. A student and a homeless person. Not just any old homeless person, admittedly, but for the time being not somebody you would leave alone in an official interrogation room with an as yet still open murder enquiry.

And a possible perpetrator.

So she would do her bit.

'Meet me here in four hours.'

First she read up on the beach case, skimming through the file. Then she got some additional information from Norway. When that had been done, she chose an interrogation room that she knew lay at a safe distance from unnecessary questions. With a couple of sets of doors that allowed Stilton to sneak in behind her without attracting attention.

Olivia had to wait at Polhemsgatan.

'We have some excerpts from the interrogations that were carried out in 1987 with you, in connection with the murder on Nordkoster,' said Mette, with a distinctly neutral voice. 'You were on the island at the time of the murder, is that correct?'

'Yes.'

Jackie Berglund sat opposite Mette. Next to Mette sat Stilton. Jackie's and Stilton's eyes had met just a few moments earlier. Both were most inscrutable. He could perhaps guess what she was thinking. But she had no idea what he was thinking. She was wearing a yellow tailored suit and her dark hair had been set up in a strict French twist.

'In two of those interrogations, the one on the night of the murder, the other in Strömstad the day after, by Gunnar Wernemyr, you claim that you were never up by the Hasslevikarna coves, the place where the murder happened. Is that correct?'

'Yes, I was never there.'

'Were you there any time earlier that day?'

'No. I never set foot up there, I was staying on a luxury yacht down in the harbour and you know that, it says so in those interrogations.'

Mette proceeded calmly and methodically. She explained, teacher-like, to the very hard-skinned former escort lady that the police, with the help of DNA on a hairslide, could prove her presence on the beach where the murder took place.

'We know you were there.'

There was silence for a few seconds. Jackie was cool and she had plenty upstairs, and she realised that she must switch strategy.

'We had sex,' she said.

'We?'

'Me and one of the Norwegians, we were up there and had sex, it must have been then I lost that hairslide.'

'Just one minute ago you said that you had never been there. You said the same in two interrogations in 1987. Now you suddenly say that you were there?'

'I was there.'

'Why did you lie about it?'

'So as not to get mixed up in that murder.'

'When were you there to have sex with the Norwegian?'

'In the daytime. Or perhaps towards the evening, I can't remember, it's more than twenty years ago!'

'There were two Norwegians on the yacht. Geir Andresen and Petter Moen. Which one did you have sex with?'

'Geir.'

'So he could verify your story?'

'Yes.'

'Unfortunately he's dead. We checked that just a while ago.'

'Right. Then you'll simply have to believe me.'

'Will we?'

Mette looked at Jackie, just caught out with a couple of pretty hefty lies. Jackie looked just as stressed as she felt.

'I want a lawyer,' she said.

'In that case we'll end the interrogation here.'

Mette turned the tape recorder off. Jackie got up quickly and went towards the door.

'Do you know Bertil Magnuson? The managing director of MWM?' Mette suddenly said.

'Why should I?'

'He had a summer house on Nordkoster in 1987. Perhaps you bumped into him?'

Jackie left the room without answering.

Olivia had walking around restlessly in Kronoberg park. She thought it was taking ages. What were they doing in there? Would they remand her in custody? Suddenly she found herself thinking about Eva Carlsén. Ought she to tell her? It was largely thanks to Eva that she herself had clung on to the Jackie thread.

She phoned.

'Hi! Olivia Rönning here! How are things?'

'Fine. The headaches have gone.'

Eva gave a little laugh.

'How are you getting on?' Eva asked. 'With Jackie Berglund?'

'It's going really great! We've got hold of some DNA which shows she was on the beach on Nordkoster. The same evening as the murder!'

'We?'

'Yes, well, I'm working together with a couple of detectives now!'

'Come off it! Really?'

'Yes. Jackie's being interrogated by the National Crime Squad!'

'Right? Gosh. So she was on the beach that evening?'

'Yes.'

'That's remarkable. And now have the police started up the investigation again?'

'I don't know, not properly perhaps, so far it's mainly me and the guy who was in charge of the investigation back then, it's us.'

'Who was that?'

'Tom Stilton.'

'OK, so he's taken it up again?'

'Yes. Reluctantly!'

Now it was Olivia who laughed and just then she saw Jackie Berglund slip out from the entrance to the National Crime Squad.

'Eva, can I call you back a bit later?'

'Yes, do that. Bye.'

Olivia hung up and saw Jackie climb into a taxi. Just as it drove away, she saw that Jackie looked out. Straight at her. Olivia met her gaze. Cat murderer, she thought, and felt her entire body tense up. Then the taxi disappeared.

Stilton came out from the same entrance and Olivia rushed up to him.

'How did it go? What did she say?'

On her way from the interrogation room, Mette was stopped in a corridor by a senior police commander. Oskar Molin.

'Was that Jackie Berglund you had in there?'

'Who's said that?'

'Forss saw her going in.'

'And phoned you?'

'Yes. And he claimed that Tom Stilton slipped past in a corridor, was he in there too?'

'Yes.'

'When you interrogated Jackie Berglund?'

'Yes.'

Oskar looked at Mette. They had often worked together and had a solid respect for each other. Luckily for her, Mette thought, as this could all look rather dodgy.

'What was the interrogation about? The murder of Nils Wendt?'

'No, of Adelita Rivera.'

'And who the hell is that?' said Oskar.

'The woman who was drowned on Nordkoster in 1987.'

'Are you working on that?'

'I'm helping.'

'Helping who?'

'Is it sensitive? With Jackie Berglund?' said Mette.

'No? In what way?'

'It seemed to be in 2005, when Stilton was getting close to her.'

'Why should it be sensitive?'

'Because both you and I know what she does, and perhaps there's something in her register of clients that shouldn't be there?'

Oskar looked at Mette.

'How's Mårten?' he said.

'Fine. Do you think he's in the register?'

'You never know.'

They both smiled. A rather forced smile.

Oskar Molin would presumably not have smiled at all if he'd known that Mette had succeeded with what Stilton couldn't manage in 2005. She had got a search warrant for Jackie Berglund's place. Perhaps not entirely by the book, but Mette had her channels.

So Lisa Hedqvist went into Jackie's flat on Norr Mälarstrand when Jackie herself was in the interrogation room. It was after all about a murder for which someone could still be prosecuted. Among other things, Lisa opened Jackie's computer and copied all the folders onto a little USB-stick.

Oskar Molin would not have liked that.

* * *

She had been walking around Flemingsberg for hours looking for Acke. Asked all the young boys she'd met if they'd seen Acke Andersson. Nobody had seen him.

Now she was sitting in Acke's room holding a pair of worn-out football boots in her hand. She sat on his bed. Her gaze had fastened on the broken skateboard. Acke had tried to repair it with brown tape. She dried her tears again. She had been crying in here a long time. An hour or so earlier, Mink had phoned and had nothing to report. Acke was missing. She knew that something had happened to him, she could feel it throughout her body, something to do with those fights in the cages. She saw all his bruises before her, all the wounds on his little body. Why had he done it? Fighting in cages? He wasn't like that. Not at all! He never fought! Who had tricked him into doing it? Ovette squeezed the football boots between her thin hands. If only he'd turn up, she would buy new boots. Straight away. And go to the Gröna Lund theme park. If only he... she turned round and picked up her mobile.

She would phone the police.

The skip stood outside a building on Diagnosvägen. It contained some old stained mattresses, a partly burnt leather sofa and lots of junk from a cleared-out cellar. The girl who peered over the edge of the skip caught sight of a DVD box among the rubbish. Perhaps there's a disk inside? With some effort, she managed to climb over the side of the skip and land on the sofa. She carefully stepped across to the DVD box. It might be empty, it might be a real find. Just as she was stretching down to pick up the case, she saw it. A bit of a little arm sticking up between some sofa cushions.

Further down the arm the letters KF had been drawn, with a ring round them.

19

Stilton stood outside Söderhallarna shopping gallery and sold magazines. It wasn't going too well. He was rather exhausted. He had walked almost two hours up and down the stone steps the previous night. During most of that time he had thought about Marianne's visit to Vera's caravan. Now one of them was dead and the other happily married. He assumed. Before he had fallen asleep in the caravan, he had thought about Marianne's hand on his. Was it just a gesture of sympathy?

Presumably.

He looked up towards the sky and saw how dark clouds were on their way. If it was going to start pouring, he wasn't going to stick around here. He packed the magazines in his rucksack and moved off. Mette had just phoned and said she had to put Jackie Berglund to one side for the time being. She would get in touch if and when it was time for more interrogations.

'Just be careful,' she had said.

'What?'

'You know what Berglund's like, now she knows who's after her.'

'OK.'

Stilton hadn't told Mette about Olivia's experience in the lift. Perhaps Olivia herself had told her? Or was it just a general warning?

When he left his pitch on Medborgarplatsen he was reminded of his hypothesis. The one he had described to Janne Klinga. That they perhaps picked out their victims here outside the shopping mall.

He was too tired to think any more about it.

He walked slowly through the last part of the forest. He was exhausted. With a long sigh, he opened the door of the caravan.

The caravan that was to be moved. But the council had not said anything since the murder so it was still there.

This evening he wasn't going to walk up any stone steps.

The Ingenting forest isn't really much of a forest, compared with the huge expanses of forest up in the north, but it is large enough and with plenty of rock outcrops it can easily hide a person who wants to hide. Or more than one. In this case some figures in dark clothes. They were completely hidden by the forest.

Behind a grey caravan.

Stilton pulled the door shut. Just when he was stretching out on one of the bunks, Olivia rang and wanted to talk about Jackie. Stilton was too tired.

'I've simply got to kip down,' he said.

'Yeah, OK… but you can at least keep your mobile switched on, right?'

'Why?'

'Because… if anything happens.'

Had Mette been talking to her too? Stilton wondered.

'OK. I'll keep it turned on. We'll be in touch.'

Stilton hung up, sank back down on the bunk and turned his mobile off. He didn't want to be disturbed any more. The interrogation with Jackie the day before had taken a heavy toll. And being inside that building where he had spent so many successful years as a murder investigator, that had really got to him. Opened lots of old wounds. Having to sneak in there like a rat so as not to have to look any of his former colleagues in the eye.

That hurt.

He felt how raw all those wounds still were. The ones that came about when he was forced to accept that he had been removed from the case. More or less written off as a detective.

OK, he did have a psychosis. It had been anxiety hysteria, he had needed treatment. But that wasn't the core of the problem.

According to Stilton himself.

In his opinion he had been manoeuvred out of the force.

Of course, some colleagues had supported him, but all the crap that had been talked about him behind his back – that had got worse by the day. He knew who was stoking the fire. And in an organisation where you work in close contact with each other it doesn't take long to poison an atmosphere. A dark word here. A vague insinuation there. People who looked away, people who didn't come near when they saw you sitting alone at a table in the canteen. In the end you simply had to give up.

If you had any pride at all.

Stilton did.

He filled a couple of boxes, had a short chat with his boss and left.

Then it was a downhill journey.

Now he slipped into an exhausted torpor on the bunk.

Suddenly, there was a knock on the door. Stilton gave a start. Another knock. Stilton supported himself on his elbows. Should he open the door? Yet another knock. Stilton swore, got up from the bunk, took a couple of steps to the door and opened.

'Hello. My name is Sven Bomark, I'm from Solna Council.'

The man was in his forties, with a brown coat and a grey cap.

'Can I come in?'

'Why?'

'To talk a little, about the caravan.'

Stilton stepped back to the bunk and sat down. Bomark pulled the door shut behind him.

'Can I sit down?'

Stilton nodded, and Bomark sat down on the opposite bunk.

'Are you living here now?'

'What does it look like?'

Bomark smiled a little.

'Perhaps you know that we need to move the caravan?'

'When?'

'Tomorrow.'

Bomark spoke calmly and in a friendly tone. Stilton observed his white unused indoor-hands.

'Where are you going to take it?'

'To a rubbish tip.'

'To burn it?'

'Presumably. Is there anywhere else you can live?'

'No.'

'You know that we've got a hostel in…'

'Was there anything else?'

'No.'

Bomark remained sitting. The men looked at each other.

'I'm sorry,' said Bomark and got up. 'Can I buy one of these?' He pointed at a little bundle of *Situation Sthlm* that lay on the table.

'Forty kronor.'

Bomark pulled out his wallet and handed over a 50-kronor note.

'I haven't got any change,' said Stilton.

'It doesn't matter.'

Bomark took the magazine, opened the door and disappeared out.

Stilton fell back onto the bunk. He hadn't got the energy to think. The caravan would be got rid of tomorrow. He would be got rid of. Everything will be got rid of. He felt himself fall deeper and deeper.

The two dark figures waited until the man with the grey cap had gone. Then they sneaked up with the plank. It was a thick plank. Together they jammed it under the door handle, quietly.

One of them then put a large stone as a brake at the other end of the plank. They quickly unscrewed the top of the little can they had with them.

Stilton turned and twisted on the bunk. He felt a slight prickly sensation in his nose. He was still in a deep torpor, too tired to react. The prickliness got worse, the smell made its way deeper and deeper into his subconscious, violent fragments of fire and smoke and the screams of women passed through his drowsy brain. Suddenly he sat bolt upright

Then he saw the flames.

High yellowy-blue flames that licked the outside. Heavy, acidic smoke that started to seep inside. Stilton panicked. With a terrified scream he jumped up from the bunk and hit his head on one of the cupboards. He collapsed on the floor, managed to get up again and threw himself at the door. It didn't open.

He screamed and threw himself at the door again.

It didn't open.

A bit further away in the forest, the dark figures stood looking at the caravan. The thick plank against the door handle worked fine. The door was completely blocked. Besides, they had poured a proper dowsing of petrol round the caravan. The fire was literally eating its way into the walls.

A normal caravan can resist fire for quite some time, before the plastic starts to melt. A caravan in this condition turns into a blazing inferno in no time.

'No time' was now.

When the entire caravan was engulfed in roaring flames, the figures turned and ran off.

Into the forest and far away.

Abbas el Fassi was on his way out of the plane. There was a bit of a crush in the exit corridor and he was tired too. He still had some pain from when he had been hit on the head. And on top of that, his body had just suffered another gruelling flight.

A very heavy attack of perspiration together with a couple of unexpected air pockets over Denmark had forced him to pull out the material under his sweater and put it inside a plastic bag. He was carrying that in his hand now. A blue plastic bag. Otherwise he had no luggage in this direction either.

He was not a man who bought a lot of things.

He had given the knives to two little boys in Mal Pais.

In the plexiglass corridor between the plane and the arrivals hall, he pulled out his mobile and rang Stilton. No reply.

As soon as he got to the end of the corridor, he was met by Lisa Hedqvist and Bosse Thyrén. He knew who they were. Together they walked into the arrivals hall. Both Lisa and Abbas pulled out their mobiles. Lisa phoned Mette and said that everything was under control. They were on their way out.

'Where shall we go?'

Mette thought about that a couple of seconds. She considered it reasonable that Stilton should be there when Abbas showed his material from Costa Rica. It concerned the beach case to the greatest degree, she had already understood that much from Abbas' short call between two planes. The police headquarters is not a good idea, she thought.

'Take him to his flat on Dalagatan. We'll meet you outside.'

Abbas talked on his mobile with Olivia.

'Do you know where Stilton is?'

'In the caravan?'

'He's not answering.'

'Really? But he's there, I phoned not so long ago and he was there then. He seemed very tired, I think he was going to get some sleep. But he said he'd keep his phone turned on. Perhaps he's too tired to answer?'

'OK. We'll keep in touch.'

Abbas come out into the arrivals hall with Bosse and Lisa on either side. They went straight to the exit. None of them noticed the man standing by a wall and looking at the croupier from Casina Cosmopol who was just cutting across the hall. K. Sedovic pulled out his phone.

'Is he alone?' asked Bertil Magnuson.

'No. He's with a guy and a girl. Plain clothes.'

Bertil processed that information. Were they people he had met on the plane? Or people he was working with? Were they plain clothes police?

'Follow them.'

Olivia sat in her kitchen clutching her mobile. Why hadn't Stilton answered when Abbas phoned? He wasn't going to turn his mobile off. Of course he would have answered when he saw that it was Abbas phoning. Had he turned it off after all? She tried to phone Stilton. No answer. Had his credit run out? But even so you ought to be able to phone him. She wasn't quite sure how it worked.

Her imagination set to work.

Had something happened? Had he been beaten up again? Or is it that bastard Jackie Berglund? Stilton had been in the interrogation room.

She jumped up.

When she came out onto the street she was very upset and made a decision.

The Mustang!

She ran across to the residents' parking area and stopped when she reached her car. She had very mixed feelings. She hadn't sat in the car since that day with Elvis. Now Elvis was dead and the car was unpleasant. She had loved both of them, and now it had all changed. It wasn't only Elvis and the car that they had taken from her, it was a bit of Dad too. But now it was about Stilton. Something might have happened to him! She unlocked the door and sank down behind the wheel. When she put the key in and turned the ignition, she felt her whole body trembling. She forced herself to put the car in Drive and set off.

There was a natural explanation for why Stilton didn't answer. His mobile lay like a little twisted plastic sausage in the ashes of what was once Vera Larsson's caravan. Now transformed into a black smouldering ruin, surrounded by fire engines that were busy winding in their hoses. They had hosed water over the last burning remains and made sure nothing spread to the forest around. And they had cordoned off the area. Mainly to keep curious locals at a proper distance.

Those same curious locals who now in whispers noted that the eyesore of a caravan was no longer there.

Olivia parked her car some way away. She ran to where some trees had been cut down, and had to argue her way up to the cordon. But then she was stopped. Some uniformed police officers standing there prevented her from getting closer.

Just behind them stood two plainclothes investigators: Rune Forss and Janne Klinga

They had just arrived and noted that the site of Vera Larsson's murder was no more.

'Some rowdy kids out for a bit of fun…' said Forss, thereby making Klinga face a dilemma. If he said that Stilton had moved into the caravan, he'd have to explain how he knew that. And that was something he couldn't really explain.

Not to Forss.

'But someone else might have moved in, after her,' he said.

'Possibly, the technicians will tell us that. If there was someone here when it burned then there won't be much left to interrogate. Will there?'

'No, but surely we must…'

'Is there anybody in the caravan?'

388

It was Olivia who had pushed her way a bit closer. Forss looked at her.

'Should there have been?'

'Yes.'

'How do you know?'

'Because I know the man who lived there.'

'Who was it?'

'He's called Tom Stilton.'

Klinga immediately felt he'd been let off the hook. Forss, however, was speechless. Stilton? Had he lived in this caravan? Had he died in the fire? Forss looked at the smouldering remains.

'Do you know if he was there?'

Klinga looked at Olivia. He remembered that they had bumped into each other in the door to the caravan a couple of days earlier, and realised that she knew Stilton. What would he say?

'We don't know, our technicians must go through the remains to see if...'

Olivia abruptly turned round and ran towards a tree. There she collapsed in a heap, completely crushed, and hyperventilated. She tried to convince herself that Stilton hadn't been in the caravan. There was no reason he had to be there. Just then. When it started to burn.

She made her way back to the car. Confused, shocked. Behind her, the fire engines slowly drove away and curious onlookers left in various directions, chatting. As if nothing had happened, she thought. She pulled out her mobile with trembling hands and dialled a number. It was Mårten who answered. With a heavy stammer she tried to tell him what had happened.

'Has he been killed in the fire?'

'I don't know! They don't know. Is Mette there?'

'No.'

'Ask her to phone me!'

'Olivia, you must…'

Olivia dismissed the call and then phoned Abbas.

He answered from an unmarked police car on the way in from Arlanda. A car that just then was barely moving. A truck had managed to jackknife and ram the steel cables separating the carriageways and caused a major hold-up in the other direction. Their direction. They couldn't get past the scene of the accident. The queues moved at a snail's pace.

The same applied to the car trailing them.

It was just a few cars behind.

Abbas hung up. Had Tom been in the caravan? Was that why he hadn't answered? Abbas looked out through the car window, there were low patches of mist hovering over the wide green fields. Is this how you get notified of a death? he thought.

In a traffic jam?

Olivia drove home. Parked the car and walked slowly up to the entrance to the building. She could hardly think straight any longer. Digest the news. She couldn't understand what had happened. But her instincts still worked, more or less. When she keyed in the door code and pushed the door open, she did so with some caution. She had seen Jackie Berglund's gaze from the taxi outside the police headquarters, and she had seen Vera's burnt-out caravan. Was that Jackie's revenge for the interrogation?

There were no lights on in the lobby, but she knew exactly how far away the light switch was. She could reach it while still keeping the door open with her foot. She stretched out her hand towards the switch and suddenly gave a start. She had seen something out of the corner of her eye. She screamed at the same moment that she pressed the switch. The light flooded over a very pathetic looking figure with scorched hair and burnt clothes and whose arms were bleeding from various scratches.

'Tom?'

Stilton looked at her and coughed. Violently. Olivia rushed forward and helped him onto his feet. They made their way slowly up the stairs and into the flat. Stilton sank down on a chair in the kitchen. Olivia phoned Abbas. They had left the queue and were now close to Sveaplan.

'Is he with you?' said Abbas.

'Yes. Can you phone Mette? I've not been able to get hold of her.'

'OK. Where do you live?'

Olivia put plasters on the bleeding cuts and scratches as best she could. Opened a window to air out the acrid stink of smoke and tried to offer him a cup of coffee. Stilton didn't say a word. He let her carry on. The shock was still in his body. He knew how close it had been. If he hadn't managed to smash a window at the back with a Calor gas tube, the technicians would now have picked up the remains of a twisted skeleton and taken them away in a black bag.

'Thank you.'

Stilton took the mug of coffee with trembling hands. Panic? He had panicked. Not surprising, perhaps, he thought. Shut inside a burning caravan. But he knew that it was something else that had triggered the panic. He so well remembered his mother's words on her deathbed.

Olivia sat opposite him. Stilton coughed again.

'Were you inside the caravan?' she finally asked.

'Yes.'

'But how did you get...'

'Forget it.'

Again. Olivia was beginning to get used to it. When he didn't want to, then he wasn't going to. Obstinate, to put it mildly. She was beginning to understand Marianne Boglund. Stilton put the mug down on the table and leaned back.

'Do you think Jackie Berglund was behind it?' Olivia wondered.

'No idea.'

It could be her, he thought. Or it could be completely different people, who had followed him home from Söderhallarna. But that wasn't Olivia's business. When he felt up to it, he would phone Janne Klinga. For the time being he let the hot coffee calm his breathing. He saw Olivia looking at him, discreetly. She's pretty, he thought. Something that hadn't occurred to him earlier.

'Are you in a relationship with somebody?' Stilton suddenly asked.

Olivia was very surprised by that question. Stilton had never shown any interest at all in her private life.

'No.'

'Me neither.'

He smiled. Olivia smiled back. Suddenly her mobile rang. It was Ulf Molin. From her class in college.

'Hello?'

'How are things with you?' he said.

'Fine. What do you want?'

'My dad phoned me a while ago, he had heard something about that Tom Stilton you asked about, do you remember?'

'Yes.'

Olivia turned away as she spoke. Stilton watched her.

'Apparently he's a tramp,' said Ulf.

'Oh, really?'

'Did you get hold of him?'

'Yes.'

'Is he a tramp?'

'Homeless.'

'Oh yeah? Is there a difference?'

'Can I call you back? I've got a visitor.'

'Oh, right. Yes, do that. Bye.'

Olivia hung up. Stilton realised who the conversation was about. There weren't many homeless people in Olivia's circle of acquaintances. He looked at her, and she looked back.

Something in Stilton's eyes suddenly reminded her of her father. From the photo she had seen at the Wernemyrs in Strömstad. Of Stilton and Arne.

'How well did you know my dad?' she said.

Stilton looked down at the table.

'Did you work together long?'

'A few years. He was a good detective.'

Stilton looked up, and now directed his gaze straight into Olivia's eyes.

'Can I ask you something?' he said.

'Yes.'

'Why did you choose the beach case for your college project?'

'Because dad was involved in the investigation.'

'Was it only that?'

'Yes. Why do you ask?'

Stilton pondered this a moment. Just as he was about to open his mouth, the doorbell rang. Olivia got up, went out into the hall and opened. It was Abbas. He had a blue plastic bag in his hand. Olivia let him in and walked ahead into the kitchen. The first thing that came into her head was the mess. Fuck, she hadn't cleaned the flat in ages!

She hadn't thought about that when she walked in with Stilton.

With Abbas it was different.

He stepped into the kitchen, looked at Stilton who looked back at him.

'How are you?'

'Feel like shit,' said Stilton. 'Thanks for Adelita Rivera.'

'You're welcome.'

'What have you got in the bag?'

'The material from Mal Pais, Mette's on her way here.'

K. Sedovic, who had received orders from Sveavägen to follow the croupier from Arlanda, was brief as he spoke on his mobile.

'The croupier went inside the building, the other two are sitting outside.'

He was sitting some distance from Olivia's building and watching the other car which was right outside the entrance. Bosse Thyrén and Lisa Hedqvist sat in the front.

'Did he have that bag with him when he went in?' Bertil asked.

'Yes.'

Bertil couldn't fathom what was going on. What the hell was Abbas el Fassi up to? A block of flats on Skånegatan? Who lived there? And why were the other two waiting outside? And who were they?

A question that he very soon got an answer to. When Mette Olsäter turned in and parked right in front of Lisa's car and got out. She went up to the wound-down window on the driver's side.

'Go back to the station. Call in the others. I'll be in touch.'

Mette disappeared in through the entrance. K. phoned Bertil again and told him what had happened.

'What did she look like?' Bertil wondered.

'Grey hair in a bun. A very large woman,' said K.

Bertil Magnuson lowered his mobile and looked out across to the Adolf Fredrik churchyard. He knew immediately who the woman was. The one who had gone into the building. Mette Olsäter. The chief inspector who had asked him about Wendt's short calls and given him a very distinct look: you are lying.

This was not good at all.

It was getting all screwed up.

'It stinks of smoke!' said Mette as she stepped into the kitchen.

'That's me,' said Stilton.

'Are you all right?'

'Yes.'

Olivia looked at Stilton. Badly beaten up just a couple of days ago, and now half incinerated. And he says he's all right. Was it just jargon? Didn't want to give anything away? Or a way to shift focus to something else? Away from himself? Presumably, because Mette seemed satisfied with his answer. She must know him better, Olivia thought.

Abbas emptied the contents of the plastic bag onto the kitchen table. A cassette tape, a little envelope and a plastic folder with a piece of paper in it. Luckily, Olivia had four kitchen chairs. She wasn't sure how well Mette would fit in hers. They were a bit wobbly.

She landed heavily. Olivia saw how the chair legs spread out a little. Mette put on a pair of thin rubber gloves and lifted up the cassette tape.

'I've already touched that,' said Abbas.

'Right, so we know that.'

Mette turned towards Olivia.

'Have you got an old cassette tape recorder?'

'No.'

'OK, I'll take this to NCS.'

Mette put the cassette back into the plastic bag and lifted up the little envelope that had lain in the leather bag. It was an old envelope, with an old Swedish postage stamp on it. Inside was a letter. Written on a typewriter and short. Mette glanced at the letter.

'It's in Spanish.'

She held it up in front of Abbas. He translated aloud.

'"Dan! I'm sorry, but I don't think we are right for each other, and now I've got the chance to start a new life. I'm not coming back."'

Mette held the letter under the kitchen lamp. It was signed 'Adelita'.

'Can I look at the envelope?' said Stilton.

Abbas handed the envelope across, and Stilton looked at the stamp.

'It's postmarked five days after Adelita was murdered.'

'Could hardly have been written by her then,' said Mette.

'No.'

Mette opened the plastic folder and pulled out a typed A4 sheet of paper.

'This seems to be more recently written, it's in Swedish.'

Mette started to read it aloud.

'"To the police authorities in Sweden!" It's dated 8th June 2011, four days before Wendt came to Nordkoster,' she said and continued to read. '"Earlier this evening I received a visit from a Swedish man, here in Mal Pais. His name was Ove Gardman and he told me of an event on the island of Nordkoster in Sweden. A murder. 1987. Later in the evening I could ascertain that the woman who had been murdered was Adelita Rivera. A Mexican whom I loved and who was pregnant with my child. On account of various circumstances, mainly economic, she had travelled to Sweden and Nordkoster to fetch some money that I couldn't fetch myself just then. She never came back. Now I know why, and I am fairly certain who lay behind her murder. I'm going to go to Sweden to see if my money is still on the island."'

'The empty suitcase,' said Olivia.

'Which suitcase?' Abbas wondered out loud.

Olivia quickly explained to Abbas about Dan Nilsson's empty suitcase.

'He must have had it with him to put his hidden money in,' she said.

Mette went on reading.

'"If the money isn't there, then I'll know what has happened, and will act accordingly. I have with me a copy of the cassette tape that is enclosed in this bag. The voices on the tape are of me and Bertil Magnuson, managing director of MWM. The recording is self-explanatory." It's signed Dan Nilsson/Nils Wendt.'

Mette lowered the letter. She had suddenly been presented with a great deal of substance for her case. Above all the short telephone calls to Bertil Magnuson from Wendt. They must have been about the missing money.

'Perhaps you should have this too.'

Abbas opened his jacket and pulled out the photo from the bar in Santa Teresa. The photo of Nils Wendt and Adelita Rivera.

'Can I see it?'

Olivia reached out for the photo. Stilton leaned towards her. They both looked at the couple who were holding each other in the picture. Stilton reacted slightly.

'They look happy,' said Olivia.

'Yes.'

'And now they're both dead. Sad…'

Olivia shook her head a little and handed over the photo. Mette took it and got up. Because she was the only one of them who officially was involved in the murder investigation, nobody protested when the lifted up the blue plastic bag with all the material. On her way to the door she caught sight of a little cat's toy on the window sill. The only thing Olivia had kept.

'Have you got a cat?' she asked.

'I had, it… disappeared.'

'That's sad.'

Mette left the kitchen.

She left the building with the blue bag in her hand and went up to her black Volvo, got in, put the car in gear and rolled away. Some way behind her, another car rolled away, in the same direction.

Bertil Magnuson stood beside the window in his office. The lights were not on. He was in touch with K. Sedovic all the time. Bertil played up a number of scenarios in his head. The first, and most desperate, was quite simply to force Olsäter's car off the road and get hold of the blue plastic bag with violence. Which meant an attack in the street against a senior police officer and involved considerable risk. The second was to see where she went. She might even drive home? Then they could do a break-in and get hold of the bag. With a lot less risk. The third was that she drove straight to police headquarters.

Which would be disastrous.

But unfortunately was the most likely scenario.

In Olivia's kitchen there was now a pregnant silence. The information that had now reached them was quite astonishing. Stilton could hardly take it in. After all these years. Finally, Olivia looked at Abbas.

'So Nils Wendt was the father of Adelita's child?'

'Yes.'

'Did you find out anything else about her? From that man, Bosques?'

'Yes.'

Abbas opened his jacket again and pulled out a little menu from the airplane.

'I memorised what he said and wrote it down on the plane...'

Abbas started to read from the menu in his hand.

'"Very beautiful. Came from Playa del Carmen in Mexico. Was related to a famous artist. Spent her time working on..." '

Abbas became silent.

'On...?'

'I can't read what I've written, there was some turbulence... hang on! Wall hangings! "She wove beautiful wall hangings. Was very much liked in Mal Pais. Loved Dan Nilsson." That was roughly it.'

'Where did they meet?'

'I think it was in Playa del Carmen, and then they travelled to Costa Rica to start a new life together. As Bosques put it.'

'And that was in the mid-Eighties?' Olivia wondered.

'Yes, and then she got pregnant.'

'And went to Nordkoster and was murdered,' said Stilton.

'By whom? And why?' said Abbas.

'Bertil Magnuson, perhaps,' said Stilton. 'After all, Wendt wrote that he was on that cassette tape, and besides, he had a summer place on Nordkoster.'

'Did he have it already then?'

'Yes,' said Olivia.

She remembered what Betty Nordmann had told her.

'Then your Jackie theory falls,' said Stilton.

'Why? Magnuson might also know Jackie. He might also be one of her customers. Perhaps she knew him already back then? Perhaps they are mixed up in it, both of them? There were three people on the beach.'

Stilton shrugged his shoulders. He couldn't cope with any more talk about Jackie Berglund. Olivia changed the subject and turned to Abbas.

'The men who did the break-in, at Wendt's house, what happened to them?'

'They regretted it.'

Stilton glanced at Abbas. He didn't know what had happened but assumed it included details that weren't for the ears of young Rönning. Which Abbas was perfectly aware of.

'But they must have been after that stuff that you got from Bosques, surely?' said Olivia.

'Presumably.'

'And then you can't help wondering who they were working for. It must have been somebody from Sweden, right?'

'Yes.'

'Soon she'll say Jackie Berglund again.'

But Stilton smiled a little when he said that. He now had enough respect for Olivia to skip the jargon. He got up and looked at Abbas.

'Is it OK if I...'

'The bed's already made up.'

'Thanks.'

A dialogue that Olivia interpreted as meaning that Stilton would spend the night in Abbas' flat.

He didn't have a caravan at his disposal any more.

* * *

It turned out that the disastrous scenario, the third, was the one that was played out. Mette drove straight to the NCS at police headquarters with her blue plastic bag and disappeared in through the glass doors. K. Sedovic reported to Bertil Magnuson.

For a few moments, Bertil wondered whether he should disappear. Leave the country. 'Do a Nils Wendt'. But he dropped that idea pretty quick. It would never work, he knew that.

And he realised what it had all boiled down to.

A question of time.

He parked the Jaguar outside the house and went straight up to the terrace. He sat down and lit a cigarillo. The summer night was clear and mild, the water glimmered. From Bockholmen he could hear voices singing. Linn was somewhere in the neighbouring district at what she herself called 'a completely uninteresting ladies' dinner with some people who called themselves Stocksund's Skirts'. A group of abandoned housewives who devoted themselves to charity and what one might call luxury Tupperware parties. Linn had almost nothing in common with those women. Except perhaps her address. But since Bertil claimed that he would be having some business meetings and perhaps would be late home, she went to the dinner.

Dressed up.

And beautiful.

Still sitting, Bertil thought about her. About how she would react. About her eyes. How she would look at him and how he would handle that humiliation. And then he thought about the reason for all of it. About the people at the National Crime Squad who just now would be sitting listening to a recording where he distinctly admitted involvement in a murder. Not only involvement, he had initiated it.

Bertil Magnuson.

But what choice had he had?

The entire existence of the company was at stake!

So he chose a different path to that which Nils Wendt had proposed.

A catastrophically wrong path, it turned out. Now.

When he went to fetch the unopened bottle of whisky in the bar, he saw every imaginable newspaper headline before him and heard every excited question from journalists across the world and he knew that he wouldn't have any answers.

Not a single one.

He was pinned to the murder.

* * *

The dimmed lighting hardly reached the thin white arm which hung down a bit from the covers. The letters that had been written there, KF, had almost been wiped off. Acke lay in the bed, unconscious, anaesthetized, with tubes in and out. Ovette sat in a chair close by and cried, quietly. Cried over everything that had gone wrong, all the time, throughout her life. She couldn't even take care of her child. Of little Acke. Now he lay there and was in pain and she couldn't do anything about it. She didn't even know how to console him. She didn't know anything. Why had it ended up like this? She couldn't blame everything on Jackie. She was after all a free agent who had made her own choices. But how free was she? At first, after she'd been kicked out from Red Velvet she had got a bit of money from Social Security. She didn't get any unemployment benefits since she'd hadn't paid tax all those years. She was outside the system. Then she became a cleaner for a while. But she didn't like that and wasn't particularly good at her job. After a few years, she returned to what she knew she was good at.

Selling sex.

But by then she had got a bit older and wasn't quite as desirable, even on that market. Besides, she didn't want to take customers to her flat because of Acke. So it was the street.

On the street.

Back seats in cars, gardens and garages.

Right at the bottom of the scale.

She looked at Acke. At the dimmed lighting. She heard the weak whooshing sound in the tubes. Oh, if only you'd had a dad, she thought. A real dad, like your mates. A dad who could help. But you don't. Your dad doesn't know about you.

Ovette swallowed a thick lump in her throat and heard how the door behind her creaked. She turned round and saw Mink standing in the opening with a football in his hand. Ovette got up and went over to him.

'Let's go out,' she whispered.

Ovette took Mink a little way down the corridor. She needed a smoke and had found a glass door giving out onto a little balcony. There she lit a cigarette and looked at the football.

'Zlatan has autographed it.'

Mink showed her a signature that with a certain amount of goodwill could be interpreted as Zlatan's. Ovette smiled and patted Mink's hand.

'Thanks for caring, there aren't many who do, you know what it's like...'

Mink knew. That's what it was like. If you were where Vettan was, then you had to suppress everything just so you could stick it. There wasn't much room to care about others. The same for everyone around her.

'I'm giving it up now,' said Ovette.

'Giving it up?'

'The street.'

Mink looked at her and saw that she meant what she said.

Just then, just there.

At the other end of the corridor stood a doctor and two policemen. They were in charge of the MHP investigation. The technicians had just told them: there was no trace of a body in the remains of the caravan. So Stilton was alive at least, Forss thought. He received the news with some relief, rather to his own surprise. Now they wanted to talk with Acke Andersson. Stilton had mentioned his name in connection with the cage fighting and his own beating-up. Now they wanted to see if they could get any tips about the perpetrators. It might even be the same people who lay behind the murder of Vera Larsson and the Trashkick films.

'I don't think he's in any condition to talk,' said the doctor.

He wasn't. Klinga sat on Ovette's chair next to the bed. Forss stood on the other side. Acke lay there with his eyes shut.

'Acke.'

Klinga tried. Acke didn't react. Forss glanced at the doctor and pointed with his finger at the edge of the bed, and the doctor nodded. Forss carefully sat on the bed and looked at Acke. Beaten-up northerners and murdered tramps, no they weren't part of what he could feel empathy with, but this was something different. A little boy. Been beaten black and blue and thrown into a skip. Forss realised he had put a hand on Acke's leg on top of the covers. Klinga glanced at the hand.

'The bastards,' said Forss, in a low voice, mainly for himself.

Forss and Klinga stopped outside the door, took a deep breath and looked in the other direction. Towards a balcony with a glass door. Out there Ovette stood smoking, and she looked into the corridor. Forss reacted, for a split second, something fluttered past. Then he turned and went in the opposite direction.

For Ovette it wasn't just a flutter. She followed his back with her gaze, a long time, until he had gone.

She knew exactly who he was.

* * *

It was pretty quiet between Abbas and Stilton. All the way to Dalagatan and right into the flat. They weren't the type of men who talked. Not with each other, not in that way. They were both very knotted persons, each in his own noose. But they had a shared past and they had a now, and the balance between them had been difficult. It was Abbas who had stayed on his feet, while Stilton had fallen, and the roles had been switched. Not an easy transformation for either of them. Stilton had gone to extremes to avoid Abbas. One of the few people he trusted absolutely. Under normal conditions. When the conditions changed, to Stilton's disadvantage, he couldn't face meeting Abbas. He knew what Abbas saw, and for Stilton that was degrading.

It wasn't for Abbas.

He had considerably more levels than Stilton assumed. On one of those levels, an absolute solidarity was anchored. In this case with Stilton. He had managed to keep an almost constant check on Stilton's situation in the city slums. On a couple of occasions when Stilton had been in his worst periods and contemplated suicide, Abbas had been there and caught him. Taken him to the people who could help him with the proper care. Left him there and sneaked off. So as not to embarrass Stilton.

And Stilton was very well aware of that.

So they didn't talk very much. They knew. Stilton sank down on one of Abbas' wooden armchairs. Abbas put on a CD with music and pulled out a backgammon set.

'Are you up to it?'

'No.'

Abbas nodded and put the game away. He sat down in the armchair next to Stilton and let the music take over. They listened to the delicately beautiful tones for a long while. A single piano, a viola, a few simple stanzas that twirled around one another, were repeated, varied. Stilton twisted towards Abbas.

'What's the music?'

'*Spiegel im Spiegel*.'

'Yes?'

'Arvo Pärt.'

Stilton glanced at Abbas. He had really missed him.

'Did you need your knives in Costa Rica?' he asked.

'Yes.'

Abbas looked at his finely sculpted hands. Stilton sat up a bit straighter in his armchair.

'Ronny gave me a book for you the other day.'

Stilton pulled out the slim tiny book from the antiquarian bookseller and handed it across to Abbas. He had had it in his back pocket in the caravan, which was lucky, his overcoat was incinerated.

'Thanks,' said Abbas. 'Wow!'

'What's the matter?'

'It's... I've been looking for this for ages. *In Honour of Friends*, translated by Hermelin.'

Stilton saw how Abbas carefully touched the slim book's soft covers, as if he was caressing a sleeping woman, and then he opened it.

'What is it?' Stilton asked. 'What's it about?'

'The Sufi world... the one beyond the corner.'

Stilton looked at Abbas. When Abbas opened his mouth to explain to a complete idiot that it was about thawing or freezing thinking ability, Mink called on his mobile. Mink had phoned Olivia and wanted to get hold of Stilton and been given Abbas' number.

'One moment.'

Abbas handed the mobile across to Stilton. Mink spoke in a low tone.

'I'm standing in a hospital corridor. Acke's been beaten up.'

Stilton had missed the news about Acke. He had had quite a lot of his own problems the last twenty-four hours. But the analytic side of his brain was recuperating fast. He immediately linked the beating-up of Acke with the burning of Vera's caravan. Kid Fighters.

'Kid Fighters?' Abbas asked when Stilton gave him back the phone.

Stilton quickly moved Abbas from the world beyond the corner to a much more concrete world with beaten-up children and murdered homeless people and torched caravans. And his own hunt for what the media had dubbed the Camera Phone Murderers.

'Just say if you want any help.'

The knifeman gave a little smile.

* * *

Bertil Magnuson was not smiling. He had quickly become quite tipsy with the help of the whisky and in that state was trying to work out what it was all about. But he couldn't get it clear. Neither what Wendt had been after, or what he had meant by 'revenge'. But it didn't make much difference now, for his part.

For his part, it was over.

Since he was the chairman of the Friends of the Cedergren Tower, a society that provided economic support towards the preservation of the old monument, he had also been entrusted with a key to the tower.

A key that he with some clumsy effort managed to dig out of one of Linn's beautiful mother-of-pearl boxes in the desk in the hall. Then he opened his private safe.

* * *

Mette Olsäter and her inner circle sat in the investigation room at the NCS. A room where just now you could have cut the atmosphere with a knife. Two women and three men sat around a tape recorder with an old recording. An old conversation. It was the third time they had listened to it.

'That's Magnuson's voice.'

'Without a doubt.'

'Who's the other guy?'

'Nils Wendt, according to his letter.'

Mette looked at the board on the wall. The crime scene photos from the shore at Kärsön. The picture of Nils Wendt's corpse. The maps of Costa Rica and Nordkoster and quite a lot of other stuff.

'So now we know what those short telephone calls to Magnuson were about.'

'Blackmail, presumably.'

'With the help of this tape.'

'Where Magnuson admits to having ordered a murder.'

'The question is what Wendt wanted, what the blackmail was about?'

'Money?'

'Perhaps. According to the letter he wrote himself in Mal Pais he was going to Nordkoster to look for money he had hidden there…'

'…and since he left the island with an empty suitcase, then he can't have found any money, can he?'

407

'No.'

'But it doesn't have to be about that,' said Bosse Thyrén, the young and sharp one.

'No.'

'It could have been about some sort of revenge, on another level?'

'And only Bertil Magnuson can answer that.'

Mette got up and gave the order to immediately arrest Bertil Magnuson.

* * *

It was very dark in the Cedergren Tower, silent, and rather spooky for an ordinary person. Or a person in an ordinary state. Bertil Magnuson was not in an ordinary state. He had a little pocket torch in his hand and was making his way up to the upper regions of the building. The tower room. The room right at the top with the bare brick walls, and just a couple of small slits out to the world.

A world that not very long ago had belonged to him.

The man who had mined coltan ore and given the electronics world its tantalum. The exclusive component that was the basis of the techinical revolution.

Bertil Magnuson.

Now linked to a murder.

But that isn't what Bertil was thinking as he climbed up the narrow winding stone steps with the help of his little Maglite. He supported himself against the brick walls now and then, very drunk.

He thought about Linn again.

About the shame.

About having to look Linn in the eye and say:

'It's true. Every word on that tape is true.'

He couldn't do that.

When he had finally clambered right up to the tower room, he was beyond physical sensations. It was unpleasantly damp and dark and that didn't bother him at all. He felt his way to the closest little opening in the wall and pulled his grey pistol out of his pocket and stuck it in his mouth. Then he looked out and down.

Perhaps he shouldn't have done that.

Far down below, in a direct line of sight from where Bertil was standing by the aperture, he saw Linn walk out onto the big terrace. Her beautiful dress. Her hair falling so beautifully over her shoulders. Her slim arm which reached out and picked up the almost empty whisky bottle and her head which turned round slightly, in some surprise, and then looked up.

At the Cedergren Tower.

And thus their eyes met, if eyes can meet at such a distance, in an attempt to reach each other.

Mette and her group arrived at high speed at Magnuson's address. They all got out and approached the house where the lights were on. Since nobody opened despite repeated rings on the doorbell, they went round to the back up onto the terrace. The door from the house was wide open. An empty whisky bottle lay on the terrace.

Mette looked around.

How long she had sat there, she didn't know. Time was totally irrelevant. She sat with her husband's bloodied head in her lap on her cerise dress. Some of his brain tissue had plastered the brick wall opposite her.

The first shock, the one that came when she heard the shot from the tower and saw Bertil's face disappear from the opening, was what had driven her up to the tower in a state of panic.

The second shock, when she had got up to the tower room and saw him, that too had worn off slightly. Now she was like a carving, in another state, slowly slipping into mourning. Her husband had shot himself. He was dead. With her fingers she carefully touched Bertil's short hair. Her tears dropped down onto his dark jacket. She picked a little at his blue shirt with the white collar. Even to the end, she thought. She raised her head and looked out through the opening, and down, towards their house. Police cars on the drive? Strangers up on the terrace? She didn't really understand what those dark-clothed people were doing down there. On their terrace. She saw a big woman who pulled out a mobile phone. Suddenly Bertil's mobile rang, in his jacket on her lap. She put her hand into the pocket and pulled it out. A strange object that she was holding in her hand, and which was ringing. She pressed the answer button, listened and answered.

'We're up in the tower.'

Mette and her team very quickly reached the top of the tower. And at least as quickly ascertained that Bertil Magnuson was dead and his wife in a state of severe shock. It was of course possible that Magnuson had been shot by his wife. But considering the background, it wasn't particularly likely. Nor considering the situation in the tower.

It was simply tragic.

Mette looked at the Magnuson couple. She wasn't the sort who got emotional when it came to crime and punishment, and her sympathy was entirely with the wife. She felt nothing for Bertil Magnuson.

No more than a second's disappointment.

As a police officer.

But her sympathy for Linn led her to explain. A little while later down in the house. Linn had been given some sedatives and she'd asked them to tell her what had happened. Why they were there, and if it was connected with her husband's death. So Mette told her part of it. As mildly as she could. She was of the opinion that the truth was the best healer, even though it could hurt when it was served up. Linn wouldn't really understand what it was about, that would be to expect too much. Mette didn't fully understand herself. Yet. But there was nevertheless some sort of explanation for the husband's suicide in that tape recording.

That was about a murder.

20

News of Bertil Magnuson's suicide was soon out in the media.

Not least online.

One of the people who was quickest to comment was Erik Grandén. In an almost furious outbreak he tweeted his indignation over the witch hunt to which Bertil Magnuson had been subjected in recent weeks. One of the most shameful houndings of an individual in modern Swedish history. To find an equivalent he had to go back to the infamous lynching of the innocent nobleman Axel von Fersen in Stockholm in 1810. "The people who have hounded him bear a despicable guilt upon their shoulders! They have whipped up a suicide!"

An hour after his outbreak, the party's governing board phoned and summoned him to a meeting.

'Now?'

'Yes.'

Grandén had mixed feelings as he hurriedly made his way to the party headquarters. On the one hand, there was Bertil's horrific suicide and his thoughts went out to Linn. He must remember to phone her. On the other hand he was rather elated about meeting the board. He took it for granted that it was about his future top post out in Europe, otherwise you wouldn't be summoned so abruptly. He was slightly irritated that he wouldn't have time to visit a barber before the meeting.

The press would of course be there to cover it.

* * *

Mette sat in her room. Shortly she would go through all the material with her team. Magnuson's suicide had changed the game plan. Made things more tricky. Now a lot would be about the recorded conversation, while neither of the two who spoke was still alive. The chances of proving who had murdered Nils Wendt had lessened radically.

The murderer was probably also dead.

What they had was circumstantial evidence. Wishful thinking, a celebrity lawyer would say to the press.

So for the moment Mette put Wendt's murder aside and started to study a print-out of some of Jackie Berglund's computer files. One of them contained a sort of card index. A register of clients. With a mishmash of sex buyers, known and unknown. But some of the names made her react.

Especially one of them.

* * *

Grandén sat down at the oval table. Normally there were eighteen people on the board. Today only a smaller group had gathered. He knew them all well. Some of them he had himself eased into politics, others he had been forced to put up with.

Such were the rules of the game. Of politics.

He poured out some water from the carafe in front of him, lukewarm. He waited for someone to take the initiative. It was slow in coming. He glanced around the room.

Nobody looked him in the eye.

'Rather an historical moment for us, all of us, not only for me,' he said.

And pulled in his lower lip slightly, in his familiar organic movement. The group looked at him.

'Tragic about Magnuson.'

'Outrageous,' said Grandén. 'We must take a stand against that mob mentality, it could hurt just about anybody.'

'Yes.'

The man leaned forward towards a little CD player on the table. He stopped his finger just before pressing Play.

'We got this a little while ago.'

The man was looking straight at Grandén who was just running his fingers through his hair and wondering if it would stick up and look silly as it tended to do when he had the wind against him.

'Yes, right.'

The man pressed Play and a recorded conversation started. Grandén immediately recognised the voices. Two of the three musketeers, he himself being the third.

'Jan Nyström has been found in his car in a lake, dead.'

'Yes, I heard.'

'And?'

'What can I say?'

'I know you're prepared to go a long way, Bertil, but murder?'

'Nobody can link us to it.'

'But we know.'

'We don't know anything... if we don't want to. Why are you so indignant?'

'Because an innocent person has been murdered!'

'That's your interpretation.'

'And what's yours?'

'I solved a problem.'

Having got that far in the conversation, Grandén began to realise that this meeting was not about his trampoline to a top job in Europe, and into the lap of Sarkozy and Merkel. He tried to win time.

'Can you back that up a bit?'

The man pressed the buttons. The conversation started again. Grandén listened intensely.

'That's your interpretation.'

'And what's yours?'

414

'I solved a problem.'

'By murdering a journalist?'

'By stopping the spreading of a whole lot of unreliable shit about us.'

'Who murdered him?'

'I don't know.'

'You just made a telephone call?'

'Yes.'

'Hello, this is Bertil Magnuson, I want Jan Nyström out of the way.'

'More or less.'

'And then he was murdered.'

'He died in a car accident.'

'How much did it cost you?'

'Fifty thousand.'

'Is that what a murder costs in Zaire?'

'Yes.'

The man turned the CD player off, and looked at the decidedly composed Grandén. The water cooler bubbled weakly in the background. Somebody was doodling on a notepad.

'The journalist Jan Nyström was murdered on the 23rd of August 1984, in Zaire. As we just heard, the murder was instigated by Bertil Magnuson, managing director of the then MWM. At that time you were on the board of the company.'

'That is correct.'

His lower lip puckered out again.

'What did you know about it?'

'The murder?'

'Yes.'

'Nothing. I do however remember that Nils Wendt phoned me after the murder and told me that that journalist had come up to their office in Kinshasa with a very serious report about MWM's project down there and asked for a comment.'

'Did he get one?'

'Magnuson and Wendt promised him a comment the next morning, but he never turned up.'

'He was murdered.'

'Apparently.'

Grandén glanced at the CD player.

'Did Wendt say anything else?' the man asked.

'He suddenly maintained that there was a lot of truth in that journalist's report and that he himself had tired of Magnuson's methods and wanted to pull out.'

'From MWM?'

'Yes. He was going to leave the company and disappear. "Go underground" as he put it. But first he would get some life insurance.'

The man pointed at the CD player.

'He took a hidden tape recorder with him and got Bertil Magnuson to admit that he had ordered a murder.'

'Apparently.'

Grandén kept quiet about the next phone call he had received. From Bertil Magnuson, the next day. In which he told how Wendt had disappeared and that almost two million dollars were missing from an account for 'unspecified costs'. An account that Grandén knew wasn't visible to the accountants and which was used to buy services from less scrupulous persons when problems cropped up.

And Jan Nyström had evidently become just such a problem.

'Where did you get this recording from?' he asked.

'Mette Olsäter, at the National Crime Squad. She had obviously heard about your Twitter contribution today and thought we ought to have an opportunity to listen to this and talk to you before it reached the media.'

Grandén nodded. He glanced around the table, slowly, nobody would look him in the eye. Finally he stood up and looked at them.

'Am I a liability?'

He already knew the answer.

A top political post in Europe? He could forget that, tainted as he was by his close association with Bertil Magnuson. Privately as well as in an official capacity. Besides, he had been on the board of MWM at the time of the murder.

He left the party office with long strides and walked across to the Old Town. He knew that his political career lay in ruins. Soon the hounds would be at his heels. They'd hunt him down. He who had lived so long with his high profile and his arrogant tweeting. They'd skin him alive, he knew that.

Without going anywhere in particular, he wandered around the narrow lanes. The lukewarm breeze made his hair stand up. He walked bent slightly forward, dressed in his smart blue suit, alone, a ghostlike scarecrow. The historic buildings leaned over the tall, slim body.

His days on twitter were over.

Suddenly he found himself outside a barbershop on Köpmangatan, his own barber. He walked in and nodded towards a chair where the barber was massaging some hair cream into the black hair of a man who seemed half asleep.

'Hello, Erik? You haven't got an appointment, have you?' said the barber.

'No, I just thought I'd borrow a razor, I've got some hairs on my neck that I want to remove.'

'Yes, sure... you can use that.'

The barber pointed to a little glass shelf on which there lay a good old razor with a brown Bakelite handle. Grandén took the razor and went into the toilet at the far end of the shop. He locked the door behind him.

One for all.

* * *

Mette was in her room. She looked at her team. They were all there, concentrated. The suicide of the previous night had been something of a nasty surprise.

Mette took charge.

'I suggest we go through it from the beginning. Theses and hypotheses.'

She stood at the very front of the room, next to the wall with the large board. Adelita's false letter had been pinned up there, next to his own 'letter of explanation' from Mal Pais. Just under that, the photo of Wendt and Adelita that Abbas had taken from the bar in Santa Teresa.

'If we start with the recording from 1984 in which Bertil Magnuson admits he ordered the murder of the journalist Jan Nyström,' said Mette. 'Since Magnuson is dead, we can put that aside, it will have repercussions on other levels. But we do know that Wendt left Kinshasa just after the murder and disappeared. His former live-in partner reported him as missing a week later.'

'Did he go straight to Costa Rica?'

'No, first he made his way to Mexico, to Playa del Carmen, where he met Adelita Rivera. We don't have any exact information as to when he turned up in Mal Pais, but we do know that he was there in 1987.'

'The same year that Adelita travelled from Costa Rica to Nordkoster,' said Lisa Hedqvist.

'Yes.'

'To fetch the money that Wendt had hidden at his summer house there.'

'Why didn't he fetch it himself?'

'We don't know,' said Mette. 'In the letter he says that he couldn't.'

'Perhaps that's connected with Magnuson. Perhaps he was afraid of him?'

'Yes.'

'Where did the money come from?' asked Bosse.

'We don't know that either.'

'Perhaps it was money he had pinched from their company before he disappeared?'

'That's possible.' said Mette.

'And all those years before he turned up here again, was he there all the time? In Mal Pais?'

'Presumably. According to Ove Gardman he worked as a guide in a nature reservation there.'

'And thought that Adelita Rivera had tricked him and taken his money?'

'Possibly. He did receive a false letter from her in which she leaves him most abruptly, a letter that was written by one of the people who murdered Rivera on Nordkoster in 1987. The most likely purpose of the letter would have been to try to prevent Wendt from investigating why she didn't come back.'

'The perpetrators must have kept a very cool head,' said Bosse Thyrén.

'Yes. But then Gardman turns up in Mal Pais three weeks ago and tells him about the murder he witnessed as a boy, and from the Internet Wendt realises that it was Adelita Rivera who had been murdered, and he goes to Sweden.'

'And now we've got to the present day.'

'Exactly, and now we have a pretty good idea of Wendt's movements. We know he didn't find any money on Nordkoster, we know that he had his recording from Kinshasa 1984 with him, and we can assume that he played parts of that recording for Magnuson in those short calls we have proof of.'

'The question is, what was he after?'

'Could it be connected to the murder of Rivera?'

'That he thought Magnuson was involved in it?'

'Yes?'

'Perhaps we can check with the help of this?'

Lisa Hedqvist pointed at the board, at the old envelope.

'That letter is signed "Adelita", and was posted five days after she was murdered, right?'

'Yes.'

'We should be able to get DNA from it, from the stamp, don't you think? And match it against Magnuson. Saliva works OK even after twenty-three years, surely?'

'Yes.'

Lisa went up to the board, loosened the envelope and went on her way.

'While we're waiting for that, we can nevertheless note that Wendt's calls must have put enormous pressure on Magnuson since on the tape he does admit that he ordered a murder. Of a journalist,' said Mette. 'The consequences of that being made public must have been completely clear to him.'

'So he tried to get hold of the tape by having Wendt murdered?'

'Well I think that's a fairly likely motive.'

'But Wendt had a copy of the tape in Costa Rica.'

'Did Magnuson know that?'

'We can't be sure, but one could well assume that Wendt had mentioned that as a sort of life insurance, after all he knew what Magnuson was capable of.'

'So Magnuson tried to find the tape in Mal Pais, is that it? Abbas el Fassi was attacked in Wendt's house.'

'Yes,' answered Mette. 'We don't as such know if that was on Magnuson's initiative, but it does seem very likely.'

'And if that was the case, then he must have realised that he'd failed and that the recorded conversation would soon reach Sweden. Reach us.'

'And then he shot himself.'

'Which means that we'll never get a confession about the murder of Nils Wendt. If it was him behind it.'

'No.'

'And nor for the murder of Adelita Rivera either.'

'No.'

The conversation came to a halt. They found themselves in a cul-de-sac. They had no technical evidence to tie Magnuson to the murder of Wendt. All they had was circumstantial evidence, a possible motive and an old investigation that was in effect closed.

If it hadn't been Magnuson who had licked the stamp.

* * *

Stilton assumed that they had followed him. From the Söderhallarna mall and all the way to the caravan which they had then set on fire. He also assumed that it was the same people who had beaten up Acke. Perhaps they'd seen when he and Mink had met Acke in Flemingsberg. Besides, he also assumed that they thought he had died in the fire. If they were to catch sight of him again, it should really stir things.

He had popped in at the editorial offices en route and bought a pile of magazines. They all asked him about the caravan. He got some warm hugs.

Now he was standing outside Söderhallarna again, selling *Situation Sthlm*.

He was very alert.

To all the shoppers going in or out he looked just the same as he usually did. Like a homeless seller of the magazine. Who stood where he had stood several times of late.

They had no idea.

When it started to rain heavily and thunder could be heard, he went on his way.

The storm clouds had darkened the sky and flashes of lightning could be seen over the housetops. Liam and Isse were already soaking wet before they reached Lilla Blecktorp park. They hardly needed to sneak through the trees below

Ringvägen. And once in the park there were plenty of bushes and trees to hide behind. And they were wearing their dark hoodies too.

'There.'

Isse pointed and whispered. He pointed towards a bench quite near a tree with a particularly large trunk. A tall slim figure was sitting on the bench holding a can of beer, slightly bent towards his knees, with the rain spraying his body.

'It fucking well is him!'

Liam and Isse looked at each other. They were still amazed. They had caught sight of Stilton outside the Söderhallarna and hardly believed their eyes. How the fuck had the bastard survived the caravan fire? Isse pulled out a short baseball bat. You could hardly see it in the poor light. Liam glanced down at it. He knew what Isse was capable of when the spring was released. They cautiously went a bit closer and looked around them. The park was, of course, empty. Nobody with any sense was out in this weather.

Except the wreck on the bench.

Stilton sat there, his thoughts elsewhere. Being alone like this, in this sort of setting, reminded him of Vera. Of her voice, and of that one time they had slept with each other, just before she was beaten to death. There was something desperate about that memory.

Then he noticed them, out of the corner of his eye.

They had almost reached the bench. And one of them had a baseball bat in his grip.

Cowards, he thought. Two against one. And even so they needed one of those. At that point, he wished that his step-climbing training had started six years earlier, or that those six years had never happened. But they had. He was still only a shadow of his former physical self.

He looked up.

'Hi,' he said. 'Do you want a gulp?'

Stilton lifted the can up. Isse swung his baseball bat lightly and hit the can perfectly. It went flying and Stilton watched as it landed several metres away.

'Homerun,' he said, and smiled. 'Perhaps you ought to…'

'Shut it!'

'Sorry.'

'We torched your fucking caravan. What the fuck are you doing here?'

'Having a beer.'

'You fucking dickhead! Don't you get it? Shall we smash your face in?'

'Like you did with Vera?'

'Which fucking Vera? Was that the bitch in the caravan? Was she your bitch?'

Isse burst out laughing and looked at Liam.

'Hear that? It was his bitch we smashed!'

Liam smiled a little and pulled out his mobile. Stilton saw him turn the camera on. It was coming. He wasn't really sure how to react.

Right at them, he thought.

'You're a couple of heaps of shit, do you know that?' he suddenly said.

Isse stared at Stilton. He couldn't believe what he had heard. How the fuck did the drunkard dare? Liam glanced at Isse. The spring would soon be released.

'You should be locked up for life and fed with rotten cat shit.'

The spring was out. With a roar, Isse lifted the baseball bat well behind his shoulder and then started a violent swing. Right towards Stilton's head.

The swing didn't go all the way. It didn't even go halfway. Before it got that far Isse got a long knife right into the upper part of his arm. He never saw where it came from, and Liam never saw the other knife either. But he felt how it went right through his hand and caused the mobile to go flying in a high arc over the bench.

Stilton was soon on his feet and grabbed the baseball bat. Isse was crouching down screaming and staring at the knife stuck deep into his upper arm. The rain was whipping against his face. Stilton hyperventilated and felt how Vera's horrific death had taken possession of the wooden bat. He held it to one side at the same level as Isse's head. His brain was black. He now gripped the bat with both hands and was about to swing a blow with the full weight of his body straight at Isse's throat.

'Tom!'

The cry pierced right into his black brain, indeed deep enough in to stop the movement for a second. Stilton twisted round. Abbas was coming forward from the large tree.

'Put that down,' he said.

Stilton stared at Abbas.

'Tom.'

Stilton lowered the baseball bat slightly. Suddenly he saw how Liam was trying to scramble away. He took two quick steps and aimed a blow straight over the back of Liam's knee. Liam collapsed in a heap. Abbas reached Stilton and put his hand on the bat.

'There are better ways,' he said.

Stilton eased up a few seconds. He looked at Abbas and tried to control his breathing. After yet a few more seconds he let go of the bat. Abbas threw it deep into the bushes. Stilton looked down at the ground. He realised how close he had been. How the degradation in the rock shelter and all the other shit had made him almost transgress every possible boundary.

'Can you give me a hand?'

Stilton turned round. Abbas had pulled the knife out of Isse's biceps and hauled him up onto the soaking wet bench. Stilton dragged the terrified Liam off the ground and threw him onto the bench next to Isse.

'What shall we do now?' Abbas asked.

'Take their clothes off.'

Stilton had to do it himself. Abbas stood to one side and wiped the blood off his knives. The youths on the bench stared at him in terror.

'Get up!'

Stilton yanked Isse up onto his feet. Liam got up by himself. Stilton ripped their clothes off as fast as he could. When they were completely naked, he pushed them back onto the bench again. Abbas stood in front of them with his mobile. He turned the camera on and held a protective hand over it, for the rain.

'Right,' he said. 'Shall we have a talk?'

The text message that Janne Klinga had just received was short but very dramatic: "The mobile murderers are sitting on a bench in Lilla Blecktorn park. Their confession is out on Trashkick."

He didn't recognise the number.

Klinga, who perhaps had a good idea who had sent the SMS, was in the park as fast as his wheels could get him there. With three constables. They found two naked, soaking wet youths who were tied to a wooden bench. Mangled and broken.

An hour later, he sat with his boss Rune Forss and the entire MHP group in a room at police headquarters. As Klinga clicked his way to the Trashkick site, he could almost smell the expectation in the room. There he found a newly posted mobile film which showed two youths sitting naked on a park bench with terrified eyes and telling how they had killed an old hag in a caravan and some guy up in a park near Värta docks and torched that caravan a bit later and some other violent activities directed towards homeless people.

In quite some detail.

Rune Forss suddenly got up. He was furious. Partly because he had been served the two people that he himself had been trying to find. Partly because the people who had filmed this and obviously lay behind it all couldn't be identified.

And perhaps above all because the youths' tattoos could be seen very clearly: KF, with a ring round the letters.

Just like Stilton had said.

* * *

First he had dropped in on Ronny Redlös and said he was sorry about the black coat having been incinerated. He was given another book to take with him. Then he had sought out Arvo Pärt who was in a sleeping bag under a bench in Fatbur Park close to Södra Station. Pärt was just as soaked as the sleeping bag. After another hour they had found Muriel just a few seconds before she was about to inject herself with an escape rocket in a cycle garage.

Now all three sat in a room at the Halt, a primary care clinic near Mariatorget.

'You can go in now.'

All three went towards the room that the nurse had pointed to. The door was open and Benseman lay in the bed next to the wall. He was a broken man, physically, but at least he was alive. He had been given a room here at the clinic. Really it was against the rules, but it's hard to send a smashed-up homeless convalescent 'home' to a dustbin room.

'We've got them,' said Stilton.

'Thanks, Jelle,' said Benseman.

Muriel held one of Benseman's hands. Pärt dried his eyes. Tears came to him easily. Stilton handed a book to Benseman.

'I looked in at Ronny Redlös' place on the way here, he asked me to give you this.'

Benseman took the book and smiled. It was a volume by Akbar del Piombo. A completely manic pornographic description of nuns and horny men.

'What's the book?' Muriel asked.

'One of those that certain male writers have to write some-time in their life to get out of their system what they can't write under their real names. Akbar del Piombo is a pseudonym for William S. Burroughs.'

Nobody round the bed knew who either of those authors was, but as long as Benseman was satisfied, they were satisfied too.

* * *

Mette stood beside the board in the investigation room. Some of the team were collecting their papers. The investigation into the murder of Nils Wendt had come to a standstill. Lisa Hedqvist came up to her.

'What's on your mind?'

Mette had been staring at the pictures of Nils Wendt's corpse. The naked body. The big and distinctive birthmark on his left thigh.

'There's something about that birthmark, on his thigh…'

She unpinned the photo from the board.

* * *

Olivia had spent the day catching up on practical things. Cleaning, vacuuming. And talking with Lenni who was going to go to the Peace & Love music festival without Jakob.

'Why?'

'Well, his ex was suddenly back in the picture again.'

'Oh that's a shame.'

'Yeah, I just can't fathom what he sees in her. The only thing she's given him is crabs!'

'How disgusting!'

'Yeah, isn't it?'

'Are you travelling up there on your own then?'

'No, I'm going with Erik.'

'Erik? Jakob's mate?'

'Yeah? What about it? You're not seeing him are you?'

'No, no way, but I thought that him and Lollo…'

'No, she dumped him and pushed off to Rhodes yesterday. You must keep in better touch, Livia, you miss everything!'

'I'll do my best, I promise!'

'But anyhow, I've got to pack now, must rush to the train soon. I'll be in touch! Love you!'

'Love you too!'

And then down to the laundry room. Several hours to do all her laundry. When she emptied the pockets of the clothes for the last load she suddenly came across the little plastic bag. The earring! She had forgotten all about it. The earring from Nordkoster that Stilton had given her. She opened the bag and looked at it. Surely it was in Jackie's boutique she had seen a similar one? She put it next to her laptop, rather excited, and found her way to the boutique's website. Under 'Products' she found lots of bits and pieces for Jackie's shop. Including a collection of earrings. But nothing that looked like the one Olivia had in front of her. Not that surprising perhaps, she thought. The earring from Nordkoster is at least twenty-three years old. She must have seen it somewhere else. In another shop? Or had someone been wearing it? Or was it in some-body's house?

Suddenly she remembered where!

And it was definitely not in Jackie's shop.

Stilton was walking along Vanadisvägen. The storm clouds had more or less passed and now it was only drizzling. He was on his way to Abbas' flat. He would kip down there one more night. Then he'd see. He wasn't comfortable with the situation. Abbas was OK with it, he knew that. The problem didn't lie there. It was him. He wanted to be on his own. He knew that he could have violent nightmares and that those screams were always waiting in the background. That wasn't something he wanted to drag Abbas into.

They had gone in different directions after the meeting with the youths in Blecktorn park. But, first, Abbas had wondered how Stilton knew that they would turn up just there.

'I noticed that they followed me from Söderhallarna, and I phoned you.'

'But you haven't got a mobile!'

'There are corner shops.'

Then they had parted. Abbas would upload the mobile film, they'd got the passwords for Trashkick. Stilton would get a new mobile. He had it in his pocket now. Abbas had forked out for it. Suddenly he heard a strange whistling sound right next to him. He turned around and looked about him. Empty. Another whistle. Stilton pulled the new mobile out of his pocket. The ringtone was set for 'Factory whistle'.

He answered.

'Olivia here! I know now where I've seen that earring!'

It didn't take many minutes for Stilton to realise that Olivia, as usual, must phone Mette.

'Now? But it's so late…'

'Detectives work day and night. Haven't you learnt that?'

Stilton hung up.

Mette did not work day and night. She worked effectively when she worked and then she portioned out responsibility. That benefitted everybody. When Olivia phoned, she was on her way home. After a lot of overtime. She did at least manage to get down to the main entrance during the conversation, but then she turned back. Olivia's information about the earring had suddenly got the penny to drop. After twenty-six years.

There would be even more overtime.

She hurried back to her office in C-building. There she opened a large cupboard and lifted out a cardboard box which was marked NILS WENDT 1984. Mette wasn't the sort of person who threw things away. They could be useful, sooner or later. She opened the box and dug out a little bundle of tourist photos. With the bundle in her hand, she pulled the blinds down, turned on her desk lamp, sat down behind the desk and opened a drawer. There was a magnifying glass right at the front. Mette took it out. On the table in front of her lay the photo of Nils Wendt from the forensic lab. Mette held up one of the tourist photos and examined it with the magnifying glass. It had been taken in 1985, from a distance, and was a bit blurred. The photo showed a man in shorts. You couldn't really make out his face properly, but the birthmark on his left thigh could be clearly seen. Mette glanced at the corpse photo of Wendt. At the birthmark on his left thigh. It was just as clear on that image. And was identical to the one on the tourist photo. The man in the photo was Nils Wendt.

Mette leaned back.

She had been in charge of the search for Nils Wendt for a while, in the Eighties, and during that time they had been contacted by a couple of Swedes who had been in Playa del Carmen in Mexico on holiday. They had taken some candid photos of a man they thought was the missing businessman. Who had vanished under mysterious circumstances a while ago. They hadn't been able to confirm it.

That it was Nils Wendt.

Strange, Mette thought. She looked at the two photos in front of her. You could hardly fail to notice that birthmark.

An hour later, they met, all three of them. Mette, Stilton and Olivia. Late at night. Mette met them down by the entrance and took them through all the necessary checkpoints. She didn't encounter any problems. Now they stepped into her room. The roller blinds were still pulled down, the desk lamp on. Olivia remembered the room. She had been here when? An eternity ago. In reality it was only a few weeks. Mette pointed to a couple of chairs in front of the desk. Stilton and Olivia sat down. Mette went and sat behind the desk. Like a schoolteacher. She looked at her visitors. A former detective chief inspector, now homeless and a slightly cross-eyed young police trainee. She hoped that Oskar Molin wasn't working late.

'Anybody want anything?' she said.

'A name,' said Stilton.

'Eva Hansson.'

'Who is that?' Olivia asked.

'She lived with Nils Wendt in the Eighties, they had a summer house on Nordkoster. Now she is called Eva Carlsén.'

'What!'

Olivia almost got up from her chair.

'Has Eva Carlsén lived with Nils Wendt?'

'Yes. How did you come in contact with her?'

'Through my student project.'

'And it was in her home you saw that photo?'

'Yes.'

'With the earrings?'

'Yes.'

'When was that?'

'It'd be ten, perhaps twelve days ago.'

'What were you doing there?'

'I was taking a folder back to her.'

Stilton smiled a little, to himself. The whole thing was acquiring the character of an interrogation. He liked that. He liked it when Mette was in good form.

'How did you know she had been on Nordkoster at the time of the murder?'

'She told me herself.'

'In what context?'

'It… well, um… we met on Skeppsholmen and…'

'How intimate was your contact with her?'

'Not at all.'

'But you were in her private home?'

'Yes.'

What is this, Olivia thought. A fucking interrogation? It was me who told her about the earrings! But Mette went on.

'Was there anything else, besides the earrings, that you reacted to in her home?'

'No.'

'What did you do?'

'We drank some coffee, she told me she was divorced and had a brother who had died of an overdose, then we talked about…'

'What was his name?'

Stilton suddenly cut in.

'Whose name?' Olivia asked, puzzled.

'The brother. Who died of an overdose.'

'Sverker, I think. Why do you ask?'

'Because there were a couple of junkies in the investigation, on Nordkoster, they had…'

'They were staying in one of her cabins!'

Olivia almost got up from her chair again.

'Whose cabins?' Mette asked.

'Betty Nordeman's! She threw them out because they were on drugs! But she said they left the island the day before the murder.'

'I interrogated one of them,' said Stilton. 'He said the same, that they had pushed off before the murder. They had pinched a boat and gone across to the mainland.'

'Did you check that about the boat?' said Mette.

'Yes. It had been stolen the night before the murder. It was owned by one of the summer visitors.

'Who?'

'Can't remember.'

'Could it have been Eva Hansson's?'

'Could have.'

Stilton suddenly got up and started pacing the room. Brilliant, Mette thought. She remembered so well that some of the people at the NCS used to call him the Polar Bear. As soon as he started pacing back and forth.

Like he had now.

'One of the junkies in the cabin might have been that Sverker,' he said. 'Eva Hansson's brother.'

'How many people were in the cabin?' Mette asked.

'Two.'

'And there were three up on the beach,' said Olivia. 'According to Ove Gardman.'

They fell silent. Mette held her hands together, twisting them so you could hear a cracking sound in the silence. Stilton had come to a halt. Olivia looked from one to the other. Mette was the one who put it into words.

'So it could have been Eva Hansson, her brother and a junkie friend of his who were on the beach?'

They all took it in.

Two of them knew that there was still a very long way to go before they had a shadow of a chance to prove what Mette had just said. The third, Olivia, was a police trainee. She thought they'd almost cracked it.

'Where's the Nordkoster material?' Stilton asked.

'It will be in Göteborg,' said Mette.

'Can you phone and ask them to check what that junkie was called, the one we interrogated? And whose boat they'd nicked?'

'Certainly, but it'll take time.'

'Perhaps it'd be easier with Betty Nordeman,' said Olivia.

'How come?'

'She claimed she kept track of her guests, of the rental cabins. A register I suppose, she might still have it. They seemed a very well-ordered family, the Nordemans.'

'Ring and find out,' said Mette.

'Now?'

The very same second she said it, she glanced at Stilton. 'Detectives work day and night.' But waking up old women out on the islands at this time of night?

'Or do you want me to phone?' said Mette.

'I'll phone.'

Olivia pulled out her mobile and rang Betty Nordeman.

'Hello, this is Olivia Rönning.'

'The murder tourist?' said Betty.

'Err, yes, that's right. I do apologise for ringing so late, but we...'

'We're arm wrestling.'

'Oh, right? Who are we?'

'We in the club.'

'Right. Well then. Yes, Betty, I've just got a little question, you told me that you'd had some drug addicts in one of your cabins that summer the murder took place, do you remember?'

'Do you think I'm senile?'

'Not at all, do you remember what they were called?'

'No, I am that senile.'

'But you kept a record, I thought you said.'

'Yes.'

'Do you think you could...'

'One moment.'

There was silence at the other end, quite a long time. Olivia heard a bit of laughter and voices in the background. She saw how Mette and Stilton looked at her. Olivia tried to demonstrate that they were arm wrestling. Neither Mette nor Stilton reacted.

'Axel says hello,' said Betty suddenly on the phone.

'Thanks.'

'Alf Stein.'

'Alf Stein? Was he one of…'

'He was the one who rented the cabin, one of the drug addicts,' said Betty.

'So you don't know what the other one was called?'

'No.'

'You don't remember the name Sverker Hansson?'

'No.'

'You don't know if one of the drug addicts had a sister who lived on the island?'

'No.'

'OK, thanks an awful lot. And say hello back! To Axel!' Olivia ended the call. Stilton looked at her.

'Axel?'

'Nordeman.'

'Alf Stein?' said Mette. 'Was that his name?'

'Yes,' said Olivia.

Mette looked at Stilton.

'Was he the one you interrogated?'

'Possibly. Perhaps. Sounds a little familiar…'

'OK, I'll phone Göteborg, they can check if it was. Now I've got other things to do.'

'Like?'

'Police work, that among other things includes your ex-wife at the SKL. Good night.'

Mette pulled out her mobile.

Olivia drove through the light summer night. Stilton sat next to her. Silent. They were on their way from the NCS and had their minds elsewhere.

Olivia was thinking about the remarkable situation in Mette's room. An active detective chief inspector and a former detective chief inspector and her. A police trainee. Who got to sit there with them and discuss a murder investigation in that way. But she felt she had filled a function. She had contributed in several ways. In her opinion.

Stilton was thinking about Adelita Rivera. The pregnant woman on the beach. He put his hand on the Mustang's worn instrument board.

'This is Arne's old car, isn't it?'

'Yes, I inherited it.'

'Nice car.'

Olivia didn't answer.

'What was wrong with it?'

'Drop it.'

She had learnt. A taste of the same medicine, and then it was quiet.

21

The morning sun washed over the yellow house in Bromma, the rays mercilessly revealing how dirty the bedroom windows were. I'll do them when I get home, Eva Carlsén thought, and closed the suitcase. She had been asked if she wanted to travel to Brazil to write about a successful treatment programme for adolescents who were slipping into crime. It suited her nicely. She needed a change of environment. The attack in her home had left its mark. All the publicity around the murder of Nils too. She needed to get away a while. She would pick up her visa in half an hour, and then take a taxi to the airport.

She took her suitcase down into the hall, put a jacket on and opened the door.

'Eva Carlsén?'

Lisa Hedqvist was on her way up the front steps. Behind her was Bosse Thyrén.

* * *

The arrest of the two people who had murdered a homeless woman in a caravan got quite a lot of coverage in the media. And there were numerous pieces speculating about Bertil Magnuson's suicide and the weird business with Erik Grandén, the cabinet secretary at the Foreign Ministry.

Grandén's links to the sensational revelation from Zaire 1984 had led to feverish activity on the news desks. They all wanted to get hold of him. In the end it was a photographer who had taken the wrong turning at Skeppsbron in the Old Town; he had decided to park his car down on the quay. And it was there he had been sitting. The political prodigy. Behind the statue of Gustav III. With a folded razor in his hand and a look of total despair. When the photographer tried to talk to him, he just looked out across the water.

'Jussi.'

That was all he said.

In the end he had been fetched by a mobile psychiatric team and taken to hospital. The Moderate Party had quickly issued a statement in which they explained that Erik Grandén was taking 'time out' for personal reasons.

Otherwise, they had no comment.

* * *

Stilton had got some information from the police archives in Göteborg via Mette. They had found his old interrogation with the drug addict on Nordkoster. He *was* called Alf Stein. The boat that had been stolen belonged to Eva Hansson. Mette had checked with criminal records to see what they had on Alf Stein.

Quite a lot.

Including an address in Fittja.

She gave that to Stilton.

They took Olivia's car to Fittja and parked close to the centre. Olivia was to wait in the car.

Stilton already had a pretty good idea of Alf Stein's present situation. It wasn't very complicated. He was almost certain to be found among the other drunks near the alcohol shop.

And he was there.

Stilton himself had no difficulty in fitting in.

He sat down on the same bench as Alf Stein, pulled out a bottle of Explorer vodka, nodded at Alf and said:

'Jelle.'

'Hi.'

Alf glanced at the bottle. Stilton handed it to him and Alf wasn't slow to grab it.

'Thanks! Affe Stein!'

Stilton gave a start.

'Affe Stein?' he said.

'Yeah?'

'Hell, man, did you know Sverre?'

'Which fucking Sverre?'

'Sverre Hansson. Blond bloke.'

'Or right, him, yeah. But that was a hell of a long time ago.'

Affe suddenly looked suspicious.

'Why the fuck are you asking about him? Has he been talking shit about me?'

'No way, not at all, he liked you, but he's croaked.'

'Oh fuck.'

'Overdose.'

'Poor bastard. Mind you he was on really heavy stuff.'

Stilton nodded. Affe swallowed a hefty gulp of the vodka.

Without a tremble.

Stilton took the bottle back.

'But what the fuck, was he talking about me?' said Affe.

'Yes.'

'Did he say anything special?'

Are you worried? Stilton thought.

'Nix. Nothing special… he said you were mates when you were younger, that you did some stuff together.'

'What sort of stuff?'

'Pretty wild stuff. Had fun, you know…'

Alf relaxed a little. Stilton handed over the bottle again and Affe put it to his lips. Thirsty bloke, Stilton thought. Affe wiped his mouth and gave the bottle back to Stilton.

'Hell, man, we had fun, yes we did. And did some fucking crazy things too. You know what it can be like…'

I know, Stilton thought.

'Didn't he have a sister, Sverre?' he said.

'What about it? Why d'you ask that?'

Stilton saw he had gone a bit too fast here.

'Nothing, he went on a lot about her, that's all…'

'I don't want to talk about his fucking sister!'

Affe jumped up and stared down at Stilton.

'Get it?'

'Easy, man, fucking cool it!' said Stilton. 'Sorry. Sit down.'

Stilton held out the desirable bottle towards Affe as a gesture of reconciliation. Out of the corner of his eye he saw how Olivia stood beside the car and watched them with an ice cream in her hand. Affe swayed on his feet and realised it would be best to sit down again.

'Forget his sister if it's so fucking sensitive,' said Stilton.

Affe took another gulp from the bottle and looked down at the ground.

'She conned us fucking bad one time, the bitch. Get it?'

'I get it. Who the fuck likes being conned?'

'Right. Nobody!'

So Stilton decided to tell a whopper to his newfound mate Affe. About how he had been conned by a bastard of a mate to help him beat up another bloke. The mate had claimed that the bloke had been pawing his girl and they had given him a good beating. Then later he met his mate's girl on some occasion who said that the bloke hadn't been pawing her at all. It was a lie, this mate of his had owed the bloke money and wanted to be shot of him.

'He conned me into beating up a bloke and he croaked, d'you get it?'

Affe sat quietly and listened, sympathetically. They'd both of them been conned, brothers in misfortune. When Stilton had finished, Affe remarked:

'Fucking heavy story. The bastard.'

Affe went quiet. Stilton waited him out. After a while Affe opened his mouth again.

'I got fucked up with summat a bit like that, or Sverre and me both, we were conned into some heavy shit by his sister…'

Stilton had all his senses on full alert.

'She conned us to… oh fuck I've wanted to forget all that shit man…'

Affe reached for the bottle.

'That's what we all want,' said Stilton. 'Nobody wants to remember shit.'

'No but it fucking well sticks there anyway… you know, Sverre and me we lost contact after that, totally. We just couldn't see each other, hell, and it was a woman too!'

'A woman?'

'Yeah! We did it to a woman! Well we… she got us to do it, his fucking sister. Just cause she had some fucking problem with that poor woman. And she was preggers too!'

'The sister?'

'No! The woman!'

Affe sunk even lower on the bench. His eyes filled with tears.

'Where did it happen?'

Stilton knew that he was pushing it, but Affe was deep inside his alcoholic memories and didn't react.

'On some fucking island…'

Affe suddenly got up.

'I've got to fucking move, man, I can't face talking 'bout this, it was such a fucking disaster!'

Stilton handed the bottle over to Affe.

'Take this with you!'

Affe took the bottle with the last drops, swayed alarmingly and looked at Stilton.

'And I took his sister's fucking money for years to keep my mouth shut! D'you get it?'

'I get it, that's heavy, man.'

Affe stumbled off towards the shadow of a tree. Stilton watched him when he fell down to sleep off his anguish. When Affe had conked out, Stilton got up. He put his hand into the inside pocket of his scruffy jacket and turned off the recording function on Olivia's mobile.

He had got what he was after.

* * *

Mette got a search warrant for Eva Carlsén's house in Bromma. It took some time to go through the whole building. But it also gave results. Including a well-hidden envelope behind a shelf in the kitchen.

Written on the envelope was: Playa del Carmen 1985.

* * *

The room wasn't particularly large. It didn't contain anything superfluous. Just a table, three chairs, a tape recorder. On two of the chairs sat Mette Olsäter and Tom Stilton. He had borrowed a black leather jacket and a polo sweater from Abbas. On the chair opposite, sat Eva Carlsén with her hair loose and wearing a thin light-blue blouse. On the table between them lay various papers and objects. Mette had asked for a good table lamp. She wanted to create an intimate atmosphere. Now she turned on the lamp.

Mette was in charge of the interrogation.

A little earlier, she had contacted Oskar Molin and explained the situation.

'I want Tom Stilton to be there.'

Molin understood why and gave it the OK.

In an adjacent room sat or stood the greater part of Mette's team and a young police trainee. Olivia Rönning. They could follow the interrogation on a screen. Several of them had note-pads in their hands.

Olivia looked up at the screen.

Mette switched on the recorder and said the date, time and

names of those present. She looked at Eva Carlsén.

'And you don't require the presence of a lawyer?'

'I can see no reason for it.'

'All right. In 1987 you were questioned by the police in connection with enquiries about a murder that had taken place at the Hasslevikarna coves on Nordkoster. You were on the island when the murder took place, is that correct?'

'Yes.'

'At the time you were called Eva Hansson, is that also correct?'

'You know it is, you interrogated me about Nils' disappearance back in 1984.'

Eva was going to defend herself. She adopted a slightly aggressive tone. Mette picked up an old tourist photo from a plastic folder and pushed it across the table.

'Do you recognise this?'

'No.'

'There's a man in the photo. One can't really see his face, but you can see that birthmark there?'

Mette pointed to the very specific birthmark on the man's left thigh. Eva nodded.

'I would be grateful if you answered instead of nodding.'

'I can see that mark.'

'The photo was taken in Mexico almost twenty-six years ago, by a tourist, who thought it was your then live-in partner Nils Wendt, who was missing at the time. Do you remember that I showed you this picture?'

'It's possible, I can't remember.'

'I wanted to see if you recognised the man in the photo as your partner.'

'I see.'

'You didn't. You said that it most definitely was not Nils Wendt.'

'And what are you getting at with that?'

Mette put a newly taken autopsy photo of Wendt's naked corpse in front of Eva.

'This is a newly taken photo of Wendt's body after his murder. Can you see the mark on his left thigh?'

'Yes.'

'The same mark as in the tourist photo, isn't it?'

'Yes.'

'At the time of Wendt's disappearance you had been living with him for four years. How could you claim that you didn't recognise his extremely distinct birthmark on his left thigh?'

'What do you want to know?'

'I want to know why you lied. Why did you lie?'

'I didn't lie! I must have made a mistake? Twenty-six years ago? Made a mistake? How should I know?'

Eva brushed away a lock of hair with an irritated gesture. Mette looked at her.

'You seem irritated.'

'And what would you be in my situation?'

'Careful to tell the truth.'

Bosse Thyrén smiled a little and made a note on his pad. Olivia couldn't take her eyes off the screen. She had met Eva twice and found her to be a forceful but friendly woman. Now she saw something completely different. A clearly tense woman who seemed unbalanced and vulnerable. Olivia started to feel herself becoming emotionally involved. She had promised herself to be professional. To try to see it like a police officer. Neutral. Like a future murder investigator.

That was already going badly wrong.

Mette put down a new tourist photo in front of Eva on the table. A photo from a bar in Santa Teresa. Brought back by Abbas el Fassi.

'This photo comes from Santa Teresa in Costa Rica. The man in the picture is Nils Wendt, isn't it?'

'Yes.'

'Do you recognise the woman he has his arm round?'

'No.'

'You have never seen her before?'

'No. I have never been in Costa Rica.'

'But you might have seen a picture of her?'

'I haven't.'

Mette pulled out the envelope they had found behind a shelf in Eva's kitchen. She took six photos out of the envelope and spread them out in front of Eva.

'Six photos, all showing Nils Wendt and the woman from the earlier photo, who you didn't recognise. You see that it is the same woman?'

'Yes.'

'We found these photos in your kitchen in Bromma.'

Eva looked from Mette to Stilton and back to Mette again.

'That's a fucking dirty…'

Eva shook her head. Mette waited until she had stopped.

'Why did you say that you didn't recognise the woman?'

'I didn't see that it was the same woman.'

'As in the photos from your home?'

'Yes.'

'How have these six photos ended up in your house?'

'I can't remember.'

'Who took them?'

'No idea.'

'But evidently you knew they were in your house?'

Eva didn't answer. Stilton noted how the rings of sweat under her arms expanded down the light blouse.

'Do you want something to drink?' Mette asked.

'No. Are we almost finished?'

'That depends on you.'

Mette pushed forward yet another photo. An old private photo, where a smiling Eva stood beside her younger brother Sverker. Eva reacted noticeably.

'You don't stop at anything,' she said, in a much lower voice.

'We're just doing our job, Eva. When was this picture taken?'

'In the mid 1980s.'

'So it was before the murder on Nordkoster?'

'Yes? What's that got to do…'

'You have a pair of very special earrings on… in the photo, haven't you?'

Mette pointed to Eva's long beautiful earrings in the photo.'

'I had a friend who was a silversmith, and she gave them to me for my twenty-fifth birthday.'

'So they were made specially for you?'

'Yes?'

'And only one pair was made?'

'I think so.'

Mette lifted up a little plastic bag with an earring in it.

'Do you recognise this?'

Eva looked at the earring.

'It looks like one of them.'

'Yes.'

'Where does it come from?' Eva asked.

'From the coat pocket of the woman who was murdered in the Hasslevikarna coves in 1987. How did it get there?'

Olivia looked away from the screen. She thought it was starting to be hard to keep on watching. Mette's way of calmly and deliberately hurting her victim.

With a single aim.

'You have no idea how it ended up in her coat pocket?' Mette asked.

'No.'

Mette turned a little to one side and glanced at Stilton. An interrogator's trick. The person being questioned should be made to feel that the interrogators knew more than they did. Mette looked at Eva again and then down at the old private photo.

'Is that your brother standing next to you?'

'Yes.'

'Is it true that he died from an overdose four years ago?'

'Yes.'

'Sverker Hansson. Did he visit you at your summer house ever?'

'On occasion.'

'Was he there the same late summer when the murder took place?'

'No.'

'Why are you lying?'

'Was he?'

Eva looked surprised. Was she acting? Stilton wondered. She must be.

'We know that he was there,' said Mette.

'How do you know?'

'He was there with a man called Alf Stein. They rented a cabin on the island. Is he someone you know? Alf Stein?'

'No.'

'We have a tape recording where he confirms that they were there.'

'Oh really, so they were there then.'

'But that isn't something you remember?'

'No.'

'You didn't meet Alf Stein or your brother?'

'It's possible I... now you mention it... I remember that Sverker had a mate with him on some occasion...'

'Alf Stein.'

'I don't know what he was called...'

'But it was you who gave them the alibi for the murder.'

'Did I?'

'You claimed that Sverker and his mate had stolen your boat and disappeared. The night before the murder. We believe it was the next night. After the murder. Wasn't that the case?'

Eva didn't answer. Mette went on.

'Alf Stein claims that you have paid money to him over the years. Have you done that?'

'No.'

'So he is lying?'

Eva wiped her forehead with her arm. She was close to the edge now. Both Mette and Stilton saw that. Suddenly there was a knock on the door. They all turned round. A uniformed woman opened, and held out a green folder. Stilton got up, took the folder and handed it across to Mette. She opened the folder, glanced at the top sheet and then closed it again.

'What was that?' Eva wondered out loud.

Mette didn't answer. Slowly, she leaned into the light from the table lamp.

'Eva, was it you who killed Adelita Rivera?'

'Who's that?'

'She's the woman who can be seen with Nils Wendt in all the photos you have been shown. Was it you?'

'No.'

'Then we'll continue.'

Mette lifted up the forged letter from Adelita.

'This letter was sent from Sweden to Dan Nilsson in Costa Rica, Dan Nilsson was Nils Wendt's alias there. I shall read it to you, it is written in Spanish but I shall translate it. "Dan! I'm sorry, but I don't think we are right for each other, and now I have the opportunity to start a new life. I'm not coming back." Underneath is a signature. Do you know who signed it?'

Eva didn't answer. She was staring at her clasped hands on her lap. Stilton watched her, expressionless. Mette went on with the same controlled voice.

'It's signed "Adelita". She was called Adelita Rivera and was drowned at the Hasslevikarna coves five days before this was posted. Do you know who wrote it?'

448

Eva didn't answer. She didn't even look up. Mette put the letter on the table. Stilton was watching Eva carefully.

'The other day you were assaulted in your home, in the hall,' said Mette. 'Our technicians found traces of blood on your hall rug and checked these to see if they came from the perpetrators. In connection with that, you had to supply a DNA sample and that showed that the blood came from you.'

'Yes.'

Mette opened the green folder she had just received.

'We have also done a DNA analysis of the saliva on the stamp on the letter from "Adelita" in 1987 and that has matched your DNA. From the hall. They were the same. It was you who licked the stamp. Did you write the letter too?'

Everybody had an edge, an edge to the precipice. Sooner or later you get to that edge if you are pushed hard enough. Now Eva was there. At the edge. It took some seconds, perhaps almost a whole minute, but then it came. In a low voice.

'Can we take a break?'

'Soon. Was it you who wrote the letter?'

'Yes.'

Stilton leaned back. It was over. Mette leaned towards the tape recorder.

'We shall take a short break.'

* * *

Forss and Klinga had interrogated Liam and Isse for a couple of hours. They had both grown up in the Hallonbergen suburb of Stockholm. Klinga had been landed with Liam. He knew more or less what he would hear. Even before what they already had on Liam's criminal record. A whole lot of shit which escalated during his teens. When Liam ended by telling how his dad used to help to inject his big sister at the kitchen table, the picture was pretty clear.

To Klinga.

Damaged children. Wasn't that what she had called them? That woman he'd seen on TV, on some current affairs programme.

Liam was an extremely damaged child.

Forss had established roughly the same topography around Isse. Originally from Ethiopia, abandoned and left to his own devices even before his voice broke. Damaged and demolished. Crammed full of aimless violence.

Now it was about the cage fighting.

It took a while before they got Liam and Isse to reveal what they knew, but it trickled out in the end. Names of the other boys who helped to arrange them and above all: when the next fight was to take place.

And where.

Out on Svartsjölandet, in an old closed-down cement factory. Now empty and fenced off.

Except for some people.

Forss had put a watch on the place several hours earlier. The strategy was to let the whole thing get going before they raided it. When the first little boys were shut in the cages and the cheers and jeers started up, it was quickly stopped. The police had cut off every possible escape route and went in with heavily armed officers. The police vans outside were soon filled to the brim.

When Forss and Klinga came out of the factory, they were met by journalists and photographers.

'When did you find out about the cage fighting?'

'A while ago, via our undercover activities. It's been a top priority recently.'

Forss said straight to a camera.

'Then why haven't you raided them earlier?'

'We wanted to be certain the right people were there.'

'And were they now?'

'Yes.'

As Forss posed for another close up, Klinga walked away.

* * *

Some of the members of the team had left the room. Olivia was still there, with Bosse Thyrén and Lisa Hedqvist. They probably all felt the same thing. A sort of relief because an unsolved murder was about to be solved, mixed with various personal reflections. For Olivia, a lot of that was about motive.

Why?

Even though she had an idea what it might be.

The trio in the interrogation room had been given coffee. The mood was low key. For two of them some relief, and somehow perhaps even for the third. Mette turned the tape recorder on again and looked at Eva Carlsén.

'Why? Can you talk about it?' she said.

Mette had suddenly changed her voice. The impersonal interrogator voice had gone. The one that only had a single purpose, to get a confession. The new voice was from one person to another, in the hope of understanding why we commit the acts we do commit.

Knowledge.

'Why?' said Eva.

'Yes.'

Eva raised her head a little. If she was going to tell them why, then she'd have to push herself through a whole lot of pain. Suppressed pain, sublimated. But she felt that she ought at least to present an explanation. Put words to what she had devoted a whole life to try to atone for.

The murder of Adelita Rivera.

'Where shall I begin?'

'Wherever you want.'

'The first thing that happened was that Nils disappeared. Then, in 1984, without a word. He just vanished. I thought he had been murdered, that something had happened down there in Kinshasa, you thought something like that too, right?'

Eva looked at Mette.

'That was one of our hypotheses, yes…'

Eva nodded and stroked the back of one hand with the other. She was talking very quietly now, and fraily.

'Anyhow he never turned up. I was desperate. I loved him and was totally crushed. Then suddenly you came and showed me those tourist photos from Mexico and I saw that it was Nils, and he was alive and had a nice tan and was in some holiday resort in Mexico and I was absolutely… I don't know… I felt horribly cheated. I hadn't heard a word, not a postcard, nothing. There he was in the sun, and I was here and mourning and was desperate and… there was something extremely degrading about it… as if he didn't give a damn about me…'

'Why didn't you say that it was him when I showed you the photo? Then, in 1985?'

'I don't know. It was as if… I wanted to get hold of him, myself, wanted an explanation, wanted to understand why he did that to me. If it was something personal between us, that he wanted to hurt me or whatever it was he wanted. Then I realised what it was about.'

'How?'

'When I saw those other photos.'

'The ones we found in your house?'

'Yes. I contacted a foreign agency, specialists at finding missing people, I told them where he'd last been seen, in Playa del Carmen in Mexico, you'd shown me those tourist photos from down there, and then they started looking and found him…'

'There?'

'Yes. And then they sent a whole pile of photos from there, of him and a young woman. Intimate photos, sex scenes, from bedrooms and hammocks and the beach and everything imaginable... you've seen them, it was terrible. It might sound... but I was incredibly hurt... not just deceived, cheated on. It was something about the whole way he had gone about it, as if I was just air, not somebody who existed, just something you could treat like... I don't know... And then that day came along...'

'...when the young woman suddenly turned up on Nordkoster?'

'Yes. Pregnant. His baby. Came with her bulging belly and hadn't a clue that I recognised her from the photos and I knew that she'd been sent there.'

'By Nils?'

'Yes? Why else would she turn up? And then I saw her sneaking around the back garden of our summer house in the evening, and I'd been drinking wine and became... I don't know, I became furious. What was she doing there? At our house? Was she looking for something? And then...'

Eva became silent.

'Where were Sverker and Alf Stein then?' said Mette.

'They were in the house. I didn't really want them staying with me but they'd been kicked out of the holiday cabins and they'd moved in...'

'And then what happened?'

'We ran out into the garden and dragged that woman into the house and she started to fight and scream, and then Sverker proposed that they should cool her down a bit, he was high on drugs.'

'So you took her to the Hasslevikarna coves?'

'Yes, we wanted to get away from people.'

'What happened there?'

Eva twisted one thumb with her other hand. She had to dig very deep to find the right words, to give them form.

'There was no water on the beach when we got there, it was low tide, spring tide, the beach stretched a long way out. And then I remembered…'

'About the spring tide?'

'I had tried to get her to tell me what she was doing there, what she was after, where Nils was, but she didn't say a word, just kept silent.'

Eva couldn't look up any longer. Her voice was very low.

'The guys fetched a spade and then they dug a hole… and put her in it… then the tide came in…'

'You knew that it would come then?'

'I'd lived on the island for several years, everyone there knew when the spring tide came and went. I wanted to frighten her, make her talk…'

'And did she?'

'Not at first. But then… when the tide came in… in the end…'

Eva became silent. Mette had to fill in.

'She said where Nils had hidden his money?'

'Yes… and where he lived.'

Stilton leaned forward a little.

'And then you left her there?'

It was the first time he had said anything during the entire interrogation. Eva gave a start. She had been engaged in a painful dialogue with Mette, the man next to her hadn't existed.

'The guys ran home. I stayed behind. I knew that we'd gone too far, that the whole thing was madness. But I hated her so terribly, the woman out there in the water. I wanted to torture her for taking Nils away from me.'

'Kill her.'

Stilton was still sitting in the same position, leaning forward.

'No, torture her. It might sound strange, but I didn't think she'd die. I don't know what I thought, it was all black inside my head. I just went away.'

'But you knew it was a spring tide?'

Eva nodded in silence. Suddenly she started to cry, quietly. Stilton looked at her. Now they had the motive for the murder of Adelita Rivera. He tried to catch Eva's eye.

'Now perhaps we can move on to Nils Wendt?' he said. 'How did he die?'

Mette gave a start. All her focus had been on linking Eva Carlsén to the murder on Nordkoster. The murder of Nils Wendt hadn't been on her agenda at all. She was completely convinced that Bertil Magnuson lay behind it. Suddenly she realised that Stilton was a step ahead.

Like in the old days.

'Can you tell us about that too?' he said.

And she did. Luckily for both Mette and Stilton since they had nothing concrete that could link Eva Carlsén to what had happened to her ex-partner. But Eva had no reason to lie at this stage. She had already confessed to a brutal murder and wanted to get the rest out too. Besides, she didn't know what they knew. She didn't want to be interrogated by Mette again.

She couldn't stand that.

'There isn't that much to tell,' she said. 'He just rang the doorbell one evening, at my house, and I was really shocked. Not because he was alive, I knew that after all, but that he should suddenly turn up like that.'

'Which evening was this?'

'I can't remember. The day before he was found.'

'What did he want?'

'I don't really know, he... it was so weird... all of it...'

Eva became silent and sank into herself. She slowly went back in her mind to that weird meeting with her ex-partner. How there had suddenly been a ring on the door of the house in Bromma.

Eva opened the door. Outside stood Nils Wendt in the weak light from the porch lamp. He was wearing a brown jacket. Eva stared at him. She didn't really know what she was looking at.

'Hello, Eva.'

'Hello.'

'Do you recognise me?'

'Yes.'

They looked at each other.

'Can I come in?'

'No.'

A few seconds passed. Quite a lot. Nils? After all these years? What the hell was he doing here? Eva tried to pull herself together.

'Well, can you come out then?' said Nils and smiled a little.

As if they were two teenagers who didn't want their parents to see them? Is he crazy? What the fuck did he want? Eva turned round, took a coat off the hook, stepped outside and closed the door behind her.

'What do you want?' she asked.

'Are you still married?'

'Divorced. Why? How did you know where I lived?'

'I googled you and found out that you'd married, many years ago, your husband was a very successful pole-vaulter, Anders Carlsén. You've kept his name.'

'Yes. Have you been keeping track of me?'

'No. I just happened across it.'

Nils turned a little, expecting her to follow him, and then walked towards the gate. Eva stayed in the porch.

'Nils.'

Nils stopped.

'Where have you been all these years?'

She knew that, very well. But he didn't know that she knew.

'Abroad,' he answered.

'And why are you turning up here? Now?'

Nils looked at Eva. She felt that she ought to go a bit closer, a bit more intimate. She went up to him.

'I need to tidy up some things from the past,' he said in a low voice.

'Oh, right, and what are you going to tidy up?'

'An old murder.'

Eva glanced around her, instinctively, she felt her neck tightening. An old murder? The one on Nordkoster? But he couldn't have known anything about that? That she was mixed up in it? What did he mean?

'That sounds unpleasant,' she said.

'It is too, but I'll soon be finished, then I'm going home again.'

'To Mal Pais?'

That was her first mistake. It just slipped out of her. The very next second she realised what she had said.

'How do you know I live there?' said Nils.

'Well, don't you?'

'Yes. Shall we go for a drive?'

Nils nodded towards a grey car that was parked outside the gate. Eva was uncertain. She still had no idea what he was after. Talk a bit? Bullshit. An old murder? What could he know about that?

'Sure,' she said.

They got in the car and drove off. After a couple of minutes, Eva asked:

'What was that about an old murder?'

Nils hesitated a couple of seconds, then he told her. About the murder of the journalist Jan Nyström that Bertil Magnuson had ordered. Eva looked at him.

'Is that why you came here?'

'Yes.'

'To get back at Bertil?'

'Yes.'

Eva relaxed. It wasn't about Nordkoster.

'Isn't it rather dangerous?'

'Getting back at Bertil?'

'Yes. Well he did have a journalist murdered, apparently.'

'He won't dare murder me.'

'Why not?'

Nils gave a little smile, but didn't say anything. They drove over the Drottningholm bridge, out onto Kärsön and towards the other side of the island. Nils stopped the car near a slope down to the water. They both got out. It was a starry night. A half-moon spread light across the water and the rocks. It was a very beautiful spot. They had been there several times, in the old days, late in the evening. Gone skinny-dipping, with nobody around.

'It's just as beautiful here as it used to be,' said Nils.

'Yes.'

Eva looked at him. He seemed calm, as if nothing had happened. As if everything was as it used to be. Nothing is as it used to be, she thought.

'Nils.'

'Yes.'

'I must ask you something else…'

'Yes?'

'Why did you never get in touch?'

'With you?'

'Yes. Who else? We were living together, do you remember? We were going to get married and have children and spend our lives together. Have you forgotten that? I loved you.'

Eva suddenly felt how she was being steered in the wrong direction entirely, by the wrong feelings entirely. But the whole situation with Nils at this spot after twenty-seven years was so absurd. The past erupted like molten hate within her, without her being able to stop it.

'That was stupid, I ought to have got in touch, absolutely. I'm sorry,' said Nils.

He's saying sorry, she thought.

'After twenty-seven years? You say you're sorry?'

'Yes. What do you want me to do?'

'Have you ever thought what you have done to me? What I've had to go through?'

'But, Eva, there's no point in…'

'You could at least have got in touch and said that you were tired of me and wanted a new life with her! I would have accepted that.'

'With who?'

That was her second mistake. But she felt that there wasn't much point in keeping quiet. There was no way she could resist what she felt deep inside. Nils was suddenly very alert.

'With whom should I have a new life?'

'You know bloody well! Don't pretend you don't know! Young and beautiful and pregnant and then you send her here to fetch your hidden money and think that she…'

'How the hell do you know that?'

Nils' eyes suddenly became icy cold. He took a step towards Eva.

'Know what?' she said. 'About the money?'

Nils looked at her long enough to realise just how wrong he had been. All the time. It hadn't been about Bertil at all. That Bertil had managed to trace him via Mexico to Mal Pais and then followed Adelita to Sweden to get hold of the stolen money. Bertil wasn't involved in the murder at all. It was Eva who had nicked the money and…

'Was it you who murdered Adelita?' he said.

'Is that what she was called?'

Suddenly Eva got a very hard slap right across her face. Nils was raging.

'WAS IT YOU, YOU FUCKING BITCH?'

He threw himself at Eva. She tried to fend off the next blow. Eva was in pretty good condition, and Nils was not at his best.

Suddenly they were fighting, furiously, grabbing at each other, kicking, until Eva got a grip on his jacket and pulled him to one side. Nils couldn't keep his balance, stumbled on a stone and fell backwards with his head straight onto a rock edge. Eva heard the muted sound when his skull hit the sharp edge of the granite. Nils collapsed in a heap on the ground. The blood was pumping out of the hole in the back of his head, over his neck. Eva stared at him.

Mette leaned in towards the light from the table lamp in front of Eva.

'You thought he was dead?'

'Yes. At first I didn't dare touch him, he lay there bleeding and didn't move and I was in shock and furious and everything.'

'But you didn't phone the police?'

'No.'

'Why not?'

'I don't know, I just sank down on the ground and looked at him. Nils Wendt. Who had destroyed my life totally back then. And now he turned up again and said he was sorry. And started to hit me. And had realised what I had done on Nordkoster. So I pulled him across to the car and managed to get him into the driver's seat, the car was right next to the slope down to the water, I only had to release the hand brake…'

'But you must have realised that we'd find him?'

'Yes. But I thought… I don't know… he had threatened Bertil Magnuson…'

'You thought that Magnuson would get the blame for it?'

'Perhaps? Did he?'

Mette and Stilton glanced at each other.

* * *

It wasn't exactly a joyful mood in Mette's car later that evening. They were on their way to the big old house in Kummelnäs. All three had something to think over.

Stilton was thinking about the unravelling of the beach case. How just one solitary event can trigger such a violent chain reaction. Two Swedes meet on the other side of the world. They share a bottle of wine. One tells the other something that suddenly explains something he has wondered about for more than twenty-three years. He travels to Sweden to avenge the death of his beloved. Seeks out his former partner. Is killed. Is found by Mette who notices a birthmark on his thigh which she recognises from some previous occasion, and at the same time Olivia has started looking into the beach case.

Remarkable.

Then his thoughts moved on to much tougher things. To what would inevitably happen in a while. At Mette and Mårten's house. And how he should deal with that.

Mette was thinking about her pursuit of Bertil Magnuson. How wrong she had been. But he had ordered a murder after all, he was guilty of instigation. She wasn't going to take responsibility for his suicide.

Olivia was thinking about Jackie Berglund. What a blunder. If she hadn't been fixated on Jackie, Elvis would still be alive today. A costly lesson.

'That must have been how it was.'

It was Mette who broke the silence. She felt that they must be given a jolt. They would soon be home in her hotchpotch house. And she didn't want to spread silence and suppressed thoughts there.

'How what was?' said Stilton.

'The people who broke in and knocked down Eva Carlsén must have been sent there by Bertil Magnuson.'

'To do what?'

'To look for the tape recording. Magnuson will certainly have checked all the hotels and seen that there was no Wendt there, just like we did, and then he'd have remembered Wendt's old former live-in partner, they would presumably have socialised back in those days, they both had summer houses on Nordkoster, and then he thought that perhaps Wendt was hiding at her house and had the tape there.'

'Sounds reasonable,' said Stilton.

'But the earring?' Olivia wondered. 'How did that get into Adelita's coat pocket?'

'Hard to say…' said Mette, 'possibly when they fought in the house, her and Eva.'

'Yes.'

Mette braked as they approached the big old house.

As they were walking up to the house, Mette received a call on her mobile. She stopped in the garden. It was Oskar Molin on the phone. He had just had a meeting with Commissioner Carin Götblad and discussed a name in Jackie Berglund's register of clients. A name he had been given by Mette.

'What did you decide?' said Mette.

'To put it on the backburner for a bit.'

'But why? Because it's Jackie Berglund?'

'No, because it would disturb the re-organisation.'

'OK. But he's going to be told about it?'

'Yes. I'll do that.'

'Good.'

Mette hung up. She noticed how Stilton had stopped a couple of metres from her and heard the conversation. Mette walked past him without saying a word, and went up the porch steps.

Abbas opened, with his arm round Jolene. Olivia got a warm hug from her.

'Now we want to eat!' said Mette.

They all made their way through the rooms to the large kitchen. There Mårten was faffing around with all sorts of ingredients for what he had promised would be the gourmet peak of the summer.

Spaghetti carbonara with frozen wild chanterelle mushrooms.

The other members of the clan had been fed a while ago, and were now spread out in various places in the house. Mårten had explained that the lady of the house wanted some peace and that her guests wanted to eat undisturbed. Those who wouldn't accept that would be sent up to Ellen in the attic and have to count knitting stitches.

It was comparatively quiet downstairs now.

'Take a seat!'

Mårten swept his hand over the laden table, where some of Mette's ceramic pieces also featured. Some as dishes, others as plates and others again as something in between. Cups, possibly.

They sat down.

Mette poured out some wine. Stilton declined. The warm glow from the candelabras glistened in the others' wineglasses when they toasted each other and drank.

And relaxed.

It had been a long day for all of them.

Mårten too. He had spent quite a lot of time thinking about what would happen in a while, and how he should deal with it. He wasn't entirely sure. It could go either way, and none of them was easy.

He waited.

And all the others did too, with the exception of Olivia. She felt how the first gulp of wine spread calm and warmth through her body. She looked at the group around the table. People who had been total strangers to her not so very long ago.

Stilton, a homeless man. With a past that she now knew one or two things about. But not enough to make a pattern.

A pattern that she was very curious about, but nevertheless. She remembered what he had looked like the first time they met, in Nacka. There was quite a difference to now. His eyes looked completely different, among other things.

Mårten, the man with Kerouac. The expert on child psychology who had got her to open up in a way that amazed her. How had he done that?

Mette, his wife, who had almost frightened her to such a degree that her legs seemed to turn to jelly, and who still kept her distance. But with respect. She had after all let Olivia come into her office and her murder case.

And then Abbas. The slender-limbed man. With his secret knife on him, and his strange scent. Like a Ninja warrior, she thought. Who was he really?

She took another gulp of wine. That was when she noticed it, or rather felt it. A sort of expectant atmosphere around the table. No smiles or quick exchanges, just a sort of wait-and-see feeling.

'What is it?'

She just had to ask, with a bit of a smile.

'Why are you so quiet?'

The others glanced at each other round the table. Glances that Olivia tried to follow from one to the other, until she landed at Stilton. He wished he had his bottle of Stesolid pills with him.

'Do you remember when I asked you in the kitchen, in your flat, when the caravan had burnt down, why you had chosen the beach case?' he suddenly said.

The question surprised Olivia.

'Yes.'

'And you said it was because your dad had been involved in the investigation.'

'Yes.'

'There was nothing else that you reacted to?'

'No… well, yes, after a while. The murder took place the same day I was born. A bit of a weird coincidence.'

'No it wasn't.'

'What do you mean? It wasn't a coincidence?'

Mette poured out some more wine for Olivia. Stilton looked at her.

'Do you know what happened that evening, after Ove Gardman had run home from the beach?'

'Yes, they… or what do you mean. Straight after?'

'As soon as he came in through the door and told them what he'd seen, his parents rushed to the beach at the same time that they called an air ambulance.'

'Yes, I know.'

'His mother was a nurse. When they got to the beach the perpetrators had gone, but they managed to get the woman, Adelita, up out of the sand and water. By then she was unconscious but still had a weak pulse, his mother tried to give her mouth-to-mouth, and they kept her alive a while, but she died a minute or so before the air ambulance arrived.'

'Right.'

'But the child in her womb was still alive. The helicopter doctor did an emergency caesarean and got the baby out,' said Stilton.

'What? The child survived?'

'Yes.'

'And what, why haven't you told me anything about that? What happened to the baby?'

'We decided to keep the baby's survival a secret, for reasons of security.'

'Why?'

'Because we didn't know anything about the motive for the murder. In the worst case it might have been about the unborn child, that it was the child they wanted to kill.'

'So what did you do with the baby?'

'We let one of the investigation team look after the baby at first, we thought we'd be able to establish the woman's identity, or that a father to the child would turn up, but that never happened.'

'No? So?'

'The police officer who took care of the child eventually applied to adopt her, he and his wife were childless. We and the social services thought it was a good solution.'

'Who was the police officer?'

'Arne Rönning.'

Olivia had presumably already suspected where Stilton was going, but she needed to hear it. Even though it was incomprehensible.

'So the child is me?' said Olivia.

'Yes.'

'So that makes me... what? The daughter of Adelita Rivera and Nils Wendt?'

'Yes.'

Mårten had his gaze fixed on Olivia the whole time. Mette was interpreting her body language. Abbas had pushed his chair back a little.

'... that's not true.'

Olivia was still in control of her voice. She was still way behind.

'Regrettably,' said Stilton.

'Regrettably?'

'Tom means that perhaps you ought to have been told about this in a different way, on a different occasion, under different circumstances.'

Mårten tried to keep Olivia where she was. She looked at Stilton.

'So you've known about this all the time since we met outside that shopping centre?'

'Yes.'

'That I was the child in that drowned woman's womb?'

'Yes.'

'And not said a word about it?'

'I was about to several times, but…'

'Does my mother know about this?'

'Not the exact circumstances. Arne decided not to tell her,' said Stilton. 'I don't know if he told her before he died.'

Olivia jerked her chair back, got up and looked around the table. She stopped at Mette.

'How long have you known about this?'

Her voice now had a slightly higher tone. Mårten realised that it was getting close.

'Tom told me a few days ago,' said Mette. 'He didn't know what he should do, if he should tell you or not. He needed help, he was extremely worried by…'

'He was worried.'

'Yes.'

Olivia looked at Stilton and shook her head. Then she ran out. Abbas was ready and tried to get hold of her but she tore herself loose and disappeared outside. Stilton tried to rush after her but was stopped by Mårten.

'I'll do it.'

Mårten ran after Olivia.

He caught up with her a little way down the road. Olivia had sunk down against some iron railings with her hands over her face. Mårten bent down to her. Quick as a flash, Olivia stood up and started to run again. Mårten ran after her and caught up again. This time he pulled her to him, turned her round and held her in a tight bear hug. She calmed down after a while. The only sound to be heard was her desperate sobs against his chest. Mårten stroked her back gently. If she had seen his eyes at that moment she would have known that she wasn't the only one who was in despair.

Stilton had moved across to the window in one of the rooms. The lights were turned off inside and with the curtains pulled to one side he could see all the way to the lonely couple on the road out there.

Mette came up beside him and she too looked out.

'Did we really do the right thing?' she queried.

'Don't know…'

Stilton looked down at the floor. He had gone through a hundred alternatives, ever since she had stopped him that first time and said her name was Olivia Rönning. Arne's child. But none of the alternatives had seemed acceptable. In the end it had felt more and more uncomfortable and at the same time harder and harder to deal with. Cowardly, he thought. I was too cowardly. I didn't dare. I had a thousand excuses to avoid saying it.

In the end he had turned to the only people he trusted. So as not to have to say it himself. Or at least say it surrounded by people who perhaps could handle what he himself was totally untrained for.

Like Mårten.

'But now it's been said,' said Mette.

'Yes.'

'Poor girl. But she knew she was adopted surely?'

'Possibly. I've no idea.'

Stilton looked up. They wouldn't get any further with that just now, he thought, and looked at Mette.

'The call you received in the garden, was that about Jackie's clients?' he asked.

'Yes.'

'Who did you find?'

'A policeman, among others.'

'Rune Forss?'

Mette went back into the kitchen without answering. If Tom gets back on his feet now then we'll deal with Jackie Berglund and her customers together, she thought. In the future.

Stilton looked down at the floor and noticed Abbas come up by his side.

They both turned towards the street.

Olivia was still in the grip of Mårten's bear hug. His head was leaning against hers and his mouth was moving. What he said to her stayed between them. But he knew that this was only the beginning, for her, the beginning of a long journey. Melancholic and frustrating. A journey she must make by herself. He would be at hand if she needed him, but it was her journey and her journey alone.

Somewhere en route, at an abandoned station, she would get a kitten from him.

Epilogue

She sat quietly in the summer night, a night that wasn't night, that was little more than a rendezvous between dusk and dawn, with the glow of that enchanting light that southerners tend to get so excited about. Sensual, and for Olivia hardly noticeable.

She sat among the sand dunes, alone, she had pulled up her knees under her chin. She had been looking out across the cove for a long time. The tide was low, very low, there would be a spring tide tonight. She had been sitting there and watched the warm sun sink low and watched the moon take over the stage, a show off in borrowed rays, colder, more blue, without any particular empathy.

The first hour she had been able to collect her thoughts and tried to think in concrete terms. Where exactly did they take Adelita down on the beach? Where was her coat found? How far out had they taken her? Where had they dug the hole? Out there? Or there? It was a way of holding back, or at least delaying what she knew would come.

Then she thought about her biological father, Nils Wendt. Who had come here one night with a suitcase on wheels and walked out to where the tide had withdrawn and stopped there. Did he know that it was here? That the woman he loved had been drowned just here? He must have known, what otherwise was he doing here? Olivia realised that Nils had mourned Adelita, that he had sought out her last place in life so that he could mourn.

Just here.

And she had been sitting hidden behind some rocks and seen it.

Seen that moment.

She breathed in, heavily.

She looked out towards the sea again. There was a lot that washed through her, inside her, and she tried to hold it back.

The cabin. He came to the cabin. To borrow her mobile. Suddenly she remembered a short moment, just as he had come in through the door, how Nils had stopped and there had suddenly been a look of surprise in his eyes. As if he saw something he hadn't expected. Was it Adelita he saw in me? For a split second?

Then came the second hour, and the third, when the concrete things and the actual things weren't enough to hold it all back any longer. When the child in her became all of her.

For a long time.

Until the tears came to an end and she managed to look out again and get in touch with her intellect. I was born on this beach, she thought, cut out of my drowned mother's womb, one night with a spring tide and moonshine, just like this one.

Just here.

She let her face sink down towards her knees.

That was how he saw her, far away. He stood behind the rocks, in the same place as before. He had seen her walk past the house a few hours earlier and she hadn't come back. Now he saw her crouching down, at almost the same place where the others had stood, that night.

He heard the sea again.

Olivia didn't notice when he came, only when he sank down next to her, crouching too, and becoming still. She turned a little and caught his eye. The boy who had seen it all. The man with the sun-bleached hair. She looked again. It was my father he talked with in Costa Rica, she thought, and my mother he saw murdered here, and he hasn't a clue about that.

Some time I'll tell him.

They looked out across the sea. Towards the wet expanse of beach that was bathed in moonlight. Small, shiny crabs scuttled back and forth across the sand glowing in the steel-blue light. The rays glistened in the rivulets between the folds of sand. The limpets clung particularly hard to the rocks.

When the spring tide came in, they left the spot.

Biographical note

Cilla and Rolf Börjlind have written twenty-six Martin Beck films for cinema and television, as well as most recently working on the manuscripts for the Arne Dahl's A-group series. In 2004 and 2009 their crime series 'The Grave' and 'The Murders', were screened on Swedish television. In addition Rolf Börjlind has written eighteen films and received a Guldbagge Award for the manuscript for the film *Yrrol*.

As well as being among Sweden's most praised scriptwriters, Cilla and Rolf Börjlind have now embarked on a new career as bestselling authors. Their books are characterized by charismatic protagonists and depictions Sweden, full of social conflicts.

Before its release, *Spring Tide*, the first book in the series about Olivia Rönning and Tom Stilton, had sold rights to twenty countries. And when published, it received rapturous reviews from Swedish critics.

Under our three imprints, Hesperus Press publishes over 300 books by many of the greatest figures in worldwide literary history, as well as contemporary and debut authors well worth discovering.

Hesperus Classics handpicks the best of worldwide and translated literature, introducing forgotten and neglected books to new generations.

Hesperus Nova showcases quality contemporary fiction and non-fiction designed to entertain and inspire.

Hesperus Minor rediscovers well-loved children's books from the past – these are books which will bring back fond memories for adults, which they will want to share with their children and loved ones.

To find out more visit www.hesperuspress.com
@HesperusPress

Cold Courage
Pekka Hiltunen

COLD CASE

Lia is horrified when she witnesses a grotesque crime scene
on the way to work. A woman has been murdered,
her body dumped in the boot of a car. With the police unable
to solve the crime, Lia takes on the detective work herself,
with help from her new friend Mari.

COLD BLOOD

Mari is an enigma. Born with an incredible ability
to read people, she runs a mysterious unit called The Studio,
a motley group of brilliant minds fiercely loyal to her.
They will do whatever it takes to put the world to rights,
even if blood is shed.

COLD COURAGE

Together Lia and Mari are playing a dangerous game,
entering an underground world of human trafficking
and brutality. With her life in danger, Lia is forced to decide
how far she is willing to go in her quest for justice…

*The first in The Studio series from the award-winning
Finnish crime star Pekka Hiltunen.*

Out Now